Rook Point

ROOK POINT

THE BLACKWELL BROTHERS
BOOK THREE

K.L. TAYLOR-LANE

ISBN eBook - 978-1-7399897-8-1
ISBN paperback - 978-1-7392089-5-0
Written by - K. L. Taylor-Lane
Cover design by – Leah Maree at Designs by LM.
Edited by - Inga Oake

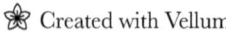 Created with Vellum

It started when I was just a boy.

My obsession.

An inheritance the men in my family seem to be gifted, one that feels a lot like a disease.

It was love at first sight.

Hair the colour of fire, eyes crafted of the deepest jade.

I was captivated by her instantly, enthralled, but it was not meant to be, our worlds were already vastly different. Destinies not meant to intertwine. My family *worked* for people like her, they didn't marry them. The Princess of the Irish Mob. The eldest son of The Firm's disposal crew.

So, I grew up, I moved on, and I spent long nights in bars drowning dangerous thoughts of her.

But, it seems, with time, things can change. One night, one debt, one single game of cards.

And in a sick twist of fate, a treasure that should never be mine was suddenly within my grasp.

Leah,

for your love, for your passion, for your heart.

Note from the Author

Please be aware this book contains **many** dark themes and subjects that may be uncomfortable/unsuitable for some readers. This book contains **very** heavy themes throughout so please heed the warning and go into this with your eyes wide open.

For more detailed information, please see pinned posts on the author's socials.

The characters in this story all deal with trauma and problems differently, the resolutions and methods they use are not always traditional and therefore may not be for everyone.

This book can be read as a standalone. However, it is recommended you read this series in numerical order for maximum enjoyment.

*Rook Point is a dark, MF, forbidden, gothic, love story. Please read with caution, the characters in this book do not and will not conform to society's standards or normalities. This book does have a *happy ever after.**

*The Blackwell Brothers series is a series of interconnected standalones, meaning this book CAN be read as a separate entity, you do not have to read the first books in this series to enjoy or understand this story. However, for maximum reader enjoyment, it is recommended you read the series in the order shown below.

Reading Order
Book 1 - Heron Mill (Hunter and Grace)
Book 2 - Heron Mill Tenebris (Hunter and Grace)
Book 3 - Rook Point (Thorne and Haisley)

🪶 X 🪶

NOTE FROM THE AUTHOR

Book 4 - Cardinal House (Wolf Blackwell)

Book 5 - TBA

Book 6 - TBA

Book 7 - TBA

Book 8 - TBA

CHAPTER I

THORNE

Navigating dark alleyways behind seedy little gentlemen's clubs is certainly not my ideal Thursday night activity in late December, two days after Christmas. Shined dress shoes splashing through dirty puddle water, a light drizzle misting the air, rain droplets refreshing on my cool skin, settling atop the wax in my hair. We take sure steps, our pace unhurried but not leisurely. Confident.

The Doyles owe me a fair amount of money, for jobs I have carefully carried out for them. With precision, tact, a professionalism they will not find elsewhere. If I take on a job, it will be done. That is why they hired me. *Chose* me.

Arrow, one of my younger brothers, walks beside me. Arms loose, gently swaying by his sides, hands relaxed, fingers slightly curled into his palms. He glances over at me, dark eyes, almost black in the dense light, ones that match my own, peer at me, his gaze narrowed just slightly from the corner of his eye as he continues facing forward. Straight black hair styled back, longer than mine, and without the wave to it, but we look very much like the brothers we are. Same olive skin tone, mine, decorated with intricate dark ink, hidden away beneath my clothes, his, untouched, virgin, and still, at twenty-six, he has no plans for marking his skin.

We continue down the alley, the scent of damp rubbish and wet cardboard thick in the air. Black plastic sacks overflowing with trash, tossed haphazardly out of back doors. Our footsteps echo off the cracked tarmac, up the high brick walls that surround us. We are both silent, listening, ears pricked like guard dogs. You never know when you might be ambushed in Irish territory, although, the likelihood for us is slim.

The Blackwells may have always run disposals for The Firm, but we also organise and oversee all clean-up crews this end of the country now. It was my idea, not too long ago, to expand, the six sons of The Blackwells all branching out into different areas of clean-up and disposal. Sometimes we are hired muscle, hitmen, none of us really minding what task we are set. It made sense to push further out. We never get caught. No bodies found. No witnesses. No trouble with the law. Our reputation precedes us.

The Swallows, the family that run The Firm, agreed with our expansion, seeing how it could benefit us all, as long as we always dealt with them first when they called. It helped tie us all in with the other organised crime factions. We are slowly making peace with the Albanians after the massacre that ensued a few years ago. Already, we are in bed with the Irish, Italians, Romanians and Mexicans. The Russians are working through spats over new leadership, so even they are now suddenly all the more eager to play nice. So, what that means for us is, we are busy, *all* the time. Busy, but organised.

It is what I thrive on.

Organisation.

Be it in the kills, the clean-ups, the disposals.

I thrive on it all.

But I *do* require payment for my hits.

And that is where the Doyle boys have fucked up.

When we reach the large metal door, rusted, chipping red paint and a sliding hatch in its top half, Arrow pounds his fist on it, once, twice, a third time. The hatch slides open, violent in its nature, dark eyes peering out at us, no light emitting from inside. I stare at the man, a deep crease between his dark brows, he grunts, slams the slider shut, and unbars the door, metal on metal grating, he thrusts the door open.

"T'orne," he grunts in greeting as Arrow and I step inside.

Door slamming closed at our backs, the sound of it vibrating up the walls as it is re-latched closed. The familiar hallway beyond, one I have travelled down far too many times, is dimly lit, the walls are yellowed, paint peeling. The entire place has seen better days, but the patrons regularly visiting this dingy, grimy, run-down little hellhole are just as dirty and grubby as the building, so it suits its clientele.

🐦 3 🐦

One of the Doyle's henchmen steps into view, appearing noisily through a door to our left, he nods his bald head, a grunt of instruction to follow. Head held high, expression blank, I sniff, and start the journey down the corridor. It twists through the centre of the old structure, more levels beneath our feet, more overhead. Every floor in this shithole set with a purpose of debauchery.

Concrete floor beneath our feet, stomped out cigarettes, half empty beer bottles and cans, litter the walkway. Arrow kicks discarded trash out of his way where he follows behind me, huffing beneath his breath with disgust. Doors line both sides of the narrowing hall, the broad shoulders of the man we follow seemingly growing as the space tightens. And just when we are so deep inside the snaking hallways that he looks as though he is going to have to start walking sideways to continue on our journey, he stops. His sledgehammer sized fist hammering on the wooden door I've frequented more times in the last few months than I would like to count. It swings open, a plume of cigarette smoke flooding out over our heads.

The guy steps aside, big meaty hand splayed over the inwardly open door, holding it for us to enter. I step through first, Arrow at my back, and then the door is slamming closed hard behind us as we make our way further in.

Four large men stand around the room, dressed in all black, arms folded over wide chests, backs to walls, all of their eyes zeroed in on me. I pay them no mind. My gaze, instead, on the three Doyle brothers sitting on the opposite side of the circular table in the centre of the room, dark green felt covers it, discarded hands of cards face down, crumpled fifty-pound notes piled in the middle.

"Ah, it's the Blackwell lads, 'ow's it goin', T'orne?" Rian Doyle rasps, exhaling a thick plume of white smoke through his nostrils, broad grin widening.

Sitting on the left of his older brother, slim shoulders, a stained, yellowed t-shirt baggy on his skinny frame. Pasty skin sullen, head of dark auburn hair shaved almost to the scalp, his thin lips blanch white as he pulls on the cigarette stuck to his bottom lip, dark eyes lit up with mocking.

He tips himself back and forth on the legs of his chair, swinging in the same way my younger brother Archer so often does. It makes my eye want to twitch, but I don't give him any further attention, altogether dismissing the brother on the other side of the man I *actually* came to see.

"Liam," I say stoically, addressing him directly, I want to get straight down to business tonight without any of the fucking games they usually try to play with me.

"T'orne, T'orne, *T'orne*," Liam chuckles, his words a cheery singsong, raspy and thick, "What's the craic?"

The spitting image of both his brothers on either side of him, his hair a little longer, thick curls, a dent in the bridge of his hooked nose, dark eyes locked on mine.

I watch his smile, false, like a Cheshire cat, a fractured grin by all accounts. Slowly, he folds his fingers together, in front of him atop the table, revealing he is not clinging onto a weapon beneath the surface of it. I find it interesting, his nerves, the way he hides them beneath a well-practised mask, but lets it all down with the tiny chink in his chain of armour. A single twitch to his left eye, it crinkles the skin at the outer corner not even a millimetre, but I catch it, see it is there.

The urge to tilt my head is strong, but I do not let my curiosity get the better of me. The smile that wants to sculpt my lips is trodden out before the desire gets too strong, and I slowly slide my hands into my slack pockets.

"I want my money."

Liam chuckles again, nodding his head overzealously like one of those dashboard dogs you get in cars.

"A course ya do, lad, a course ya do."

Staring at him, Arrow silent and sentry at my back, we wait for him to continue. When he does not, I sigh, just a little dramatically and shrug my shoulders, the movement tight beneath my black suit jacket.

"Where is my money, Doyle?" I already know he has not got it, but I am not leaving here tonight without it.

"Well, ya see, I actually want'cha to do another job for me first, there's a gi-" I stop him with a single raise of my hand, palm in the air to shut him up.

"You do not have my money, for the work I have *already* carried out for you." A statement, not a question, he blanches at that, but I continue. "But here we are, *you*, asking *me*, for yet, *another* thing. How can I trust that, after doing yet *another* job for you, I will ever get paid?"

"Let's make a wager on it," Gobán, the other brother, bonier, more skeletal even, than his two brothers, says teasingly. Dark eyes sharp, green glinting in his irises, "A game a'cards," he shrugs, leaning forward on the green felted table. "What d'ya say, T'orne?"

Slowly, single brow tracking up my forehead, I shoot him an unhurried look. Knowing I am almost unbeaten in card games, does not matter what I play, I always just seem to have a good hand, Lady Luck on my side. But Gobán is not in charge here. I allow my curiosity to gloom its way through then, darkening my already ebony eyes. My head cocks of its own accord, twisting on my neck to stare over at Liam.

"What are the proposed stakes?" I rumble, feeling my brother's very minute rush of breath at my back.

Arrow is always nervous. It is one of the reasons why I keep dragging him out with me on extra jobs. The man is soft, but he can be a viper when backed into a corner, he just needs to be able to tap into that at will and whim. I will help him get there, he has to stop letting his emotions bleed into these things, they will tear him apart inside. I already know the things we do keep him up at night.

"Winner takes all or nuthin'," he almost squawks out, the adrenaline lining the inside of his wiry veins, a lowly spurt of excitement unhinging his *don't give a fuck* attitude.

I stare at him for a long moment, silence in the

room, Rian placing all four of his chair legs gently back down onto the ground, no longer rocking in place.

"I do not think that seems quite fair," I say quietly. "Considering what you already owe me is payment for jobs well done," I right my head on my shoulders, both eyebrows lifted delicately. "I am glad I know you a little better than that, Liam," his name rolls off of my tongue like I am laying out a red carpet. "Because if I were any other man, I would think you were trying to make me look a little daft… Or, I don't know, perhaps, fuck. Me. *Over*." It is a low growl, a rumbled warning, I may appear cool, calm and collected, but I am a dangerous fucking beast with a soul and conscience as black as my heart.

Liam sputters, both brothers blanching, eyes widening at the threat in my tone, and the sick satisfaction I get from the smell of their fear as it fills the air is enough to get my dick fucking hard. But as it goes, this is not the time, nor is it the place, for that.

"Double our debt if you win, cleared if you lose."

"Doubled debt is also not going to benefit me, is it, Doyle?" I cluck my tongue. "If you cannot even pay what you owe now…" I look between the three of them, almost cowering in their seats, even their guards, placed strategically around the room, look a little uneasy. "Double what you owe me will put you into seven figures of debt, Liam," I state. "You are sure that is something you want to *risk*?" And even as I say the word, curling off of my tongue like smoke, my insides heat just a little.

Risk is what employs people like me, *needs* people like me. Risk requires services that very few others, outside of The Blackwells disposal services, can offer. I am very good at cleaning up messes made by risk-takers; I also happen to be *very* content in my job role.

"I could just bill your father instead," I shrug loosely, knowing a threat like that would never bother me.

But not these boys.

The three sons of the infamous Brádach Doyle. Brádach is a notoriously violent man with large fists, a temper that flares quicker than the speed of light and a man solely responsible for beating two of his *own* sons to death for their insubordination. He is also the head of one of the five families running the Irish mob, best friend to the leading family, The Kellys. So if I were these men, I would be a little concerned by my threat too.

Liam leans forward, almost mimicking the younger brother to his right, eyes on mine, slight scowl to his mouth.

"'S'that so?" he hums, considering me, suddenly looking much older than his twenty-six years. "You's a single man, T'orne," he rasps, accent thick, his eyes shine with something new. "How 'bout I throw you in a woman? Got 'em all trained up real nice, obedient. Know how to suck dick, too," he says it blankly, like he has sold all of this to a hundred others before, does not matter that I know he has, he is trying to pitch me a prize he hopes I will be interested in.

He watches me for reaction, as if I could not find a

woman for myself, and might actually snap up his ridiculous offer of trading skin. I keep my face blank. Getting nothing out of me, he tries again.

"Or get ya some women if ya win, hm? Take ya pick, as many as ya want, have a wild nigh' a fun, a weekend, week, month, wha'ever ya want. Could do wha'ever you want with 'em. And I'll still owe double. I'll *get* ya double, we don't need to be bringing anyone else into this, let's keep it between us."

He is panicking now, a trickle of fear slithering beneath his skin. Palpable, something I can feel vibrating through the smoky room. And because the sadist in me likes to watch the suffering…

"I do not want your women," I say coldly. "I do not want your blithering either." Flicking my gaze onto my brother, feeling his unease surging through the pores in his skin. "We can make an arrangement," I state firmly, swinging my gaze back onto Liam. "I am a fair man." I let that sink in for a few long seconds, long enough to have Gobán fidgeting uncomfortably in his seat. "*I* win, you owe me double. To be paid within five days." I eye Liam, watch the information swirl around his irises, settling. Then I say, "And if you win, your debt is cleared, and I will do whatever job it is that you wanted to give me when we first arrived. For *free*."

All three of their faces light up like Christmas trees on a timer, as though they have already won. It should probably make me anxious, the unknown task, but all it really does is have excitement pulse, albeit dully, through my veins. Did I mention, I am *really* content in my job?

"And we want to know what the job entails *first*," Arrow says from beside me now, large body standing tall and unyielding on my right.

I feel proud, but I do not react. Everyone knows the Blackwell brothers are as thick as thieves, but they do not know my younger brother has a slight aversion to what we do.

"We 'ave a girl we need rid of, dead, buried, never existed," Liam states with indifference.

"Age?" is all I ask; I am not killing children.

"Twenty-three."

I nod, her fate already sealed, be it by my hand if I lose, or by some else's if I win, it does not matter to me.

"What she do?" Arrow asks and I bite down on my tongue, because it does not matter what she has done, we do the job regardless, it is better not to know, not to humanise targets.

"She killed her cousin, Cian Kelly," Arrow's brows reach his hairline with surprise, and I must admit, even mine have the urge to climb my forehead, but they do not, my reaction remaining indifferent.

"She's a Kelly?" is what my brother asks next, and I want to roll my eyes, already tired of this bullshit, it does not matter because I am going to be the one winning anyway.

"Mm, only a middle daughter, not even a fucking virgin," Gobán spits, like it is the most despicable thing he has ever heard, as though, a tiny piece of thin skin nestled high between a woman's thighs means fucking anything. "Coulda sold her off ot'erwise."

He shrugs, dismissively, and even as I feel my spine stiffen at his words, it is nothing to do with me. The Irish trade in skin and sex, that is how it works, always has, and as my dad reminded me as a very small boy, there is nothing I can do, I cannot stop it even if I would like to.

"Haisley's a fucking cunt, anyway," is what Rian snarls next, and I swear, the blood in my veins turns to ice.

I blink, sound in the room dropping until it is nothing more than a muffled echo. Arrow's deep rumble at my side is there, but I cannot make out his words. My skin crawls, clothes suddenly feeling much too tight, sweat beads at the nape of my neck, my hands fizzing, fingers numb. I do not blink, or breathe and it feels like too much time and not enough time passes all at once. And then my hearing comes back with a pop, my eyelids clear my cloudy vision with a solid blink, and my chin lifts back up the tiny fraction it dropped.

Everyone in the room completely unaware that my brain just imploded. Liam stands, as do his brothers, his hand outstretched across the table, I eye him, my gaze on his and his alone.

I feel triumph as I speak my next words.

"But if I do lose, this will be the last job I ever do for the three of you," and then I grasp his hand, cold and clammy, I shake it firmly in mine before he can utter a single other word.

And I resign myself to the fact that this may just be the first card game that I lose.

CHAPTER 2

THORNE

Lady Luck is, unfortunately, most definitely on my side when I lift my two cards revealing a Ten *and* a Jack of Clubs.

I want to bash my head into the fucking table. My heart burns inside my chest cavity. Acid thick in the back of my throat. Every baser instinct inside of me is growling and snarling with rage. Thank fucking Jesus, Mary and Joseph that I am able to exchange my cards, because when I do, I am left with a measly two of Hearts and Six of Diamonds. The cards facing up in the centre of the table cannot fair me any better and for the first time in my life, I want to smile at the prospect of losing.

But as is best, I keep my well-practised face blank. My gaze lifts from beneath my thick lashes, dark brow dropped. I eye Liam across the table. His dark eyes already on mine, and there is a glint in them, a twisted little sparkle that lets me know he thinks he has already won.

The smirk that kicks up just one corner of my mouth, an involuntary reaction to being beaten, could not be stopped if I chewed my own lips off. The shock on Liam's face at that, has him paling, thinking I am cocky because I have a good hand.

Arrow at my back, a sentry soldier. I know he will not have seen my cards, my hands covering them when I checked them. Movements done purposefully, because I can imagine him not being able to hide his shock or surprise if he had seen my starting hand and then watched me switch them out.

No one knows about the feelings I harbour for a girl I cannot have. Feelings buried so deep inside of me they are burrowed away in my fucking marrow.

A sickness.

Liam is silent, his brothers on either side of him still, I am hoping he is as much of a cheat as everyone says he is, that way it is a sure thing that I will be the loser. They think they are beating me, conning me out of money I am rightfully owed, but I do not care about money. I do not really care about anything other than my family, Dad, younger brothers, sister, nephews. Everything else is insignificant, meaningless, living in an endless void of dull and lifeless shades of grey is my current status.

If only they knew, though, that when I lose, I will be the richest fucking loser these idiots have ever challenged. Everything I have ever wanted is being offered to me on a platter. If. I. *Lose.* I can hardly believe it.

It makes me think back to when I was younger, always competitive, wanting to win, beat my brothers at every game and challenge we played, until one day, I learned that life is not about winning everything.

I had just turned twelve when I was tasked with my first disposal, assisting, learning. Dad explained how our world worked, our *real* world.

It opened my eyes to what I already harboured.

The bloom of darkness that had been locked away inside of me, something that every Blackwell carries, uncoiled like dense smoke. Infecting every part of me, rushing through my veins, seeping into my organs, my bones. I felt as though I had just been reborn, the entire process feeling natural. I welcomed it, unfazed and unconcerned with what my new purpose entailed, the direction my life would inevitably lead. I understood our place, our role, our duty.

I was proud.

To be a Blackwell, to carry my name, to fulfil the duty my ancestors before me laid out.

I have built up quite a reputation of my own, the eldest of the Blackwell brothers, stoic, expressionless, unfeeling. A heart as black and burnt as my soul. Carries out any and all jobs with a callous professionalism that remains unmatched.

I let myself think of her now.

Haisley Kelly.

Thick red hair in heavy curls that drop past her waist. Enchanting green eyes lined with thick pale lashes. Light coloured freckles covering every visible inch of her creamy skin. I think of the last time I saw her, two years ago on her twenty-first birthday, remember the expression she was wearing when she thought no one was watching her.

I want to frown, the thought of her in that club making everything in me feel heavier, like trying to wade through mud. My gut twists and my heart thuds and I feel every muscle in my body stiffen. Everything chaotic and uncontrolled.

I fucking hate everything about her.

My twitchy fingertips almost jump as I run them over the back of my cards. Face down beneath my other hand on the table, trigger finger feeling just a tad too impatient to get on with my task. It will not be that hard, killing a girl for crimes I am neither the judge nor jury on. I am only one thing, the executioner.

The air in the room is thick, cigarette smoke swirls high above our heads, but it has got nothing on the cloud of tension that fills the rest of the space.

My lungs claw to draw in air, filling my insides with nothing more than humid pressure. I want to tear off my jacket, strip out of my shirt, yank at my too tight collar, despite the top two buttons already being open. Skin slick beneath my clothes, I flick my gaze back up, watch Liam cock his head to the left just the smallest fraction, and I know he has a good hand.

Time feels irrelevant, suspended, the game seemingly dragging me through time and space, and also not moving me forward at all. When Gobán lifts a brow, Arrow clearing his throat almost silently behind me, I make a show of checking the cards beneath my hand. We manipulated the rules slightly for this game, three rounds with the ability to trade out our cards, giving us the opportunity to get the best hand we could. No folding, or I would not have given a fuck about what I actually had because no one would have seen them.

Without any further words, I flip my cards. Keeping my eyes trained on Liam, a toothy grin quickly stretches wide across his face, he bangs a fist down onto the table, victory rife in his gaze.

He flips his cards, Spades, giving him a flush. He bounces out of his seat, chair clattering back to the floor, his brothers cheering and slapping him hard on the back as all three of them fly to their feet. I stand slowly, Arrow shifting ever so slightly.

"Well played," is all I say, firm, confident, unfazed, and even so, Liam swallows, all three pairs of Doyle eyes roving onto me. "A deal is a deal."

I wait, Liam's gaze flicking over to a guard, the big guy nods, disappearing through a door in the back.

"Just getting' ya job, T'orne, then ya can be on ya's way, lads," Liam grins, and I nod expressionless.

Despite the fucking thudding inside my temples, blood rushing through my veins with a roar as violent as a rough sea, I stand still, like I am carved of stone. I blink every twenty or so seconds, of which there are too many occurrences of, making it look like I am still *in* the room. The minutes tick by, the Doyles offering us drinks, none of them gloating, being *gentlemanly* for a change, knowing they are lucky. Because that is what they are.

I could have walked out of here, won, left with them owing me double, but I heard her name and an explosion happened inside my skull.

The door the henchman disappeared through is forced open, ricocheting off the wall as it swings wide. My head wants to pull my gaze in that direction, my eyes burning in their sockets to catch a glimpse of her, but I keep my focus on Liam. Monitor the deep crease carving down the centre of Gobán's eyebrows as his attention is diverted to the door. I take in a slow breath, even as my lungs want me to pant for them, and it has never been harder to control my body's natural reactions than it is right now.

Even when I think of Mum, and my brain swims with toxic memories, hearing the rush of water, the pounding of blood in my ears, the twisted pain in my chest. I manage to keep it together.

But right here.

Now.

I can feel myself slipping.

My hands want to fist, eyes narrow, but I keep my composure. Even though, beneath the pressed suit, the blank stare, my heart thuds hard and fast behind my ribs. I struggle, because this, being in the same room as *her*, even though I am not looking, the anticipation of what is to come.

I have never felt so out of control before.

And I hate it.

I can feel my mind fracturing, all of these years of keeping it together, my body, my heart, my soul, all of these sharp, razed edges I have held together inside, start to splinter and crack. Slicing me open to ooze and spill and bleed an endless river of black.

Rian is the first to move, a snarl curling his top lip over his teeth, he tucks a cigarette behind his ear as he strides toward the door.

Arrow shifts at my back, stepping up beside me, his wide body angled in their direction.

That is the thing with Arrow, he is so *good*, he cares too much about things that are *nothing* at all to do with us, the boy wants to be everyone's hero. I wonder when he will realise that Blackwells are anything but.

He nudges me with his elbow, a swift, sharp jab to my side whilst no one else is watching. I glance at him from the corner of my narrowing eye. His head nodding towards what I know is my target, in so many more ways than one.

Reluctantly, too slowly and too fucking fast, I laser focus my attention in on the open door. The guard blocking the door frame, Rian's back to me, his body curled forward, a smaller person I cannot see, trapped between them.

Her, her, her.

Rian starts speaking, a low, dull muttering, that I imagine, from the look on his face before he turned to her, is a threat or warning of some sort. He is so close to her, his breath must be blowing across her face, and the tips of my fingers physically ache to curl into my palm.

Before I have a chance to snap like a frayed slingshot bungee cord, he straightens, turns back towards us, his nose wrinkling as he sniffs hard in irritation. He eyes his brothers briefly, and then steps to the side.

My lungs seize in my chest. Her body hidden beneath a too big, baggy tracksuit, black hoodie, grey bottoms, dirty trainers on her small feet. Cloth bag over her head, hands behind her back, I cannot see them, but I imagine they are tied. She is silent, and I think of someone shoving something over her mouth, stopping her speaking, making any noise. Perhaps, she is just, resigned to her fate.

Or maybe she is a good girl who does what she is told.

The muscles in my stomach tighten, a cold sweeping chill, prickling the skin at my nape. My tongue feels thick and heavy in my mouth, dry and uncomfortable, like it could choke me if I swallowed right now.

I cannot really *see* any of her. It could be *anyone* under that sack.

And I know what I should do. Take her from here, bundle her into the car, let Arrow lead her so I do not have to touch her. I swallow then, at that thought, throat scratching like sandpaper and nod my head towards my brother.

Without anyone in the room uttering another word, head nods and silence, I turn, one of Doyle's men pulling open the door, another of them on the outside as I turn, the one who brought us in just over an hour ago. No one speaks, no one moves. So I hear when Arrow gently clasps, what I imagine is, her elbow, and I hear her soft footsteps shuffle along with my brother's without hesitation. That wash of heat comes over me again and I have to grit my teeth to get my feet to work.

The corridor is narrow before it widens out and I cannot hear any of the noise that I could when we first arrived because of the buzzing inside my head, reminiscent of a shaken up box of flies.

Maggots, one's I had for fishing when I was a boy, I had neglected to refrigerate them, allowing them to develop into flies. The sound horrified me as a child, and I feared being reprimanded for my lack of care. All that had come of it was Dad releasing the flies out of the box and explaining why they are kept cold, to stunt their growth. But as I lay awake in bed some nights, it was as though I could hear them, they haunted me, the noise. Even now, flies make my skin crawl.

I think of Grace then, my stepsister, something more to one of my brothers. Hunter's obsession with her has only helped her come out of her shell, their three sons are just as obsessed as their father when it comes to their mother. I think we are all just a little bit under her spell. But I think of her softly spoken requests, when she finds an insect inside the house, asking me to lift her up onto my shoulders, so she can capture whatever little thing it is, gently cup it inside her hands. I hate it, insects, bugs, especially flies, but I do not tell Grace that, let it deter her, life is very precious to her, *all* life. Freedom.

It shoots a shiver up my spine as I wonder what she would think about my killing Haisley. Would she be the one to dice up her corpse? Grace likes the pretty ones presented on the slab; her eyes always glimmer for days afterward.

I suddenly wonder what it is that *I* think about killing Haisley. I am not sure, for what feels like the first time in my life, if I really know what I am doing.

I am ripped violently from my thoughts when I am bumped from behind, and I realise I have stopped walking completely, lost inside my own head. I blink, and it is only then I hear it, over my own thrashing heartbeat, the rush of blood in my ears, the pounding inside my head, a gasp. Whimper, muffled and almost silent to me, but I hear it, and then I feel her again, almost burrowed against my back, and I wonder how close my brother is to hers.

I am six-three, Arrow much the same, the small girl between us not much more than five-five, and I think of snapping her spine. How it would not take much, I could make it quick, keep that sack over her head, twist her neck on her shoulders in one clean crack.

She would not see it coming.

She would not have to suffer.

I fist my hands at my sides, start my steps forward again, clearing my cloudy vision with a few fluttered blinks, and try not to think about the burning patches of skin on my back where she just touched me. Even through my clothes, everything feels like it is on fire. I breathe in deeply through my nose, smell the smoke-filled air, an underlying waft of something musky, damp, and sex. That is what goes on in the lower levels of this building, just below my shined dress shoes, orgies and defiling acts fill the rooms. Some of it consensual, most of it probably not.

But it is not my business.

I cannot change what is.

The only thing is this life I have control over is myself and my actions. *That* is something that has been carved into my insides for as long as I can remember.

When the exit door is pulled open and the cool winter air hits my clammy skin like knives, I welcome it. It is easier to breathe out here, we are closer to our car, parked just at the end of this alleyway, not quite wide enough to fit a small vehicle down, let alone a much larger one like my Mercedes GLC. But I blocked the entrance by parking directly across it, helping keep us a little safer.

I feel my pace picking up when I hear Arrow's gentle voice whispering soothing words to our, *my*, new task. I feel a strange pang of jealousy, I want it to be *me* that offers her comforting words, reassurances of safety, but that is not me, and it is not how I work and that is absolutely not how this is going to go.

I feel like I am unravelling, losing control of myself, my head already spinning, and as I walk, I feel the earth starting to tilt beneath my feet. I blink again, shaking my head just slightly, trying to get it on straight. Taking the car keys from my trouser pocket, my thumb on the door handle unlocking at my touch, I wrench it open, slide into my seat, slam it closed, face forward, hands on the wheel.

Put her in the boot.

And even as I think it, I know what Arrow's going to do and I should stop this before it happens. I should tell him absolutely not, under no circumstances is she riding in the car like a passenger as opposed to a prisoner. But when he opens the rear door on the opposite side to me, predictably ushering her onto the seat and fastening her seatbelt over her, all I can do is engage the child locks and squeeze the wheel a bit tighter.

I flick my gaze onto Arrow, watch in the rear-view mirror as he walks behind the car, coming to sit in the seat directly behind mine. The swoosh of his trousers against the leather as he slides into place. Click of his seatbelt not a second later when he pulls his door closed.

That is the first real sign of life in her, a flinch at the slam, I hear it more than I see it, the rustle of fabric, and I have to close my eyes, avoid the mirror, think of literally anything else to get myself back under control. I count to five, exhale through my nose, start to drive.

Rain patters against the window, sheeting down now, the wind blowing against us, making water slash over the windows, and in the dark night, I drive and I drive and I do not know where I am going. With no destination in mind, I finally pull into a layby on the side of the road. I have made it out of the city now, but not quite into the country and I cannot take this girl to Heron Mill. My family home, where I no longer have a room anymore because I have numerous properties scattered across the country instead. So when I stay overnight, on a rare occasion, like Christmas, I use a guest room instead.

I drop my head forward, forehead touching the top

of the steering wheel. Nothing but the loud sound of rain battering the roof. Yet, beneath it all, I can still hear her breathing, it is a little too fast, and I imagine what she would look like now, beneath that sack, with my hand tight around her neck. Arrow shifts in the seat behind me, also quiet, his breaths, too, just a bit too fast. He has no idea about my connection with this girl, a fallen mafia princess that I have been told time and time again throughout my life, is *'out of my reach'*. And all I can focus on is the pain thrashing around inside my skull, the tension in my shoulders, tight grip on the leather wheel. My brain feels like I am sifting through sludge, I squeeze my eyes so tight, white flares across the inside of my eyelids and then they are snapping open. I sit up, flick my gaze to Arrow in the rear-view mirror, and get out of the car.

"You need to call Archer to pick you up," I tell Arrow as he joins me outside of the car, knowing Archer is the closest.

If he has finished his assigned job, he should be close enough to collect Arrow on his way home.

"You're leaving me here?" Arrow blinks at me, as if that is not what I have just said.

The rain is like ice, beating against our skin where we stand on the side of the empty road.

"Yes," I confirm without explanation.

It is all I can think to say. I find myself completely incapable of thinking about anything other than getting my brother out of the car and out of my way.

"Thorne…" Arrow murmurs, his dark eyes on mine,

wet hair plastered to his forehead, weight shifting from one leg to the other.

He glances at the car window, and I know he cannot see her through the tinted glass, definitely too dark to be road legal, but he is looking right at where she is sitting anyway. It is as though hackles rise on the back of my spine, his hand cupping his nape, fingers squeezing the muscles in his neck. We are a few feet from the car, gravel and puddles beneath our feet, and we are drenched right through from the freezing rain. I stare at him, and his thoughts are *so* loud and disapproving, I can practically hear them, but I do not say anything further.

Slowly, swallowing, Adam's apple bobbing harshly in his throat, he returns his gaze to me, dropping his hand and I expect him to protest. Not because I am going to abandon him on the side of a road in the pouring rain, the temperature below four-degrees, and the wind violent. But because he has a soft spot for people in distress, particularly women. It is not that that is a bad quality to have, it is just that in our family's line of work, it can only really ever complicate things.

He blows out a breath, licking his lips quickly, his jaw clicks as he grinds his teeth and then, reluctantly, he nods. Reaching up, hand curling over his shoulder, I squeeze the muscle there, and nod in return. I turn away, knowing he is watching me, and as my icy fingers curl around the handle to the driver's door, he calls behind me.

"Make it quick, Thorne."

#

CHAPTER 3

HAISLEY

A door opens and closes, a second vibrating slam quickly following the first, and I think I'm alone, but I can't be sure. I know there's at least two, but one of them didn't speak. I don't know if he's the driver or if there's a third, perhaps there's more.

The one that sat in the back seat with me whispered kind words, something to soothe me, no doubt, but all they did was have bile burn up the back of my throat, and make my stomach churn like an empty washing machine. I don't want to be sick, my mouth sealed shut with tape so sticky I know if it ever gets peeled off it'll be taking the gnawed skin of my lips with it. I'll likely be dead before that happens, and I can't say I mind.

The flesh beneath my eye is swollen, my cheekbone aching with every tremoring exhale, and I just want it all to stop. I don't want to die, but I don't think I really want to live either. I feel… suspended. Like time has lost all meaning. I'm only twenty-three, I thought I'd have escaped the binds of my family by now. I'm no one important, not to the men in my family, not even really to my mother. I have siblings, full and half, but being a daughter of the Irish mob is more a show than anything else. I'm only a piece of currency, something to be used for transactional purposes, but only if the tiny membrane between my thighs is intact.

That's why I find myself in the back seat of this car.

I try to breathe slowly, keep calm, not lose my head, but beneath this sack, tiny spots of light filtering through the heavy material, it is incredibly hard. Eyes closed, I strain my ears, trying to hear anything beyond the hammering rain, it pings off the metal roof of the car, sounding like pelting stones. It almost sounds like hail, perhaps it is now, it is December after all, and the weather in England is unpredictable at best.

I'd give just about anything to feel the rain, the hail, sleet, God, even snow at this point, and I hate the stuff usually. I like to be warm, even though my freckled skin disagrees, burning up tomato red with even just the briefest exposure to it, but I like it all the same. A tear squeezes free, rolling down my sore cheek, an injury gifted by my father before my banishment to the Doyles. A backhanded smack to the face for killing my cousin.

Cian Kelly.

Another tear falls at that, and then another, my chin dipping towards my chest. I sniffle, trying hard not to cry, because if my nose gets blocked, I won't be able to breathe at all, and I'm already working hard not to panic as it is. I take a deep breath, one that rattles my lungs, shifting my shoulders, it pulls at my bound hands, making me wince, my numb fingers having enough life in them to sense pain.

I hope they make it quick, whoever *they* are. I don't need any more lectures, I don't need to tell my story, what happened and why. Eoin Kelly didn't care, my own father, he called me my older sister's name twice before a guard of his corrected him with a terribly fake cough to cover it. I suppose that's what you get when you only feel pride at the birth of a son, discarding the girls to numerous nannies whilst you try to re-impregnate your wives with a boy instead.

A gust of wind whips around me as a door up front opens, the smooth shuffle of fabric as someone slides across the leather of their seat, the door closing more quietly than when they closed on their way out. But nobody gets back in next to me, the empty space beside me making me feel impossibly small, and I'm already little.

Five-five, with wide hips, thick thighs, and a curved belly, and sometimes, next to my sisters, all taller than me, but who spend their entire lives on a diet, I feel like the biggest person in the room. I realise now, I kinda like that feeling, despite it having made me feel awful in the past, I think I'd give anything right now to be made to feel bigger again.

My body starts to tremble then, the cold air blowing in reigniting my fear as the car shifts into gear. My teeth chatter behind the tape and I curl my numb fingers, knuckles carving into the base of my spine where my hands are bound behind my back, squashed between me and the seat. I squeeze my eyes shut, and as the car starts to pick up speed, the road not smooth, fear wrapping itself around my spine like barbs, I get the overwhelming urge to pee. Attempting to take a deep breath, shuddering as air is pulled rapidly through my nostrils, I press my legs together, squeeze my eyelids shut so tight, stars shoot across my vision, and every breath burns.

"I am not going to hurt you," a thick, rumbled voice, something that's rough but smooth, dense like coiling smoke, heavy with *truth*, says from the front seat and my breath stills completely.

I want to laugh suddenly, because I'm not sure that even really worried me before, the thought of hurting. I don't think I've even *thought* of pain until this man mentioned it. Tears cascade down my face, despite my mixed emotions, all tangled and twisted, because as much as I am at his mercy, bound and silent and scared, it sounds like a truth.

"Breathe, Haisley," the same voice from up front instructs and I can tell he's still facing away from me, but the vehicle feels as though it's slowed a fraction, like despite his eyes not boring into me, I still have the majority of his attention.

His voice makes me feel like I'm liquid, muscles dissolving into the leather of the seat, the way he almost caresses my name as it leaves his lips.

My ears burn, my throat tight and my bladder, thankfully, feels less likely to release itself, so I just drop my head back against the headrest, taking slow sips of air through my nose. My ears are pounding, heart racing, but it all starts to slow as I follow his instruction.

And when my breathing, still too quick, my pulse jumping in my throat, begins to slow, the vehicle speed picks up again, the road evening out beneath the tyres, and I hear him murmur beneath his breath.

"Good girl."

I'm not meant to hear it, and I'm a million percent sure he didn't mean to say it. Nevertheless, the words ripple their way up my spine, a flush heating my chest, spearing like slow sliding tentacles up my neck, igniting my face in a cherry red bloom. And I'm suddenly very grateful for the sack over my head.

Time feels, altogether, too fast and too slow, in the same way that it has over the last three weeks. Since Cian, everything's been a blur. I've been pulled from pillar to post, safe house to safe house, not that any of those places were actually *safe*. When the Doyle brothers' guard threw a mismatched tracksuit at me and told me to put it on tonight, I just felt numb. I didn't struggle whilst he taped my mouth, tied my hands, my only thoughts, really, were thank God this is it. It's finally going to be over.

I think of my cousin, his green eyes, much like mine, but angrier, full of something possessive and downright petrifying and I squeeze my eyes closed. I replay that night over and over inside my head until it spins so much, I feel dizzy and sick. And it's only when my eyes snap open, my chest heaving as my nostrils flare, desperate to claw in as much air as possible, the rough fabric of the sack sucking in with my erratic breaths, that I realise the car's stopped.

It's still dark, no light filtering through the woven fabric covering my head, and the rain is beating harder than the organ inside my chest. There's a pinging sound, beneath the rainfall and I strain my ears to listen, trying to work out if it's-

"Hail," the driver says quietly, cutting off my thoughts, and my heart jerks into a stampede tempo beneath my ribs.

His voice wraps around me like a lasso, loose at first, but slowly, it tightens with every breath I take, and I feel like I'm just waiting for it to snap into place around me and squeeze.

"I was waiting," he says slowly, his voice so, *so* deep, unhurried but precise, practised, as though he's always got the undivided attention of anyone he's ever spoken with before. "To see if it stops."

My brow creases as he continues, wondering why he's explaining himself to me, or even, speaking to me at all. I wish I could close off my ears, cover them, stop his deceptively alluring calm from lulling me into a false sense of safety. I don't need to know anything about this man to know that he's dangerous. Everyone that is connected to this, my family, the mafia, even through something as loose as a friend of a friend of a friend. None of it will ever be good. And I'm not bound and gagged in the back of this man's car for him to talk me to death.

I wish I could tell him, scream at him to just get the fuck on with it already, I'm ready, I just want this to be it, the end. I'm not ready to die, but I'm still more ready to die than I am ready to live. I've spent the last three weeks fighting, and now, I'm just, *done*.

But then a car door opens, *my* door, the wind whips around me, small droplets of rain misting over me as someone leans across my body, unsnapping my seatbelt. Their fingers find my right thigh, the gentlest of touches and I flinch so hard the back of my skull collides with the headrest.

"Relax," the driver's voice says, his face so, so close to me, and I find myself calming now that I know it's *him* hovering above me in the open door and not another stranger. "Swing your legs around," he rumbles quietly, a chill ripping its way up my spine as I do as I'm told.

I think of him calling me *good girl* and I half want to die with embarrassment, but I swing my legs around, feet dangling, and his large hands curl over my hips, igniting something in my chest. Lifting me down to the ground. He steadies me, my legs feeling like jelly, and then his touch disappears and I'm panting beneath the sack over my head, wishing I could see.

"I am going to hold onto your arm, just so you do not fall."

His voice, so proper, words so polite and perfect. It's a caress, warmth sliding down my spine and my danger receptors start to run haywire inside my head, because I'm about to die. But my body's hot, my skin on fire, even though the outside air is so fucking cold my teeth chatter as I'm assaulted by the rain. Just as he said, the car door closing at my back, the man takes my arm, his grip light, and I could run. I could twist out of his grip and run, and I might not get far, or I might turn and smack headfirst into a light pole, but any of those things, the outcomes of my escape, would indicate I value my life, and I'm just not so sure that I do.

So I let him lead me by my elbow, his long fingers scorching me through the fabric of my hoodie. The one that's dirty, smells of smoke and sweat that isn't mine and the thought of what someone possibly did whilst wearing these clothes makes me want to heave. But there's tape on my mouth, sealing my lips and as we take a slow step up, and then another, a sloped incline, small rocks beneath the soles of my trainers, before another few steps. My body guided by the man who's going to take my life.

I gag.

It's loud behind my closed mouth, echoing in my chest, my nostrils flare and my eyes water and I need this fucking bag off of my head. Everything suddenly feeling much too real, too close. Claustrophobia, something I've never much thought about, always living in a large house with an oversized bedroom, so much space, and too much emptiness. My eyes stream, and I try to keep my rolling stomach from lurching, but I can't, and it does, and I heave so hard it pulls the bunched muscles in the top of my back, shooting pain down my spine.

Ears buzzing, heart thudding, blood rushing through

my ears, I wonder if I should let myself be sick. If only to choke on it. End this shit myself. Not give anyone else the satisfaction of doing it for me.

Fuck Cian, he deserved what he got.

Fuck my father too.

I hate him.

I hate our family.

I hate all of them.

Everything.

I can't breathe, the heat of my body suddenly replaced with a burning cold, ice spearing its way through my veins. Tears track down my cheeks, I heave again, my nose running, white spots dotting my vision, and I think I really might be sick. But then the sack is torn off of my head, tape ripped violently from my face, my mouth popping open on a gasping exhale as my head whips to the side, the skin of my cheeks stinging.

My arse hits the floor first, feet flat, knees bent up by my ears as I'm roughly shoved forward, head hanging between them. My greasy hair curtains limply on either side of my face, eyes closed, nose running, tears falling from my watery eyes. I breathe hard through my mouth, spit dribbling from between my swollen lips, dripping to the ground between my open thighs. I pant hard, getting my breath, my hollow stomach settling almost instantly because I can finally breathe.

My shoulders pinch as warm hands cover mine, I flinch forward but I feel so drained I don't try and further get away. Cold metal of a blade slides over the skin of my wrists, slicing through the rough fabric of the rope binding me. My limbs part, dropping forward heavily, grainy wood beneath my knuckles as they graze the floor beneath me. My breath rushes in and out of my mouth, the freezing air burning my lungs, my throat dry and irritated, I keep coughing, trying not to vomit bile and the pins and needles in my hands are starting to hurt as blood rushes through my arms.

I don't even bother opening my eyes, just stay slumped forward, and as my breathing slows, my hearing starting to come back, sounds other than my own rushing blood, start to filter their way through. It's his almost silent footsteps that prick my ears first, echoing as they disappear away from me, and I finally blink my eyes open.

The room is dark as I lift my head, my neck stiff and shoulders aching. I use the ditch of my elbow to wipe my face, then drag the cuff of my sleeve across my nose, my chin. I rub my knuckles into my eyes, swiping over them with the backs of my hands.

The floor between my legs is wood, old and dark and not well looked after. I lift my gaze further, eyes slowly rolling around their sockets to peer through the gloom, discovering I'm alone.

Wind rattles the small, high windows at my back as I take stock of my surroundings, glance over my shoulder, rain lashing the thin glass panes. I scope out the room, low ceiling, walls painted white, their surface shadowed and slightly uneven. A bright flash fills the room, lighting it up for just a second, illuminating the mostly empty space, highlighting its cobwebs, a couch, armchair, fireplace. Thunder rumbles, and I imagine the clouds outside to be dark and low, it feels as though the walls shake with the second clap of thunder and I jump a little, a shiver running down my spine.

I stretch out my legs, the muscles aching as I lay them down, flex my toes towards me, the tight muscles pulling and burning, but it feels good, destroying the ache. Bringing my hands up, tugging up my sleeves to inspect my wrists, the pale skin torn and red from the rope bindings. I sigh softly, the cold air making them burn more, and then I hear *him*.

His footsteps are so quiet, I keep my gaze lowered, eyes lifted beneath my lashes so I can monitor his approach. And I don't want to look at him, I don't think I want to see the man that's going to take my life.

I don't want the very last thing I see to be my monster.

CHAPTER 4
THORNE

She is still where I left her. Hunched over on the floor, her hands on her knees, fingers blanching where she squeezes them tight. I wish I knew what she was thinking. Why she has not tried to run. I left her alone. The door is five feet behind her. Unlocked. I kind of wanted her to. Not to chase her, that is not really my thing, just to, I don't know, let her go?

I will not be good for her.

I *cannot* be.

I am not *good*.

She would have to escape, evade my capture, but if she had left just now, ran out into the rain and wind and hail, hurried through the storm, I would have let her go.

And she would have died, the elements would end her, and it would be painful, but my job would be done.

Let her go.

But I cannot. I already know, despite never chasing anything in my entire life, I would.

For her.

I stare at her small fingers as I approach, chipped red polish on short, rounded nails. Fair skin decorated with light freckles, the backs of her hands peeking out of the too long sleeves of her hoodie, snaked with pale green veins, like ivy climbing its way up beneath her flawless skin, wrapping itself around her bones.

Gently, I place the metal tub I am carrying down onto the floor between her feet and mine, my fingers slow to uncurl from the handles on either end of it. Her head is still bowed when I glance up, my body still folded in half, bent forward, and she is not looking up at me, but I know she is watching because the tiniest of flinches rips through her, but she is trying hard not to react.

I straighten, step back, turning out of the room again, I take the two steps down, ducking through the doorway as I do, a narrow, square archway leading to the kitchen. The electricity is still off because I was having issues with it last time I was here, I will get it fixed once daylight rolls in. I was not expecting to be here.

It is off the grid, out of use, a lighthouse that is now just a listed building, but not one anyone wants, and the small attached house that we currently reside in. None of it cannot be structurally renovated. No one would stumble across it unless they shipwrecked on the rocks below and scaled the hundred-plus feet of white cliffs to get up here. Being here feels like I am on the edge of the world. Forgotten and lost and alone.

Perhaps that is exactly why I bought it.

Fortunately, everything else is still connected, gas, water, but the water is cold. I check the gas stove, the four pans of water I placed there, already starting to boil. Little bubbles rushing to the surface, I listen, my head twisted just slightly to capture any noise she might make.

I never thought I would be in a position like this.

And I do not even know why I have brought her here.

I am supposed to kill her.

I *have to* kill her.

I *want* to.

I take two pans off of the gas burner, carry them back through to the front room, bare except for the large empty fireplace, a small worn couch and battered old armchair. And the girl in its centre.

She does not look at me.

Slowly, I drop into a crouch, pour both pans of heated water into the metal tub, return to the kitchen for the others. I do this twice more and then I dip my fingers into the metal tub, swirl the tips of them through the water, testing its temperature. I glance up at her, her position unchanged, head still bowed, and I want to see her, a face that I have memorised so well. Does she still look the same way I remember? I want to see it all before it is removed from this planet for good. It feels cruel, to be gifted this girl, only to have to tear her from this life and force her violently into the next.

But I do not form attachments.

And I think of all the times that Haisley Kelly has overtaken my thoughts, filled my head with dreams and wants, I know I can never have. And it feels like a punishment.

Perhaps, that is why I pretend to hate her so much.

Something inside of me repels against it all, but I still have a job to do. Why did I not leave this shit for someone else? Why did I not even try to win, take my money, leave those Doyle boys in debt and never think of her and what became of her again. Why did I hear her name and have to have her for myself. To *kill*.

I find my gaze on the smooth surface of the water, dark in colour, like the room, bathed in shadows and gloom and something more sinister. The air feels suddenly electrified, my teeth grinding as I think about what I have to do. Everything feels dangerous, *I* feel dangerous. The guns strapped to me, one holstered beneath my arm, the other at my hip, and they feel so heavy, if I were to throw myself off of this cliff, their weight would drown me. But it is not real, and this situation is, and I wonder how long I will get to have her for.

The girl I cannot have.

I peer up from the water, brow low, eyes lifted beneath my lashes, and I watch her. Small, and silent, waves of thick red curls fallen free from the mess tied on the back of her skull. I want to comb my hands through it, twirl the lengths through my fingers, twist it tight and lock it around my knuckles.

My elbows rest on my bent knees, and I flick the water droplets free of my fingers before pushing my hand through my hair. Straightening, I look down at her, try not to notice the way she seems to shrink in on herself.

"Haisley," I say her name softly, I think of my sister Grace, the gentler tone of voice I use with her, but I do not think that will work here. "Get up, please."

It takes a minute, a minute that feels like an hour, but slowly, she does as I ask, and I feel like I breathe a little easier because of it. My chest feels tight as she stands on wobbly legs, her knees trembling, fingers curling into fists at her sides.

But she does not say anything, and she *still* will not look at me.

I think of all the things I could say, something to reassure her, maybe, something kind, encouraging, something that would make her feel safer, at ease. But Blackwells do not tell lies. So instead, I take a small step back, briefly glance down at the water and swallow.

"Take off your clothes."

And her eyes finally snap up to meet mine.

CHAPTER 5
HAISLEY

I stare at him in the dark, trying to swallow his quietly spoken words, and my breath catches. Lungs full, desperate to empty, but I just... can't.

I didn't want to see him.

And now I can't stop looking.

He is *nothing* like I expected. I've seen contract killers before, I'm assuming that's what this arrangement is, my view of them always on the sly. Through door cracks, stair railings, creeping through shadows, my back flush to a wall. But what I've learnt from my time spying around the house, is that these people, hired solely for grisly deeds, are usually great huge men with bald heads and greasy skin, dirt and blood in equal measures on their hands. Scary looking guys with scars and weapons and sweat patches under their arms, none of them have *ever* looked like this.

It all just feels wrong.

Terrifying.

His dark eyes bore into my own, so captivating, so dark in colour they look black, only enhanced further because his face is in shadow. Chin dipped, head angled slightly down, he looks up at me through a thick fan of black lashes, and the way he has his head cocked, it's almost… childlike, boyish. Something curious, dangerous, the way his lips don't lift at all, his top and bottom lip the same thickness, a gentle curve to his cupid's bow.

His gaze burns me, heat razes across my flesh, goosebumps prickling beneath my donated clothing, and I will my eyes to fall, away from him, my attention to divert to *anywhere* else.

I blink, eyes dry as I strain them hard in the dark, his thick wave of black hair pushed back neatly on his head, but a single tendril has dropped forward, falling across one dark eyebrow, the tip of it resting in his lashes. He makes no move to shove it back, his eyes firmly locked on me, waiting. He shifts his shoulders, black suit jacket over a black shirt, matching slacks. My eyes rove over his attire, it's pressed and straight and perfect.

It's all… *wrong*.

I lick my lips, split, dry and cracked, my tongue dry too, and I manage to drop my gaze again. Peering at the metal tub between us, half filled with water, a waft of steam swirling from the top of it and I almost pass out on the floor.

Take off your clothes.

I suddenly wish I'd run; I know he'd catch me, but I could have at least tried. I thought I came here to die. And now he's…

"What?" I whisper, my voice cracking and I have this insane urge to cry.

I don't want this strange man to see me naked. I don't want anyone to see me naked. I don't want anyone to *see me.*

A shiver rips up my spine, tears gathering in my eyes, clinging to my lower lash line, and my skin flushes hot, but cold spears through my veins too. Icy and sharp. He doesn't say anything, he just watches me, and I wonder if it'd be better just to take them off, save myself any more humiliation and just… do as I'm told.

Good girl.

The memory of his words in the car just a few short hours ago fill my cheeks with heat, and I'm sure I must be glowing a cherry red. And now that I've seen him, put a face to the voice. A voice that feels reminiscent of silk caressing my skin like strong fingers, a face that would surely make angels weep. His jaw is sharp, strong, angular. Cheekbones high, shadowing the hollows of his face, he looks like a demon, something that would creep from the shadows in the corner of your room at night.

A monster.

"*Now*," he rumbles quietly, a warning.

I'm going to die.

He studies me as I take a deep breath, and slowly, so fucking slowly, my entire body trembling, I pull on the cuffs of my sleeves, slipping my arms into the inside of the hoodie. My eyes water as I stare at the floor, the wood dark, grainy, I pick out one little section, a teardrop shape in the woodgrain, so dark in the middle,

I wonder if there's a hole at its centre. I push my arms together, bring them up the centre of my chest and using my hands at the neckline, I slip my head inside the fabric. A single tear falls as I push the bunched fabric up and over my head, hair slapping at my back.

I keep my head down, blurry gaze on my chosen focal point in the floor, hoodie balled up in my hands, held tight before me, still covering my front from his view.

"Drop it," he whispers, raspy and thick.

Throat tight, I swallow, my arms shaking, chest heaving, I let go of the sweatshirt. Without waiting for his instruction, I go for the rolled over jogging bottoms, the strings pulled tight and knotted in a bow over my navel. Fingers trembling, I pull the tie-string free, slip my thumbs beneath the waistband at my hips and push my bottoms down. I toe off both trainers, kicking them to one side of me, and step out of the joggers.

The room is ice cold, standing in my underwear, goosebumps erupt across my skin, and I watch as my tears drip from my chin, splashing against the floor. I bring my hands up, balled fists hiding my breasts, and I think of all my imperfections, bruises, injuries, hideous things I've kept hidden for the last few weeks when he finally shifts.

Regaining my attention, I look up a little from beneath my lashes, my head still bowed, I watch his feet, shoes shined so perfectly I bet he can see his own reflection in them.

He steps around the tin tub, his footsteps silent, and

I feel my breath catch in my throat as he stops before me. I squeeze my eyes closed briefly, sucking in a deep breath. He smells like metal, like gunpowder and iron and leather, salt like the sea and ice, something sharp like ozone. That strong scent you sometimes catch during a lightning storm, the one that alerts you to danger if the flashes in the sky fail to do so.

This man feels like a storm, a calm, lucid exterior, but beneath the surface of those dark eyes something menacing and turbulent lies in wait.

I watch as his hand slowly comes up, my teeth chattering with the cold, fear. Rain and hail thrashing against the thin windows outside. We stand in the shadows, me on display for this hungry predator. His finger and thumb find the tip of my chin and I jolt as his warm skin touches my cold.

"*Shh,*" he coos, lifting my face, I keep my eyes downcast, his fancy shoes covering the little wood grain I was studying. "Look at me," he whispers, his warm breath between us, fanning over me, ruffling the little loose hairs around my face, his big body radiating a scorching heat.

I swallow hard, the lump in my throat like a stone blocking my airway, and it takes everything in me to finally lift my gaze. His face is so close, our lips almost brush, I suck in a sharp breath, filling my lungs with everything that is him. It's intoxicating and lethal and it feels like I'm consuming poison. But he just stares at me, his head tilted in that curious way, eyes like an abyss, swirling black vortexes, but this close, I can see them more. My own eyes wide with fear, I study his, discovering the black flecked with gold, like there's some sort of goodness trying to reveal itself through a veil of pitch darkness.

But I know it's not real.

It's my hope. For something better.

Mercy.

I let my gaze fall, unable to look at him any longer, stomach knotting, and then there's cold air replacing his warmth. I shiver, glancing up beneath my lashes, watching him track his steps back across the floor, his eyes still firmly on me. He manoeuvres effortlessly around the tub of water, stopping on the other side of it. His head drops back into that boyish tilt, chin dipped, eyes flicked up, and it's so… *strange* on his harsh features. He reaches out his arm, hand open, fingers outstretched, an eyebrow barely lifting on his forehead, silently beckoning me forward.

Come, he summons silently, I can feel his words in the silence thick between us.

I've been trained to follow orders, to submit to men, to do as I'm told. I'm a primped and pruned princess of the Irish mob and despite that not really being how the inner workings of my family actually go, it seems, even on the brink of death, I'm unable to rebel against a lifetime of conditioning.

The silence is so loud it's deafening, my body trembles, feeling the cold, hearing the rain. The flashes of lightning flare like alarm signals, casting the room in sudden bursts of blinding light, it's all much too fast, the sheeting hail *tap, tap, tapping* against the window. And this dangerous man's dark eyes burning a hole right through my soul, I feel high and flustered and I think I *want* to place my hand in his.

"Come here, Little Cub, let me see you," he whispers, cooing, coaxing, the pet name sending a rush of heat through me, because the way he says it, it feels like an endearment.

His gentle words extend a deceptively looking golden thread, one that doesn't want to guide, but wants to strangle, to choke, and you know this, but you still can't seem to resist its pull, walking knowingly straight into its deadly tangle. Sacrificial.

I swallow hard, that rock in my throat joined by another, but my feet take me forward. Cautious, tentative steps. Eyes locked on his, he compels me toward him with nothing more than a look. And I'm swept up in his storm, electricity bolting through me, I let one of my arms fall away from my heaving chest, slowly outstretching, until the tips of my fingers are dancing in the palm of his open hand. His fingers close over mine one finger at a time, igniting me with every new touch like he's the spark and I'm the gasoline.

I jolt, he smirks and my stomach sinks and levitates all in the same breath as I see him immediately smother the curl to his lips. I'm panting, my skin on fire, my blood like ice, my chest heaving as I stare at him. I don't look away as he guides me into the water, hot on my feet, warmth rushing up my ankles as it laps at my flesh, my calves, a different heat hitting me in the apex of my thighs.

Embarrassment floods through me, revealing itself in my pale skin, my entire body covered in pale tawny-coloured freckles, dark mottled bruising, but nowhere near enough to hide the red flush as it blooms over the entirety of my body.

But he doesn't look at my battered body, even when he says, "Drop your hand," a slight nod to the arm still held up over my chest. "Let me see you," and he's still staring into my eyes, but I'm suddenly aware that *he's* aware of everything.

Lace bra the only thing covering my top half. I drop my arm, the cold air tightening my nipples, the rough lace a welcome friction on my skin.

That's when his eyes drop, it's only a quick glance, barely even a half a second of a look, before his eyes are back on mine, a blank expression on his face. It feels like concern, the way his black orbs flicker between my own, but he's so relaxed, stoic, the fear I had moments ago slams back into me in full force.

His grip on my hand tightens, his other going to my left arm, strong fingers curling around my elbow.

I keep staring, unable to take my eyes off of him, watching his face for anything. For an expression, a crease between his brows, something to make him human, just a man, just for a second, or maybe I'm waiting for something else entirely, something to reveal his true self.

A monster.

I think, in this moment, that perhaps, I want him to be something else. Not changed but still something different. This dangerous man with the dark eyes, the stoic face, but who smirked at me like he was the devil. Unguarded and wild and dangerous.

He's going to kill me.

He's *my* monster.

His hand on my elbow slides up my arm, thumb smoothing its way to the pressure point in the front of my shoulder, his fingers flex over the ball joint. His chin dipped, he steps right up to the metal tub, his shoes tapping the side of it as he does. Fingers on my shoulder grazing slow, lazy circles over my skin and then the tips of them slip beneath the thin strap of my bra. Eyes still locked on his, trapped, enraptured, held captive. He watches me, inches from my face, his breath on my cheeks, he guides the strap down. My eyes snap closed, a tremble wracking through me, my legs feel like jelly, and the warmth from the water, the cold air in the room, the scorching heat from *him*, is making me dizzy.

"Keep your eyes on me," he whispers the order, his words fanning my lips, my chin trembles, bottom lip wobbling as he slips the other strap down. "I am not going to hurt you," he tells me again, and I swallow down a shaky breath, blinking, I lick my lips, refocus my attention on him.

Dropping my hand, my fingers tingling, he reaches around me, my body quaking, his large hands smoothing over my cold skin, everywhere he touches burns a trail across my flesh. And then my bra is snapped open, I swallow hard, my eyes watering and my head is spinning again, but I let it fall free. I let him take it away from me, so I'm left in nothing but my knickers.

His hands are so big they smother me, but he still doesn't touch me inappropriately, and I hate myself because I think, maybe, I would let him. His hands slide down my back, feather light and almost not touching at all, but his heat glides over my skin, pricking me with goosebumps, like little electric shocks as though he were. His thumbs trace the back of my underwear, just the cotton edge, his face so close to mine, he looks blurry, it feels a little like I'm drunk, with him this near, warm water on my aching feet and his hot hands running over my flesh.

He draws back, just enough to look into my eyes, to see me properly, those dark orbs flicker, just once, between my own and then he pushes my knickers down. He guides them down my thick thighs, his touch tingling as they finally hit my knees and fall to the water. I don't look down and he doesn't look down, the rain is still hammering against the window, sounding like bullets against the thin pane of glass. The wind whistling through this old decrepit building, howling like screaming fox cubs. I shiver, still trapped in his gaze, ensnared and bleeding and broken and…

"Please, just kill me," it's a whispered plea.

My sanity barely hanging on by a thread after weeks of shit just like this, no, not like this, I don't know what is happening here, but *this* is something else. He doesn't blink, he doesn't move, react, like he knew what I was going to say before I did. He says nothing when I keep staring at him, keep silently wishing he'd just do it already.

"*Please.*"

The sob gets lodged in my throat, my eyes don't water, his hands by his sides, my underwear removed, floating around my ankles, my hands not even trying to cover my naked body now.

"I am not going to hurt you," he tells me again, a whisper too, like we're both in this moment, and neither one of us wants to break it by speaking too loud, shatter the gloom.

He sounds like he wants to say more, something else, but he doesn't, and I don't wait for him to. Dropping my gaze, I lick my chapped lips, a split in my bottom one spearing its way down further than the line of my lip, edging into the skin of my chin. It pulls when I move my mouth too much, I wondered if it needed stitching when it happened, but it's started to heal now, slowly, it's been three weeks and I can still taste blood.

"I am going to bathe you, Haisley," is what he finally says, my eyes drifting shut at his gentle words, because despite how they sound, they don't really feel gentle at all.

Feet and ankles in the water, I curl my toes as he takes a small bar of soap from his pocket, something he must have brought in from the other room and drops down in front of me. I stare at the top of his head, thick wave of black hair pitch as night. His hands with a cloth I hadn't noticed before, dipping into the water, his fingers slowly close around my ankle, cloth in the other hand, my breathing laboured as he glances up at me. We hold each other's gaze as he lifts each of my feet, one at a time, removing my underwear from my ankles in the water. And then the warm cloth is sliding up the inside of my calf, his other hand still holding onto my ankle. A cuff, a shackle, long fingers protective in their hold, grounding me. To this moment, to this experience, to *him*.

He moves the soapy cloth up to the back of my knee, all the while his eyes are still on mine. Enraptured, hypnotised, enthralled, I keep my eyes on his as the cloth climbs higher, momentarily leaving my skin to dip back down into the water. I don't know what's happening to me, but I don't feel fear, something else capturing me instead as I keep my eyes on my captor.

A whimper escapes through my teeth as he reaches the back of my thigh, still bruised and tender from the lashings of my father's belt. He stills at the sound, his hand with the cloth still there, his touch so light, it makes me want to cry. My teeth sink into my sore bottom lip, pulling it into my mouth and locking it behind my teeth as tears prick my eyes. Without words, he starts to turn me around, never once looking at my body.

He doesn't react when I'm finally turned away from him, my eyes now on the rain lashing against the small window set high in the wall. I feel suspended for a moment, time standing still, and then it's like nothing happened at all as he continues to wash my skin clean, being careful over the backs of my thighs. He's gentle, switching hands, one always firmly around an ankle as he runs the warm cloth over my legs, his hold switching carefully to my hip when he has to stand taller to reach my back.

He squeezes the cloth, water and soap suds sliding down my skin, and the feel of his gentleness, his care, makes me moan under my breath. It's barely more than silence, the tiny, escaped noise, but he hears it, his fingers flexing on the flesh of my hip, tighter, and he feels closer, his breath drifting over the back of my neck, and I think I'm losing my mind.

What am I doing?

I stand tall, I stay still, motionless, even as my naked chest heaves with breath, my breasts rising and falling as his fingers slide up my back, beside the hand with the cloth and his hand is suddenly clamping over my nape. Eyes wide, I stare straight ahead, suck in a sharp breath, his lips graze my lobe as his face stops beside mine, chin over my shoulder, his eyes burn a hole in the side of my face, but I don't look.

He hums lowly with something like satisfaction, I feel it vibrate through his fingers, ricocheting down my spine.

"*Mmm*, you are a good girl, aren't you, Haisley?" I tremble at the question that's not really a question at all, shaking so hard my teeth chatter. "So *fucking* good," it's a rasp, strained, a confession he didn't want to admit, one, if voiced any louder, he'd likely snap a tendon, and it breaks me.

My knees buckle, ankles roll, but his firm hold on my neck keeps me up, he holds my weight like it's effortless, my feet dangling just above the bottom of the little metal tub.

"I am not going to hurt you," he reassures me again, still whispering, breathy now, and I can feel his heart hammering in his chest at my back, despite him not touching me. "I am just bathing you. That is all."

His breath slides down the side of my throat, my body like a battle of ice and fire, I feel myself nodding, his grip still so tight it makes me wince, but as he lowers me back to my feet on wobbly legs, horrifyingly, I realise, I don't want him to let go.

"*Please*," I hear myself say it, a whispered begging, I don't recall telling my mouth to form the word, but he pauses, listening to me, waiting, so patiently. "Please," I lick my lips, swallow, those rocks in my throat starting to crumble. "*Please*," my eyes fall, my insides twisting, *"Don't let go."*

He exhales at the same time I do, a rush of breath like we've both been holding onto it, and I wonder what the fuck it is I think I'm doing, because this is my executioner. The faceless monster that's been haunting my dreams for the last three weeks. And I'm tired, I'm so tired of fighting, I thought this was my end, but my body seems to want something else entirely.

Of its own accord, my hand comes up, reaching for his but then all at once, I'm stopping myself from falling forward, my shins hitting the lip of the tub, both of his hands leaving my body. A gasp whips its way up my throat as the cloth is thrown violently into the tub at my feet, water sloshing over the sides. I spin around so fast the floor feels like it's tilting beneath me but all I can do is watch the tense muscles in his back shift beneath his suit jacket as he exits the room.

Quickly, I finish washing myself, my cheeks flushing with shame, I keep my gaze down on my toes, nails still painted a bright red that hasn't chipped yet. Such a stark contrast from my normal life, bathing in a little tin tub. I may not be a revered child of the Kelly clan, but to the outside world, I'm still a princess of the Irish mob, and so I'm treated as such, if not only for appearances sake. I'm used to a large house, with butlers and maids, chefs and masseurs, hair and make-up teams on call. I've been a pampered princess despite the shitty things I've had to put up with. But there are lots of us, some of my sisters, younger and older alike, are prettier and skinnier and have perfect skin, better manners, less attitude. They're the ones married off in a deal first, they're tamer, more amenable, less *murderous*. Anyone I was offered to would have thought my father had been scraping the barrel, they'd probably think I were an insult rather than a gift.

Foaming the cloth with the small bar of soap and rubbing it over my skin like I'm trying to scour it off. I can't wash my dirty hair in this water, not much more than a puddle, but I *can* scrub at my skin. Embarrassment floods my veins, replacing my blood with fire.

'Don't let go.'

Jesus Christ, I'm such an idiot. What in the fuck is wrong with me?

Shaking my head, I rush through washing, making sure I'm careful of my bruises, the one's on my belly and arms don't really hurt anymore, they just look nasty, but my chest still aches if I breathe too deep and the back of my thighs, my arse, all of the fleshy parts of me still make me wince. It's only when I drop the cloth into the lukewarm water that I realise I don't have a towel.

Except I do.

As I glance up, the darkened doorway my executioner disappeared through is filled again. He stands there, my captor, a large blue coloured towel in his hands, his eyes are back on mine, his head dipped in that curious tilt making my stomach flip. I feel my cheeks heat as he approaches, my gaze dropping, I shiver, my body aching and tired and so *done.*

He stops before me, the towel held between his outstretched hands, open, waiting, and I don't move, I can't. I'm waiting for him to lose his temper, shout at me, beat me. *Kill me.*

Kill me, kill me, kill me.

But he doesn't do any of those things.

"Come here, Little Cub," he says softly, tears pricking my eyes with the kindness.

It's not real.

I breathe hard through my nose, trying not to look, hating myself for wanting to. My fingers curl into fists, nails digging into my palms, and I'm waiting, still waiting, for him to do something. I smell him again as he closes in on my front, his breathing so deep and even, it's like he's walking around asleep. So at ease, comfortable, relaxed. Something spikes in my chest, my teeth clamp down on my bottom lip as it threatens to tremble.

"Come," he says again, so quietly, so calmly, and I feel my blood getting hotter, irritation at his coolness.

Skin prickling, tears drying, anger suddenly starts to simmer low in my belly. I'm not this, I'm not afraid to die. I don't need to be spoken to like I'm a child. I'm a twenty-three year old woman, I'm intelligent, I'm resourceful, I'm not *this*.

I'm a murderer, too.

Inhaling a long, slow breath, filling my lungs, the air heavy with dust and an old musty smell, presumably because this place has been closed up for a long time, but it still can't cancel it out, *him*. Gunpowder is rich, strong, heady, and leather, the sea. I'm dizzy and angry and just a little bit frightened, but I'm not seeking comfort. I'm not seeking comfort in anyone or anything. I've been alone a long time, left to my own devices, watched and monitored but alone. I don't need to find comfort in anyone, especially not the man holding out a towel with the patience of ten Saints. My executioner.

Demon.

Devil.

Monster.

Definitely not him.

Slowly, I step out of the tub, gaze trained on my feet, I watch water droplets run down my ankles, curling over the small bones in my feet. The towel is draped around me, the man turning me in his light hold to swaddle me in rough fabric. I'm covered now, hidden from view and I feel better, covered in a worn towel. But his compulsion is strong, the way he's so close but feels too far and I'm almost panting with my uneven breaths because the proximity is all too much. I feel like I can't breathe as he watches me, and I'm not moving, I'm stock still but he's right *there* and I want to look, have my gaze lock back on his dark one because I felt something, and I wish I didn't.

"Breathe," he whispers, his breath on my cheek, lips brushing my skin, a shiver tearing through my body, my breath catching in my throat. "Relax, I am not going to hurt you."

My gaze snaps up then, hooking on his, his eyes dark, so fucking dark, swirling little vortexes of nothingness, and I finally find my voice.

"Kill me," I say, it's loud, the bubble of gloomy confusion we were in just mere moments ago shatters like an exploding lightbulb, sharp jagged pieces firing across the room like daggered missiles.

He stares back at me, his face blank, eyes dead, that head tilt he wears so well nothing more than a fleeting memory. I blink, he continues to stare and then he's grabbing hold of me, heaving me up and over his shoulder, my body jarring as my face hits the base of his spine. I inhale him deeply, his scent intoxicating me, blurring my thoughts and overwhelming my senses.

"Put me down!" I scream, the sound rattling its way up my throat, trembling free from my lungs with a screech as I pound my fists into the back of his thighs.

I arch my back, my muscles burning, my skin tight over my bruising, craning my head up, my neck twisting. He carries me through narrow walkways, dark and damp, my ears buzz, my chest heaves and my fists hammer against his solid flesh. He doesn't stop, slow down, he just keeps walking, calm and cool and I hate it. The silence, lack of reaction.

"Put me down! Let me go!" I screech so loud I can't even hear myself, but his smooth, gravelly voice cuts through all my noise.

"If you were not already injured," he says softly, "I would spank you so hard, you would wear my handprint on your arse for the next month."

I pant through my open mouth, staring into the darkness, my thighs aching and tightening and everything getting so fucking messed up inside my head. Tears prick my eyes, and I'm suddenly grateful for my bruises, but he's not finished.

"You will not wear anyone else's marks ever again."

It's like a spear through the heart, his promise, but not one of safety or reassurance. Something dark and sinister, ominous.

The tremor in my body quakes through me, I drop my arms, releasing my fists, go limp.

"Good girl," he praises, and I grit my teeth so hard they squeak, my eyes crushing closed, tears squeeze free, dripping up my face, running into my hairline where I hang upside down.

"You're a monster," I whisper, hating that my voice cracks on those words.

There's silence as he continues moving through the house, rain still battering against the windows, the roof, until we pause, his footsteps slowing and then stopping. He dips down, the creak of old hinges loud in our silence as he slides me back down over his shoulder, slowly, carefully, making sure I get my feet under me.

I stare up at him, my face a mess, eyes blurry and wide, his, completely unreadable, unfeeling, and I want the man that bathed me back.

He stalks towards me, the tips of his shoes brushing my bare toes as I stumble backwards, falling into even more darkness, the only thing visible is his movements. The backs of my legs hit the edge of something, and I flop backwards, an old mattress creaking beneath me as I drop to my arse, clutching my towel to my chest. He doesn't stop coming, climbing over me as I scuttle backwards over the musty sheets, the mattress springs poking into the palms of my hands, my towel unravelling beneath me.

That's when the fear hits me, his much larger body looming over mine, he grabs both my hands in one of his and I squirm under him, dreading what's to come as he pins me beneath him, not touching me, but his body is right there, trapping me to the mattress.

"Please, please, *please*," I cry. "I'll be good, I'm sorry, I'm sorry, *please, not this*," I sob then, real tears streaming down my face. "I'm sorry," I cry, huge wracking sobs vibrating through my bones.

I turn my head to the side, pressing my face into the sheets, crying harder than I think I've ever cried before, him still looming over me, my hands locked in one of his. His chest heaving, expensive shirt and jacket brushing my bare breasts, his panting breath on my neck.

His other hand fumbles between us, his belt buckle clanging as he undoes it, ripping the leather through his trouser loops, his knuckles grazing over the skin of my pelvis. I cry harder, even though I fight like hell not to, my head aching, my heart lurching, my pleas and begging unintelligible as I sob. My stomach coils with dread, my insides churning with sickness. The leather of his belt slaps against my skin making me wince, but then it slides up my chest so fast it burns, continuing past my head and my eyes blink open wide as he wrenches my arms up above my head, my shoulders popping in protest making me cry out with the pain.

The backs of my hands collide with cold metal bars, the bed frame, and then the warm leather is encircling my wrists, I glance up at him from the corner of my eye. Watching him work above me, blank face lacking any signs of concentration, or feeling. He doesn't look annoyed, irritated, angry, nothing, and I think that's scarier.

My hands are secured as I stop squirming and I squeeze my eyes closed as I feel him shift, my breath held in my lungs because I'm not ready for this, he told me he wasn't going to hurt me. Maybe everything he said was a lie. Everything he said *is* a lie.

"Go to sleep, Haisley," he orders quietly, and then his heat is gone, his weight disappearing from the bed, mattress springing up beneath me, I blink my eyes open. "I told you, I will not hurt you," he says from somewhere in the dark, my eyes squinting now, trying to seek him out.

A thick blanket is draped over my naked body, the texture rough and scratchy but I know it'll keep me warm. I freeze, hearing his footsteps now, moving away from me, the ones he keeps so silent, as he heads to the door.

"I am a monster," he confirms calmly from somewhere at the foot of the bed. "But I do not tell lies," he finishes, and then he's gone.

The door clicking closed with his exit, my held breath rushing out of me. I find myself alone once again when I realise, I think I might want to be anything but.

CHAPTER 7

THORNE

Arms hanging limp over the armchair, elbows resting on the worn leather, hands loose, I stare out of the window, watch the rain race down the flimsy pane. Feet flat to the floor, legs spread wide, head dropped back, I sigh so heavily it feels like my lungs shrivel as they deflate.

She cried.

I made her cry.

And I do not know how to feel about it as I sit here with a rock-hard cock and regret in my chest.

I frightened her after everything that she has been through for who the fuck knows how long. I think of the bruises on her perfect skin, so dark they are like a bloom of storm clouds across her flesh, but I could not make them out fully in the dark, and she was exposed enough without me prodding at her.

I did not want to scare her; I do not think… I just wanted- I blow out a breath, shake my head, pinch my eyes closed. I do not know what I wanted, I do not know what the fuck I am doing.

I listen to the wind, howling through the small, dilapidated house, feel the constant draft of cold wash over me. It is eerie, this house, built adjoined to the derelict old lighthouse. I bought this place because I like the sea. I like the sound of the violent waves breaking and crashing against the rocks, the white cliffs.

I like that there are no people here.

I like that I can breathe here.

Currently, I cannot hear the waves over the rain, the pinging and tapping of hail, but I imagine I can. Head dropped back, I breathe in deeply, inhale musty air, feel a clawing at the inside of my chest because I can still hear her.

Crying out.

And I hate myself because my dick is hard as fucking stone beneath my slacks, and it is taking every fucking ounce of self-restraint to keep it to-fuckin-gether. I blow out a breath, squeeze my hands over the arms of the chair, worn leather soft beneath my palms, and grit my teeth.

She is crying out.

For me.

Even after everything. The man that has taken her, made her strip naked, and then restrained her. And she is calling for me. I know it is only because she is alone, she has no idea if I have left her here, abandoned her, maybe forever, maybe to die, maybe for something worse. I can only imagine what she thinks is going to happen to her. She knows I am the one that is going to end her. Supposed to. She does not know the circumstances, but it tells me a lot about her crime if I am her punishment. I know the Doyle boys say she killed her cousin, perhaps she did, but she does not look like your everyday murderer, it was not done for the thrill of taking a life.

Or maybe it was, and she is just as dangerous as I am.

My lips curl at the thought, but I shake my head clear.

I know the Irish do not particularly value their women, not unless they are earning the family a pretty penny, sweetening a business deal, merging with another powerful household. Something that is beneficial to the Kellys, but they do not usually punish them with a death sentence, regardless of the crime. It makes me wonder what details I am missing.

What happened to you, Haisley Kelly?

The wailing continues from just down the hall, echoing through the confined space, and it shreds apart my insides like monster talons trying to claw their way out of my soul. I keep my eyes closed, tension in my face, my neck, my shoulders, muscles taut and strained. She wails. Like a siren. She calls to me, anguish, pain, the pleading. Thank fuck she does not know my name. I cannot get close to her.

I already got too involved; I almost lost my head.

But it is the sorries that are killing me.

The begging I can deal with, but the sorries, I can

hardly function. And I want to go to her, to calm her, to soothe her, to just let her know that she is not alone. *To hurt her.* No. I cannot stop her cries, only induce them, I should just leave here, I should just let her go.

Let her fucking go, Thorne.

If I let her go, the consequences for me, the danger it puts my family in, it does not bear thinking about. I have nephews now, tiny little boys who need to be kept safe. And I will. Keep them safe. Even if it means, I have to murder the girl with the deep jade eyes and fire red hair. Even if it means, I will lose myself once I have done it.

I do not know why I hate myself so much. I mean, that is the only explanation, is it not, I must really, truly hate myself to be putting myself through this shit. Finger and thumb pinch the bridge of my nose as my hand comes over my face. I squeeze my eyes shut tight, exhale through my nostrils, wonder what in the ever loving fuck is wrong with me, and my phone buzzes in my pocket.

Pulling it out, I stare at the screen, watching it ring and ring and ring before it cuts off, immediately starting up again. He is going to want to know where I am, if only so he can get to sleep tonight, well, this morning. It is four-eleven-am, the sun will not rise for hours yet at this time of year, and it is supposed to rain all day, nothing but thunder and lightning storms forecast for the remainder of the week. What a way to end the year.

On the fourth call, I pick up.

"Jesus Christ, Thorne," Arrow exhales through the phone in a rush of breath. "Is it done?"

I think about what to say, the lies and lies and more lies. And then I think of Mum.

Blackwells do not tell lies.

"No," is all I answer, unable to even attempt an elaboration as erratic thoughts rush through my brain.

"Fucking hell, Thorne, what the fuck are you doing? Where are you?" he demands, panic rife in his voice, he sounds a little choked and I worry, not for the first time, about my younger brother's anxiety.

"I will be home soon," I tell him, and it is not a lie, but *home* is not really anywhere for me.

Not the mill I grew up in, not any of the six properties I own, so where *home* is exactly, I do not know.

"When? When will you be home?"

And I know he means Heron Mill, where my dad still lives, my younger brother Hunter, our sister Grace, their sons. Where we all seem to drift in and out of like we just cannot bear to ever really leave. Homebase but not home.

"Thorne?" Arrow's voice pulls me back from the barrage of thoughts, feelings.

I run my knuckles over my chest, hand curled into a fist, the other squeezing the phone so tight to my ear I hear the plastic squeak.

"I do not know, Arrow," I want to sigh, to, for once, not hold everything inside, and let him hear just how tired I am.

But I do not, even when he does. I want to tell him

everything is fine, that he has nothing to worry about, but I cannot force myself to lie, it is as though my very soul rebels against it.

Blackwells do not tell lies.

"Thorne-"

"Arrow, you have your own jobs to do, I will be home in a few days, everything is fine."

I cut him off, imagine him pacing his room, not able to rest until he has tried to fix everything he thinks requires it.

"This is what I do," I say calmly, reassuring, "trust me, brother."

"What about New Years?" he asks me next, and I continue staring out of the high set window, only able to see the sky, mesmerised by the rain running down the glass.

"It will be done by then."

And then I hang up, let her crying filter back to me, close my eyes. Wish my fucking dick would go down and the headache behind my eyes would die.

Four days.

In her sleep, her chest rises and falls with deep, even breaths. Arms bound up above her, elbows bent, relaxed on the pillow, bracketing her head, fingers curled around the leather of my belt. I think about where that belt usually sits, tight, low on my hips, mere inches above my cock which twitches as I think of it. I inhale sharply through my nose, nostrils flaring, my jaw ticks as I grit my teeth, lean myself in the doorway, clean clothes, for her, in one arm, other shoulder pressing against the jamb. I have to duck a little, the old doorways not built for anyone over six-foot, but I do not mind.

Thick splay of bright red hair spreads over the dark green pillowcase, the usual bouncy curls lay limp, heavy with oil, the ends frizzy and wild from not being looked after. But her face, her pale skin, her freckles. The way her nose is a little squashed on her face because it is so tiny, but her lips are full, thick and dark with a rounded cupid's bow. Pale lashes, strawberry blonde fans hiding those big jade-green orbs. They go up at the outer corners, her eyes, just a little, and it makes her look like something out of an ancient Egyptian carving, a little fox like.

The sun is up, it is a little after ten, I have already been out, run my errands, interference, and the rain continues to beat down, as expected. What was unexpected, though, was the kitchen roof leaking, and discovering that the bathroom ceiling also leaks and now there are three metal buckets collecting water in the living room also, as rain drips steadily through the ceiling. I can fix it. When the rain stops.

Approaching the bed on silent feet, shoes still on because it is fucking freezing in this house, despite the fire I just built in the front room. I place the pile of clothes at the end of the bed, reach over her, carefully release the steel buckle from around the bedframe, unthread the leather. My knuckles graze the inside of her wrists, I eye the fading bruises on her skin beneath the pink marks from the leather restraint, but they are not bad, they will disappear by night like they were never there, I feel a spike of irritation at that but I temper it down.

Her skin is so soft, I cannot help but trace a single green vein a little way up her forearm, the tip of my finger gliding over the raised markings, the bruises that look like finger marks. It makes my heart thud hard in my chest, my breaths a little rough, anger clicking through me at the thought of anyone putting their hands on her, well, anyone *else*. She is so pale, she is almost translucent, and the further up her arm I trail my finger, the more bright veins I find to follow. Blues, greens, violet, freckles smothering it all like decoration.

I do not notice it until I am closer, finding myself leaning into her just a little too close, her breathing changing, quickening like a hare escaping a fox. I do not look at her, she does not try to squirm away from me, but I pull back, my fingers itching to touch her again. And she does not speak, but I can hear her fear, heart drumming in her chest, it is the only thing I *can* hear over the rushing of blood in my *own* ears. I keep my gaze down, on the old wood beneath my feet, see my reflection in the toes of my shined shoes, take a couple steps back.

"There are clothes," I swallow, glancing at the folded pile, "Water, and a bathroom," I look up then, at her, but not her eyes, she still has not moved, naked body still hidden beneath the wool covering. "Just here," I tap the wall to my left, swallow again, "I am going to cook," I inform her then, a slow breath drawing into my lungs. "Anything you do not like?" I ask politely, despite already knowing, I have spent years watching her.

She does not answer, and I wait, keeping my eyes trained on the floor just beside where she lies in the bed. I am patient, I have taught myself that things I really want are worth the wait, regardless of how long that wait might be, and what I really want, in this moment, is to hear her. Even though, since the first time I laid eyes on her, I was sworn off her, told she was not meant for me. But this, having her here but not really having her… it feels like torture, self-inflicted, a slow acting poison trickling its way through my veins as opposed to flooding them.

"Eggs, I don't like them," she says quietly, still unmoving and I feel the corner of my mouth twitch, she clears her throat, "Shellfish," my head tilts, ears pricking, every single sense I have all tuning into her frequency. "I'm allergic," she whispers, and I realise how much I love that, her quietness.

I remember the first time I ever saw her; she was six, and she was screaming at her older brothers. Her sisters looked horrified at her standing up for herself, that is what made me take notice, and when she was hauled off of her three older brothers for beating the ever-loving shit out of them, that was the moment it stuck. She was not going to turn out like them, her sisters, she was going to be different.

She *was* different.

And I have always been drawn to different.

It was not anything weird or wrong, the way I watched her that day. I just appreciated the fact she had big balls in a world built and designed to obey and worship men. But even at just six years old, she was defying it all. I did not see her again until eleven years later.

That was when it began.

My obsession.

I think about the quiet, how I was never accustomed to it, before my sister Grace came to live with us, Dad's ex-wife's daughter, her aversion to loud noise after growing up in an asylum. We have always been noisy, a family of seven men, a father, six sons, all very, very close in age, constantly talking over one another, how my mother used to tell us to shut up, scold us for her headaches.

My fingers flex, wanting to curl into fists as I smother thoughts of my mother, flash my eyes up onto Haisley, allow myself just the briefest of looks. She is peering over at me, those fox-like eyes wide, curious, and I drop my gaze, nod, gesturing to the clothes at her feet with a tilt of my chin and turn from the room, leaving the door open at my back.

CHAPTER 8

HAISLEY

He leaves me alone, his steps silent, I listen, straining my ears, to see if he's still there, just outside the open doorway, hiding from my view. I glance down the length of my body to the clothes by my feet, glance back to the door. Holding the knitted blanket to my chest, I sit up, instantly shivering with cold as an icy draft crawls down my spine. I reach for the bundle of fabric, pull the dark, forest green sweatshirt towards me, soft fabric bunched in my fists, I bring it up to my nose, smell metal, leather, and the storm. *Him* and nothing else, and my lips curl as I cover my face with it, hide the smile that should absolutely not be there.

One arm banding over the blanket to my chest, I haul the other clothes in the pile into my lap, find a long sleeve t-shirt, gather the material, poke my head through the neck, one arm in the sleeve and then drop the blanket, thread my other arm through. Blanket pooling at my waist, I pull on the sweatshirt next, flick my hair free, and then hurry to pull on the black cotton knickers, arching my hips, shoulders to the bed beneath the blanket, then slide my legs into the matching green tracksuit bottoms.

Everything's baggy but it's warm and clean and the thick white fluffy socks feel like the nicest thing I've ever owned. I don't question where this came from, I'm just grateful to be in something clean or new, something that feels like mine even if it's not really.

Feet swinging down to the floor, the wood like ice beneath them, I shiver, pull my sleeves down, over my hands, peer around the room, seeing it in light for the first time. There's no window, but low light filters in from the open doorway, daylight streaming in from somewhere down the hall. The room is bare, the walls a wash of white, my hand lifts to touch the cold surface, fingers roving over uneven rock, like it was carved rather than built, smooth insides of a cave. The bed I slept in is just a metal barred headboard and mattress, there's nothing else in the small space except for a rickety looking wooden chair in the far corner.

Taking a deep breath, I edge my way out into the hall, making my way to the bathroom on my right. It's simple when I step inside, taking the two steps down into the rectangular shape room, like it was never actually meant to be here, but it is now. There's a toilet, a sink, no mirror above it, and a shower curtain pulled open over a clawfoot tub that looks less like one built for luxury and more like it's an antique. It's feet a dull grey where I think, once upon time, were probably gold. I do my business, wash my hands, finding fresh soap, a roll-on deodorant and new toothbrush, paste and washcloth.

Once I've taken full advantage of using everything left, presumably, for me, I place the palm of my hand on the rough wood of the door, other hand curling around the brass handle, and quietly pull it open. Steeling my spine, the smell of bacon piquing interest in my rumbly belly, I blow out a breath, pretend to be brave and go to turn back, past the bedroom, head to the main space. But just a couple feet further to my right is the end of the hallway, and my eyes, curious as ever, even if it could get me in trouble, peer over.

A hexagonal shape space, with darkened doorways like alcoves, set deep into the walls, their destinations hidden behind heavy wooden doors, leading off of it. I step into the centre, a small circular window in the top of the external wall at my back, and a huge old mirror propped up against the internal wall opposite, heavy red drapes parted to show it off.

Glass a little rusted at the edges, little dark spots missing their reflective shine, set in an intricate gold edging, carvings of angels and flowers, thorns and vines make up its frame. I step in closer, gazing up at the top of it where two little cherubs are touching cheeks, looking down at whoever glances upon their reflection.

I drop my gaze, breath catching in my throat as I lay eyes on myself. Eyes circled with deep, dark rings, my usually round cheeks almost gaunt, hair greasy and flat, my curls all stringy and dry. I take a slow breath, heart pounding in my chest, I look down at my toes, think of what damage is hiding beneath my new clothes. Wonder if I should look, if I even want to see.

I think of that first beating I took, the blood of my cousin still warm against my skin, I don't think it hurt. The kicks, the fists, whip, I'm not sure I really felt any of it at all. Numb. My body trembled, my knees jointless, and my lungs forgot how to breathe when Shane, my cousin's best friend and my father's favourite muscle, forced his way into Cian's bedroom. Found me standing over my dead cousin, his best friend's blood spurting from his neck. How I'd never seen blood like that before, the way it arced out of his throat like a garden sprinkler we would run through together in the summer as kids.

Hot, thick, metallic.

The taste of it on my tongue when I accidently licked my lips, the overwhelming smell, heady, violent, *calming*. Then it all crashed into me, the way it happened, what he did, what I did, all of it made my stomach roll.

Before I realise what I'm doing, my fingers are curling around the thick ribbed band of elastic along the bottom hem of my sweatshirt, yanking it up along with the t-shirt beneath it, exposing my belly. Eyes unblinking, I stare into the aged mirror, my skin mottled like some sort of macabre camo print skinsuit. Blues and violets, green, black, greys, all swirling together like a tropical storm. Bile claws its way up the back of my throat, and I almost choke on it when I lift the fabric higher, hold it up beneath my chin, bare my breasts.

I can pick out each individual fingerprint bruise on my waist, the print of a boot on my ribs, teeth marks... I squeeze my eyes shut, nostrils flaring, tears splashing down my cheeks.

Every inhale-exhale hurts, my bones feel like they're creaking, I breathe hard, heart hammering like drums beneath my ribcage. Every expansion of my chest cavity making them bend and bow, crack.

My eyes pop open as a warm grip snaps around the back of my neck, firmly collaring, squeezing the pressure point so tightly I stop breathing. I stare at him in the mirror, behind me, his eyes, like black storms, on mine in the reflection. I want to swallow, to pull away, to shake his hold off of me, drop my fucking shirt. But I'm swept up in his wave of darkness, and it makes me want to submit.

To drown.

In him.

With him.

In the gloom that seems to keep descending down around us.

Kill me, kill me, kill me.

"Haisley," he says my name so quietly, so calmly, it's dark, it coils and I want to yield.

Elegantly spoken words, his deep voice, all of it crashing over me like a violent wave, I'm drowning and drowning and drowning.

When his other hand moves from its place at his side, slowly coming around the front of me, I can't tear my gaze from his eyes, swirling like raging storms, captivating me, holding me prisoner. Bones trapping me inside my skin, blood pounding through my veins, breath held in my lungs, and it feels as though it's all by his command. The knuckle of his thumb brushes the tip of my chin, his fingers curling over the bunched fabric beneath it, he gently pulls it away from me, rolling it carefully back down, covering my exposed flesh, the back of his long fingers grazing over my tender skin.

And then he's done, but he's still holding my gaze, gripping my neck, and we're caught on one another, I don't want to blink, break the moment. My legs sway beneath me, I feel myself wanting to tilt back, he's so close, but there's too much space and I don't want to feel the cold air between us for even one more second. My lips part, my chest heaves, and he is perfectly calm. And I do not know this man. And I'm waiting for my death, something that never seems to come. I feel a sudden wash of rage collapse over me, like I'm resurfacing, and it isn't fair, that even in death, I do not know this man's name and yet, he seems to know me.

"Who are you?" I whisper, it's breathy, the way it sounds sends a blush blooming across my cheeks, but I hold his eye, even though my eyes are burning in their sockets to drop to my toes.

Gaze still locked on mine, he doesn't flinch at my question, he doesn't blink. His tongue sweeps out slowly, bathing his bottom lip before he tucks the corner of his lip between his teeth, top teeth snagging the dark peach flesh. And then his eyes fall down my face, hooking on my lips, I snap my mouth closed, my chest heaving.

"Death," he whispers, I watch him, a tiny curve to the corner of his mouth.

It's gone as quickly as it appeared and then his body is plastered to my back and my eyes are slipping closed at his sudden cloak of warmth.

I crave it, his closeness, his attention, anything this man gives me, will give me, even *that.*

"Whose?" I breathe, my lips trembling, barely parting on the question, his grip tense on my neck, his body hard against my soft.

My head only coming to the centre of his chest, I can feel him watching me even without opening my eyes, because those swirling pits of darkness burn and freeze me all at the same time. His breath ghosts down the side of my throat and I feel myself wanting to look, not wanting to, my hands limp at my sides, the palms clammy, my body so, so cold everywhere he isn't touching me. My heart is hammering against my sternum, I want to rip apart my chest cavity, tear it out and stomp on the fucking thing, let the hole in my centre finally breathe, bleed and ooze and hurt.

It's then that I feel it, his hardness pressing into the base of my spine, and my eyes flare wide, immediately latching onto his in the old, gold mirror where he still stares at me. We're in the gloom, no light but a sconce on the wall to my right, but the candles aren't lit, and it feels better, somehow, being in the shade.

My body stiffens, like rigor mortis setting in, preparing itself for what's to come, the inevitable, like a practice, trial run. He dips his chin, his head tilting in that curious way, predatory, but I'm not sure this very well put together man even knows what he's doing when he drops the tip of his nose to the spot beneath my ear. His eyes still tracking me in the reflection, I don't move, my muscles starting to relax, to melt, or perhaps they're just dissolving when he inhales me, slow and deep. Filling his lungs, mine seem to shrink as his expand as though he's stealing the very air from me. I feel his chest at my back, his cock pressing hard into my spine and the little breath I have left rushes out when he turns into me. His lips against my skin when he murmurs into my flesh, eyes still on mine as I tremble at his mercy.

"I made you breakfast, Little Cub," I suck in a sharp breath.

Arousal, fear, confusion, a morbid curiosity, pulse through me like a second heartbeat and then he releases me so suddenly my palm flies out, slapping against the rusted glass. Breath fogging the mirror, I watch him step away from me, his eyes still on mine, everything so intense and I want to cry, to claw him back, let him consume me, tuck inside of him. Be whipped up in his storm, carried out to sea, drowned and consumed and devoured.

"Come," he orders lowly, and then his eyes finally drop, falling away from me, making my skin burn with embarrassment, he turns away from me, a gentle clearing of his throat. "Eat."

And then he's disappearing down the hall, past the bedroom, and taking my last little piece of sanity with him.

Beautiful jade-green eyes haunt me, the ones currently shuttered with a thick fan of pale lashes, her head low as she carefully eats the food on her plate, bacon, spinach, avocado, a handful of berries. I watch her lift her fork, those thick, dark lips closing over the metal cutlery, fourteen chews before she swallows, the fork making a quiet scraping sound against the mismatched china.

The black and white tiles beneath my feet are cold even with my shoes on, this makeshift table I pulled in from outside is rickety, its old legs wobbly on the uneven floor. My chair rocks if I breathe too hard, and this kitchen, a galley shape but a little wider, is freezing, the electricity is still not firing and I am slightly concerned I am going to need help. Which I do not want because it means bringing someone to this house and I do not want anyone here. With her.

Her thick hair hangs around her face, but I can still

see her so perfectly, her curvy body sitting directly across from me. I know she knows I am watching her, can probably feel my gaze on her, but I cannot bring myself to look away.

I am too close. I got too close. I am supposed to be disposing of her. I am a hired gun. A macabre magician, making sure people disappear as though they never existed. I wonder how long I could keep her. Keep her hidden, a buried treasure of sorts. I wonder how long before I would kill *for* her. I stare at the top of her head, freckles, even in the parting of her hair, she quite literally is covered in them, and I want to trace each one with the tip of my tongue, see how they shine connected to one another with a trail of my saliva.

It vibrates again, my phone, burning against my thigh, I already know it will be Arrow, and I itch to switch it off. I have no reason to keep it on, except to take another job, organise my siblings. Check in on my brother Archer and ensure he *is* actually where he is supposed to be and not fucking his way through another political party's gaggle of wives. I do not remember the last time I turned it off. Stepped away. Took a day off.

Control.

It has been that way since I was a child, something inside my brain needing it, enjoying things in even numbers, pencils sharpened to the same length, all of these things keeping me up at night if they were not *just so*. An incessant need to be the one in charge. Even with Dad, he's still young, but he's stepped back, a little less hands on, but he is still very much there. He could take over for a few days, just until I deal with this. But then I would have to fill him in on why, and he is the only one who already knows about Haisley, my… *draw* towards her.

"Does it hurt?" her soft voice has me snapping back into the room, I blink, looking up at her.

She sits across from me, knife and fork placed together atop her now empty plate, hands hidden beneath the rickety table, but from the pull of her shoulders I imagine they are clasped tightly in her lap. I stare at her, her gaze, those eyes, wide and round, flicking between my own. And I realise it then, a smirk wanting to lift my lips, but I have already shown her enough weakness, so I stare back at her, blankly, waiting. She shakes her head, twists her face away from me, and I want it back, her attention, crave it, her, those eyes on me.

"Does what hurt?" I ask quietly instead.

It is gentle for me, my voice deep and gravelly, I am naturally a little loud but not with her. I want to hear her even when I am speaking, her breaths, the beat of her heart, the flutter of her pulse, blood rushing through her veins. I want to be so attuned with her that I hear it all above my own.

Slowly, her gaze swings back to me, she blinks, tucks her split bottom lip between her teeth, the curve of her cupid's bow blanching at the top as she chews on her lips.

"Thinking that hard," she finishes, her cheeks flaming, her creamy skin dotted with freckles, practically glowing.

I do not think it is really supposed to be a joke, but it feels a little funny to me all the same, and I usually am not one to find humour in things. She is nervous, with her question, and I feel my cock hardening once more. I hate myself for it because my thoughts spiral then, wondering what she would look like beneath me, her lips violet, cheeks tinged blue. My dick grows uncomfortable beneath the tight confines of my slacks, and I shift in my seat.

"No," is all I respond.

She swallows, her throat working, rolling, I picture my belt around her dainty neck, her tendons straining against the taut black leather. I blink, catch her eyes on me.

Rain hammers against the window at my back, her eyes not wavering from my own. I still cannot hear the waves crashing against the side of the cliff, the storm still raging, dominating it all.

"Are you going to kill me?" she asks even quieter, and in this moment, I hate myself, my job, every fucking thing I have ever done in my life.

Her eyes are sad, and I feel something swirling low in my gut. It feels like shame and I am disappointed in myself for already dragging this out too long. I should have just shot her in that fucking alley, thrown her in the boot of the car and tossed her to my brother at the mill. I have waited years for this woman, girl, she is still so young, her life is just beginning, yet it is already over. I have watched her from afar, stalked her from shadowed corners, stared at what I knew I could never have. But she is here now, isn't she, so young and fractured. Vulnerable.

I think of her bruised skin, the reflection in the mirror, the teeth marks I saw in the side of her breast, that deep split in her lip. Watching her, once again, from the safety of shadows. I bite down on my molars, grind my teeth, it is none of my business, what she did, what happened to her, she is not my responsibility. And yet, it feels as though she is. I have kept her alive, a full thirty hours longer than I should have. I am supposed to be in charge here, I know my place, my role, I gave myself this task, to what? Punish myself? And yet, I fear I'm beginning to fall so wildly out of control.

I have ten years on her, but the moment I saw her, exposed her to me in the room right next door to where we sit now, it felt like the first real night of my life. The first time I have ever taken a full breath in my entire existence. It feels like she is mine even though she is not, even though she never could be.

How could I keep you?

"That's why they gave me to you, right? Because of what I did." The words are said like an echo of my own, unfeeling, resigned, cold.

Lifting my eyes unto hers, she stares back at me, holding my gaze, strong, even as I see her chin quiver. It makes me want to leap across this table, take her into my chest, bury her beneath my bones to keep her safe.

From me.

"Yes," I reply honestly, "That is why they gave you to me."

She trembles, even though she tries to hide it, her chest rising and falling a little quickly, but she holds my gaze, does not look away. The rain beats against the window harder, the pane of glass sounding as though it could crack into pieces at any moment. She reaches up, fingers curling through a lock of red hair, she tucks it behind her ear, tilts her chin up just slightly.

"I was given to you for you to... *dispose* of me," she says quietly again, and I realise now, how much I really, really do like that soft voice she has.

I feel compelled, with those big eyes on mine, green emeralds split with shards of ocean blue-green, framed in long, pale lashes, to give her whatever she wants in this moment. Like she is stitching an invisible thread through me, something set deep beneath my flesh that she can tug on and I will dance to her tune because she has unknowingly had control of my soul since the very moment I caught sight of her again on her seventeenth birthday.

I do not think I wanted her then, not in the way I do now, I just wanted to give myself to her for whatever the fuck she deemed me worthy of doing for her. It is why I have grown a hate for her, something to try to repel me. A faux hatred. But I kept myself hidden from her view, always just out of sight even when I was right fucking there. All to keep her safe, from so many things, but maybe, most of all, *from me.*

It is different now, we are older, *she* is older, twenty-three to my thirty-three, she is old enough for me to feel for her now. Really truly feel whatever it is that makes blood sing in my veins, my cock harden like steel and my heart hammer like it is a beating drum.

I keep my head, blood heating, heart rate increasing, I can feel my pulse thrashing in my neck but I keep my eyes trained on hers. My face stoic, my renowned self-control starting to feel like it is going to peel away and crack.

"Yes," I finally confirm, and I watch her chest still, breath held tightly in her lungs, I stop too, restricting my own intake of air, waiting for her to speak.

I will tell you anything you want to know, baby girl.

"What's your name?" she whispers then, the room dark because of the weather, like we're sitting in the centre of a storm cloud right here in this very kitchen.

Anything but that.

I cock my head, finally giving in to the urge, curiosity always revealing itself with this exact move-ment. I find everything about her curiously fascinating, and surprisingly, my name is not what I expected her to ask for.

"You are afraid," I say instead, watching the flut-tering of her pulse fly beneath her freckled skin. "Of me?" I ask, another question before she can answer, "Or of death?"

She licks her lips, swallowing, her eyes flickering down before she looks back up at me from beneath her lashes.

"I don't feel afraid," she confesses like she's

ashamed, and I feel myself wanting to lean in, let her words brush against my lips as she speaks them, but I hold back, sit still.

Control.

"What *do* you feel, Haisley?" the air is charged, lightning pulsing through me, readying to strike, I curl my hands into fists, fingers trapped beneath my thumbs.

"I didn't want to look at you," she tells me in a whisper, doing just that, her eyes still on mine.

I am captivated, hypnotised, entranced, I feel dizzy, like she is gripping her hand around my neck and squeezing.

"Why?" I find myself whispering back, wanting to coax her along, keep her confessing.

Nostrils flaring just slightly, she swallows again, the tip of her pink tongue peeking between her lips as she wets and rolls them together.

"I didn't want to see my executioner," she whispers. "Because, if you had a face, then you were real and it was real and everything was going to end here," she flicks her eyes between my own, "With *you.*"

It rushes out of me, my breath, at the way she says *you*. Like I mean something to her in some way, like she does not see me as a one dimensional end to her life. And it feels… confusing, too fast. I suddenly realise, I think, I thought I wanted her to want me, but this just makes everything so much harder. I bite down on my teeth, clench them together, feel the back of my jaw popping as I do. Because this *does* all need to end here, by New Year's Eve at the latest, that is our timeline and I wonder if she knows she has missed Christmas, if she even cares. What she was doing, where she was, what she was being put through. I think of the bruises on her flesh, the fear in her gaze, the dead look behind her eyes and I feel my skin getting incredibly hot, despite the plummeting temperature of this icy room.

Her eyes boring into me, we hold each other's gaze, I am seeing her the way I always have, even when she thought she was alone, when she cried on her seventeenth birthday, on the balcony looking down, alone. She was never alone, she just did not know it, and now she is finally seeing me. After all these years of me always, *always* seeing her, and she is finally here, and yet, it feels like *I* am not really here at all, and I wonder if this is nothing more than a dream.

"Please," she whispers, her back straight, shoulders still pulled taut, "Tell me your name."

Compulsion.

That is what twists around my guts. The fear that comes with it, slithering around the discs in my spine, constricting.

It feels pleading, the way her chin trembles, her cheeks flushing pink, she pulls her sore lip into her mouth, wincing as she sucks on the cut. Courage, that is what it took for her to ask me a second time. Time gets incredibly slow, my heart thuds a strong steady rhythm, but it feels like this moment is something it absolutely should not be. I watch it all happening, like a car crash, the collision, see it all playing out inside my head, the repercussions of something as simple as a spoken name.

But nothing is stopping me and time is speeding back up again, too quickly, too fast and I am slamming into my own walls, feeling them crumble to dust beneath me.

"If you know my name, it will mean your end, Little Cub," is what I tell her in a low growl, her eyes do not shy away from mine, she holds me captive, but she does not speak.

She does not change her mind.

The world gets impossibly smaller and I wish I did not know my name at all, then it would not be uncomfortable to keep it from her. As it stands, I am a Blackwell, and as such, I do not tell lies.

"Thorne."

Her eyes flare with shock, her lip popping free, parting on a small inhale, gasp, and I feel my insides twisting and knotting and fucking celebrating because I have given in. Already, it is far too easy to give this girl what she wants. And I am picturing a future where I keep her hidden, locked away and shackled to me in the only way a Blackwell knows how.

Blood.

Blood and blood and more blood.

Oozing and rushing and gushing.

And what that means for her now.

Her life.

Her death.

My control.

"Are you going to make it hurt, Thorne?" she whispers, breathy and almost wanting, the way her chest heaves on my name, perhaps it is fear.

But I know fear. I see it every day. Breathe it in. Let it fill me. Occasionally, I let myself revel in it, and this, *this* does not feel like that.

I do not want her fear.

I want her surrender.

Am I going to make it hurt?

What is going to hurt is the mess we just fucking made.

She has broken my resolve without even really trying. The second I got her in my grasp, I felt it. Deep primal need to keep, protect, devour. Obsession creeps its way through my veins, finally breaking free of its shackle and chains.

I think of all the times I have seen her over the years. Watching from afar. Playing nice with her family. Hoping to catch a glimpse of her somewhere, a party, a dinner, event. I searched for her face in places I knew she would never be, yet my eyes still wandered, no matter where I went. Bars I sat myself at, drinking too much. Searching for just the right redhead, that I could do nothing more to than fuck from behind, because I could not bear the thought of seeing their faces not being *hers*, whilst I fucked away my forbidden desires.

Forcing myself to hate her. Anything associated with her. Just to get through my day.

But that was another lifetime.

I could never hate her.

I see that now as I stare at her, across the rickety table, splinters poking up, jagged in the weathered wood. I watch her face, the blush flaring in her cheeks, she swallows again, but she is oh, so quiet.

I do not think she realises what I am.

She thinks I am her end.

And I will be.

Just… not right now.

I stand slowly, brushing my hands once down my legs, smoothing the creases in the thighs of my pressed trousers. I flex my shoulders back, straightening from the wobbly chair. Her chin tilts up, lips parted, her eyes still locked on mine as I step out from between the table and chair, take the four very short steps towards her, stopping at her back. She twists her neck on her shoulders, peering up at me, head tilted back, tendrils of fiery red hair spilling over the back of the chair. I want to bury my hands in it, fist the roots, wrench her head back further, expose every inch of that pretty little neck.

Instead, I place my hands delicately on her shoulders, it electrifies my fingertips, her head tipping so far back her crown almost brushes my lower abs. I glance down at her, without dipping my chin, staring down my nose, and give into the smallest urge I have right now. I bring one of my hands up, rest my thumb beneath her eye, let my fingers fan, curl delicately over her cheek, the side of her jaw, chin, the tips grazing the soft skin of her throat. She swallows, her breath ghosting over my skin, short and sharp, as she keeps peering up at me. I step into her, the crown of her head pressing into me now, her hair trapped between us.

"I am not going to hurt you, Little Cub," I almost coo, whispering, a hush to my voice.

She sucks in a sharp breath, holding it in her lungs, and I let my fingers dance a little way down her throat. The silky feel of her skin beneath my rough is addictive, and I cannot help but glance at my fingers. Dark against her light, my natural olive skin tone much warmer than her icy freckled skin.

But then I realise that statement is not quite true.

"At least, not in a way you will not like."

And then I'm twisting away from her, my touch leaving her cool skin, little flares of electricity jolting in my fingertips as I leave the room.

CHAPTER 10

HAISLEY

Thorne.

I watch him work. Feeling braver, since our encounter over breakfast just this morning, I follow him around the dilapidated house like the little cub he calls me, soundlessly shadowing his every movement. Silently, he gets the water on, hot, steam clouding from the taps, electricity firing, even though there are no bulbs in the light fixtures in this crumbling building, and the basket beside the fireplace is now stocked with dry wood.

In the sunken kitchen, alone, after a shower, hair finally washed and a fresh black tracksuit on, one that miraculously appeared at the foot of my bed whilst I was in the bathroom. I peer over my shoulder, through the darkened doorway into the front room, two steps up. Fingers curled over the edge of the sink, I press up onto my tiptoes, lock my elbows, shoulders bunched, I try to get a glimpse of outside. Every tiny window in this old house is set high up, in the rooms that even have a window. The bedroom doesn't, but I think I kind of like it that way.

Teeth gnawing on my sore lip, I wince, tasting blood, eyes still firmly on the darkened space over my shoulder. He told me not to go outside, *Thorne*, warned me with low, hushed words, deeply spoken all the same, that I would absolutely regret it if I tried. His words: *'Do not test me, Little Cub, for you are far safer with the monster you think you know than the one you do not.'* But it was sometime before that, whilst there was still food on my plate, my gaze lifted to watch him as I slowly chewed, his face blank but… *not.* That I'd already decided I wasn't going to try and run.

Rain lashes the window as I heft myself up onto the kitchen counter; it creaks loudly as soon as my full weight is pressing down on the palms of my hands. White socked feet dangling above the floor. I haul myself up, knees bending, I pull my legs up, tuck them beneath myself. One of my hands going to the wall above my head, bracing, fingers splayed, I rest forward onto my shins, knees balancing me as I wriggle forward.

When the surface doesn't feel like it's going to buckle beneath me, I glance back over my shoulder, watching the darkness for him through my drying curls, springing up into tight ginger coils as they do. Seeing nothing, I stretch up taller, my fingertips clinging onto the edge of the window, chin flush with my knuckles, breath fogging the glass, I peer out and still.

Grey, grey, grey. Crushing and swirling and frothing. The sea stretches out before me as far as I can see. Wild water, violently crashing waves leaping over smaller ones, the wind whipping spray in all directions. Eyes dropping, I spy nothing but a cliff edge and it makes my head spin, how close we are to it. The terrifying ocean, an endless grey vortex that could swallow me whole. My fingertips blanch white as I put more pressure on them where they cling to the very slim edge of the window setting. The tip of my nose becomes flush with the thin rattling pane of glass, my eyes roving over everything I can see.

Water.

Storm clouds.

That's all there is.

I'm not sure what to feel about it.

Considering I've never seen the sea before.

It feels a little like awe, amongst other things, maybe, perhaps, mostly fear.

It's then that I feel him before I see him, little hairs springing up on the back of my neck, a light sheen of sweat spotting the space behind my ear. He moves like a spirit, soundlessly, but his presence is undeniable, compelling the room.

"What are you doing?" he asks slowly, unhurried, unconcerned.

I want to look, but I don't. Keep peering out of the window. I think of his eyes, how much they should frighten me, the darkness in them, but there's those little slivers of gold too. Those make me feel warm inside and

I don't think that's the reaction I should have to this man who is going to kill me.

"Where are we?" is what I ask, but I don't really care about that, I think I'd just sort of like to go outside, despite the weather, I want to see.

He's silent at my back, which is what I expected, he doesn't seem to be the type of man to speak unless it's absolutely necessary. I keep watching the sea, waves colliding and battling one another, thick white foam and swirls of violence, it all consumes me and I wish I could hear it, over the hammering of rain.

He steps closer, and I want to look, I want to see, I don't currently feel fear with the man who told me he does not tell lies, but I continue watching the turbulent water, the swirling cyclone of storm clouds above. There is something comforting in that. He said he won't hurt me; he does not tell lies, and that in itself, feels like truth. He hasn't once touched on the subject of my death, not really. I'm not naïve enough to think he would keep me alive for any reason, but I do wonder why it is he's stalling. I haven't tried to run, he said I was given to him, and he is a monster.

I should run.

But I don't.

Won't.

He is a violent, raging storm, dangerous with its bright bolts of lightning, but my fingers want to reach out and touch it all the same. I always did like things that were not good for me. Fighting with my brothers when I was a child, when my sisters would be too afraid,

I would always fight back. I would scream and shout and kick and punch. Until I was older. Eight years old was my first beating, my father's belt over the backs of my thighs, the lecture I was given about doing as I was told. Follow my brothers' orders or there would be more punishment. And there was.

A shiver rolls through me like one of the waves I'm watching, cold sweeping down my spine. Thorne steps up beside me, the sink before him, my body on the counter leaning far over it to cling onto the little window. I want to look but I don't.

"The coast," he finally speaks, it's cold and honest and makes my lips twitch with the sudden urge to chuckle, I cling on tighter to the little window ledge. "There is nothing else here," he tells me next, a cool detachment but something like content buried in there somewhere.

I swallow, keeping my gaze trained on the view beyond but I'm not really seeing anything now as I listen to his voice. Let his quietly spoken words soothe me somewhat like a child's bedtime story.

"I like it," I whisper, my breath fogging the glass before my nose, despite me also being cold, outside it must be far worse. "Can we…" I trail off, licking my lips, about to finish when he speaks first.

"I think it would be better if you did not start sentences using the term *we* in a question without an ending."

My neck practically snaps as I throw my head over my shoulder, fingers clutching onto the ledge the only thing keeping me from tumbling to the floor. My eyes catch on his instantly, his posture relaxed but still straight and perfect, unruffled and pressed. His dark hair is wet, a wave to it on the side of his head where it's been combed back, he smells fresh, clean, like a musky soap but still like him, leather, salt, metal. It dizzies me as I look down at him, towering high above him on the kitchen surface, and he only looks back, no expression on his face at all, but his eyes seem to dance with warning in the way his head is angled once more.

"Please," he says then, so politely, one of his hands sliding free from his pocket, pressed slacks pristine, black shirt tight across his chest, the buttons look as though they could burst free at any second. "Come down," his hand open, outstretched for mine.

I glance down at his fingers, his skin is smooth, despite the little rough patches I've felt when he touched me. Chin dipped, I glance at him through my lashes, his ebony eyes on mine, it's intense, the way he watches, clocking my every breath, every blink, as though this is merely natural to him. Monitoring me so closely. Intensely.

Carefully, I release one hand from the window, blood rushing back into my fingertips as I let go. Fingers sliding into his palm, his own curl over mine, strong and sure like he's not going to be letting go. Something bubbles inside my chest at the thought, my hand staying permanently inside his, much larger than my own. The little spark that zaps through me, the way he grips my hand, pulsing its way up my arm, hits me straight in the chest and I don't know what this is. What is even happening here, because I don't want him to let go.

My hand in his, he locks his elbow, his other hand sliding free of his other pocket, he offers that one to me as well. I shuffle on my knees, turning my body around. I watch my feet as I bring them out from beneath me, letting this silent man hold my weight, balance me as I twist. One white sock appearing before the other. I swing my legs down, arse to the counter and as I sit fully on the icy surface, I think of Thorne telling me he would spank me so hard, I'd wear his handprint for the next month.

A full blush heats my cheeks at the memory, my hands still held tightly in his. I can feel them growing impossibly clammy with the fire racing across my flesh under my heavy tracksuit, the long sleeved t-shirt beneath. Gaze dropping, I can't look at him, I study my socked feet as he tugs my hands gently, gesturing for me to hop down.

Only, when I slide off of the cabinet, my socked feet slipping on the tiles, he pulls me tight, my front colliding with his, breath knocking out of me as I fall into him. His grip impossibly tense on my hands, fingers going numb, he steps into me, my back hitting the counter, his hips becoming flush with my belly. Breathing hard, I keep my eyes trained on the straining muscles beneath his tight shirt, his chest perfectly calm as mine rises and falls rapidly, bumping into his hard body with every breath.

Slowly, his hands loosen, but his touch doesn't leave

me. Twisting my insides tighter and tighter like a boa constrictor is strangling my organs, crushing the life from each and every one. One of his hands slides up my forearm, thumb resting in the crook of my elbow as his other leaves me completely. Disappointment starts to flood through me and I breathe harder and harder as he seems to be getting nearer and nearer even though neither one of us is moving.

The knuckle of his finger slides across my chin, still dipped, my eyes focused on one of the small black buttons of his shirt. I know what he's going to do, how he's going to move my face, before he's even applying any pressure. So when he does, tilt my face up to meet his, I keep my gaze averted, the blooming red in the fire of my cheeks screaming with steam. I keep focused on his little black button, the tiny loop of cotton that hasn't quite been pulled all the way through one of its four holes, securing it in place.

"Look at me," he commands it without threat, a smooth rumble, "Let me see you," he says quietly, and my entire being moves unconsciously at his words.

Eyes flicking up, his face tilted down, I lift my chin in the space between us, his lips almost caressing my brow. I swallow hard, tip of my tongue wetting the cut in my lip, his eyes watching the movement. He glances back up, his breathing soft, the faint scent of toothpaste filling my nose. The rough skin of his finger beneath my chin, I hold the air in my lungs, watching as his head slowly cocks, dark eyes studying me, flicking to the hammering pulse in the side of my throat.

"I've never seen the sea," I whisper between us, his eyes very slowly lifting from my pulse to look into my own.

His hand beneath my chin switches so suddenly I flinch, fingers sliding over the side of my jaw, down my neck, his thumb hovering over the split in my lip. He glances at my mouth, my lips parted, an exhale whistling quietly between them, his thumb presses down on the wound. It hurts and it burns, but I don't dare move and he watches as he does it, pressing harder and harder until my lip is crushed to my teeth and a tiny whimper escapes me with the final spark of pain.

He blinks, the pressure releasing, his hand lifting in the space between us, blood tinges my taste buds and I watch him staring at the pad of his thumb. A smudge of dark crimson on his warm olive skin, his dark eyes flash back to my own, and then his thumb is pushed between my parted lips, my teeth scraping over it as he forces his way between them. More blood on my tongue, his thumb in my mouth, the pad of it forced to the very back and he's pressing down hard all over again. My throat constricts, and I gag as his fingers hold firm on the side of my face, the tips of them at my hairline.

"Suck," he whispers, my eyes watering as my throat tightens, but my lips close around the digit all the same.

The cut stinging, he pushes his thumb in as deep as he can, depressing my tongue, I suck on his skin, my stomach tightening. His eyes glinting with those slivers of gold, they slice through his darkness like treasures buried in a cave, luring the hunter deeper into the dark before swallowing them whole. Then his thumb is popping free of my mouth, I'm gasping and swallowing and flushing hot all over again as saliva dribbles down my chin. He swipes his wet thumb back over my lip. Smearing the blood, pressing the wound too hard, I feel it bleeding, swiped across my lip, over my chin. He watches me, popping that same thumb into his own mouth, sucking on it with a groan, his hollow cheeks hollowing further. His eyes are on mine all the while, breath stalled in my constricting lungs. His lips part, thumb slipping free, the tip of his tongue flicking out over the pad of it as he brings his hand back to my face.

"You taste like something I should not indulge in, Little Cub," he breathes the words against my skin, something forbidden and haunting thick in his words, his hands gripping the counter at my back.

I can't control my breathing, the way his eyes are locked on mine, his lips so close to my face. He feels familiar, even though we had never met before this, the way he watches me doesn't unnerve me, despite it being so intense. I think, perhaps, Thorne is just an intense man, whether he is pinning his next target to a kitchen counter or simply shooting them in the back of the skull. *No.* I don't think that's something he would do. He would shoot them head on, he would make sure they saw him coming.

His fingertip is tapping softly at the centre of my forehead, my eyes blinking back into focus.

"Where did you go?" he asks me gently, hand dropping back to the worktop, that curiosity back in his dangerous gaze.

It shoots a thrill through me like a bolt of lightning, electrifying my nerves.

His interest in me.

He is the storm, and I am the lost cub who does not know how to hide from its elements.

I don't answer his question.

"Take me to the sea, Thorne." I lick my lips, my request nothing more than a breathy whisper, "Please."

He watches me, his face blank, his breathing quickening just a fraction. I keep my focus on him, my eyes staring into his, the gold like shards spearing through his darkness. His head dips down towards me, like he just can't quite help himself, I don't move as I watch him, his nostrils flaring.

"Let me see it before I never can again," my lips almost brush his, his eyes on them, gaze downcast as he watches my mouth move. "I won't run," I promise him then, and I realise just how true the whispered statement is.

Torturously slowly, his hips still pinning me in place, the curve of his hip bones pressing into the softness of my belly, the heat of his body warming me all the way through to my chilled bones. He lifts his gaze, long, thick fans of lashes curling into his brows as he does. Round brown orbs move slowly between my own, the tip of his nose brushing mine, and I'm frozen, waiting, hoping, lost in whatever this is with him.

"It is raining," he breathes, licking his lips, "You will

catch a chill," he almost whispers, his eyes intently on mine, making me blink.

"What does it matter?" I half snark, anger biting me. "You're going to kill me, what the fuck does it matter?" I snap out.

I don't have time to catch my breath as he smothers my mouth with his palm. The side of his hand crushing across my nostrils, tip of his thumb clamping beneath my chin, fingers curling into my cheek. He is composed, perfectly so, and it is the most terrifying thing I have ever seen. His eyes are black holes, blank, evil, emotionless. My chest aches, hands coming up to his arm, my fingers lock over his forearm, his wrist, I pull with all my strength, panic firing its way through me, nails gouging at his skin. Legs flailing as I try to kick him, but the way he has me penned in I can hardly move my feet.

"Do not speak to me that way," he says quietly, calmly.

It's eerie and I cannot breathe, and I think I want this to be it. Because I'm having a rush of feelings flood through my system, pain in my face, panic in my lungs. This man, the way he tilts his head, the way his eyes glint, the way he doesn't smile. His hands on me, his breath on my face. It's been two days, what would happen in another two, a week, a month. Something is wrong with me because the thought of being locked up in here forever with this brutal man crushing the bones in my nose doesn't even remotely put me off.

Kill me.

Kill me, kill me, kill me.

I chant it in my head, over and over and over. My eyelids squeeze closed, and the panic seems to die off the longer I'm deprived of air, because I'm ready for this, and I wonder if I've been ready since the day I left my mother's womb.

Suddenly, my head is wrenched backwards, a fist in the roots of my hair, neck cracking as I bow backwards. Thorne tears his hand away from my face, my lungs heaving to draw in air, his hips still pressing into the curve of my belly, my back aching where it digs into the counter.

His hands come up to my cheeks, gently lifting my head, my lips parted as I claw in air, his thumbs brushing beneath my eyes, collecting the moisture there. I stare at him, eyes wide, his face blank of anything. He sweeps my hair back, his hands sliding over my entire face as he threads his fingers into my curls, caressing my skull with both hands, large enough on either side of my head to crush my bones if he so wished. And then he speaks, his breath on my skin.

"I will not hurt you, Haisley," and it feels like he means it but is unsure of the reason why. "But do not think you can push me because of it."

The way he looks into my watery eyes, I taste blood as I suck on my lip, iron heavy on my tongue, breath panting wildly through my nose. I want to tear away from him, shove him back, get him to take his fucking hands off of me. But it feels as though I am truly incapable of doing any of those things, I don't even remember dropping my hands from his arms.

"I will take you outside," he speaks lowly, his deep voice smooth and controlled, "When the rain stops."

I peer up at him, heart hurting inside my chest, the dull thud of it echoing loudly in my ears.

"When the rain stops," he promises, taking a step back, his heat no longer infecting me, his hands by his sides, my entire body trembling as he turns and walks away from me.

Nothing left in his wake but the poisonous stench of my fear.

And something *else*.

For three days, it doesn't stop raining. Each morning Thorne wakes me, a fresh tracksuit waiting at the foot of my bed, his large, suited body leaning in the door frame. I use the bathroom, I eat at the kitchen table with him, he doesn't eat, but he's there, he watches. Making sure that I do. I avoid the hallway with the darkened doorways and the rusting mirror, never venturing further than the bathroom at that end of the small house.

On the worktop again, leaning over the sink, the tap leaking a very steady drip of water. I count to four, and each time I say the word silently, my lips forming the word without sound, it drips.

I stare at the sea, less choppy today, the sky a little clearer, heavy, dark clouds still low, the glass of the window I cling onto is like ice against my fingertips. A gentle waft of warmth at my back, from the fire in the front room, socked feet dangling over the edge of the counter, the soles of them feeling the heat the most. But I shiver regardless, it is forever cold and gloomy in here. The only time I'm ever warm is with *him*.

Thorne hasn't touched me again, since he smothered my mouth, promised me the outside when the rain stopped. It hasn't. I wish it would. I want to see the view. His perfectly dressed frame battered by the sea air. I imagine his hair dropping forward, the wave to it curling over his brow, the wind whipping at his shirt collar, his big, dark eyes lit with daylight. How the gold in them might look, if I ever see the sun again. It feels like this storm will never end.

Sighing, my chin resting on my knuckles, blanched white from my grip on the little window ledge, I push up, sit down on my haunches, release my hold on the wall. Swivelling around, I unfold my legs, drop them over the edge of the counter and slide down. White socks bright and new against the worn chequered flooring, fingers sweeping over the little table as I pass it, I hop up the two small steps into the living room.

Thorne sits in the old leather armchair, the material of it nothing more than threads in some parts. He doesn't look up at my entrance, scribbling away in a black, leatherbound journal, but I'm not a fool, I know this man is aware of everything I do. Every blink, breath, sigh.

Heavily, I plop down onto the sofa, drag the soft pumpkin coloured blanket over my lap, legs folded beneath me, I finger a loop of the knitted fabric, my eyes trained on my chipped red polish.

I feel his eyes on me, my body letting me know he's watching by pushing a bloom of heat to my cheeks. I flush as red as my hair at his attention, but he's unaware I know he's watching me. I listen to the crackle of the fire, the scratch of his pen, the occasional *swish* as he turns a page. Smell the burning wood, the fresh scent of rain from the bucket collecting droplets on the floor between us, but his stormy, salty scent overpowers it all.

Despite the scratch of his pen on paper, I know he's still watching me. I don't look up. Even though I want to. But having his attention, as much as it feels suffocating, I crave it. Long for it. For those dark eyes to captivate me, make me forget, just for those few seconds. Who I am. What I've done.

"I am leaving tonight," he announces quietly.

Fingers tightening in the blanket over my lap, head jerking up, his ankle atop his knee, black slacks, black socks, shined black shoes. Gold pen resting on his closed journal, leather bound papers secured with a thin lace of the same material. Large hands folded together, fingers clasped, he stares at me across the small space, no more than ten feet stretch between us. The fire before me, candles burning on the mantle above, black and white wax dripping down onto the stone hearth beneath because the lights in this house, despite having electricity now, are not reliable. So we sit in the gloom, natural light from the grey sky creeping in through the small windows, flickering candles and the fire, all we use for light. But, together, it isn't so bad. It's almost… nice.

Our bubble a dense, tense, storm cloud of gloom.

'I am leaving tonight.'

I want to ask what happens to me now.

But I don't.

We both know how this ends.

I end.

I swallow, drop my gaze, nod my head, blink hard, breath like sludge travelling through my lungs as I try to draw in air.

Thorne is a dangerous man. Hands bathed in blood, eyes hard. I'm unsure if he's the violent waves of the ocean readying to drown me, or the raging storm circling over my head, electricity charging to strike me down.

Regardless.

I want to be consumed.

By him.

In whatever way he deems me worthy.

It feels intoxicating, his attention, the way I crave it.

"Haisley," he says softly, practised.

The way my name rolls off of his tongue, something dark and ominous, like he's been speaking it in the darkness forever, and I just never heard him.

"It's okay," I whisper, voice tremoring, panting, eyes squeezing closed, I nod again, "It's okay," more reassurance, *for him.*

None of this is okay, but this is my life. Women do

not mean anything to a man in this world unless she is a pretty, mindless virgin. One that obeys, doesn't speak out of turn, and whimpers but does not scream during a beating. We are conditioned.

Princesses of the Irish Mob.

What a fucking joke.

I want to laugh, despite emotion clogging my throat, tears burning the backs of my eyes. My tongue feels too big for my mouth, lips dry, throat tight, I swallow hard. Fisting the blanket, nails biting into my palms even through the material, I try to breathe deeply, nostrils flared.

Please make it quick. Please don't make me see.

Kill me. Kill me. Kill me.

Suppressing the panic that pricks my skin, I try to slow my breathing, heart drumming in my chest. I gasp as his warm hand suddenly collides with my cold skin. Arm beneath the blanket, fingers circling my ankle, he squeezes softly, my eyes snapping open. He's crouching before me, looking up, his dark eyes wide on mine, his jaw shaved clean, hollowed cheeks, high cheekbones, sharp angular jaw, all defined by the gloom of shadows.

"I am coming back," he hushes, deep, almost melodical, I blink at him, sucking in a desperate breath, the rough pad of his thumb rolling over the soft skin of my ankle bone. "I want you to stay inside," he continues, but all I can concentrate on is the heat of his hand caressing my foot, almost absentmindedly. "You will be safe here," he says next and I drop my gaze, lick my lips.

"For how long?" it's something we haven't discussed, me too fearful of reminding him what he's supposed to do with me in case I urge him to get on with it quicker, but the psychological torment of the unknown is torture. "When does this life end for me, Thorne?" I glance up at him, from beneath my lashes, watch his jaw tense, tongue rolling across his front teeth.

He licks his lips, tightens his hold on my ankle, I know he likes it when I say his name.

"Is that what you dream of, Little Cub," he whispers, "My hands closing around your pretty little neck?" his fingers dig into the bones of my foot. "Or is it something else you think of?" his bottom lip curls into his mouth, his canine tooth snagging on the peach-coloured skin. "What do you imagine when you dream of me killing you?"

I tremble, my breaths laboured, his fingers around my foot twisting my skin until it burns, but I don't make a sound. He pushes up, his other hand planting beside my thigh, he leans in toward me, his weight on my ankle, his grip strong, unrelenting. I think he could snap my bones with a mere flick of his wrist if he so wished. I don't think I would hate it.

I think of his hips pinning me to the kitchen counter, the way he held me down on the mattress the first night here, bound my hands with his belt. The way I cried out for him, despite it all, being frightened, until I exhausted myself, because I wanted my killer not to leave me in the dark by myself. How, for the last few nights, I have pictured him doing it all over again, but he stayed, this time he stayed. His brutal hands bruising my skin is something that woke me with heat in my core and slick between my thighs. He's going to kill me and as sick as it is, I think, I'm probably going to like it.

"Tell me, baby girl," he demands, his words a deep whisper, his breath fanning over my lips, "Tell me all of your sick little fantasies."

He says it like he knows, like he's pried his way inside my head, cracked my skull, gouged my brain, manipulative fingers creeping through me, bending and twisting my insides.

Lips brushing the shell of my ear, breath ghosting down the side of my neck, pressure on my ankle that makes it feel like the bone is going to snap.

"I want to know everything inside that beautiful little head of yours," he whispers, tongue flicking over the shell of my ear with his overly pronounced words, breath held in my lungs so tightly, they feel shrivelled. "Feed me with your darkness. Infect me with your sickness, Little Cub." Breath rushes out of me, my fingers fisted in the blanket, slowly, I lift one of them, let my fingertips ghost over his back. "Poison *me*."

Letting my hand connect with him, slide down the flexing muscles in his back, I feel him shiver, the first touch I'm giving, his grip tightening, fingers beside my thigh fisting the blanket that separates us. I find what I'm looking for when I reach his waistband, and then I shove at his chest. Throwing him off balance in surprise, his grip tightening on my ankle as he tries to steady himself, weight on his toes. I kick out at him, watching him stumble back a step as he straightens, releasing my foot. Standing quickly, the blanket pooling at my feet, I click off the safety, the black gun in my hand trembling, I raise it up and aim it at him.

I don't know what I'm doing, what the fuck is possessing me, but I spread my feet a little wider, lock my elbows, stare at him down the barrel. A shot of pain hits my heart, the organ stuttering with my own unease, but I exhale slowly through my nose all the same.

Thorne stares at me, the room in shadow, his face haunting with the gloom, but his eyes seem to glitter in the light from the fire. Black candles on the mantle above, the steady drips of wax collecting on the cracked hearth below. My palms are sweating, my skin cold, hair prickles the back of my neck but I keep the gun trained on him.

Slowly. *So*. Fucking. Slowly. He lifts his hands into the space between us, his chest no more than two feet from the gun, palms outstretched, his fingers splayed, he raises them higher. Focus on me, he licks his lips, his head tilting in that slow, methodical way that he does, curiosity blazes in his irises. It no longer feels like a reflection from the fire, but like his insides are dancing with flames instead.

"Do it," he says next, rough voice calm, his chest rising and falling evenly, no panic in his gaze, just a scorching smirk playing on his lips. "I am not afraid to die," he whispers. "Are you?"

Panic surges through me, my arms tremble, tears prick my eyes, and I want to squeeze them closed, tighten my lids, hide the moisture collecting there. This dark, dangerous man is unafraid, *amused* by my threat of ending his life. And I realise, with a sharp stabbing inside my chest, that if I were going to actually shoot him, then I would have already done it.

He knows this, I know this, and yet, I'm still holding up the gun.

I stare into his eyes, wide and dark, thick lashes, gold fragments fracturing through the black abyss.

"I'm afraid," I whisper, still holding the gun out before me, my finger trembling on the trigger, but I'm unable to move.

"Tell me your fears," he whispers back, smirk gone, tone serious.

He doesn't tell me to put down the gun, there's no force from him, he doesn't demand anything at all from me. He just waits. Patiently. For my answer which I'm suddenly unable to give.

I swallow, my arms trembling, spine ramrod straight, sweat beads at my hairline but I am so, so cold. My insides feel knotted, my head a mess and the only thing I can think to do is surrender. I flick my gaze down to the gun in my hand, it's getting heavier and heavier, harder and harder to hold up. I feel weak, my elbows ache and my muscles are burning. My knees hit the floor first, the gun still aimed at him, his lower half now as I fold down onto my haunches.

I am captive, in more than one sense of the word.

Nostrils flaring, I pant for breath, fingers numb, white spots dance across my vision as I keep my eyes on the man before me, but don't really see anything. I don't want to die. I don't want to have killed Cian. I don't want to have all of these fucked up feelings for this dangerous man with violent, pretty words, but I don't want to live for nothing either.

Thorne lowers himself before me, his hands still raised, two feet of distance still separating us. He rests back on his haunches, our positions mirrored, and I inhale a sharp breath as I catch his scent, it supersedes every other aroma in this room.

"Let me feast on your fear, Little Cub," it's spoken softly, louder than before, I feel mesmerised, sick, twisted and broken. "Let me take it from you," he breathes, my eyes locked on his, tears roll over my lower lashes, dripping off my chin. "I will devour everything that has ever hurt you," it feels like a promise, one of darkness and blood and the tarnishing of souls. "I will be the only thing left for you to fear." My eyes feather closed, the gun still raised, but the action redundant. "But I will never hurt you."

Breath catching, eyes pinging open as he pushes up onto his knees, his chest becoming flush with the gun, he presses against it, the barrel digging into his sternum. My arms shake harder, my chin trembling, and I don't know what I'm doing, what I want, my intentions. Everything is muddied and unclear, cloud upon cloud of confusion swarms my skull, blanketing my brain in darkness.

"You can do it, Haisley," he coos, "If you want to, just squeeze the trigger."

Breath sails through my lungs, catching in my throat. The cords in his neck are strong, veins protruding, pumping life through him. This will be my only chance at escape, to run away and disappear. I'm sure, some-where, I'm already dead, existence evaporated like rain-drops in the sun from my family tree. But I will be running forever, always looking over my shoulder. I don't know how to get a job, not really, I don't have a pass-port, a birth certificate, I don't even have any money. The thought chokes me as I blink the blurriness from my gaze, suck my bottom lip into my mouth.

"You are so confused," Thorne breathes, his words bleed into the air around us and I swallow so hard I almost heave. "It is okay," he reassures me, in the same placating way I did him not minutes ago. "I will not hurt you."

Those words do not translate into *'I won't kill you',* despite my every hope and prayer since I arrived here wishing otherwise. I blink, my tears dissolving, my cheeks flushing red, I stare at this man. Captor. Monster. One that, despite everything, has clothed me and fed me and bathed me.

Protected me.

I feel heat on the back of my neck, the little hairs on my arms standing on end. I'm going to fall in love with this man and the brutal things he does to me. Then he is going to end me and I will die with a broken heart. I feel it in my very marrow. Someone like me was not built to endure such things.

My breath stutters, a new resolve washing over me,

and it's the first thread of real emotion I have ever seen in him as a small crease forms between his dense brows. The cool barrel of the gun feels like ice beneath my chin, my hands steady now.

"I am not afraid to die," I whisper the words between us, my chin tilted up, eyes downcast, his hands are still raised in the space between us, and I can tell I've surprised him. I feel a truth on my tongue, and it can't be contained, "I think, perhaps, I was born to."

His thick neck works in a gulp as he swallows, his breathing picking up just a little, Adam's apple bobbing. I hear buzzing in my ears, blood zooming through my veins. Crackles from the fire spitting, the droplets of wax dripping from the mantle, hissing as they meet cold stone, and I feel calm. I feel *free*.

"Little Cub," Thorne says softly, his deep, gravelly voice smooth as velvet. "Please."

His eyes wide, another *please* from this man, so polite, calm, always meticulously well-spoken. I think of each one he has offered me, all sincere, none quite so much as this.

"It's okay," I say then, "I'm not afraid," I whisper, my lips curling up on my face, a tear spills from the outer corner of my eye, running into my hairline. "Not anymore."

"Let me have the gun." His voice cracks, it sounds raw and I watch as a bead of sweat rolls down the side of his face, his fingers in the space between us not entirely still. "I am not going to hurt you," he reminds me, and I smile at that, let my eyes fall closed. "I could never hurt you," it's a whispered confession, my eyes burn, throat tight, I shake away the thoughts of what that could mean. Suddenly, quieter, he speaks again, less emotion, "Do you hear that, Haisley?" he whispers, my eyes slowly blinking open. "The rain has stopped."

And I release the gun.

Wind whips across my face, the clouds hanging low, I watch her thick flames of red hair soar in the storm, head tilted back, face towards the heavens. I feel shaken, my nerves fizzing as I re-pocket my phone, having made my excuses to not head to the mill, it feels a little like relief. I cannot leave this broken girl here alone. I do not want to leave this broken girl anywhere I am not.

Hands sliding into my pockets, phone buzzing beneath my palm, *Arrow*. I ignore it, train my eyes on the girl at the edge of the cliff. The old lighthouse towering above her, she looks like a lit match, a flame dancing in the wind before it fizzles out. I want her to thrive, I want her to drown, I want her to live and to die and to be only for me.

She looks so young and I feel so old, but only ten short years sit between us. There was a time, I, too, held a gun beneath my jaw. The difference being; I pulled the trigger. I think of my mother, how she did so many awful things, but the one that tore at my insides beyond repair was when she sent my younger brother Hunter away. It was only three days before I managed to get hold of Dad, who went to fetch him immediately, but those three excruciatingly long days felt like my life was imploding.

Dangerous thoughts infected my brain, ones I had always managed to suppress, a seed of sickness beginning to grow. After that, my carefully crafted control, sometimes, would slip, a blind rage where I saw nothing but red, a possession, dark and twisted and violent would engulf me and I never could remember what I had done.

"Haisley," I call, needing to draw myself back, away from poisonous thoughts, ground myself. "Please," I say calmly, despite my heart hammering inside my chest cavity, "Come away from the edge."

There is no panic in my voice, despite it thumping away in my heart, but she is too close to the edge of the cliff, one that crumbles and shrinks every year as the crashing sea erodes it. Stones skitter, but her small feet track her back, a new pair of dark green Chucks, fresh out the box, one I had stowed in the back of my car. I worried if she had shoes she would try to run. I wish now, perhaps, she had tried.

It means she wants to live.

I do not know what this beautiful girl wants.

I am supposed to kill her.

The girl who has haunted me from the moment I

laid eyes on her at the tiny age of six years old. She was seventeen when my obsession truly began. But thoughts of her have forever consumed me.

"Mafia Princesses are not meant for men like us," Dad says, his tone weary as he pushes a hand through his slicked back hair, dark and wavy, just like mine.

This is not the first time I have heard this lecture; I am twenty-seven now. I am not a boy. I could likely recite it by heart, should that be his request. Instead, I clasp my hands together, rest them on the kitchen table.

"I know," I respond, emotionless, despite the claws of obsession hooked deep in the vertebrae of my spine. "I will not make any advances on her, I know my place."

Dad sighs loudly, elbows planting themselves on the thick plastic tablecloth, yellow and white checks with little bumblebees printed on it. Mum would have liked this.

I hate it.

"Thorne," Dad says, resigned. "I wish there were something I could do, my boy," his large hand lands on my shoulder, strong fingers gripping the taut muscle.

It feels comforting, despite my coldness, I always have to be so in control of myself, I cannot allow myself to become emotional or it will end badly for everyone.

"We are cursed, the men in this family, we become obsessed, it is a toxin in our blood, passed down through generation and generation of the Blackwell clan. It cannot be scrubbed out, so it must, when necessary, be controlled."

"I understand," I repeat, pushing all thoughts of the fiery redhead clear from my mind. "I do not long for her."

Dad's head snaps up, his gaze hard on mine.

"Blackwells do not tell lies."

"Thorne?"

I blink, Haisley's soft voice a lullaby for my cursed soul. Looking down at her, her lip tucked between her teeth, she has gotten incredibly close to me in lost seconds I do not recall blanking. I think of her, not an hour ago, a gun pressing into the softness of her chin. *My gun.* Panic like lightning through my veins, the soaring of my heart, the way it dropped into my stomach and has not yet clawed its way back out.

She blinks up at me, eyes wide, round and green and sparkling, no redness, no tears, no clumping of her lashes. Nothing of what was; a mess on our living room floor. *Our.* My heart thuds, harder and harder, and I worry I might be having a heart attack.

"Thorne?" she speaks so quietly, it settles me, low stimulation, nothing that will set me off, no loud sounds, no harsh movements, things I have always struggled with, but overcome despite it all because this is my life.

I want to tilt my head, assess her, strip her bare with my gaze. Absentmindedly, my fingers outstretched, they loop through her curls, twirling in the bottom of her red tresses, a bright orange-red, like a summer's sunset when the sky resembles the hue of fire. Soft silk ribbons between my fingers, I twirl and loop the little strand around my thumb, hooking in it enough to tug. I bite down on my back teeth, clench my jaw, release her hair, sweep a hand through my own.

"Are you leaving?" she asks me innocently; hope, she tries to hide, thick in her question.

I shake my head once, voice carried on the volatile wind, "I am staying."

A smile curls her lips, her head dropping, she tries to hide it, gaze on her feet, I bite my tongue, inhale a slow, practised breath, try hard not to reciprocate it.

I am not sure what is happening to me, but this was not a good idea. I feel a little like a child on Christmas morning, being gifted the puppy everyone in his household told him he could absolutely never have. And it is, also, probably, not a wise idea. To gift the brutal boy something soft and fragile, when he is always dripping toxins and bathing in blood, followed closely by a shadow built from depravity.

"I like it here," her words gentle, she shifts her weight from one foot to the other, eyes flicking up, chin dipped, gravel scuffing under her shoe.

I do not respond, even as my heart swells, because most women, of her calibre, would be complaining and whining, and I *know*, this is nothing like the house she comes from. Having been inside it, seen the luxury, I know this is a stark contrast for her. I have penthouses, apartments, a manor house, homes abroad and expensive cars. But of them all, I like it here too.

I like it here too.

I want to say it, see her smile again, maybe this time,

I shall be gifted with it, but, I cannot allow myself to give her these parts of me. So my mouth stays closed, my tongue caught between my teeth, hands achingly clenched in my pockets.

She turns, body angled towards me, head over her shoulder, ringlets of hair covering half of her. I ache to reach out, coil it around my fists and cover her lips with my own. I have never wanted to kiss someone before. Apart from the first kiss I ever had, which was nothing more than two nine year olds pressing their lips together before quickly wiping them off on their sleeves. I try to remember a time I have ever kissed anyone since...

"Can we go in there?" she is quiet with her words, they are slow when she speaks, and her accent is hardly noticeable, something I am sure, has been forced out of her with strict schooling.

I glance up over her head when she brings her attention back to me, avoiding her gaze, my eyes catching on the old lighthouse. White paint peeling, door rusted, I do not think I have ever entered it more than once. It is falling apart inside, and I want to tell her no, because it is too dangerous, all parts of it, and the house we are taking refuge in, are barely fit for use. But as I glance back down at her, fingers knotted in front of her, twisting together with nerves. It took courage for her to ask for something that she wants. A strange thought occurs to me then. What will happen if she needs something I have not already provided, how will she request something that might make her uncomfortable?

Why am I thinking about this long term?

"Yes," I tell her then, that smile she tries to smother curling her mouth, but this time she does not look away. "But you must stay close to me; its structure is not sound."

She dips her head again, a flare of pink rising high in her cheeks, "Okay, Thorne."

I swallow, the way she says my name, a direct link to the charred organ inside my chest, it sparks something rotten in my brain, twisted and sick. I step forward, past her, putting distance between us both, for her safety and for mine. I am already attached, I have been inevitably tied to this woman before she ever knew I existed, but I cannot let myself go with her. I cannot lose my control.

I have to kill her.

The door is unlocked, but it is weathered, rusting, the hinges half crumble as I shove my shoulder into it, fist tightly curled around the handle. With a thunk and a creak, it opens, dust and rust particles sprinkling down, I crane my head back, out of the way of the crumbling debris, palm flat to the door, waiting for it to settle. But before I can even glance at the redhead behind me, she is peering around my body, clouds of filth falling into the top of her hair.

"Haisley," a scold, which she ignores, and I am suddenly aware that my control over her is non-existent.

I think of my brother Hunter; the way he is with our stepsister Grace. She has all the control. He is a slave to her desires.

What happens when a man who has only ever

known control, requires it, can suddenly no longer grasp it?

Her small hand comes to the base of my spine, curly red tendrils spilling around her face as she arches forward, resting on me so she does not fall through the doorway. I am rigid. The first voluntary touch from her that has not resulted in gun theft, shocks me to my core. Her cold skin sinks through the thin cotton of my black button up shirt, my warm skin cooling at the light touch. Her fingers barely brush me, but they do, I am frozen, and I want her to press harder. I want the bones of my spine imprinted into her hand, bruises from her fingertips as divots in my back.

Touch me.

Even as I think it, I know it is a very bad idea. I will not be able to control myself with this girl. I will hurt her, I will kill her, and I did not bring her here to make a mess. I am meticulous, my skill is refined, I do not like to play with my prey. But I think, staring at this woman, lips plump and parted, blood fresh on her skin from a cut that was *not* put there by me, that, perhaps, I may like to play with this one.

CHAPTER 13
HAISLEY

The sea crashes below me, sky rumbling above, it won't be long before there's more rain falling. But while it's not, I get to breathe in air that smells like the man who holds my life in his hands. Thorne is the salt of the sea, the storm of the sky, and my fingers curl into fists at my sides at the thought of being drowned in it.

My toes, in new, dark green Chucks, shuffle me closer to the edge, dirty puddles beneath my feet, gravel underfoot. I peer over the edge, down at the white foamy waves climbing and colliding with the base of the cliff. I stare for what feels like an eternity, the swirls and whirls of the murky water. It's violent. I wonder what it would feel like.

"Haisley," Thorne's voice echoes on the wind, infecting me with the decadent smoothness of his tone. "Please," he calls calmly, my heart hammering inside my chest at the way he is just so polite, "Come away from the edge."

My tummy flips, even though his words are delivered cold. It feels like he cares, my father would never care enough to call me away from the edge of a cliff. In fact, he'd probably order one of my siblings to run past and shove me over it. Doing as I'm told, I step back, three large steps, my eyes still focused forward, on the point where the sea meets the sky in a line of gloom.

Thorne is staring right at me when I turn to face him, unable to keep my eyes off of him for long. I have a desperate craving, like a creature clawing away inside of my flesh that wants to tear free, slice its way into his and bury itself there.

His dark eyes are blank as I approach, gaze over top of my head, on the point I was just standing, as though he's unaware I've even moved.

"Thorne?" I whisper, I tuck a lock of hair behind my ear, the wind instantly throwing it back across my face.

I study him, his face expressionless, eyes unseeing, I can't bring myself to touch him in case he shatters like glass.

"Thorne?" I say it a little louder, he blinks, looking down at me, reaching out, his fingers spiralling in the bottom length of my hair.

Twirling it around his finger, he inhales slow and deep, and I find my frantic breaths wanting to slow, to match his, be in sync with him. He releases the tendril of hair too quickly, sweeps the same hand through his own, a thick black wave styled neatly, precisely, away from his face.

"Are you leaving?" I enquire gently, hopeful he'll tell me he's staying.

I saw him make a call, his head dropped forward so I was unable to attempt to make out his words.

"I am staying."

He says with a single shake of his head, and a smile breaks my lips, I drop my gaze, stare at my new shoes, scuff the toe of them in the wet gravel, trying to hide my happiness at his answer. Warmth blooms in my chest, despite my coldness, the icy air, it's winter, and it's been unusually cold and wet the last few weeks, December's usually drier than this.

"I like it here," I announce, my words quiet, eyes flicked up as I trace the toe of my shoe through a muddy puddle.

He stares at me, blankly, and I want him to say something, maybe tell me he likes it here too. But he doesn't, and the disappointment I feel in my heart weighs much more than it should. Perhaps this isn't even his property, he's a man that dresses impeccably, drives a fancy car, a large black Mercedes that sits not too far from where we stand. And I'm used to the finer things, too, but… I like it here.

Maybe more so than anywhere I have ever been before.

I think I'm losing my mind, perhaps being in such close proximity with a man as sharp and dangerous as Thorne is corrupting my soul.

Perhaps I have always been this way.

Imagining my death at the hands of this killer and liking it.

My cheeks heat, I glance over my shoulder, towards the lighthouse that I had no idea was here, not in view from my little kitchen window I peer out of inside the house.

"Can we go in there?" it's a request I didn't really mean to voice, but the words have tumbled free now, I can't take them back.

When I turn back to face him, his dark eyes on the lighthouse, focus over my head, I study his angular jaw, the hollow in his cheek, memorise it.

"Yes," he answers, dropping his gaze back onto me, a smile curls my mouth, and I don't look away. "But you must stay close to me, its structure is not sound."

There it is again, that carefully constructed order, politeness in every word, instructions meant to protect me. My cheeks heat again, hotter, brighter.

"Okay, Thorne."

He stares back at me like he'd very much like to place his hands around my neck and snap it. The look in his eyes is gone as quickly as it appeared, he steps around me, making sure there's a distance between our bodies. I instantly miss his heat, the way it seems to radiate off of him, seep into my own, curl beneath my skin, sink deep into my bones.

I follow behind him, desperate to see the inside of the lighthouse. I've never seen one in real life before, and it makes me antsy wanting to get closer. Thorne's steps are double the length of one of mine, his long legs quickly eating up the space. Hurrying to catch up, I slow my pace when he reaches the door, large hand curled around the handle, green and blue veins thick beneath his warm skin. I hover just behind him, his shoulder pressing into the large door.

Rook Point.

The name is inscribed into the old door, a curve at the top of it, white paint yellowing and peeling in large flakes with rust. The writing is blue, aquamarine, and I imagine that the sea is this colour under the rays of the sun, something that is currently still hiding behind clouds of grey. Head craning back, I stare up at the imposing building, the top of it climbing into the heavens upon this white cliff. A beacon of light, something that can shine for miles, cutting through even the darkest of nights.

With a thump, Thorne cracks the door open, shouldering it like a battering ram, he leans far back, his body almost touching mine as he avoids clouds of debris tumbling through the air. I stare at his side profile, his jaw strong and defined, I swallow, turn my attention to the open door, step into him, so close we're almost touching but he seems oblivious to my nearness. Tongue running over my bottom lip, tasting blood, I suck it into my mouth. He doesn't flinch away, excitement zapping up my spine, my fingers flex into the palm of my hand before I bravely extend them. Placing them gently against his lower spine, I try not to hold my breath as I feel him stiffen at the contact, peering around him

instead. Shoving my head into the doorway, dust particles smothering me.

"Haisley," it's a thrill, his tone, a sharp, yet softly
spoken warning, but I don't react, I keep staring inside
the gloom.

Eyes squinting, I peer upwards, a white spiral staircase curls its way up, dust lacing my lashes, I blink my
eyes, shake my head. Puff air out between my lips.
Thorne's hand comes to my chin, I still. I don't blink,
my fingers trembling where they rest like feathers against
his lower spine, my breaths coming in quick succession.
A bird caws overhead, making me swallow, its flap of
wings reverberating around the tower. I ache to look, to
see, but I'm frozen, his grip firm on the tip of my chin,
my jaw clenching, he turns my head, back towards him,
gaze over my shoulder.

"Let me go in first," he says calmly.

His face carefully blank once more, I long for a reaction, a curious head tilt. But then his thumb darts up,
swiping slowly over my split lip, too hard, too rough, the
pad of his thumb plucking at the torn skin. Lips parted,
I watch his dark eyes focus on his thumb, keep still, lungs
seized, throat locking up. I realise, with a strange feeling
in my heart, that even when he's hurting me, I think, I
want it to hurt more. So, I force my face closer, his palm
beneath my chin, cupping it, somewhat affectionately,
even as he brutalises my bloody lip.

Hand stilling, he blinks, dark eyes troubled as they
snap up to meet mine. Breath sails through my lungs
in a rush, the tip of my tongue glides over my bottom

lip, tasting iron, salt, catching the tip of his thumb and his chest rises with a sudden, sharp inhale. Then he blinks again, eyes suddenly *seeing*, he straightens, releases me, steps out of my hold, breaking whatever this is.

Lacing my fingers together before me, I watch as he steps through the doorway, dust settling where it falls. His shined shoes leave footprints in the white, my eyes darting all over the space as I follow him inside, without waiting for his say so. I step into the centre of the circular space, crane my neck back, blink up. Lips popping open, I laugh a little, a smile on my mouth.

"Wow," I breathe, staring up in awe, everything rusting, chipped paint, the metal stairs flaking large clumps, white edged in orange-brown.

Birds resettle above us, Thorne at the base of the stairs, I spin a little, slowly, peering up at the ceiling. Caws and flapping wings are all I can hear, as though the clashing of waves outside has died, the inside of this lighthouse safe from outside elements.

"Rooks," Thorne says softly, my eyes falling onto his, head still craned back, his hands slide into his trouser pockets as he watches me. "A Parliament of them."

I blink, straightening my neck, the bones protesting as I finally force my head upright. Fluttering my lashes, I step a little closer to him. Open door at my back, wind whipping through it, gaze darting between the birds circling our heads, and the dangerous man watching me.

"The stairs are not safe, Haisley," he informs me, and for a man who doesn't tell lies, it feels a little like an untruth, but I let it go, offer him a small smile, one I couldn't hide if I tried.

"Okay."

I lick my lip, the wound weeping, it stings but I want him to touch it again, rip it open every time it heals. *Scar me.*

Glancing back up, high above our heads, the metal stairs clinging to the walls, curling around the structure, I eye the platform at the top, wonder if he would let me *try* to reach it, at least give i-

"No," his voice like silk, threads its way to my ears, my mouth curling into a smile, broader, *real.* "I know what you are thinking, and *no,* you cannot *give it a go.*"

I laugh at that, a real, full laugh, one that jiggles my belly, and brings tears to my eyes. I wipe a fist over my closed lids, pushing dust and god knows what else into them, but I feel *good* and I don't care if I have to wash out my bleary eyes, because as I glance back at Thorne, he's *smiling.* And I stop laughing instantly, swallowing hard, his lips, the top the same thickness as the bottom, a curve to his cupid's bow, are tipped up, it's not toothy, his hollowed cheeks dimpled, cheekbones lifted. I blush, drop my gaze, pray for something.

Maybe him.

Maybe death.

Because that is all that is going to happen here.

Curled up on the couch, legs tucked beneath me, knitted blanket pulled over top, my hands fisted beneath it. I'm in two sweatshirts, a long-sleeved thermal t-shirt beneath, leggings and track-suit bottoms, thick white socks. It's cold, really cold, rain lashing the windows. It's dark out now, from the rain, and the absence of day. Fire roaring, spitting and crackling, candles on the mantle above, steadily dripping wax, it feels cosy, even though there are metal buckets catching raindrops from the holes in the roof.

Thorne comes in from the kitchen, stopping beside me, two mugs, one black, one green, in each of his hands. His dark eyes penetrate me, analysing my every movement, since he closed up the lighthouse an hour or so ago, told me to get inside and wash my face, I have sat here, on this old, uncomfortable couch. Unmoving, because I'm not sure what is happening to me, but I'm going to die by this man's hands and I wonder if I want them on my body in another way before that happens. It feels a little like I scare him, the way he avoids me, until he just *can't*.

I don't think about his gun, the weight of it in my hand, the smooth metal pressing into the underside of my chin. I think of the real words he spoke to me instead, the way he looked startled, just for a second, that masterful control dissolving. How it felt like some sort of win.

"Thank you," my hand reaching out, steam wafting across the top of the green mug as he lowers it down to me.

My fingertips brush his, he blinks, but doesn't pull away and it feels like fire is lighting beneath my skin. I don't know if it's him, maybe it's me. Perhaps I am sick and twisted and wrong.

A murderer.

But I feel safe, here, with him. Existing in the gloom, a gothic array of black candles creating a haunting display over the mantle. Something sinister tainting the air, the taste of it not all that unappealing the longer I live in it. I breathe him in, not subtly, salt and metal and leather, he turns away from me like he doesn't notice, body angled towards the armchair he seems to have claimed as his own, mine the sofa I currently sit on by default.

I inhale the tea, *rose*, and my head snaps up.

"Thorne," it feels like an accusation, a crack of electricity in the air.

He stops, part way across the room, his back still

towards me, one hand by his side, the other curled around his black mug, his fingers don't twitch, he doesn't turn to look at me.

"This tea…" I trail off, eyebrows furrowing, I glance down at the steaming liquid, swallow past the tightness in my throat. "How do you know this is what I drink?" Rose tea with black pepper is absolutely not a standard flavour.

His head dips, he still doesn't look back, instead, takes a step forward.

"No," I say slowly, louder, stilling him, my spine straightening, I sit up taller, "How did you know about the tea?" Hairs are risen all along the length of my arms, the back of my neck, a chill like skeletal fingers creeps its way down my spine. "Thorne." Irritation is spiking, insides twisting and churning, I think of his eyes on me, how they felt comforting, not unfamiliar. "Tell me, right now," my voice trembles, but it isn't with fear.

My socked feet hit the cold floor, iciness instantly climbing up my legs, I step over the fallen blanket, squeeze the mug tighter in my hand, the heat of it scalding my skin. I'm a mere foot away, his back still to me, his black suit jacket tight across the hard planes of muscle in his back. I jut out my chin, teeth clenched, I am boiling with the sudden rush of temper as it floods through my system.

"What are you doing, Little Cub?" he whispers, still looking away from me, and I feel like jelly instantly, at the nickname, shame heating my cheeks at my outburst, but I stand firm. "Are you upset with me," breath stutters through my parted lips, "For knowing something about you that you did not share with me?" spoken so softly, the question dousing my fire in ice.

So calm, so cold, he turns his head, chin dipped, face shrouded in shadows. High cheekbones carving his face like a skeleton mask and I feel myself wanting to push forward, move closer, the anger that was present only seconds ago, dead and buried twelve-feet deep. Smothered by consecrated ground, I can smell it, grave dirt, sweet and earthy, foreboding, it smells like my future.

And yet, I close the gap between us. Head held high, I find myself an inch from his back, his head still angled towards me over his shoulder, our eyes connecting with something like a dare. Heat from the fire suddenly feels scalding, heat singeing the side of my face, but the room is cold, my skin prickling, with goosebumps, awareness. And that flare of anger I thought had died, swoops back in and morphs into something else.

I want to hold onto it, that tethering of violence, it makes me feel better, hate in my heart, for this man, this place, the situation I unavoidably got myself in. Perhaps I should have let Cian destroy me instead. Evaded all of *this*.

It feels like I want to explode, or shrink, to take up all of the space and none at all and all that screams inside of my head is who the fuck are you, what do you want, why are you here? What in the ever-loving fuck is happening to me? All questions aimed at myself. Confusion wars inside my brain, I don't know who I am. I've never had time in my day to really, truly, be myself, and for once, I feel glad. Glad that I haven't had to suffer quite like this ever before. Because it is soul destroying. And even *that* no longer belongs to me, it hangs between realms, life and death, the veil dividing the two, one foot in the grave, one out and it's all in this man's bloodied, brutal hands. And I think I might just want him to squeeze.

I flinch, as he turns, and he is so, *so* hard to be angry with, I have so much of it to channel, rage, and this man makes it almost impossible to be my target. My captor. I'm not even sure I want to push him for the right reasons, I think, maybe, I just want his attention, and the shame from that burns hot in my cheeks. So many unspoken confessions, I want to blurt it all out, the way his dark eyes, cut with honey, slash through my soul.

He takes the mug from my hand, carefully unpeeling my fingers and I'm not sure when he placed his own drink down, but it reminds me of the tea and my insides roil again.

"I-"

"It is New Year's Eve, Haisley," is what he says, cutting me off in the most polite manner.

I blink, the low flickering light of the room only carving up his shadowed face, flames dancing off of him, the wall at his back. Rain beats against the windows, the leaky roof, and I try to calculate when I missed Christmas. Being kept in that tiny back room, towels on the floor for bedding, food once a day, some-times every other, two bathroom trips that they didn't always remember to collect me for. My bladder aches at the thought, phantom pain in my pelvis, tears prick my eyes and I swallow thickly.

"I stayed," he says, as though that weren't obvious, what with him being right fucking here, but my anger dries up as quickly as it blooms when he says, *"To be with you."*

Gaping up at him, crease forming quickly between my brows, I puzzle what he's trying to say, the sincerity and truthfulness of every word. Something clenching in my stomach, my heart thundering like the storm outside, rib bones rattling, I lick my lips, cracked, dry, bleeding, feel completely blindsided.

"I do not have to be here, there are ways of making you stay without me."

I think of before, a room, with rope, the haze of smoke. Then I got here, and I smell leather now, my wrists aching at the thought of Thorne climbing over the top of me, binding my hands with the warmth of his belt. Skin crawling with horror at the thought of being here, *without him*, alone. I realise, again, just how much I crave this killer. It is sick and twisted, how much I do.

"I will stay here with you." A statement. "Because I *want* to."

His face dips forward, the tip of his nose almost brushing mine, the way he angles his head, half of his face alight with the orange glow of fire. I am frozen, caught in a cloud of confusion once more, and it is destroying every single part of me.

"I will not hurt you," he breathes the words over my

parted lips, and I gulp them down on a sharp inhale, hold the breath in my lungs. "Even though I am *dying* to."

Body trembling, the tip of his nose finally makes contact with the side of my face, I sway into him, my hands by my sides, I am enchanted, in his thrall. He runs his nose over my temple, to my hairline and I curl my fingers into fists, I want to reach out, but I think I would shatter this delicate moment and I want to hold onto it for as long as I can. Refraining, I hold as still as I can. Thorne's large hands remain perfectly still by his sides, eyes closing, I try to keep my breathing calm, even as his lips skim my cheekbone, nose in my hair. His mouth moving beside my ear, breath hot and humid down the side of my throat and I wonder how he is always so warm, hot. A shudder wracks through me, my skin always cold, like it knows its destiny.

Corpses are cold.

Death, foreboding, is like a cold wave settling over my skin, drowning me beneath it.

I wonder what this monstrous man thinks about death.

His own.

Mine.

"Thorne," his name a plea as it whispers through my teeth, my cool breath over his skin, his heat warming me through my layers of clothing.

He makes a strangled sound in the back of his throat, and I tremble as he steps into me, his hard body like solid marble against my softness. His breaths grow harsh, my hands quivering by my sides, but I can't be the one to touch him, I will ruin whatever this is, and no matter what that says about me, I do not want it to.

Hot and fast, his breath rolls over my pricked skin, his nose pressing into the sensitive skin just beneath my ear. His bottom lip parted from the top, rests against the side of my throat, the way he's bent forwards, dropped to my height, his head angled like a predator waiting to sink teeth into my artery. He towers over me, engulfing me in his scent, his body curled around me, but his hands still hang by his sides, and I want to touch them. Large, strong hands, olive green veins snaking beneath warm coloured skin, my fingers flex, his face almost buried in my neck, it's overwhelming, the way my heart thuds so hard it hurts.

"*Thorne*," it's a breathy whisper, a quiet melody sung directly into his ear, a shiver works its way through him, making my breath catch in my chest.

"Little Cub," he whispers back, husky and rich.

I feel him lick his lips, his tongue flicking over my pulse as it slides over his bottom lip, a crushed whimper clawing its way out of my throat, even though I try to strangle it.

A rumbling sound, reminiscent of a growl, thunders its way through his chest, his body rattling with the force of it. I flinch, inching closer into him, letting my temple just graze his shoulder, my face angled in towards his throat, the same way he's curled into mine.

"Thorne," a bare whisper, but it's spoken into his

flesh, his lips parted, pressing into the skin at the side of my own throat. "*Please.*"

He breathes hard through his nose, hot and humid, "Do not do this, Haisley," he says, lips trembling over my pulse, his nose drawing down the column of my throat. "I was not made for someone like you."

I blink, the statement ricocheting through my insides as if I've swallowed barbed wire, mouth dry, breath held, anger quakes through me like a hurricane, but he doesn't part from my flesh. His lips, nose, breath, all still very present, and my words refuse to come out as anything more than the practised whisper I've learnt to use so well since I arrived here. The way we speak to each other, always in these quiet, intense moments, nothing is ever more than a whisper.

"Someone like *me?*"

He freezes, his breath held, nothing hot fanning against my neck, but then his teeth graze over my pulse, and it's such a gentle scrape, I wonder if I really even feel it at all.

"A princess."

Breath rushes out of me, tucking my cupid's bow between my teeth, I lick over my top lip.

"I'm not a princess, Thorne." I let my eyes flutter closed, speak directly into his neck, my lips plucking at his skin. "I'm nothing more than a breathing corpse."

A dark chuckle falls from his sinister slash of a mouth, making me jolt with surprise, the sound loud and harsh in my ear.

"You will make such a pretty one," he breathes next,

hissing the words through his teeth, "But I am not finished with you yet, Little Cub."

I shiver at his words, a rush of heat pooling at the apex of my thighs, something vile and perverse unfurling inside my belly, a craving for what he's going to do. What I think I want to happen. I exhale hard against his skin, his own shiver raking its way down his spine, he feels impossibly huge, towering over me, nothing to see, smell or feel other than him. His hard body pressing against the length of mine, something even harder digging into the soft curve of my belly, my breath catches, lips parting.

One of his hands ghosts up the length of my body, not touching, just moving through the air, shaping out my body. Until he reaches my upper arm, curls a spiralled lock of hair around one of his fingers, tugging gently, lips against my ear once more.

"Horror will charm its way into your heart. Death will lure your soul into the dark."

I blink, the slowly spoken macabre words soft as silk prickling my skin, all this talk of death, his body too close but still too far, his words on my skin, the heat rolling off of him.

"You know what else is in the dark, Haisley?" there's something raspy in his undertone, his finger twirling my hair, my breath hot and fast.

"What?" I whisper, curiosity pinching me.

His nose catches the shell of my ear, his lips over my lobe, *"Monsters."*

I tremble, the strand of my hair coiled tightly

around his finger, he pulls it so sharply, my neck cracks, my temple colliding with his own. I whimper as his free hand snaps up, fingers wrapping tight around my throat. He angles his head in that seemingly innocent tilt, curious like a young boy, his thumb and forefinger digging dangerously hard into either side of my throat. Pulse fluttering like the restricted wings of a humming-bird, his fingers carve bruises into my neck, he tilts my chin, our eyes meeting. Electricity fizzes through me, wet heat gathering between my tense thighs.

His gaze flickers to where his hand is wrapped around my throat, my hands come up of their own accord, closing tightly around his forearm as he effort-lessly lifts me up with his grip on my throat. Lifting and lifting until my toes just skim the floor, and his head is still angled down towards me. Lips slanting over my mouth, he squeezes tighter, firmer, and the whimper I can't lock down tries to escape in nothing but an empty exhale from my burning lungs. Tears roll down my cheeks, blurry vision still on him, his face a hazy contor-tion at the closeness.

I can hear his words in my head.

'I will not hurt you, Little Cub'.

How he told me he does not tell lies. More tears slip down my cheeks, eyes spotting with black, and I keep my hands wrapped around his forearm, I should push him away, it's what my body's survival instincts are screaming inside my head. But, instead, I grip him harder, gouging my fingers into his arm over his long sleeved shirt, black suit jacket, and tug him closer, forcing my body to become flush with his arm, my toes brushing the tips of his shoes.

Do it.

I am aching.

Kill me.

I fucking dare you.

And then he's loosening his grip, still holding my throat, breath burns as it syphons into my lungs like gasoline for the fire already in them. He lowers me, slowly, my eyes blinking furiously, I keep my grip on him tight, as tight as I can and it feels insane, the thrill. My heart hammers behind my breastbone, nerves, excitement, *need.*

"This is a dangerous game," Thorne tells me, his grip still firm on my neck, bruising, windpipe half closed with the brutality of it.

I want to play.

I convey it with my eyes, not knowing where these feelings come from, but they're there and I want to explore this. *With him.* My green orbs flicker between his dark depths, cheeks hollowed, shadowed and carved out like something sinister from a ghost train or haunted house at the fair.

It is beautiful on him.

I am enthralled.

"Not tonight, Little Cub."

His hand releases me, and he is oh so careful as he places me fully on my feet. My eyes tracking him as he licks his lips, his gaze trailing its way down and then back up my body. Heat flushing even hotter in my veins, my cheeks undoubtedly blooming with a bright blush.

"Sit with me," he whispers, his fingers tucking a wild curl behind my ear. "Let's wait up together to draw in the new year," he says it with a deadly half smirk that does things, it absolutely shouldn't, to me, but he's going to further give me his attention.

And no matter how desperate it may seem, it's all I seem to crave.

So I do, and in doing so, I forget all about the rose tea.

Heat burns the entire left side of my body, and for one single millisecond it feels like too much. I am always warm, but this is something else entirely and I am not sure I like it. Eyes pinching before I force them open, the fire barely lit, my brow crinkles, and I forget where I am for a moment. Until I do not.

She must have moved into me whilst I was asleep. Which is concerning, letting my guard down enough to fall into unconsciousness. Not to wake when she rolled into me. The fingers of my right hand flex beside my thigh, desperate to touch her, to bend her, to break her.

I think of the things I need to do. I have nanny applications to sort through, background checks to carry out. Dad insisted I hire someone to help my sister. Hunter and her having three boys under five is a lot, and Grace is *struggling*.

The heat curled up into my side, freckled face

pressed into my shoulder, hands balled, tight beneath her chin. I stare down my nose at Haisley, trying desperately not to move. Admire the way she is folded up into the tiniest ball, nestling into me.

Haisley is always cold. I actually quite like that about her. In comparison to the heat that seems to constantly radiate off of my own skin, probably something to do with the scorching hellfire that forms part of my blackened soul. It is a nice contrast. Keeping my breaths even, I watch her, unable to tilt my chin in case it bumps the top of her head. Willing my heart to stop thundering in my chest, galloping like a horse at the races, I study her beneath the light of the dying fire.

Her small nose wrinkles, an eye twitching, her pale, strawberry-blonde lashes fluttering on her left eye. Her breaths are a little fast, fingers flexing inside her fists. Dreaming, perhaps something more sinister, a nightmare. I wonder what she thinks about when she sleeps. Does she dream of monsters? Evil, wicked men who hold her life in their hands, locking her up inside crumbling lighthouses? She whimpers, making my pulse spike, adrenaline simmering in my veins at the sound, the way I imagine she would squeak with my foot pressing down on her throat.

Without dipping my chin, I tilt my head to the side, drag my eyes down her twitching body, it is an awkward angle, but it is worth it, the strain in my neck. To see her. Her lips purse, nostrils flaring, her beautiful pale skin flushes red, a deep crevice forming between her perfectly shaped auburn brows.

I should not touch her.

Touch her. Touch her. Touch her.

I lick my lips, my breaths too hard now, too fast, my chest heaves in the same rhythm hers does. Like I, too, am stuck inside the nightmare playing out inside her head. I do not want to interrupt it. I want her to wade through. Be strong.

Suffer.

Her whimpers grow louder, her legs, bent at the knees, pressing into the side of my thigh, twitch and tremble. I lick my lips again, trying to kill my insatiable appetite for hurting this perfect girl. There is something sick inside of me. The way my brain wants to control, to perfect, to *break*. Haisley is everything I need. I want. Have wanted.

I want to strip her of her pain, replace it with something worse, but she will want it, crave it, *need it*. I want to push her to the edge and stop, push her and stop. Push her, *stop*. Like a madman, still watching her very obvious suffering, I grin, it is sardonic, the feeling of my lips curling up, my teeth flashing. I bite down on the inside of my cheek, ache to make her hurt more.

I think she would like it.

If it were me.

"Haisley," I whisper her name into the top of her head, her thick curls like a shield, a barrier, something to keep my infectious words seeping too quickly into her mind.

Do not touch her.

My fingers curl into a fist, she whimpers again, and I

pound my clenched hand into the outside of my thigh, huffing breaths erratically through my nose. I do it over and over, the muscle in my leg starting to fizz with pins and needles as I punch myself repeatedly. Rhythmic, solid pounds, my teeth clench, jaw knotting beneath my ear, the thumping of my fist jostling my body more than hers is twitching in her sleep.

My control is a fractured, dissolving thing, I am barely hanging on by a thread. My desire, desperation, obsession, to love and hurt this girl so completely, the idea warring, warping, and simultaneously binding together like pieces of glass and silk inside my head. It is disturbing. The feelings I am locking down and smothering inside of me.

Despite myself, I raise my hand, my thigh thumping all by itself now with my pulse hammering beneath the hot, painful skin. The muscle burns, and I know it is probably bruised. But it feels good all the same, the pain. Perhaps, the fact it is self-inflicted, makes it feel all the better.

My arm sweeps across my chest as I stretch my hand out towards her, her body is curled up so tight it looks painful. She is small, short, maybe five-five, she has thick thighs, a round tummy, smaller breasts. The tops of her arms a little chunky, these cute little dimples sit in the tops of her elbows when her arms hang straight down by her sides. She has all of these curves, and they sit in all the right places, even when they do not, it makes me ache with a bone deep desire to run my lips across her every inch of beautiful flesh.

But I know I have to be careful with her. *Gentle.* The way I have watched her for so many years, curling her shoulders forward, hunching in on herself, trying to be less noticeable, hide herself from the world. She could never hide from me, partly because she did not know I was there, partly because I actually *see* her.

I am obsessed.

With her every tiny twitch, blink, breath.

It consumes me, the need to covet her.

Tips of my fingers brushing lightly over the front of her hair, thick red tendrils curly and hanging across her face, I brush them back, barely touching, but the locks of soft hair move as I direct them off of her face. Her brows are pulled together, lips pouting, and I think, not for the first time, about how they would look turning blue, perhaps violet, as my hands worked around her pretty neck. I did not let it get that far earlier, anger, controlled, still burst out of me, my brutal hands assaulting her throat. I can still feel the tendons taut against my palm, her pulse fluttering, desperately, violently, against my clenched fingers.

I can smell her, so close to me, our scents like waves, crashing and melding together like a riptide. The intense metallic-leather sharpness of me, the deep peppery-plum of her. My nostrils flare as I breathe her in. Deep and powerful, the way that alone messes with my head.

I trail my fingers down her cheek, her usually cool skin heated by my own body temperature, a pink blush sitting high on her cheekbones. My thumb plucks over her bottom lip, my eyes fixed to the way her deep red skin blanches at the light pressure, the deep cut scabbed over. I shift my thigh, dead from punching it so hard, trying to spread my leg, allow my growing cock a little more space.

I like control.

But even I know it is not always possible to have it all of the time.

Running the rough pad of my thumb over the wound, I try not to give in. My eyes honed in on the dark purple-red beneath the scabbed over covering, but then I catch the corner of it with the short, rounded edge of my thumbnail. My eyes flicker up then, sound in the room filtering back in, when I zoned out, I do not know, but large jade-green eyes are peering up at me, into, what I am sure, are not much more than matching black abyss'.

Thumb stilling on her lip, I watch her face, the serenity of it only spurring me on, the challenge, the dare, the *submission*. Lips parted, her tongue rolls out, catching on the very tip of my digit. Her eyes still on mine, I violently hook my thumb across the scab, feel it rip away beneath my nail, a trickle of hot blood immediately running down the inside of my hand.

She whimpers, something desperate in the way her throat works with her needy whine. I shiver at the sound, unable to control my reaction, thumb still pressing into her lip, the curled knuckle of my forefinger beneath her chin. I stare down into her eyes, gaze flicking lower to her parted lips and all of the blood in my body rushes straight to my cock. It throbs beneath the tightness of my slacks, painful and swollen, I lick my lips, feeling the small trail of her blood curling around the inside of my wrist, beneath the cuff of my black shirt.

I smear it across her lips, thumb circling around and around her mouth, turning it redder and redder, bloodier. Her breaths pant, hot and heavy against my skin, head still pressed to my arm, relaxed into my body like she was made to fit right here. She is in the exact same position she was when she was sleeping, the thought of what was going on inside her head making me feel a little insane. The not knowing. Wanting to.

"What did you dream about, Little Cub?" I ask her in a smooth voice, louder than our usual whispers, but still not at full volume.

I keep my attention on her mouth, then my thumb, following it as I smear sticky dark crimson all across her pale face, tracing lines of blood up her cheekbone; I brush my fingers down the side of her face. She lets me, never once locking up, looking at me with fear.

Is it me you dream of, Little Cub?

I find my tongue tangling around the question; I want and do not want an answer to. I am saved from asking it, her words whispered first, barely audible above the rapid thrashing of my heart.

"You."

Gaze locked on my thumb, I still at her honesty. Confession. Swallowing overly hard, ignoring the ridiculously painful hardness twitching uncomfortably in the front of my trousers. It takes everything inside my head to smooth, even out, ironing baser needs, primal instincts, into submission. Into coherent thoughts as opposed to the biting blackness edging my vision, my blood pounding hard, demanding to take, fuck, kill.

Slowly, controlled, I drag my eyes up to hers. We are so close, my chin still unable to dip without bumping her forehead now, her neck craned to look up at me, see more of me with those big jade eyes. She is a picture, bloody, flushed, an entire galaxy swirling in her eyes. She looks at me as though I am death. And it is not with disdain, hatred, fear. There is need seeping out of every pore in her pretty skin.

"What happened in this dream?" I ask her quietly, drawing my attention back to my thumb, continue to paint her with her own lifeforce.

She licks over her teeth, holding herself back from licking the lips I have painted. The blood drying out, I bring my thumb to my mouth, watch her throat as she swallows, suck on the tip of it. A tangy assault of copper and salt hits my tongue, and I hold back the groan itching to tear free. Wet thumb back on her skin, I continue my ministrations. Curling my thumb into a 'T' shape on the delicate skin beneath her left eye.

"The first night," she breathes the words, they capture me, everything inside of me compelled to pay attention.

Unable to break free from the need, I curl my fingers over the side of her face, cupping it in a too tight grip, fingertips slippery with the mix of her blood, my saliva, sliding into the front of her hair, little finger tracing the smooth skin behind her ear. To her credit, she does not flinch. And I know it must hurt, the punishing hold I have on her skull is crushing. I can be gentle, but it is not *real*, not true to my nature. I do not want to pretend to be someone else when I am with her. That thought barrelling into me like a bullet to the head.

"The first night..." I repeat carefully, "*Here?*" thinking back to exactly that, her, bound and gagged in the back seat of my car, all less than a week ago.

She licks her lips, my thumb still resting just beneath her bottom one. Her eyes flutter closed, lashes thick fans over her cheekbones.

"You left me alone," she whispers, and my fingers tense in the fight to not tighten further. "I think of you staying." She swallows hard, her throat working, jaw tightening beneath my hold. "What it would be like," she glances up at me, eyes wide and watery, "If you had stayed."

"And what would it be like, Haisley?" I ask, "In your head, if I had stayed?" I whisper it then, my breath aiding in drying the blood decorating her pretty face.

This time, she does not look away, peering up at me, eyes still unblinking, glistening, the dwindling fire flickering across her skin.

"You would stay," she breathes, pepper and plum, "And lie with me."

I watch her eyes from beneath my own lashes, she keeps them on me, her cheeks heating further, because I have not forced these words from her, but she spills them like a gushing wound all the same. She could have said no. I would have let her say no. For whatever it is she tells me next, is likely to put her in further danger, confessions always do when there is tension as taut as ours. I am unsure where it has come from; I have always been the only one of us feeling tension, purely because she did not know I even existed.

But now she is here.

She *does* know I exist.

And the power of that, *me*, being the only presence in this time period of hers, hovering between life and death. The rush of power that gives me makes me dizzy. I just need to stay in control, not lose myself to the feral beast jailed behind my ribcage.

"How?" I whisper then, my thumb dragging out her bottom lip, it comes willingly, her lips parted for me, eyes unable to look away, it is empowering, having her under my thrall. "How would I lie with you?"

I want to make her say it. Whatever it is she is intent on keeping to herself. Maybe, I just want to hear something that will finally make me lose my mind. The threads of sanity are already so thin, fragile, fraying, I have always wondered what it would take to finally throw me over the edge. The blacking out with anger, the Blackwell sickness, obsession, one I have nurtured and cared for like a seed.

"Close," her words are so quiet, spoken just for me, despite us being alone, I like the thought that, if anyone else were here, they would not hear these dangerously quiet confessions.

"Close?" I mimic it back as a question, voice thick,

thumb still caught on her lip, exposing her bottom row of teeth, short and white and straight.

"Yes." Her breaths fan over the skin of my hand, hot and humid.

"As close as this?" I ask, because we are sharing breath, my eyes finally flicking up onto hers, dragging my attention from the blood on her face is almost painful, she is magnificent.

But when I stare into those big, watery green eyes, so focused on my own she does not even blink, my heart thuds so fast it feels as though it might kill me.

"Closer," she breathes, my thumb popping off of her bottom lip, *"So much closer."* And I think she is finished, the words feeling final, but then she says, "With your belt," she pauses, licking her lips, and it is so fucking distracting I almost miss the next words, "Tight around my neck."

Breath shudders out of me, my spine collapsing as I practically crush her head in my hand with the grip I have on her so tight. She does not flinch, and it does something to my insides. I feel the aching in my tight balls, lower abs crunching as I move like liquid, fluidly throwing my leg across her body, my hands pulling her down beneath me. Her legs drop to the floor in a heavy thud, contrasting with the soft gasp escaping her lips. My hand fists in the back of her hair, knocking her head back sharply, fingers needling through her thick red curls. My knees drive into the couch, straddling either side of her belly, her hips barely balancing on the edge of the worn couch.

Breaths heavy, I dip down, curving over her limp body, her hands over her chest, not clasped, not balled, relaxed and loose. Nothing in her posture tight or withdrawn, nothing emitting fear. And it makes me hungrier. I keep my own hips lifted, despite every baser instinct screaming at me to press myself into her, let her feel. But I know there is no coming back from that, so I strain with the effort it takes not to give in, and I feel it show on my face, the burn in my thighs.

Her gaze flickers over my face, dropping slowly down to the inch of space between our bodies, her fingers twitch, my other hand on the back of the couch, fingers curling over the worn fabric. The whole thing creaks as I shift slightly, dropping myself even closer. Her chest heaves, but her breath is held, her neck arching backwards in my hold on her hair, I allow her the movement, tipping her face up to meet mine.

"This close?" she sucks in a sharp breath at my question, nostrils flaring because it is all me, my scent, my breath, my fucking face. "Or closer?"

Her breath hitches, I can feel her head straining in my hand, attempting to lift, body squirming beneath me, trying to buck up, so I shift my knee, press it down onto her right hip bone. Let my weight keep her down. Her breath hitches again, but there is no wince with the pain, eyes growing suddenly wider, still locked on mine.

"Closer," she breathes the words directly into my mouth.

I could latch my teeth onto her bottom lip, drain

blood out of her, but I hold still, my hand trembling with the effort it takes to keep it fisted in her hair.

"You think you want me closer, Little Cub?" I throw her a sinister smirk. "You still think that?" it is cruel; the way I ask.

Darkness seeps from my pores like smoke, I want it to infect her. I am stuck in the rain, the noise, the thunder, the light, the dark, gloom slithers through me, poisoning my rapidly beating heart.

"You think you like pain?" mocking, a dare, I want her to react, to submit, to fight.

I don't really know what I want.

She attempts to nod, my knuckles grinding into her scalp as she does, strands of snapped hair loosening between my curled fingers.

"Speak," a snarled demand.

"I do," she whimpers out.

"You do what?" I am unhurried, despite the urgency in my blood demanding an answer.

"I like pain," she whispers, "I want it," lip trembling, the words slither out, "With *you*."

Heat flaring even hotter in her cheeks, already so flushed and red, I feel satisfaction roll through me, her reaction to me. I press my own cheek to hers, lips at her ear, allowing myself just this small touch of our skin, because if I permit myself to sink my mouth against her pillowy lips, blood streaked and distracting, I know I will not be able to pull myself back.

And I will hurt her.

Break her.

And I am not done with her yet.

I should be.

She should be dead.

This should have already been finished.

Except it is not.

Instead, I am straddling her, grinding my knee into the soft flesh covering her hip, driving the point of my kneecap unforgivingly into the curved bone. It hurts, it will bruise and I will ache to make it worse when I see it. My cock is irrevocably hard, so close to where I have dreamt of it being.

"Thorne," she breathes, still trying to move beneath me, her body jostling only the slightest amount, where I have her pinned, but it is not to get away, it is not to escape.

Eyes falling closed, I drag in a lungful of her, tart, strong, dark, my tongue catching the lobe of her ear when I lick my lips.

"If you knew," she swallows as I whisper the sick words into her ear. "What it is I have longed to do to you, you would cower beneath me." I swallow then, nostrils flaring at her breathy whimper. "You would wish you were already *dead*."

"Please, *Thorne*." I rear up, our noses touching, so close I can see nothing but blurred green and red from her eyes and hair.

"You asking for death, Little Cub? You think because I have dragged it out this long, I will keep you alive forever?" A sinister laugh crackles from my throat, raspy and thick and filled with heat.

"However long I'm with you is enough," she whispers and my breath stalls in my chest.

I am deathly still, her chest rising and falling too, too quickly beneath me, my fingers scoring the back of the sofa.

"You could do anything," she whispers again and she is the only thing I hear, "And I would want to be here," everything else is irrelevant as she speaks to me. *"With you,"* her words stroking a horrid, rotting part of me. "Anything."

I throw myself back so fast I almost slip on my shoes, the dying fire still manages to blast me with heat as I stumble away from her. I stare at her across the space, she pushes herself up, slowly, her eyes still on me. Face shadowed and curious, she smooths her hands down her thighs, wincing as her palm glides over her hip. My eyes instantly honing in on the motion.

"Go to bed," I order, my voice shattering this messy, gruesome gloom I formed around us.

She stares back at me, lips parted, eyes wide, her bottom lip bleeding and trembling, she tucks it between her teeth. My chest heaves, blood like ice when I look at what I have done to her. Curls wild and knotted on the top of her head, bloody face, fingerprints on the pale skin of her throat. It disgusts me as much as it turns me on and the feeling of combustion is morphing into a dense cloud of red.

"Now."

CHAPTER 16

HAISLEY

Two weeks is a long time for silence. Dark eyes watching my every move, except, when I look back, they're not, but I don't need to see him watching me. I can feel it. It makes my skin burn and my blood heat and my lower belly cramp and churn. The more he watches me, the worse my insides knot, like I'm just waiting for the viper of death to strike, sink in his fangs, fill me with deadly toxins.

Poison me.

He has hardly spoken to me since he straddled me on the couch, painted my face with my own blood, but now, every day is the same silent routine.

There is breakfast. He watches me eat the food he prepares, all while not eating any of it himself. Then we take our usual seats in the living space, I on the sofa, he in the chair. I watch him scribble in his journal, sometimes he takes calls, sometimes he stays during them, sometimes he leaves. I listen to the words he says, the way he speaks, so polite, firm, proper. He seems to have a large family that he won't tell me anything about. I pay attention, but Thorne is nothing if not deceptive. He talks in code for most of his calls, but I know he hired a nanny, someone he didn't seem to feel any kind of way about as he confirmed with someone on the phone that she was *clean*, after flicking his gaze between me and his phone for almost six hours before that.

It feels like a dare, when I watch him and he catches me, like he wants me to look away, but I don't and he grinds his jaw in irritation, his face remaining expressionless all the same.

I miss the head tilts and the sinister smirks that twist his face into something macabre and violent.

He watches me watching him. I get time outside; I wander until he calls me in, like a prisoner, something, I forgot for just a moment, I was. I lay awake at night, straining my ears, listening for his movements, but there never is any. He is silent and I am... *restless*.

Blowing out a breath, I look down at the water one last time, rain soaking me through, waves crashing into the base of the cliff, before I decide to dash out of the wet, flatten my spine to the side of the lighthouse. My lungs heave in the cold, breath clouding in the icy temperature, my thick tracksuit sticking to my skin, heavy on my shoulders as the water weighs it down. I glance left, towards the house, know that Thorne isn't there, at the little front door tucked inside the arched alcove, because he is fixing a leak in the bathroom.

There are weeds and mud and patchy grass, as I

skirt around the lighthouse, my goal the door. I bet in the spring this place looks beautiful. Green grass, bright sun, wild flowers sprouting up in between, but I'm not stupid enough to think I'll be here then to see it.

We must be halfway through January, my expiration date long since passed. I'm just waiting now, and it is torturous. I don't feel any less pain inside my heart, I swallow thickly as I think of my cousin. My lungs seize when I think of Thorne, what he will eventually do to me. The fact I don't exactly feel put off by any of it. I wonder if he will drag it out, make it slow, tease and torture and play with me first.

I hate that I hope he does.

There must be something wrong with me.

I am sick, somewhere deep in my marrow, something toxic and poisonous seeps its way into my skin, I suppose it could be used as armour or disease. I wonder if I'll ever have the chance to find out.

My breaths are heavy, from the cold, the rain, running through the wind to take shelter here, up against the lighthouse, I swallow down my feelings, fear, wants, ignoring it all, and push off of the wall. Readying to head back inside the little house that, sadly, sort of, now feels like home, even with the new haunting silence echoing around its walls. I've never had somewhere feel like that before, but since I've been here, safe and warm and dry, no threat of beatings for insolence. I've found solace here in this strange, decrepit little building. The leaks, lack of power, cold showers, badly sputtering taps, I find myself smiling just a little at how silly it is to like it all so much, when I hear a noise, distracting me from my thoughts.

My eyes rove across the wet ground, gravel, sand and mud all washing together in murky puddles. My dark green Converse splash through them, splatter sploshing up my legs, the tiny noise growing louder and louder even though it's so quiet I have to strain my ears to follow it. A little screechy whimper, barely there, but I can hear it, it's different to the caws and cries of the rooks, high up in their royal tower, nesting and fluffing, readying for their babies in the spring.

I crouch low, peering into the small crevice between lighthouse and cottage, shoving my hair back with my forearm, rain heavy in my lashes, blurring my vision.

Thorne will come soon, but he won't scold me for being drenched, not anymore. The things I thought were perhaps there, something inside of him that might have, maybe, one day, wanted to keep me, I fear are long gone now. His silence is readying me for my grave.

It's a tiny thing, my fingers getting scratched by thorny bushes as I part the leafless shrubs, all curled up, dark grey and wet, all of it so wet, eyes closed, tail curled into its belly. A baby something… shoulder driving into the curved wall of the lighthouse, I reach into the gap, my neck straining as I reach through, head angled over my shoulder as I strain. My fingertips claw through mud, filling beneath my nails, I reach in farther, my entire body trembling with the stretch and effort to get in there. I close my eyes, take a deep breath and then I touch fur, matted and wet and icy cold, I push harder, my shoulder popping, I grit my teeth, bare them, eyes squeezing so tightly I see stars and then I'm scooping it, dragging it through the mud until I can claw it up into my palm, the little wet ball.

I collapse back onto my bottom, puddle water immediately soaking through to my underwear, but the little tiny fox cub in the palm of my hand is worth it. Pushing to my feet, I head to the house, shoving my wet curls back off my face.

The fire crackles, warmth heating me as soon as my squelchy feet step onto the worn wooden floor. I'm so focused on the little thing in my hands, its cries having fallen silent that I'm worried it's already too late, when his shoes come into focus. I stop, look up, Thorne's eyes on mine, silence is heavy between us but I refuse to be the one to break it.

I step around him, and he lets me, but I feel his gaze as he turns, watching as I hurry into the kitchen. I run the hot tap, my free hand wiggling fingers beneath the sputtery stream, waiting for some warmth to heat my icy skin. Filling the washing up bowl, I drop the tea towel into it, wring it out and then start wiping down the little fox. Cleaning him free of mud and cold, I wipe up his face, over his ears, little tail all curled into his belly, tiny pink feet starting to appear as I clean up his paws.

Thorne stands in the doorway when I turn, intending to head to the bathroom, and just when I think he won't move, some sort of trick into making me speak first. My feet on the second step up, he moves to the right, sliding smoothly out of my way.

I hurry down the hall, my shoes squeaking and squelching with every step. Grabbing a towel, I bundle the little fluff ball up, rubbing him gently in my hands. I turn again, trotting down the corridor back to the front room, stopping in front of the fire, my knees hit the floor, wax covered hearth beneath them, a metal grate protecting the flames.

I feel him stop behind me, his presence always felt despite his steps being silent.

"What are you doing?" Thorne asks softly, my eyes slipping closed as I continue to rub the little fur ball dry.

Everything inside of me commands me to look, give him my full attention, it's like a physical ache that is tugging at my core.

"I found this fox outside," I start, unsure what the fuck it is I'm even doing. "I don't think it's doing well, and-"

"Put it back outside," Thorne says, smooth, emotionless, almost charming. "It is the runt, it is too soon for it to be born, this is not supposed to happen until March."

My eyebrows crease, the little creature in my hands finally, *finally*, making some sort of movement.

"No, it's fine, it's-"

"It is going to die, that is its destiny," he whispers, and I hate the emotionless words spilling from his mouth, just as much as I crave them.

God, I've missed you.

It's ludicrous, really, the way a shiver ripples up my spine, eyes sliding closed, a satisfied hum desperate to make itself known. It's that syndrome, the thing kidnapped people get when they develop feelings for their captor. That's what this is, whatever it's bloody called. Either that or I'm just as fucked up and insane as my father always said.

I was never a good girl, I was always fighting with my brothers, my cousins, their friends, their brothers, sons of the other four families. The girls were never fun to play with, well, not my sisters, I just wanted to fight. Take my frustrations out on something when everything felt so unfair. The beatings started then, first, with the boys ganging up on me, and then my father, his right hand man, the muscle with iron fists, Brádach Doyle, leader of his own family, one of the five. Even thinking his name feels like a curse, something dark looming over me.

"You are soaked through," Thorne supplies, like I didn't know, but there it is, that thread of irritation.

I can tell he instantly regrets it, and I wonder if he's more upset that he showed some sort of emotion, speaking first, breaking the silence *he* instigated, or if it's truly because I am wet and muddy and cuddling a dying fox.

"I'm just going to warm it up, he's so tiny, his eyes aren't even open yet," I frown with my defence, wondering if Thorne is right, and it's going to die.

It really is too early in the year for this cub to have been born, I wonder if there are others. There usually four or five to a litter, sometimes more, but this one definitely shouldn't be above ground yet, tucked safely inside of its den with its mother, siblings. It can't be more than a few days old.

"I'm going to get some milk," I place the bundled towel down, pushing up to my feet when Thorne's fingers snap tightly around the nape of my neck.

"No," he says firmly. "You are not. You are going to get yourself into that bathroom, strip off those disgusting clothes and scrub yourself clean." I shiver, his hot skin on my cold, wet hair trapped beneath his palm, forcing my neck to arch into him. "You are a mess," he hisses in my ear and I freeze, the disdain in his voice has me swallowing hard, a lump forming in my throat. He steps into me, his lips to my ear, "Do not make me tell you twice," he turns sharply, shoving me forward, my feet scrabbling to stay under me.

I twist violently, back to face him, but I'm already dismissed to him, his focus and attention now on the bundled towel.

"Thorne," I almost whimper, voice cracking, tears filling my hot eyes as he glances back over his shoulder, dark eyes smouldering, "*Please.*"

"Shower." A pause, eyes peeling away from me so slowly I hold my breath. "Now."

CHAPTER 17

THORNE

I t is stupid, I know it is, the way my eyes narrow in
on her. Her curvy legs folded up beneath her on
the floor before the fire. I glare at the white towel
in her hands, will it to spontaneously combust, the little
whiney, mewing sounds coming from inside it making
the insides of my ears itch.

Three days, it has been three days since I allowed
her to keep this attention seeking little rat inside of the
house. I consider it to be my biggest mistake yet. The
cuttingness of her attention, the little tuts, the fuss, and
the *smiles*, all of it *not* for me.

My hands ball into fists, the tendons in my arms
straining beneath my shirt, veins rising sharply along the
backs of my hands. I feel heat in my chest, a sheen of
sweat prickling the nape of my neck, and I watch her,
her curvaceous body curled up on the floor before the
fire. Tattered cardboard box beside her, one side of it

was damp from being pressed too tightly up against a wall, I tore it off, stuffed the white towel, currently in her small hands, inside it and dropped it beside her seat on the couch. The tiny, writhing, wet little thing tucked up inside of it.

She stared at me, those big green eyes, too much blue in them to be purely green, jade, beautiful all the same. A grateful smile curved her plush lips, healed without a scar, despite my constant picking at the wound she came to me with. I am pleased, her perfect features still just so. The only scars I want to see on her should be mine anyway. From me, my hands, my knife, my teeth. I shift my legs, the throbbing bulge between my thighs needing more room than what it has beneath the tight confines of my slacks.

She sits there, soft voice gentle, a baby's medicine syringe in her hand, milk inside of it, she drips it messily into the little cub's mouth.

Little Cub.

I am suddenly regretting that endearment, I have my Little Cub, and now, she has hers. My teeth ache as I clench them again, grinding them together like a pestle and mortar. Jealousy. That is what this is. Over a previously dying fox cub.

Fuck, Jesus, I hope that thing is a girl.

The surge of anger swirling in my gut makes me even more irritated. At her, at *it*, at myself. Strange to think I have spent my entire life never having felt jealousy before, but I know that is what it is. Like a festering disease it infects, slow at first, warm and foreign, but I do not mind the warmth so much, it triggers the other little parts of me that want to work harder for what I find myself already having. In one capacity or another, but then the warmth morphs into an uncomfortable hot fire, bubbling lava and a dense cloud of black.

And then I am striding over to her. Looming over her where she kneels on the floor, her head turning up over her shoulder. Big jade eyes laser focusing in on me as her neck arches, head craning, and all I can think about is how close her perfect pout is to the steel pipe trying to escape my trousers.

"I have to go on a job, Little Cub," I say gently, the surge of anger slipping out of me like smoke as she gives me her full attention, little dying rat bastard long forgotten as she listens to my words.

Crease forming between her brows, the soft wrinkle to her nose, I want to smirk at the lack of attention she gives her new pet. Bestowing her entire focus onto me and me alone, despite the towel nest cradled in her small hands.

"Are you coming back?" she whispers it then, the smirk I am suppressing completely dying behind the pursing of my lips.

"Of course, I am," I give in to the temptation then, my fingers delicately stroking over the top of her head.

She swallows, neck arched so far back, leaning into my feather light touch. I think about how easily I could snap her spinal column with the barest twitch of my hand. My fingers instinctively weave and tighten in her hair. Her eyes flutter shut at the touch and triumph sings through my veins. She blinks hard, nostrils flaring, she purses her lips, licking them so quickly I almost miss it, and then her eyes are glossy, watery. Her chin quivering and something in my chest aches and bleeds and heats all at the same time. Instantly, I am dropping into a crouch, a crease starting to carve its way between my brows, and I smooth my hand over the crown of her head, releasing her thick curls.

Weight on my toes, I lean forward, dipping into her at her side, so close we share breath and it is like my lungs fill properly for the first time all day. I hook a knuckle beneath her jaw, sweep it forward to the tip of her chin, tilt her face up. My gaze flicks between her eyes, wide and watery and wet, my cock kicking beneath my slacks, I lick my lips, relax my features.

"What is this fuss for, Little Cub?" I whisper over her mouth, plump lips parted, I envision the split she had in it, think about biting her a new one, make sure it scars this time.

"I don't want you to leave me here alone," she whispers vulnerably, that hammering organ in my chest constantly pumping black tar into my bloodstream, but since her, a little lightness is seeping its way through too, something golden and fragile.

I think about what she knows, where she came from, what sort of man she thinks I am, one that would carry out a job of dangerous calibre. That is when it hits me, that it is not about *me*, it is about me not making it back here, because then I would be dead and she would be trapped here, alone. It has nothing to do with her wanting me here and everything to do with being alone in a dangerous world, no captor, essentially, keeping her safe from worse things. I breathe evenly, despite wanting to inhale sharply, that little drip of gold in my veins quickly being snuffed out by the sticky black tar.

I push to my feet. Hands sliding into my pockets. I stare down at her, all those soft emotions dying quicker than *I* ever would on a dangerous job. Peering down my nose at her, her neck arching and arching, I think about it again, the crunch of bone, the puncture of skin, lifeless jade eyes staring up at me. And it makes my insides die just a little more. The anger. But then, it is wiped out as quickly as it starts to form.

"I don't want to be anywhere without you," she whispers it, soft, gentle, coaxing, and the shock renders me speechless.

She blinks, swallows, looks slightly startled by her confession, and then her head drops, eyes leaving me in a punishing state of shock. My brain backfires, hearing fuzzy, mouth dry. I think about what she just said, wonder if it is manipulative, does she think it will make me softer? I am not sure anything on the planet could make me soften, not even her. It is a worrying thought, one I quickly bury down deep, refocus my gaze on her, her head bowed forward, over that fucking fox cub. My blood fizzes like acid, fingers twitching in my pockets, wanting to wrench her head up, force her gaze back onto me. The heat of my body only rising, I bite down hard, my molars screaming as my jaw cracks.

"Thorne?" I blink, staring down into her eyes, neck craning back once again, her hands empty.

I flick my gaze over to the towel in the box as she pushes to her knees, swivelling to get to her feet. Quickly, I offer her a hand, the other still secured in my pocket. Her skin is so soft against my own, still cool, her fingertips sliding down the inside of my wrist, I pull her up, grip just a little too tight. Releasing her as soon as she is up, I slide my hand, burning from her touch, back into my pocket, lock my gaze on hers. She pushes her hair behind her ear, her eyes, so bravely, on mine.

"Will it…" she trails off, eyes dipping, shoulders folding forward, I wait silently, patiently. "Will you be safe?" she whispers without looking at me.

Her voice like a haunting echo, nothing more, nothing less, it sets my insides spiralling all the same. Heart thudding hard, I relax my chest, ensuring my breath does not hitch as I inhale. I lick my lips, shift my weight from one foot to the other.

I think of all the things I could tell her, all of the things I should not, will not, cannot, say.

"I am going to be with my brothers," I swallow, her chin still dipped, her gaze fluttering up to view me from beneath her pale lashes.

I tuck a lock of hair behind her other ear, my hand almost trembling as I remove it from my pocket, reach out in the space between us, calloused skin caressed by soft silken locks, I curl my index finger over the shell of her ear.

"We keep each other safe," I tell her confidently, her eyes pinching slightly, not in disbelief, more like wonder.

I eye her then, my dark orbs flicking between her green ones. She blinks hard, pink rising high in her cheeks, she dips her chin further, knotting and squeezing her fingers before her, wringing her hands together.

"Okay," she whispers, glancing behind her, through her hair, over her shoulder. "Okay, Thorne," she says more confidently, tipping her head up now, her eyes moving over my face. "You're coming back?" she asks again, and I feel my lips wanting to tip up at the corners, I suppress the urge, giving her a firm nod instead.

"Stay inside," I instruct, her face blooming an even darker pink, nodding in submission, it is a fucking beautiful sight, but I cannot let her know that. "You wait inside until I return," I watch her face, dipping my own chin, canting my head to the side to make sure she sees me, *really* sees.

"Yes, Thorne," she says quietly, my eyes wanting to roll into the back of my head at her easiness, *eagerness* to obey.

It might be out of fear, but I do not think it is.

The further I drive away from Rook Point, the faster unease piles high in my throat. It is choking, an acrid taste on the back of my tongue. I have left her a few times, for supplies, always when she is asleep, always in the dark. Never for more than an hour at a time. Always within a ten minute drive back. This is not like that. This is further, much further, a warehouse in central Southbrook.

Notifications and text messages ping up on the screen in the centre of the dashboard. Signal at the point drops in and out, and honestly, it is nice. Not being needed. Well, by anyone else.

I answer the first call when it comes in, thumb clicking a button on the steering wheel.

"Raine."

"Dude, are you almost there? I spoke to Simon who spoke to Mikey, who heard from Danny, that Sam said Rubble was calling you and you didn't answer. Archer said that-"

"Raine." I cut my youngest brother off, his usually laid back, over easy attitude, completely absent as he spits excited words through the phone. "Why are you manic? Have you taken your pills?" I ask seriously, eyes on the road, his silence deafening. "Raine."

"Dude, chill," he stammers the hurried words, "I will, but Arch said that Rubble sa-"

"Raine." It is a bark, his breathing hard, "Take a deep breath," I order, and I listen as he does. "Slow down, find something to focus on," I instruct, increasing my speed as I start the short final mile to the warehouses.

"The stars are beautiful, huh, big bro?" Raine's

wistful voice snags something in my chest, tugging on a loose stitch. "The sky's so black."

"Raine." I lick my lips, overtaking on the inside of an arctic lorry, my heart stampedes in my chest. "Focus."

"Right, yeah, dude," he rushes, I hear doors opening, closing, the shuffle of him moving around.

"I am almost there."

"Arch is there, so's Wolf," he says slightly calmer, I imagine him pushing a hand through his hair.

"And you are…?" I ask calmly, knowing I will likely hate the answer. He laughs, this far away sound that rumbles as he tries to cut it off. "Raine, are you at The Crypt?"

"Thorne?" he whispers, a chill races down my spine, there is suspicion in the way my name falls from his tongue.

"Yes?" I swallow after I speak, my ears buzzing as my tires hit the gravel, little stones skittering beneath the rubber, flicking up the sides of the Merc.

"It's a fucking blood bath," he whispers even more quietly, I pull my car up beside Archer's, his large form resting back against the matte black bonnet. "The walls, ceiling," Raine gasps like it is in awe, "They're bleeding."

"Raine, how long ha-"

"I gotta go."

The call goes dead, and I turn off the engine, unclip my seatbelt, lay both hands on the wheel, curl my fingers around it, squeeze until it creaks. Something roils in my gut, but this is routine for Raine, one of his episodes, drugs, stimulants, him constantly chasing a high, just another thing to interfere with the fragility of his mind.

Wolf raps his knuckles on my window. I look up at him, through the tinted glass, give him a single nod, pull in a deep breath. Throbbing in my temples makes me cringe, and I swallow against the feeling of something being wrong with *her.* No one knows she is there, no one knows about Rook Point, the only person that might be a danger to her is herself, but I dismiss that quickly, her running is not an issue, she has a reason to stay.

I am her reason to stay.

'I don't want to be anywhere without you.'

My heart thuds heavily, mouth going dry, perhaps I *am* the reason she would stay. Not run. But then I am thinking about that stupid fucking fox, and I dismiss the quick hit of longing, sharp like a blade in my chest. She is clinging to me as her lifeline because I am death. Hers specifically. And maybe she just wants me to feel a certain way about her, so I keep her alive longer. But then I think about it again. Those words, *without you,* and something heats low in my belly.

"Thorne!" Wolf barks, and I release the wheel, my knuckles aching, I sweep my way out of the car. "Jesus H Christ, I wanna get on with this shit," he huffs.

Wolf runs a hand down his face, lips parting as his palm slides over the lower half of his features, grazing his stubble. Archer's dark eyes glinting with his smirk under the muted orange glow of a lone bulb. Long lean legs straight out in front of him, ankles crossed, arms folded over his chest. He looks me up and down, a crease forming between his brows.

"What's wrong?"

This is the problem, being so close, the six Blackwell brothers knowing each other inside and out, unable to lie or hide or evade questions when one is simply a little-

"Rumpled. You look all *rumpled* and… what's wrong with you?" Archer pushes up to his feet, off of his car, and the first thing that pops into my skull is my Little Cub, but then I think of Raine, and the emotion evaporates off of my face.

He is shadowed, Archer, orange bulb, the sky above dark, the air is cold, clouds low, and even in the pitch of night I think I can make out rain clouds. My head is tilted back, my eyes flicking down to watch his approach. I drop my chin when the three of us are in a loose triangular huddle.

"Raine," I say, hands sliding into my pockets, both sets of dark eyes flicker between my own, waiting for me to elaborate on what they both already know. "He called, I think he is at The Crypt," I flick my gaze up as the first drop of rain splatters against my cheekbone.

"Is he…?" Archer starts, his hair longer than it has ever been, shorn on the sides, black length on top flopping into his right eye.

"Manic?" I raise a brow as I say it, glance at Wolf, his dark yellow eyes fixed on me, I think of our mother, her eyes much the same, duller, lighter, less life in them. "Yes," I say, "He sounded as though he were at the peak of his high."

"Ahh, *fuck*," Archer hisses, shoving a hand through his hair, scuffing the toe of his boot into the gravel.

"Leave him there for now," I say solemnly, knowing that, although he is out of his mind, The Crypt is a somewhat *controlled* environment. I straighten, look both brothers in the eye, "Do we know what we are dealing with?"

Wolf sighs, glancing over to his black private ambulance. The words *Cardinal House Funeral Home* painted in gold calligraphy on the side.

"Hack and slash job," Archer says cheerily, easy smirk sliding back into place as though it had never left. "Friday Fight Night got ugly as fuck," he shrugs, bringing his hands up, he rubs them together, white teeth glinting in the dim glow of the orange light at Wolf's back. "Blood and limbs probably," he grins.

Wolf sighs, "You're sounding more and more like Hunter every day," clicking his tongue, he glances at the door over his shoulder. "Best get on with it."

We start towards the door, all of us holding the same posture, Wolf's hair tied back in a small bun at the crown of his head, his wide shoulders square, broad back rippling with defined muscle beneath his black shirt. The door opens before we even knock, Rubble, The Firm leader's right hand man, stands just inside the brightly lit hallway, his usual scowl on his face, icy blue eyes staring right at me. The Blackwell's leader.

"Thorne," he nods, my name not much more than a grunt. "Wolf, Archer," he nods to each of them, stepping to one side and turning his head towards the end of the corridor. "Main room," he says as we start making our way down the hallway.

Wolf leads, I, in the centre, Archer at my back, but this is safe territory, nothing to fear, no enemies here. These people, The Firm, are not only our employers, we may not be blood related but they are family all the same. Our relationship with them dating back generations.

Wolf enters through the double doors to the main room, holding them back whilst we walk through. The large open space echoes with soft chatter, a small huddle of people on one side. It is dimly lit, large spot lamps the only things that light this room, but they reveal enough of the shadows to let me know what we're dealing with.

"Fuck me," Archer whistles, eyes on the centre of the room, long strides carrying him to the river of blood steadily pooling outwards from the side of the 'ring'.

The illegal fight nights, bare-knuckle, are brutal affairs and this would not be the first time we have been called in to clean up a mess. However, it *would* be the first time there is a child to bear witness to it.

His wide yellow eyes are the first thing I see. Watching me from over one of his fathers' shoulders, little fists tight in the shoulder seam of Maddox Swallow's t-shirt. His little head, covered in thick blonde hair, tilts into his dad's neck, chin resting firmly, eyes locked on my approach. Tracking my every confident step until I stop a couple feet away, he buries his face into his dad's throat just as Maddox turns to face me.

"Thorne," he greets gruffly, one arm tight over his son.

"Maddox," I nod, hands sliding into my pockets.

His bright blue eyes glance over my shoulder, where Wolf and Archer gather, my own flicking to the large man he was talking to before my arrival. Cameron Swallow, the usually quiet Fight Night boss, his shock of white hair pulled up into a loose bun on the back of his skull, piercing green eyes bright and alert, even as congealed blood hangs in his lashes.

"Cam," I blink, somewhat surprised by his state, considering this is a man with even better self-control than I have.

He does not fight anymore, *'Fists of Fury'*, not after the last incident.

"Thorne," he says slowly, palming his throat, smearing the blood coating his body all around, there is not an inch of skin not painted red.

It makes me think of the girl I have at the point, locked away and hidden for safe keeping. Something my self-control is battling with the longer I am not there. She would look really beautiful in red.

"You can go," I nod at him, turning my head over my shoulder, seeing the boys already halfway done before looking back, his bright eyes veiled with darkness. "Leave all of your clothes in a bag by the door of the locker room and shower."

His haunted eyes shutter, and silently, he walks towards the locker room as instructed. Maddox following close behind, his little boy peering at me once again, I tilt my head, flash a predatory grin and then he giggles into his father's neck.

I think of being here earlier tonight, what I would have seen, been a witness to, the violence, the blood, the two mangled bodies just a few feet behind me. My nephews flash through my mind, how we have shielded them thus far, despite the goings on in the sublevels of their own home. Heron Mill, the sinister secrets decaying in its basement. I think of the Swallows' son, the way he stared at me with no fear, nothing to show on his face but contentment, despite the mess of his uncle, the corpses.

Perhaps my nephews should not be hidden from such things, maybe the transition into our real world would be easier to handle if they grew up never knowing a difference. It is not my decision.

I was twelve, introduced to disposals, it was not shocking to me, but it was for my brother Arrow. He had nightmares after his first look into what life was going to be like for us, for him, the murder, the decay, the numerous tasks and skills required to never be caught. Persecution and confinement is not something he would ever survive so he learnt fast, but he is driven by fear and fear alone.

That is a monstrous thought burning like wildfire inside my brain, sparking through my veins, pulsing like a livewire, *unease*. And I am immediately filled with thoughts of my captive. My insides twist and turn, dread suddenly filling my gut and I spin on my heel, marching past my brothers.

"You two have everything under control here?" I ask on my way out, not slowing pace long enough to hear their answer.

Only one thing spurs me on, *terror,* and it is not for me.

CHAPTER 18

HAISLEY

L ittle whispers hit my ears and I look up in a panic, heart thudding hard in my chest. The wind. That's all it is. The lights kept flickering before they went out, the electricity never a sure thing here, so I'm used to it, but my eyes glance around the shadowed room all the same, seeking out phantoms and ghouls.

Shoulders going lax, I draw in a deep breath, let it calm my racing heart, listen to the wind whistle through the old house. I place the towel, wrapped around my fox cub, back inside its box, the one that Thorne pulled together for me, despite wanting to toss the dying creature back outside. It pulls on the corner of my lips, the need to smile, heat flushing my cheeks at the thought of him doing it for me.

I place the box on the couch, the seat beside mine, pushing up to my knees, I reach over, close one of the flaps over the top.

Thorne has been gone for a few hours, he didn't leave until late and I know I should go to bed, *like he told me to*, but I know I wouldn't sleep whilst he's not here. Regardless, I stand up, gather the box into my arms and head towards the bedroom, the candles I lit upon the mantle allowing me a warm glow at my back, just enough to find the steps down into the bedroom along the hall. I place the box on the bed, stare down at the striped pyjama pants, the long sleeved t-shirt I've been sleeping in, folded into a neat pile. Something I do only for Thorne. I know he doesn't like mess.

I pull the cuffs of my black hoodie down over my cold hands, only my curled fingertips peeking out, red nail polish now completely worn away. I shiver, the house cold at this end, the only fireplace in the front room. Rain lashes the windows, and I stare into the darkness of the bedroom, no window, no light, I would like it like this usually, when I was at home in my room, everything had to be pulled tight, to banish the light. But now the cloak of pitch makes me feel uneasy, since having a sack forced over my head, the thought of dark spaces horrifies me.

I think of Cian, how he appeared out of the darkness in my bedroom, the dim corner he'd been watching me from nothing but a space concealed in shadow. He'd been there the whole time, his eyes on me, and I had no idea. Until I did, and I-

My head snaps over my shoulder, a creaking sound snaring my attention, which, in this old house, I tell myself, is nothing unusual. I force myself to relax, calm my breathing, my heart racing like it's competing with a track car at the finish line. I slowly turn my head back into the room, little fox inside his box, shadows not hiding anything sinister. Grabbing my pyjamas, I tuck them beneath my arm, turn back to the door and make my way to the bathroom.

I brush my teeth, wash my face, change into my pyjamas, finger comb my curls back and pull them into a loose braid over my shoulder, tying off the end with a black elastic. It flops against my chest as I let it go, my eyes dipped down to view it without a mirror in the room. I twirl the end around my finger, think about mottled skin hidden beneath my clothes. How the bruises and cuts have gone now, healed like the split in my lip, no scars, not a trace of what was there on my pale skin. Nothing but the memory.

When I close my eyes, I can still feel it, that first spray of warm blood. I think that's what shocked me the most, how hot it was. The shock of it, the metallic taste as I licked my lips, an involuntary movement, I swallowed it all the same.

I wonder, not the first time, how Thorne will do it, if he'll feel my blood splatter his skin, slitting my throat, slashing an artery. All of it seems unlikely. The man would never give up his control, not in life, not in death, it would be something clean, quick. A bullet perhaps, to the centre of my skull, a bag being secured tightly around my head to keep the mess from spreading. All things I should never have seen, but have.

Sometimes I forget about it. My life. What it was,

why I'm here, what I did, and then it flashes through my mind, blinding me to whatever it is that I'm currently doing. But then I hear his voice, *Thorne*, summoning me back to the land of the living. I wonder how far through the veil I would drift if he never came back. Where would I go? Lost forever in the in-between.

I hear it again. The *creeeeak*. Just outside the bathroom door and my entire skeleton locks up. I'm in the dark, and it really is *dark*, I can hardly see my hands in front of my face, but as the creaking stops as quickly as it starts. My heart pitter pattering behind my ribcage, the muscles in my stomach clench, thighs trembling and sickness starting to swirl in my gut. So much fear. But I am alone. There is no way Thorne would leave me anywhere that someone might find me. Not that anyone is looking. I am dead as far as the world wants to believe.

I stand stock still for the longest time, ears strained to listen, but all I hear is the wind, whipping against the outside of the house, rain thrashing, eerie howls through the halls, ones I'm well adjusted to now. It's all the wind. Finally, I shake out my hands, my legs feeling like jelly, I breathe deeply, filling my lungs, take the two steps up to the door, and curl my fingers around the handle. Before I can think too much into it, I wrench it open, my eyes having adjusted to the darkness, I can see the wall opposite me, the nothing in between, everything exactly as it should be, except for the prickling in my chest.

I step out into the hall, pulling the bathroom door closed at my back, glance left and then right. As my eyes sweep to the right, the end of the hallway, the hexagonal shape space, with darkened alcoves and doorways set far back into the walls leading to places unknown to me. I feel compelled. To go in that direction, fear and fire pricking my veins, my muscles recoiling, fingers flexing, I shake my head against the invasive thoughts of ghosts and boogeymen, think about being brave instead.

I could retrieve the long matches from the mantle in the front room, drag the chair from the bedroom, step up onto it to reach and light the sconce. Thorne put fresh candles in it, I watched him stretch up, just the other day, muscles rippling in his back beneath a tight black shirt as he placed them inside, but we haven't lit any of them yet. I never venture past the bathroom.

But tonight, I do, forcing myself to move. My body shivers with cold, bare feet chilling further with every step across the icy wood. If it's even possible, it gets darker and darker and my eyes blink hard as I step into the centre of the space. A shiver rips up my spine, the hair on the back of my neck prickling. I hold my breath, eyes watering, I don't blink, staring hard into the dark. Slowly, I turn around, a slow pace, peering into every sunken door frame, alcove, as I turn in a full circle. Seeing nothing, I start to relax, my muscles burning where I hold myself so tensely.

I stop once I face the mirror, the gold frame haunting, the cherubs peering down from the top, looking more like little demons in the dark than the golden, angelic beings they are in the daylight. I stare at them for too long, my eyes flicked up, the darkness easing, sight becoming clearer, I lick my lips, glance at my reflection, the seven-foot length of glass spotted and rusting and it feels like it doesn't belong here just as much as it *does*.

I think of Thorne, how this mirror came to be. Did he bring it, was it here already, is this mirror just as out of place as I am, but it's been here so long now it's starting to feel like it belongs? Like *I* belong? I stare at my reflection, think of the last time I stood here. Thorne at my back, appearing like a spectre from the dense shadows, his eyes hard on mine, even though my flesh was on display, bared to him for who knows what length of time before he finally made himself known. But I know he didn't look. Not because he couldn't see but because he wasn't focused on the parts of me worth any value, he was only focused on the expression on my face.

He may be sinister, ominous, something clouded with black and red and something dark and unknown, but I feel safe with him. There's a longing, a serpent coiled in my chest, an ache, a toxin, something sick and venomous that craves his attention. The darkness of his gaze, the stiffness of his posture, the way he is just so, *so* proper. I lick my lips, think of his mouth over mine, wish he had given in to whatever is happening here between us.

Is there something?

Is it all inside my head?

I feel my frown before I see it, dropping my gaze to my feet. My cheeks heat with shame. Delusional, that's what I am, what this is. I'm a discarded piece of property balancing on a knife's edge, the blade being life and death, that is all there is for me though, *death*. It will come, one day soon, and I will enjoy it when it does.

Movement over my shoulder catches my attention, my heart beating so hard it feels like it's climbing its way up my throat. I peer into the dark, and when I see him, everything just sort of *stops*. His dull grey eyes seem to glisten, and I don't know if they really are or if it's just my deliberating fear heightening it all. The longer I stare at him the harder I tremble, my entire body quivering, muscles screaming at me to run but this isn't real. It can't be. There is no way that this is actually happening.

I close my eyes, squeeze them tight, ball my hands into fists, breathe hard through my nose as I try to calm my erratic heart. My lungs seize in my chest, hair on the back of my neck standing to attention, an alert telling me to open my goddamn eyes. And when I do, there's nothing. My entire body deflates, muscles turning to liquid, bones jelly-like and overly fragile, but I huff a soft laugh, breath easy to inhale, exhale, relief like a tsunami crashes over me as I shake my head. Berate myself for being silly.

But as I adjust my feet, the darkness around me swirling almost comfortingly, my nightmare finally takes form in the reflection of the mirror. Behind me, stepping out of the shadows, his gait slow and easy, stance confident and cocky. The cracked smile on his face broad, knowing.

"Din't t'ink ya'd see me again," he tuts, strong Irish accent thick and dry. "Did ya, dead girl," it's not a question.

He steps forward, menacingly, still far enough away he can't grab me, but too close.

"Funny t'ing, t'ough," he taps a finger to his lips, tattoos like vines climbing up his hands, over his fingertips, I don't need to see them to know they're there.

Those hands have made intimate contact with every part of my body, in punishment, in anger, in thrilling, passionate beatings.

"Din't t'ink I'd ever be seeing you again, eit'er," he shrugs, a brow lifted on his forehead, so high it almost reaches his hairline.

He is impossibly large, broad, wide, tall, demonic looking in every sense of the word. His dark hair and scary eyes, the way they bore right through you like a bullet to the brain.

"Yet," he licks his lips, pausing to run his lecherous gaze, a sneer on his mouth, down my body. "'ere you are."

My trembling body is frozen to the spot, feet planted like they're superglued to the floor. I swallow thickly, my eyes wide, tears gathering in the heat at the back of them.

"You manipulate 'im or summin?" he chuckles darkly, sliding his hands into his pockets. "T'orne fuckin' Blackwell, a perfect god amongst us all," he laughs again, shaking his head, mocking and disappointment.

My eyes never leaving him, he starts to prowl, not coming any closer, the darkness between us nothing like the shield I wish it were. I think of this devil's hands around my neck, the bruises and croak left in his wake, the violent contrast to the way Thorne has handled me, much the same, but *not*.

It crashes through me then, the reverence of it all. Thorne may have crushed my windpipe, but he never intended it to damage. Not in the way that Shane O'Sullivan had.

"T'e first job he ever fucked up, and it's for t'e likes of a wor'hless, murdering slut like yous," he sneers, body angled away from me, head snapped back over his shoulder.

It burns, the fire in his gaze, acid in his words, the small space we're locked in full of heavy, humid air, despite it being freezing. Panicked perspiration licks my skin, every inch of me trembling as he slowly turns back to face me. My gaze remains locked on him in the mirror, his eyes raking down my body, before clawing their way back up.

"He'll get his," he hisses beneath his breath, shrugging again, teeth glinting with his slippery smirk, even in the dark.

When his gaze is back on mine, my heart dead in my stomach, his brows lift on his forehead, head canting to one side, he says, low and menacing, *"Boo!"* and I bolt like a horse out of the gate.

My bare feet hammer across the warped wooden floor, his heavy steps loud and echoey as they race up behind me, the sound bouncing off the stone walls. I whip down the dark hall, but I'm not fast enough, my short legs barely half the length of his, he gains on me immediately.

Long fingers fist in the curls at the crown of my head, tearing me backwards, a cry ripping out of my throat. My back slams into his chest with an oomph, air whooshing out of my lungs. His forearm comes to my neck, the crook of his elbow across my throat, forcing my chin up, my neck arching, his fist in my hair pulling and tugging.

My eyes stream, his hot, panting breaths puffing down the side of my throat.

"How d'ya want this ta go?" he huffs in my ear, "Knife, gun, fists," he hums as though he's really thinking through his options. "Let's start with a good ol'-fashioned beating."

I whimper as he wrenches my head back further, my oesophagus feeling like it's going to burst straight out the front of my throat and then he's throwing me to the floor. I gasp for breath, coughing hard, my hands and knees slamming unforgivingly into the solid wood floor as I land, his foot connecting with my stomach before I even get the chance to catch my breath. His shoe connects with the underside of my ribs, kicking me onto my side, I gasp, crying out as his foot collides with my sternum.

"Get up!" he shouts, spitting on the floor beside me.

Saliva hangs from my lips, dripping to the floor, bile burning its way up the back of my throat, I swallow it down. Rolling onto my front, arms and legs shaking so hard it takes everything inside of me to push up onto my hands and knees. I cough, spluttering, he crouches down beside me, twirling my thick braid through his fingers, I flinch away as he winds it tight around his knuckles. Licking his lips, the light from the fire illuminating the madness in his eyes, he smiles, sickeningly, and then he's springing to his feet, dragging me up with him by his hold on my hair. Strands snap and tear, ripping free from my scalp, my feet scrabble beneath me, trying to get me up as he drags me towards him.

In my panic, I claw at his hands, gouging at his skin, he shakes me off, using his free hand to land a punch to my stomach. I go lax in his hold, the only thing keeping me upright is his hold on my hair. My stomach rolls, sickness swirling, tears spill free from my tightly squeezed lids, stars shooting across my dark vision.

I think of the last time this happened, this man, these hands. He's spitting and cursing at me, but I tune it out, the buzzing in my head louder than the flies that will eventually feast on my corpse. I think of Thorne, coming back here, finding my body and the whole thing feels like a hot blade searing through my chest.

This isn't how it's supposed to go. This isn't it for me. It's not supposed to be Shane. This isn't right. This is not my end.

Pain screams in my temples, drumming through my skull, but I get my feet under me, kick my leg out catching him hard in the side of his knee, and he's not expecting it. He throws away from him, my body slamming heavily into the wall, my chin bounces off the stone, blood pooling in my mouth, but my hands slide over the rough painted surface, locating the door handle.

Slinging it open behind me, I rush out into the rain. My braid flies over my shoulder, thumping my back in timed rhythm with my pace. Bare feet pounding through the mud, splatters of puddle water flicking up my legs. Stones and gravel slice into my feet like upturned kitchen knives as I rush forward. I hear Shane kick the step with the toe of his shoe, slowing him no more than a fraction of a second, but it helps propel me forward.

The cliff is suddenly there, the sea beyond, my toes fly over the edge, and I throw my arms out, desperate for balance, a scream catches in my throat. Rain pelts down, large, hard droplets, the wind battering me. I throw my weight onto the heels of my feet, landing hard on my arse with a splat. I claw my way to my feet, the darkness, the howling wind, all of it in my favour as I race through sludge. I glance behind me, seeing Shane stumble through the door just as I throw myself into the thorny shrubbery at the base of the lighthouse.

Breathing hard, lightning flashing violently over-head, thunder drumming and cracking and rumbling. I draw my legs up to my chest, brace my head in my hands and try to breathe through the pain.

There are no weapons in this house, no sharp knives, razors, and Thorne removed his toolkit, placing it in the car when he finished with it earlier. So I've not even got a bloody screwdriver.

Think, think, think.

Rain pelts down harder, soaking me thoroughly, my teeth chatter, blood coating my tongue, painting my throat. Pain pulses in time with my heartbeat, I risk a glance up, knowing I won't be able to hide here for long, there aren't many hiding places out in the open, there aren't really any in the house either.

Please come back to me, Thorne.

Terror rolls through me, blanketing me with fear, intense, crushing, chilling. I wait for Shane to dart past me, his gaze on the sea, head whipping side to side, stilling over the treeline to the left. I crawl free from the bushes, thorns and sticks stabbing and prodding at me, snagging my clothing as I slither free. I push to my feet silently, the rain my cover, I bolt for the front door, slip back inside. The fire dying, candles having blown out from the force of the wind, leaving the house in almost complete darkness. I leave the door open, and head back through the house to the end of the hall.

Trying all of the doors in the hexagonal dead end, the only one unlocked isn't easy to push open. I shove my aching shoulder into it, water falls from my clothes, the eerie dripping sounds splatting against the wooden floor. Fear heightening my senses, straining my eyes, my ears, I don't hear Shane coming back.

Finally, the door shifts, scraping over the floor, enough for me to squeeze through, escaping into further darkness. The space around me feeling impossibly large, I rest my back against the door, palms flat against it, I push hard, force it closed, but leaving a gap just enough that I can pry my fingers into the jamb to get back inside the house.

It's my first mistake.

I'm inside the lighthouse, I quickly realise, the rooks

nesting in the top of the tower flapping and fluffing their wings. The wind whistles around the space, icy air chilling me to the bone. I heave in breaths, pressing a hand to my expanding ribs as I do, pain ricocheting through my bones. I clench my teeth, squeeze my eyes closed.

Thorne enters my head, his voice smooth and calm, firm, I imagine him telling me to breathe. I felt like I was suffocating beneath that sack in the back of his car, but I wasn't, I didn't. I'm not under that sack now, I'm not bound and gagged. Breath enters my lungs easier at the realisation, and I blink the water from my eyes, wipe the back of my hand across my face.

And of course, just as I start to slow my breaths, pressing against my throbbing side, that's the moment the outer door to the lighthouse cracks open, hard and fast, the hinges screeching in protest.

Shane steps inside, a flash of lightning revealing me to him as he steps over the threshold.

"Do you know what I've seen T'orne fuckin' Blackwell do ta little girls like you?" he hisses, upper lip curled over his teeth as he slams the door closed at his back. "The man's an animal," he growls. "So what makes you so fuckin' special?" he asks, looking at me with disgust.

He doesn't want an answer, it doesn't even require one. I'm not special, I don't *mean* anything to Thorne. I don't think I really mean anything to anyone.

"Sloppy t'ough, real sloppy," he hums spitefully, a menacing chuckle on his lips. "I followed 'im so many times, wondering what the fuck he was up to. I had my suspicions it was pussy distracting 'im, he hardly even checked his surroundings before coming back here. Turns out I was right. The Doyles should have put a fuckin' bullet in you themselves," he spits. "I was goin' ta wait, report back ta the others, tell them about your lover boy's disloyalty, you still breathin', but then he left, and me? Well, I couldn't resist taking vengeance for ma boy right fuckin' now."

"Maybe Cian had the right idea after all," he ponders, stepping closer, his words low. "If the leader of the Blackwell Boys has kept ya alive all this time, your pussy must be fuckin' golden," he spits the words as my nails snag and claw over the door at my back. "Maybe I'll 'ave ta see what all the fuss is about, you think fucking T'orne is gunna keep ya alive forever, you little cunt? Well, we'll just see, shall we?"

He lunges forward, rough hands fisting my wet t-shirt as I try to fling myself away, his fingers driving into my shoulders. He drags me forward, my nails snapping as he tears me away from the wooden door. I hammer my fists into his side, battering his ribs, kicking my legs out, my feet scuffing over the ground as he drags me away from the door. I claw at his hand, dig my nails into the back of it.

"Keep fightin'," he laughs darkly, a tremor pulsing through me at the sound. "It only gets me dick harder."

"You'll never fuck me, you fucking psychopath," I spit at him, fighting with everything in me, the skin on the back of his hand collecting beneath my fingernails.

"Never!" I shout through gritted teeth. "Look what happened to Cian!" I scream at him.

His eyes flare, narrowing tightly, his fist balls in the front of my shirt as he pulls me forward before slamming me back into the wall. My head ricochets off the stone, layers of steel and concrete making itself known as he bashes my head back into it a second and third time. Bile burns my throat, eyes streaming, he slams me again and again into the wall. His teeth bared, lips in a snarl, spit splattering my face with every terrifying threat he shouts in my face.

My arms drop to my sides, head swimming, my body starts to slide down the wall, knees buckling. Shane grabs a fistful of my hair, tight at the roots, pain shooting through my entire body from that alone, tossing me onto the ground. My face smacks into the concrete. My eyes go black, body limp, but I can still feel when he climbs over me, heavy body straddling the backs of my thighs, it electrifies every part of me with a sudden jolt of awareness.

His hands claw at my pyjama pants, the wet cotton sticking to my skin. His scarred knuckles graze my bare flesh as he shoves my bottoms down, exposing my backside to him. I have the urge to heave, sickness swirling in my gut, but it's like my body's given up, even though my brain is screaming.

It's the clink of his belt buckle hitting the floor that forces the last bit of adrenaline to bolt through my bloodstream. I buck up at the same time he lifts onto his knees, hands busy working his jean's button and zipper. I get my palms flat under me, elbows locking even though my muscles feel like jelly and I throw my head back as he tries to come down on me. The back of my skull connects with his face making him roar, I see stars as I buck up again, managing to get one knee solidly under me and twisting so I land with a thud on my hip, barely managing to roll him off of me.

My leg flies out, kicking at him as I scrabble away, my toes just catching him in the groin. He curls into himself, hands cupping his dick as he snarls at me, gnashing his teeth.

My hands slap onto steel, fingers curling onto the first step of the spiral staircase. Torn nails catching on the railing pole, I grab it with both hands, wrenching myself up. I crawl as quickly as I can up the spiralling steps, which is not fast at all. Every inch of blood, muscle and bone shoots a pulsing pain directly into my skull with every move I make.

I keep my eyes shut tight as I drag myself up the stairs, the industrial steel creaking and groaning with every subtle move I make. And I think about Thorne. The last time we were in here. What he said to me. How he said these weren't safe, but I don't think I really believed him, despite him telling me, more than once, that he does not tell lies.

But I think, now, I finally believe him.

As I wish for death.

Pray for life.

Crave the sweet black oblivion I thought I was to be gifted by the monster of a man keeping me captive.

My monster.

My death.

With those obsidian coloured eyes and hair of the blackest night. The cant of his head when he's curious and doesn't show it in his expression, but it's revealed to me all the same with the way his head cocks to assess me.

My body.

My lies.

My truth.

My secrets.

My heart.

That's what pounds hard in my chest, even as my lungs feel like they're slowly stilling. I heave myself up another step, rough, unforgiving fingers closing around my ankles, squeezing the bones until I swear, I hear them creak. My chin smacks off of the edge of a step, my teeth chomping down on my tongue, the inside of my cheek, as Shane tears me back down the stairs. Hands clawing at anything I can reach.

And *finally*.

The realisation of the last few weeks barrelling into me unforgivingly, like that storm circling menacingly overhead shoots a bolt of lightning directly into me. Awareness rips through me like my soul is trying to tear itself away from my skeleton.

I cry out.

For the one thing I want, *need*, above all else.

Hoping my pain will raise him from the nothingness,

call him forth in a swirling vortex of dark magic, summon him from the deepest pits of hell.

I fill my lungs with all of my anguish and scream. "THORNE!"

And as my cheekbone smashes into the edge of the stairs, my eyes flying open, one hand clawing over steel, the other wrapped tightly around a railing post. I glance down. Over the edge. Blurry gaze revealing nothing but a plunging hole of open darkness. My grip tightens on the railing, harsh sharp tugs on my feet have my head bumping into the bars. I cling on tighter, whimpers falling from my mouth, my tongue feeling so dry I fear I might swallow it and choke. And then the stairs shake, *moving*. Their rusted bolts start raining down onto the concrete below, the curved corner I'm on starting to warp and bow.

Metal groans and creaks louder than the thunder crashing overhead and it feels like I'm falling as the steel structure starts to peel away from the wall. I feel dizzy and sick and my eyes squeeze even tighter together.

And then I *bump, bump, bump,* sharply down the steps, my grip forcefully yanked free of the railing. Rolling onto my side, I cry out, my legs kicking and flailing with the fight of my life when I realise nothing is there. No fingers, no pain, no twisting pinch of skin around my bones. I blink my bleary eyes, vision skewed and warped, and not only from the darkness of the space, but something else, the stairs groan beneath me, and I scrabble with the railing, one hand of fingers curling loosely around the rusted bars.

My head pounds, trousers and underwear still pulled halfway down my legs, but I can't even lift my arms enough to pry them up with aching fingers. It's like my muscles have melted away, the joints of my bones stiff and dry.

I peer down the stairs, a frown on my brow, confusion making me blink harder and harder. That's how I find him, a flash of lightning filling the space, illuminating his presence like an angel sent from the heavens. I see him through blurred eyes, the demon from my dreams and nightmares. Dark eyes blown, stare locked on me, his jaw clenched. Lightning tears across the sky outside, streaking through the cracked glass at the very top of the lighthouse, rain and wind finding its way through.

Thorne stands at the foot of the stairs, feet planted, hands in great fists at his sides. I crane my neck up, every last dying bit of strength forces my head forward, fingers slippery on the railing, I breathe slow, despite being out of breath, my heart thudding much too hard. It feels as though it might explode inside my chest. The look Thorne shoots my way is like fire licking over my flesh. A lift to one of his dark eyebrows and he's turning away, effortlessly hefting Shane up by his hair and slamming him down into the concrete floor.

Thorne hovers above him like a beast, snarling, hackles raised, he looms over him in a black suit. Never once looking more like Lucifer himself than right in this very moment. He slams Shane into the floor, towering above him, bent at the waist, one hand still balled at his side. It's as though Shane weighs nothing, one of his hands curled around Thorne's forearm, the other uselessly batting at him.

It's the next flash of lightning that I catch sight of it, Thorne straddling Shane's hips, the silver glinting in the light as Shane's blade arcs through the air. I scream, too late, as the knife stabs into Thorne, so many times I can hardly count. Tears stream from my eyes and I force myself to move, dragging my bottoms up a little, I start to slip down the steps on my bottom, slowly, one at a time, I didn't realise how high up I am. Almost to the bottom, the stairs make the most almighty sounding groan as my portion of the staircase completely breaks free from the building.

The steel sways out into the centre of the room, back towards the wall, I cling onto the railing, nothing keeping me safe on the side that's peeled free from the lighthouse's structure. I freeze, everything locking up when I look back down to Thorne, a sob choking my throat, but I don't want to distract him.

They're side on, my view of them, Thorne straddling Shane, a knife handle sticking out of Thorne's shoulder or chest. I can't make it out from up here in the dark, but Thorne doesn't even seem to notice as he pins Shane's hands beneath his knees. Pressing into the backs of his hands with his weight. I watch as his back flexes, illuminated every now and then by the storm. His right arm draws back, connecting with Shane's face in a punch that crunches so loudly, it echoes around the haunting space. And then he does it again, and again.

Shane's legs go from kicking and flailing to lead still on the floor. But Thorne keeps punching.

His arms draw back, one after the other, fists colliding with Shane's face over and over. I watch enraptured, the steel structure I'm on swaying, but I don't call out. I don't interrupt him, a black cloud of rage swirling around them, Thorne releases everything trapped inside of him. His always perfect posture, slicked back hair, expressionless face, the way he never shortens his words, everything slow and properly pronounced. The epitome of perfection. But it has cracks, deep down inside, this dark swirling smoke laid dormant, until now.

I don't know how long it goes on for. My eyes heavy, the pain in my head pulsing in time with my heartbeat, drowning out sound every now and then. I'm tired, so tired, physically and mentally. I drift in and out of consciousness, but when my hearing flits back in, all I can hear is the consistent *crunch-splat* of Thorne's fists smacking into what I can only imagine is left of Shane's skull.

A light dusting of rain filters in with the howling wind through the cracked windows above, the storm cancelling out the protesting caws of the nesting rooks. But the icy sprinkling of water feels like a blessing as it falls onto my overheated skin.

Bile burns up my throat, the staircase creaking and groaning, my grip slipping from the railing, the back of my hand hitting the step with a dull thud. And then there's nothing but silence. No buzzing, no crunching, no splats, no grunts, no screams or shouts. But the image of a knife handle poking out of Thorne has me snapping to. Neck burning, tendons straining, I crane my neck forward sharply, pain radiating down my spine as I lift my head forward.

Thorne's still there, on his knees, his chest heaving, knife sheathed inside of him, back straight, chin dipped, his fists are hanging by his sides, loose, uncurled, dark in the shadows. I imagine them split, bleeding, brain matter, blood splatter. And all I want is for those hands to be placed on me. In any capacity.

In love.

In death.

My head finally drops back with a thunk, unable to hold it up any longer, and I hardly even feel the pain slicing through my skull on impact. My ears ring like booming church bells, echoing throughout my body, I feel them vibrating in my bones, and it helps me slip into that strange place, to escape the discomfort. A gentle wave crashing and breaking, cool water lapping at my toes, I go with it, drifting as the current takes me in. I breathe easier, deeper, but then the gentle water fills my lungs like a tsunami, I bolt up, spluttering on the imaginary liquid. Groaning in pain as my spine snaps straight.

I look down at him again, and he's still there, just the same, but his breathing is even, his chest rising and falling rhythmically. A trance, that's what it looks like to me, even from so far up, I can tell he's lost inside himself down there. But I want him back. Desperately.

"Thorne?" I call softly, my voice cracking on his name because relief slams into me as I give into my instincts, call out to the man who is my very own grim reaper.

His head snaps over his shoulder, predatory eyes tracking upwards, a crease between his brows, confusion on his face as he takes in his surroundings, as though he's seeing it all for the very first time. Effortlessly, he pushes onto the balls of his feet, rising from a crouch, he sweeps one hand down each thigh, smoothing his slacks as he does. Something that's instinctual, a necessity to the immaculate parts that make him up even with an injury.

"Little Cub?" he calls to me, his gravelly voice so tight, its usual smoothness gone, in fact, it sounds like his vocal cords are about to snap. "Do not move," he says calmly, suddenly serene, his head craning back to look up at me. "I am going to get you down, okay?" and I know he means it.

"Okay," I whisper, voice not much more than a scratch up my aching throat.

I watch his shadowed form stride towards the base of the stairs, one foot on the very bottom step, what feels like so many more between us.

His footsteps slow and cautious, the storm raging outside casting him in eerie shadow. Thunder crashes overhead making me flinch hard, the metal creaking. Thorne stops his ascent, his eyes never leaving me. He nods slowly, another step, a groan of swaying metal, rust and parts tinkling as they hit the concrete floor below.

"Stay still. Focus on me, baby girl," and I nod gently,

inhaling sharply, keeping my eyes on his as best I can in the dark.

A flash of lightning illuminates the space, one quick, sharp spark has me gasping.

"Thorne!" I cry out, my breaths harsh, "Your shoulder!" it feels like a scream gets trapped in my throat, my gaze now firmly locked on the knife handle protruding out of him, before my vision is quickly re-stolen by the absence of light.

"I am fine," he says reassuringly, still taking slow steps towards me like he doesn't even feel it. "I will get you down from here. Do not worry about me."

Compelled, I slow my breaths forcefully, try hard not to shift uncomfortably. I let my eyes flutter shut, swallow the taste of blood, the sticky residue of it thick and strong on the back of my tongue.

"Haisley," Thorne calls, plucking me from unconsciousness. I blink hard, my eyes slits, "Do you think you can sit up for me?" I look down my body at him, a few steps away, so fucking far, so fucking close, I want to sob with relief. "I need you to try and scoot down a couple of steps. I cannot climb any higher without risking your safety."

I lick my lips, slowly sliding my hands down by my sides, palms flat against a step, my fingers curl over the edge of it. I look back to Thorne, my breathing immediately picking up because of the weapon in his shoulder.

"Calm," he soothes, hands relaxed by his sides, you would never look at this man and think there was anything wrong. "Push yourself up, move very slowly."

I nod, bottom lip trembling, the wind howling through the echoey space. I inch up to sitting, my eyes squeezed tight, I grit my teeth, force myself upright. I can do this. I can be brave. When I'm finally shifted, steel cold beneath my bare backside, my eyes flare open, and I know he's realised, *seen me.* My cheeks flush bright, and an apology is on the tip of my tongue.

But then his eyes lift to mine and the sorry dies on my lips, his gaze murkier than I've ever seen it, anger and something much, much darker permeate the air around us. Hands balling into fists at his sides, his body seems impossibly larger, taller, broader, more intimidating. Normally, I would want to shrink back, but instead, in this moment, something like the need for reassurance surges through me instead.

"He didn't," I choke out, ignoring the scowl starting to form on his face, an emotion, something he never usually shows, chewing hard on my inner lip, wincing at the bloody taste. "I'm okay."

The whispered words don't seem to penetrate, but he extends a hand out towards me, softening his expression back into his usual blank mask.

"Come, Little Cub," he whispers, and it's the loudest sound in the room, the endearment, the way he summons me. "Slowly," he coaches.

Knees wobbling, bare feet scraped and bleeding, I push to my feet, the staircase swinging further away from the wall as I do.

"Thorne!" I yelp in panic, grasping at air for him, his hand finds mine, long fingers ensnaring my own.

"I have you," he breathes in the air between us, "I will always have you," my legs give out at the same time I give into the overwhelming urge to cry, a sob wrenching up my throat.

Thorne draws me into his chest, unconcerned with the way the spiral staircase is collapsing around us, groaning and screeching. Even one handed, he gathers me to him, lifting my feet from the floor, he takes my weight, twisting without hesitation, he takes the stairs down, the staircase swaying beneath us. Groans and creaks of metal, a high-pitched keening, his feet plant on solid ground as I watch over his shoulder, part of the staircase completely separating from the wall fixture, collapsing in a heap in the centre of the room.

My hands raise to cover my ears, palms clamping down over them, Thorne's grip tightens, and I've never felt safer in my life. Tears stream down my cheeks, blood in my mouth, the scent of metal in my nose. But it's Thorne that brings me back, his comforting familiarity, leather, salt, gunpowder. I bury my face into the side of his neck, my hands fisting in the expensive fabric of his shirt.

That's when he wavers, his legs quivering, but he even manoeuvres falling to the ground in a neat and controlled way. Folding me into him as his knees hit the concrete, his shoes squeaking as they fold at the toes, he seats himself back on his haunches. Never once letting me go.

I lean back from him, and it's the first time tonight I'm truly able to look at him and *see*, and it almost takes me by surprise. The beauty of him. Nose to nose, his gaze flickers over my face, mine on his dark eyes, pupils blown as black as his irises. We share breath, mine fast, his slow and steady, and I try to match it, calm my racing heart. But the way he looks at me, his other hand, despite his injury, finding my waistband, pulling the elastic up just enough to cover me completely, restore a little of something someone took away from me.

"Thorne," I breathe in the space between us, and I wonder what he sees, looking at me this way.

Both of us hurt, injuries and wounds, our clothes wet and soiled, mud and rain and blood. So much blood. I know what I see, when I look at him, *my death*. And instead of fear, something else pulses through me.

He saved me.

I don't know who moves first, but my mouth is suddenly on him, our teeth clash, lips mauling at each other. I breathe hard, taking and giving, my lips sucking on the corner of his mouth in my desperate search for his lips. The arm wrapped around me slides up my back, fingers fisting in my hair, he moves my head, pressure on the base of my skull, guiding my lips to his.

He devours me as our mouths finally find each other, I feel pain, need, delicious desire overwhelming it all, soaring through every part of me as he ravages my mouth. Thorne is the most controlled man I have ever met.

Until he kisses.

He is wild and primal, his teeth scrape over my chin, lips sucking hard bruises into my skin, my jaw, my neck, down my throat. My hands grab at him desperately, snagged nails clawing down the side of his neck, I squirm violently in his lap, his free hand helping heft me over him, my knees going to rest on either side of his folded legs, straddling him.

I curl my arms around his neck, careful of the blade in his shoulder, my nails clawing and gouging at his nape, he holds me tight, breath stilted in my chest, his teeth score into my top lip, and they don't stop. The force of his jaw locking, my cupid's bow squeezing so tight it feels like it might go *pop*. And then it does, a bloom of fresh blood coats my tongue, pain bolting through my entire head, and Thorne groans into our kiss, so desperate and needy, feral, like an animal. Something that is all instinct, the tip of his tongue parts the wound, lips sucking on it hard, teeth nipping and tugging at the broken flesh. I hiss in pain, but press closer to his chest, my hands clawing at him like I want to crawl my way inside of him, let him keep me protected forever.

I kiss him like I will die if I don't. And in this moment, I truly believe I might. My lips sip greedily at his skin, mouthing down his chin, across his jaw, but then his hold on my head is moving my lips back to his like he can't bear them to be parted from his. His tongue slips indulgently into my mouth, urgently swirling over the fresh cut, long desperate laves of his tongue over mine. I grind myself down on the hardness in his lap, but he pulls back suddenly, tearing a needy whimper from my chest in objection.

"*Mors Mea*," he whispers between us, *My Death.*

His lips immediately come back to mine, but there's a firmness in his hold that lets me know not to try that again. And I hear him loud and clear, his words echoing around inside my skull, my time in catholic school studying Latin giving his whispered words away. And I already knew that Thorne Blackwell was going to be mine. I just had no idea that I might also be his.

CHAPTER 19

THORNE

Her lips are like a hit of heroin. Euphoric, addictive, a high I could never find anywhere else. I have waited so long, so, *so* long, to have her like this—to own, to claim every single inch of her. So, it takes every ounce of energy I have left to pry her off of me. Lifting her slightly off of my lap, my cock swollen and throbbing with every brush of friction she offers.

But not tonight.

This is not how it is supposed to be.

From trauma.

If I took her now, I would devour her until I drained every last drop of her essence, suck it into my soul, absorb all of her golden threaded goodness inside of me, dissolve it into my darkness. Selfishly feast on it until there is nothing left inside of her. I do not want a living corpse in my hands; I do not want a corpse at all.

"Haisley," I whisper between us.

The throbbing in my shoulder barely a dull thud of my heartbeat in my ears, my hand firm on her skull, I turn her to face me. Her plush lips bloody and parted, split top lip oozing crimson down her chin, finally something that is all mine, decedent and violent. I am a savage. Her eyes are half-lidded, gaze weary but focused, her body swaying gently in my hold, hands fisted in the top of my shirt. A cut in her hairline trickles slowly down her temple, streaking along her cheekbone and jaw, meeting the steadily dripping blood from her lip.

I lean back into her, my hold on her head tight, soft curls tangling around my fingers. Tongue following the stream of red back up, the flat of it lapping at the source, a small gash in her forehead, blooming purple bruising framing it, unfurling around the site like a blossoming flower. I clean her up, my lips and teeth sucking and nibbling away all traces of her injuries. I mouth along her forehead, down her temples, nibble the high arc of her cheekbones, and lick down her jaw. Little puffs of warm breath skate down my neck, a shiver slowly slithering down my spine as her hands fist tighter in my shirt. Her little finger of one hand stroking my skin gently between fastened buttons.

This is intimate and heavy, a lot and not enough, but she does not protest, does not pull away. Letting me take care of her in the most baser, primal, instinctive way.

See the hurt, be the hurt, cure the hurt.

She sighs as my mouth dips to her chin, her heavy eyes falling shut. My lips suck across her skin, cleaning the traces of blood left by me and someone else. She sighs in contentment and it makes me stall, my eyes wide on her face, the serene, slack expression on it. Warmth unfurls low in my belly, something like pride curling my abdominal muscles, shifting and rolling beneath hot skin.

I massage the back of her head and she hisses, face scrunching in discomfort, making me freeze, anger spikes like lava in my veins, knowing someone hurt her. *Someone who is not me.* But I keep my calm, continue swirling my tongue over her skin. She resettles, relaxing her tense muscles, her small body melting back into one side of my chest. Her hold on my shirt is vice-tight, her face turned into me as I taste and take and consume everything that happened here tonight. Absolve it.

"I am never letting you go," I whisper the promise against her damp cheek, glistening like diamonds from the trail of my tongue. "You are mine, Haisley Kelly," I declare. "And I will keep you safe forever."

"I'm not sure what to do," Haisley says quietly, worrying her bottom lip, the top one red and thick and swollen, bloody.

My bite.

Satisfaction thrums through me, my claiming mark on her, my consumption of her blood. Realisation of our situation, something I am not going to concern myself with just yet.

The fire is dead, the living room floor wet, there is a body in my lighthouse and his blood is on my skin. Newly lit candles hold her bright eyes, trained on my shoulder, that is what has my attention, her focus on the blade's handle protruding from it. I glance down out the corner of my eye at my left shoulder, flick a surveying gaze over it. It is a short knife, the handle much longer than the blade. The slow pounding pain gradually becoming deeper, the muscles aching, but it does not feel as though the blade has knocked on bone. There are many options with something like this, however, the only one currently available to me is the grittiest one.

I look up into her tired eyes, a frown between her brows, small traces of drying blood on her freckled skin, little patches I missed whilst cleaning her with my tongue. Right hand reaching up, my eyes on her face, so expressive, the parting of her lips, the soft, almost silent gasp, falling from them. My fingers curl over the handle, my knee sliding towards my other, just enough to knock her back a few paces, get her out from between my thighs. Fingers tight, I tear the blade free with one sharp motion, my teeth grit, but there is no spurt of blood, and I am grateful, possibly for the first time, that the wound is not something life threatening.

"Thorne," my name gasped in panic from her lips, "Is it… are you-"

"I am fine," I say, sweeping her wild curls back from her pretty face. "It will be fine," I nod, dipping my chin to catch her fallen gaze.

"Thorne," she says, swallowing hard. "What do we

do now?" whispered words, her eyes finally lifting to mine, my chin still dropped to my chest, head angled to see her.

"*We*, do nothing," I reassure her, her eyes heavy and sad, the stress in her features making my heart clench. "I am going to clean you up, and then you are going to bed."

Her intake of breath is slow and deep, but her shoulders peel back, spine straightening, she winces but tries to hide it, and I have the insane urge to grin. I wonder what she would think of that, me smiling like the lunatic I am at her.

"I want to take care of you first," she says gently, stepping back between my spread legs without invitation, the outside of her thighs brushing the inside of mine.

Her pyjama pants are wet, soaked through, clinging to her skin, and it reminds me of just how low they sat less than twenty minutes ago. I clench my teeth, pop my jaw, but I do not react outwardly. I think of the man, Shane O'Sullivan, dead on my property, his concave skull I seemingly destroyed with my bare hands. How I would like to bring him back from the dead, resurrect him, just to spend my time ripping his fucking head from his shoulders.

"Take off your jacket," Haisley instructs, quiet and soothing, her eyes on mine.

Small hands slowly come up to my chest, and it takes everything inside of me not to body slam her into the ground, rut into her tight, wet heat until she screams for death, to make it end, for me to drive her to the brink of insanity.

Let us wallow there.

Together.

In the gloom.

I want to decimate her.

This delicate, beautiful woman, my ache for her something rotten and twisted.

Pressure on my jacket, a soft tug on my lapels pulls my attention, my hands flying up, capturing her slight wrists in the circle of my fingers and thumbs. Her breath stills, eyes wide, green and watery in the dark. I lick my lips, unable to stop the movement as I re-taste her blood on my tongue.

Holding my gaze, my hands still shackling her wrists, gently, she pushes my jacket back, over my shoulders, my hands and arms moving with the motion of hers. Hesitantly, she twists one of her hands inside my hold, her fingers uncurling my own, but she does not look, and neither do I, as she unpeels me from her wrists, my hands dropping to my thighs. She pushes my jacket over my shoulders, carefully taking each bloody-knuckled hand in hers to thread the sleeves down my arms. Watching my face, she brings my jacket up between us, folds it neatly over her arm, before folding it once more, placing it down on the couch cushion beside me.

Her movements are slow, less like she is hurting, even though I know she is, and more like she is trying not to spook me, do something that might make me pull away. Because she does not realise it yet. The power she has over me, it is life changing, *threatening*. Because whatever happened in that lighthouse just now has changed me, inexplicably.

I cannot say what it is, my memory of the chain of events hazy and blurred, but something in my soul leapt out and attached itself, *us*, to her, I just have to wait for her to feel it too.

And I realise something I think I have always known, from the very moment I first saw her, the second, third, fiftieth time, I was never going to let her go, and I did not even quite have her yet. But now she is here, and I do have her, have finally gotten a taste of her. And it made me realise how much I really do own her. Fractured mind, body and angelic little soul. All the parts that make her up, make me up too, my golden tether in the gloom, and I am never going to let her go.

CHAPTER 20

HAISLEY

His eyes scorch my skin, my fingers fumbling nervously as I start to undo his shirt buttons, the two top tortoiseshell-coloured ones open. It occurs to me, as I snap open the next two, hands trembling softly, my eyes fixed to the task even as his burn a hole right through me, that I have never seen Thorne in anything less than a shirt and trousers. He doesn't wear a tie, and his top two buttons are always open, but everything fits impeccably, I don't think I've even ever seen him without shoes on. I think about him hiding ridiculous novelty socks beneath the leg of his trousers, the thought so absurd it rattles my chest with a huff of laughter, my teeth chewing my sore lip inside my mouth.

"What is funny?" Thorne asks quietly, my eyes blinking hard, I lick over my top lip, feel the imprint of his teeth, the open wound, dried blood.

"Nothing," I whisper, raising my eyes just enough to

look into his, his stare dark and penetrating, the hollows of his cheekbones sharp in the shadows, one side of his face glowing with the flickering candlelight.

Dropping my gaze, I continue making my way down his shirt buttons. I told him what Shane said, about not having told anyone about me yet, in more or less words. And the absence of urgency in having to move or run, to hide, is a welcome relief. His body limp, loose, arms relaxed by his sides, my knuckles graze his warm skin as I reach his waistband. I flash my gaze up, my fingers hesitant to venture lower, not knowing how long this version of Thorne is going to last before his control requirements jump back to life.

"Lift," I breathe between us, his head cocked just slightly, craned back a little so he can keep his attention focused on my face.

He shifts his hips up, allowing me to thread my arms around his back, plucking his shirt tail out of his slacks, my fingertips ghost over the leather of his belt and a shiver rushes through me. Thinking about it, where I want it to be, my confession about it, all of it making my cheeks flush with incredible heat. His breath slides down the side of my neck, warm, a little humid, forcing goosebumps to ripple out across my skin. And I still, feeling his face turn into the side of my throat, his lips brushing a kiss over my pulse point. It makes me sway, my hands fisting the silky cotton of his black shirt, I lean into his feather light touch.

"Thorne," I breathe against the shell of his ear, our

faces so close, it makes me want to live and die all in one big confusing mess.

Hovering for barely a moment, he turns away, breaking the spell, and my hands suddenly remember how to work again, plucking the rest of his shirt out from his waistband. When my cold fingers finish working the final button, I step back a little, thumbs smoothing beneath the collar. I caress the fabric between my finger and thumb, keep my eyes averted, draw in a deep breath and then push the wet fabric, a mixture of blood and rain stuck in the fabric, over his shoulders.

My thumbs run down his back, over his shoulder blades, the wet cotton clinging to his wounded shoulder. I peel it away slowly, flicking my gaze to his with every peel of fabric, he is unbothered, no expression, nothing revealing pain. Eyes going back to his skin, I push his shirt down the rest of the way, along his muscular arms, letting it pool around his wrists where his palms are planted on the cushion beneath him. Deep warm skin is revealed, golden with olive undertones, blue and green veins climbing beneath. All of him complimented by an array of black fine line tattoos over his arms, chest, abs. He is, put simply, perfection. But my eyes hone in on the deep purpling surrounding multiple stab wounds.

My eyes tighten, gaze narrowing in on the mess of carvings, heat flushes my cheeks but it's different this time, there's no embarrassment, anger and desire in equal parts pulse in time with one another, both battling to come out on top. I want to go back into that light-house just to kick a goddamn corpse. I bring my hand up hesitantly, my forefinger slow to trace over the half-inch long wounds. Thorne doesn't even flinch, but he watches me, just my face, intently, the entire time.

"Does it... do they hurt?" I whisper, that thick, airy bubble descending around us again.

It feels like safety and warmth, the privacy of the feeling, protection shielding us both inside.

"Not when you touch it," he rasps, it's thick, his tone, heavy with feeling and I swallow at the emotions it drags up inside my core.

"I'm going to clean it up," I say, eyes still fixed to the wound, blooming purple beneath thick, sticky claret.

I glance at him then, my fingertips stalling the tracing shapes they were making against his torn flesh. Thorne's dark eyes lock me in, holding me captive, my breath halted and trapped in my chest. Something heavy passes between us, something I don't want to think too hard about. No words are spoken, nothing anyone could overhear anyway, because sometimes we speak without words, and all I know is, if I let myself fall into it, this feeling, *longing*, it will give me a false sense of security. Of *promise*.

"You are mine, Haisley Kelly. And I will keep you safe forever."

I blink, wondering if his whispered promises include protection from himself. Unsure of the answer, what it would be, what I would *want* it to be.

So I push back, break our stare, the intensity of it dying like the flame of a candle, causing an ache to develop in my chest that I don't fully understand the weight of. I take myself to the bathroom, limping and sore, dragging my painful, punctured feet across the wood, intending to collect up the first aid kit, towels, washcloths. Instead, I find my hands bracketing either side of the sink, grip clinging on like it's the only thing keeping me standing. My head drops forward, the porcelain ice cold beneath my clammy palms, the only thing I know is real as my head spins, whooshing sounds in my ears.

I swallow back the bile in my throat, think of Shane's hands on me, a second time, another beating, almost something else. My stomach churns, but it's empty, nothing to come up but bile and acid and my throat constricts in protest keeping it all down. I brush a thumb to the corner of my lip, blood and salt and Thorne on my tongue. It helps me take a deep breath, soothing me, relaxing me down to sinew and bone. The way he devoured me, aggressive and brutal, passionate.

I inhale deeply through my nose, the scent of blood the only thing I can smell, and I'm not upset by it, if anything, it draws a sudden heat to life between my thighs. Stomach muscles tensing, a forced chill diving down my spine.

I lift my gaze, blinking in the darkness, I release my hold on the sink, smooth a hand back over my hair, my side braid still secured at the end, the rest a matted mess on the back of my skull. I turn then, exhausted and weary, worrying about Thorne, how deep those injuries drive, and it must be my thoughts that summon him, an invisible tether.

He stands in the doorway, tall, dark, imposing, his upper half bare, and I can't see his face, get a read on his expression, likely the lack of, but I feel him like a livewire kicking across the room all the same. The tension is thick, a heady cloud of whatever's been brewing between us like a physical haze, it's suffocating, but I don't think I hate it. I've never wanted anything more than how much I want, *need,* Thorne.

We stand, staring at one another, him on the top step, me in the centre of the sunken bathroom, nothing but gloom surrounding us. It feels like it fits, not quite darkness, but there's no light. *Gloom...* It feels right, like in the daylight we couldn't do this, be, whatever it is we really are, but in this thick, dense absence of light, it lets us get away with existing in its ominous wave.

"Shower," Thorne says, not a question, it cracks through the silence like the thunder still circling above.

That's when my hearing returns in full, the rain slashing against the windows down the hall, none in this room, no lights either.

"Okay, I'll just get you something-"

He cuts me off, fingers on his good arm closing over the door frame, barring my exit as I start towards him.

He licks his lips at the same time I lick mine.

"Together," he whispers silkily, looking down at me, his chin dipped, my neck craned back, toes almost brushing the bottom step, him still two up. "I want-" he glances away, the warm glow of candlelight drifting down the hall highlighting his high cheekbone, hollow cheek. "I *need* you to get in with me," he breathes slow, deeply, drawing his eyes back to mine, two bottomless pits of black. "I need to wash him off of you." I swallow as he takes a step down, closer, closing in on me, I don't move, sway, shift in place. "If I do not, it will drive me insane," the whispered words are a breath over my mouth, "I just need…"

He trails off, but I understand, because our short time together is the only thing I feel like I've ever really known. My life feeling like it's long forgotten, I struggle to remember much of my daily mundane activities, what I was doing, where I'd go, who I was supposed to be. I was brought here, to Rook Point, to die. But now, finally, all I want to do is live.

"Control," I whisper, finishing for him, his eyes sharp like daggers on mine, a single slow nod, he takes the final step down, his bare abdomen brushing my breasts, trapped inside a wet shirt. "Tell me what you need, Thorne," and it's like it sets off something inside his brain.

He sweeps past me, slow and elegant, fingers brushing against the back of my hand as he passes, strangely intimate, the way in which he touches me with reverence. Bent at the waist, I watch him, reaching over the edge of the tub, twisting the squeaky taps, a harsh stream of water shuddering through their rickety pipes. He turns back to face me, waiting, and I realise it with perfect clarity. Neither one of us needs words, instinctively I know what he wants, what he needs, what he's asking, all without any sound at all. And I… I want to take care of him in this moment.

The bathroom door open at my back, I close the distance between us, my heart racing in my chest, breathing a little fast, and for the first time since I met him, Thorne's chest is rising and falling in time to match mine. It shoots tingles up my spine, my legs feeling a little like jelly. I hold his gaze, and with a confidence I don't know how to place, my hands go to his belt, cautiously unthreading the leather, the buckle clinking as it hangs open, my thumb flicking his button and zipper free, I hook my thumbs beneath his waistband.

I lower at the same pace his slacks do, dropping gently to my knees, I peer up at him from the ground, his chin dipped, eyes hard on mine, his chest heaving with silent breaths. Releasing his trousers, pooling at his ankles, I tug on his shoelace, untying the bow, slipping my fingers beneath the crisscross of string, tugging to loosen it. I curl my fingers around his ankle, gesturing for him to lift, and I slide his polished shoe, black sock, free, doing the same to the other. I focus on my task, listening to every breath he takes, sharp, fast, and then I lift his feet again, one at a time, to pull his slacks free.

Taking Thorne's offered hand, he helps me to my feet, my body aching in protest, my head still a bit spinny, but I feel safe. In here. *With him.* Free hand holding onto his clothing, I fold the trousers, Thorne watching, I lay them down on top of the closed toilet lid, place his socks inside his shoes and slide them beneath the sink, tucking them out of the way.

When I straighten again, Thorne's there, our fronts brushing, him in only tight black boxers. I survey him as best I can in the dark, his warm skin, delicate inkings, nothing I can make out in the absence of light, but I want to swirl a finger across the shapes all the same. Dip down the valley of his abs, follow the short dark hair down from his navel.

"Your turn," he whispers, breath blowing across the top of my head.

I hold my breath, nerves finally fizzing to life, butterflies swoop low in my belly, my fingers wanting to curl at my sides. My ears buzz as his fingers, warm against my cold flesh, trace the line of exposed skin between the hem of my long sleeved t-shirt, the waistband of my striped pyjama pants. Thorne's hands shift beneath my shirt, palms large and warm and flat, run up over my sides, pushing up the wet fabric, clinging to me like a second skin and I hiss in pain as my arms stretch up, pain pulling tight in my ribs, my shoulders.

Thorne glances down, a soft crease between his brows, long fingers circling my elbows to bend and free my arms, the top being removed over my head. The end of my braid slaps against my bare back, and it makes me want to shrink, my hands coming up quickly at the same time Thorne's eyes and hands drop. His fingers latch around my wrists, warm and tight, slowly, eyes on mine, he tries to bring my hands down, uncovering me for him, but I hold firm, keep my elbows locked.

"I will never hurt you," he whispers in the space between us, his breath warm, my skin ice cold. "Let me see you, Little Cub," he coaxes, voice melodic, soothing, calm, but he doesn't pull, there's no force.

I take a deep breath, my watery eyes on his, he offers me an encouraging nod. A gentle tilt to his head, dark wavy hair flopping forward making him look younger, like a small boy watching and waiting for something he is curious about but is hiding from at the same time.

I swallow, making my ears pop, and I release the tensity in my arms, let them relax into Thorne's hands. He lowers them down, smoothing his thumbs over the insides of my wrists before letting go. He keeps his eyes on mine, and then those thumbs are sliding beneath my waistband, pyjamas and underwear dragging down my legs, his tall, lean body falling at the same rate, the same way I undressed him. Except, this is not the same, he stays down on his knees, at my feet, my entire body flushing the most glorious red, and I'm thankful for the early morning darkness that I'm somewhat hidden from view, no sunlight to peek in from the hall.

"Thorne!" I gasp, fingers suddenly flying to the top of his head to keep me steady as his lips press to the inside of my knee, those big dark eyes still flicked up on mine.

His hands glide up the backs of my calves, fingers tickling over the backs of my weak knees. Grip tightening to more of a hold as my legs waver, his lips skate just over my skin, my fingers clench tight in his thick, wavy strands. He traces his fingers up and down my legs, heat boiling beneath my skin, uncomfortably conscious of how close his face is to my cunt. My muscles tense, and the gentle stroking stops as he feels a change in me. Cheeks flushed red, I pull my free hand up to my face, curl it beneath my chin, knuckles grazing over my swollen jaw.

"I will not hurt you," Thorne reassures me again, but I feel like the phrase is starting to frustrate me rather than reassure me.

I think of his words from before, how he won't hurt me, closely followed by *'even though I am dying to,'* and then my own words slip out before I even have a chance to clench my teeth to keep them in.

"What if I want you to?" I whisper, my nails scratching lightly over his scalp, muscle in his jaw ticking, and I stare at his shoulder again, licking my lips.

It's as though I move without conscious thought, my body sinking down, his hands sliding up the outside of my thighs, I feel every bruise and ache as his hands raise with my body lowering. Thorne holds me steady, his usually harsh grip barely even registering in my nerve endings where he's being so careful with me. It makes me want to cry, his care, at the same time I hate it.

I lift my chin, stare into his eyes, slant my lips over his dark peach-coloured mouth, his top and bottom lip the same thickness, parted, a soft curve to his cupid's bow. I lean in slowly, flick my tongue over the smear of red on the corner of his pretty mouth, groaning almost silently as I taste my own blood on his skin. It brings the pulse back to life in my throbbing lip he tore into, and I love it, the reminder, the pain. Drawing my face back, just enough to see him, flicking my eyes between his, fluttering beneath closed lids, fanned with thick, dark curls of lashes. His fingers never tighten, his hands a firm foundation on my hips for me to allow myself to fall into. Strong. Stable. Secure. *Safe.*

"I always feel safe with you, Thorne," I whisper, my lips brushing his with every word, but I don't close the space, not brave enough to initiate a real kiss.

I lick my lips, catching his with the tip of my tongue, a low growl rumbling in his chest. He needs the control, and I think, perhaps, I just need him. I drop my attention to his shoulder, puncture wounds, bruising, drying blood. I let my lips pluck gently at the lacerations, no teeth, no sucking, no violence, just tender, light pecks of my lips peppering his wounds. His fingers drive into my hip bones, harder and harder with every press of my mouth, slow, drawn out lick of my tongue. Pain rattles around inside my skull, my body in *agony*, but with him, I don't care enough to let it stop me. I just want his hands on me in any capacity I can get them.

"I never liked to be touched," he says quietly, his calmly spoken confession having me draw back, his fingers tightening into a harsh pinch. "Do not stop, Little Cub." One of his large hands smooths up my spine, "Keep going," he encourages, but I hesitate, tilting my head back to catch his eye, "I like *your* hands on me, baby girl."

I shiver, his hand firm, growing bolder, secure over the centre of my spine, he holds me to him, pulling me into his chest, and only when our bare skin touches do I remember just how exposed I am, my spine stiffening almost immediately.

"Nu-uh," Thorne hushes, "It is just me," he says, widening his legs.

Both of us sat on our haunches, he pulls me between his thighs, my knees and shins scuffing over the cold stone floor.

"Touch makes me…" he hums, eyes still on mine, "Itch."

I huff a laugh, momentarily dropping my gaze, before refocusing my attention on him, his lips curled up in an almost smile.

"I do not like the feel of things on my skin," he watches me, giving me something, a piece of him. "Mess, dirt, mud," I wince at the reminder of the day I crawled in the mud, reaching for a dying fox, the horror on his handsome face. "I like things to be in their rightful places, it makes me feel…" he glances away, a soft crease between his brows.

One I reach up to smooth out with my thumb, letting my hand drop to his chest when his gaze turns back to me.

"Uncomfortable, I suppose now," he blinks, canting his head. "I do not really like people," he confesses next, and I feel myself blush when I nod my head slowly in agreement.

"Me neither," I whisper, heat rising in my cheeks.

Until you.

Neither one of us says it, but I feel it, the way it flows through his touch, and I hope he hears it inside his head, my voice, my words.

"I have spent a lifetime adjusting to others' expectations, to social and societal normalities, but I am not-" he pauses suddenly, a little tense before it dissolves, his words confident. "I am not comfortable with them. The way it is expected of me, to behave, to think *normally*... it is all just something I cannot quite grasp."

I tilt my head, watch his face, study his perfect appearance, godlike and demonic all rolled into one.

"I do not feel that way with you."

It's a statement, strong and honest and true. The feeling echoes around inside my hollow chest, heart thudding faster with it. His feeling, matching my own. A testament to our time here, forced together by circumstance, trapped in a small space, never able to be anything but ourselves. There's no place to hide here.

"I have a lot of siblings," I say, stating something I'm sure he already knows, everyone knows my family in this world. "Lots of noise. Everyone always shouts over one another. There's lots of bodies, the house is always crowded and overwhelming, and there's not really any of them that I even like."

"None of them?" Thorne murmurs, gently coaxing, I swallow, his fingers caressing my skin.

"Not really, 'cept my big brother Cillian. Well, half-brother, we're all mixed in our house, different mams," I shrug unashamedly, my father has seven wives, countless mistresses, it is not so unusual in the mob. "He'll make a good leader one day," I flash my eyes onto his, "Better," I finish instead, "He'll be better."

Thorne hums in quiet agreement, his eyes never once leaving mine.

"But I don't feel comfortable with any of them," I tell him vulnerably. "No one." Letting my eyes flicker between his, I confess, "Only you."

Thorne stares at me, his gaze penetrating, he briefly drops his gaze, breaking the intensity of our moment.

"Shower time, Little Cub," he says quietly, "Need to get him off you."

I nod, his hands loosening before falling away, he stands first, the hard bulge in his tight boxers level with my face, I drop my gaze, his hand there, once again, to guide me up. It's the first time I hear it, the shower spray. A gasp whooshing through my parted lips, the shower being on all this time.

"Thorne, the water," I say, watching a cloud of steam float along the ceiling, drifting out of the open door.

That's when I feel the icy coolness of the room too, a shudder making my teeth chatter.

"It's cold," I mutter, hunching my shoulders forward, curling into myself, my body feeling a little numb, and I'm grateful for it in the moment, not to feel pain.

"Come," Thorne says, his hand beneath the water, "In you get," his smooth voice quiet.

I take his offered hand, allowing him to hold my weight, lifting one achy leg and then the other over the lip of the bath. The shower spray instantly hammering down over my head, making me hiss as it assaults my new bruises. The water soaks over my head, my hair saturating, I squeeze my eyes closed tight, my arms tightening inwards, my teeth chatter, lip wound pulsing in time with my heart.

Shower curtain rings click as they shimmy across the rail, my eyes flashing open. Thorne opposite me, his body so big and imposing, even in the dark you can make out his beauty, but he's still silent, his movements to join me untraceable. Reaching across the small space between us, the white plastic curtain closing us in, he pinches the end of my scraggly braid, pulls the elastic hair tie free and slides it over his swollen knuckles, raw and bloodied for me, snapping the thin elastic around his wrist.

I bite my bottom lip, the top one so fucking painful it makes tears gather in my eyes, but I'm so… *happy* about it being there, that it makes more tears form. I hold the sound inside, the sob a lump in the centre of my chest, the salty water clinging to my lashes washing away with the hard spray of the shower. Thorne's fingers work through my plait, freeing my curls. My eyes study his shoulder, the dark bloom of mauve, the puncture wounds he assures me aren't deep. But they must hurt, inexplicably so.

"What do they feel like?" I find myself asking, my voice sounding far away, the pound of the water hitting the knotted muscles in my shoulders.

My hand lifts between us, fingertips gliding over the gouges, maybe half an inch in length, paper thin slices, there's hardly any blood, and none of them are jagged or uneven, they're neat. It makes my lips curl, wondering about Thorne's reaction to them.

"They're tidy," I say quietly, and I feel his muscles uncoil, glancing up at him, his dark eyes black in the shadows. "Neat," I say, stroking my fingers over them. "Five of them," I glide my thumb over each one. "Do you think they need stitches or something," I wonder aloud, more to myself than Thorne.

"Glue," he answers quietly, his body so steady, I think about touch, his aversion to it.

'I like your hands on me, baby girl'.

Dropping my hand, I step into him, bold and unafraid, but nervous, our skin almost brushing.

"Let me do it?" I whisper the question, my face tilted up.

He glances down at me, not dipping his chin, his eyes almost shuttered closed as his eyeballs drop to the very bottom of their sockets to peer down at me.

"Shower, Little Cub," he instructs me, his hands slowly coming to my upper arms, directing me back under the water.

I wince as he does, the flow too harsh. And then suddenly he's spinning me around in his hold, his front plastering over my back, his heat making me shiver, that's when I feel the hard cock pressing into my spine. I gasp so hard I almost splutter on air, but neither one of us addresses it.

His hands drift beneath the water, one going to the soap tray. I watch as he lathers the white bar, foaming bubbles, between his tan fingers, and then those hands are on me. Palming my throat, thumb and forefinger smoothing down my jaw to the tip of my chin. Suds gliding down my chest, his other hand flat, fingers splaying, over the softness of my belly.

"I need to get it off," Thorne speaks directly into my ear, a shiver wracking through me. "*Him*," he growls lowly. "No one else is going to touch you," he rumbles, his usually smooth voice, rough and dangerous. "*Ever.*"

I swallow down his words, let him continue soaping up my skin, the harsh spray pounding down over him instead, a light spray of it dusting me as he works. Thorne's warm hands rub over me, methodically, making sure he doesn't miss any single part of me. Clinically he runs a hand between my legs, thumb sweeping over my inner thigh, I grit my teeth, close my eyes, heat racing down my chest. His hand moves in front of me again, fingers reaching for shampoo, my bottle's green, his is black, and it's that one he places a large dollop of in his opposite hand, working it through my lengths, following it up with his own conditioner.

I smell like him, his soap, his shampoo, his skin pressed against my own. I mull over his words from tonight, whispers of safety and ownership. Something I don't understand, my time here is still just that, *time.* Limited. And now one of my father's favourite lackeys is dead. Worry courses through me, Thorne's hands still washing my skin. Fear seizes me, an uncomfortable clenching in my stomach, crease twitching between my brows. The repercussions for this are going to be severe. My father's going to find out.

We switch places when he hums, satisfied I'm clean, his hands turning me gently under the spray. He clasps the soap in his hands as the water washes the suds away, but I take it from his hands, lathering it in my own, blinking water from my tired eyes. His wavy black hair sticking to his forehead, he cocks his head, watching me as I copy him.

"May I?" I whisper, flicking my eyes between his.

Subtle nod enough, I run my hands across his hard chest, muscles tensing in his pecs as I rub my fingers in small circles. Using the palm of my hand, I wash his wound, making sure I get all the dried blood. My fingers run down the valley of his abs, soap suds bubbling over the ripples of muscle.

I keep my eyes averted from his, focused on the task, smoothing from shoulders to forearms to swollen knuckles. Knuckles swollen to save me, I dip my head, at the same time I lift his hand. Limp in my own, his fingers relaxed and curled over mine, I press a kiss to them, slow, tender pecks with my swollen lips. I run my mouth over each one, down the length of his fingers, over the curve of his thumb, veins and tendons ridged beneath the skin.

His breathing is as ragged as mine when I finally release his fist, letting it go by his side. Using more soap, I move to my knees, wash his feet, dragging slow circles up his calves, back of his knees. My arms reach up, roving over the coarse hair of his thighs, I can feel him watching me, muscles flexing, his hands clenched into tight fists at his sides. I glance up, just slightly, brave enough to finally look, hidden in the darkness. His cock stands out from his body, long and thick and *so* hard, the breath rushes out of me, making it twitch and I drop my gaze again. Licking my lips, I reach up, heel of my hand brushing over his sack, he shudders, and then my fingers are closing around his shaft, running, just once, from root to tip, feeling every raised vein in his length, before moving to his hip bones.

"You're done," I say quietly when I stand, twisting out of his way so he can wash off under the spray, the water quickly cooling.

Silently, he does as instructed, watching me as I select the green bottle of shampoo, a smile curling my lips.

"Turn," I whisper, watching as he abides, and then I lather *my* shampoo in his hair, leaving him to smell a little like me, as I do, him.

CHAPTER 21
THORNE

I wrap her short curvy body up in a large white bath towel. A smaller towel twisted low on my own hips, the fabric of hers so large it drags over the floor, draping over her from shoulders to toes. I rub my hands over her upper arms, her teeth chattering, I lead her up the steps, out into the hall, pausing briefly to check the door leading into the lighthouse. She watches me as I wander back to her, gloom and shadows and tension sitting heavily between us.

Silently, she steps down into the bedroom, cardboard box on the far side of the mattress, I pause on the top step, eyeing it with something like envy, knowing that what is inside of it requires her rapt attention more than I do. It simmers, though, the jealousy, rather than boils, but I wonder if I am just too tired to let myself fully feel it. But then I think of her hand wrapped around my cock, slippery and wet, tight, and I let the simmering dissolve.

Haisley fusses with the creature, one arm sneaking out from inside of her towel, reaching into the box, then she lifts it, closing a cardboard flap over the top and placing it down on the floor.

Slowly, she turns back to face me, my jaw clenched. This is where we part. Every night is the same. I make sure she is safely tucked in from my place in the hall, letting the darkness of the old house envelop me in its shadows, waiting until I hear her first deep breaths, then I sit in the chair in the front room, think of what I should be doing. All the ways I should kill her, *could*, fast, slow, with pleasure, pain, and then always decide to put it off for just one more day. Closing my eyes for a restless sleep, ears always open and alert, listening for her movements.

"Thorne?" she murmurs, shifting her weight from one foot to the other.

I cannot see her fat lip from here, but I know it is there, a mark of mine, and a swell of something like ownership rises in my chest. She did not get upset, or tell me to stop, no complaints or hesitation, if anything, she leaned into my bite, and it made me want to tear her open.

"Into bed," I say quietly, the same words I speak every night, but she doesn't move, standing still at the foot of the bed, dressed in dark sheets.

"Could you…" she shifts again, I suspect uncomfortably, I picture the flush in her cheeks, the heat of her skin, everywhere else cool to the touch. "Please," she whispers, "Will you stay with me?"

I contain the deep growl attempting to rip its way up my throat, locking it inside my chest, imprisoning it behind my ribcage. I take the two steps down into the room, my skin prickling with goosebumps at the low temperature inside the house. I step up to her, her head dropped forward, hands fisting the inside of her towel, keeping it closed. My fingers glide down her jaw, feeling the swelling beneath my fingertips, I swallow, fighting the urge to press into it, make it hurt.

"Not tonight," I whisper, hooking a knuckle beneath her chin, guiding her attention upwards until her gaze settles on mine.

I smooth my thumb up her jaw, fan my fingers over the side of her neck, behind her ear, thumb pressing to the top of her cheekbone. Then I dip my chin, press my lips to the centre of her forehead, breathing deep, she shudders beneath me, as I inhale her scent, mixed with mine, it makes me want to claw my way inside of her, mark her on the inside as well as on the outside. And then I step back, my hand falling away from her face.

It is only later on, when I am back out in the hall, my clothes pulled on, her deep breaths evened out and steady in the bedroom, that I slide down the wall beside the open door and let myself indulge in the sounds of her slumber.

It is after lunchtime when I tell her.

We seem to have skirted around one another for most of the day. She applied glue to my shoulder just before breakfast, delicately pinching the severed skin together. I checked her lip, her head, the multitude of bruises decorating her skin, shins and stomach, seeming to have taken the brunt of it.

I think about it all day. The Doyles, Shane, The Kellys. How, I cannot understand, why, Shane would come here, watching me for God knows how long. What possessed him to check up on any of my work. Was it just his hate for this girl, the one currently sat on my living room floor, curled up beneath a quilted blanket she wears around her shoulders like a cape? I wonder who he might have told, despite what he said to Haisley. But it does not take me long to decide on nobody. There is no way, because he would not have come here alone, he would have tracked me, found out the truth and destroyed me and her with his selected reinforcements before we even had time to blink.

Shane was close with Cian, that much I do know from various clean ups, the two of them always making the most mess on a job, thick as thieves. I need to find out what happened between them, Cian and Haisley.

"Haisley," I say her name quietly, closing my leather journal, gold pen resting inside its pages.

She twists her head on her shoulders, peering up at me where I sit in the armchair. Legs crossed, ankle resting atop my knee, I drop my leg down, shift forward, forearms on my knees.

"I need to go to my family," I say quietly, watching

her big green eyes widen further. "It will not take long, but I..." I lick my lips, glance to the fire beyond her. "I need one of my brothers to come and help with the body."

I watch her take it all in, eyes wide, growing glassy, she starts to shake her head, turning to face me. She clambers to her feet, the quilt slipping from her shoulders, black leggings, one of my black button-up shirts drowning her. I like seeing her in my clothes.

"No, no, *no,*" she pleads, and I did not know what her reaction may be, I thought it would be negative, but in my head, it was not quite this. "Please, *please,* Thorne, don't go, can't you just call them here? I'll help! Tell me what to do, teach *me.*" She lunges forward, not hesitating in grasping my shirt in her hands, fingers curling into the fabric, she drops to her knees at my feet. "Please, don't leave me here."

"Haisley," I say gently, my hands coming up, prying her fingers free of my shirt. "I will be back, and I promise you, you will be safe here."

"No, *no,*" she cries, a single tear slipping down her swollen cheek, the skin blotchy and red, bleeding beneath the skin, matching the purple marking along her jaw, her chin, split with a small gash. "I don't want to be here alone, take me with you."

"Shh," I whisper.

Taking both of her hands into one of mine, drawing them to one side, resting them on my thigh. I lean forward in the chair, slide a lock of her hair behind her ear with my free hand, smooth my thumb gently across her cheekbone.

"It is going to be all right," my eyes flicker between hers, a second tear joining the first.

I lean into her, keep her hands locked in one of mine, ignoring her struggles to break free, her frustrated huff of breath at my easy overpowering of her. I dip my head, brush my nose over hers, she stills instantly at the contact. Her breathing sharp in her chest. The flat of my tongue glides up her cheek, lapping at her tear, salty and sharp, a slight tang of copper still present on her skin. I drop my mouth to hers, tenderly and affection-ately, brush my lips over her split one, think of the scar it could leave, *my* mark. I shudder then, drawing back just enough to catch her eye.

"I know you do not want me to go," I murmur, my waist bending far forward to hold eye contact. "I need to take care of something so that I can get back to you. It is not safe for you to come with me." I swallow, "You and I both know that," I whisper, watching the resignation settle in her features.

She looks up at me from beneath pale lashes, big jade eyes watery, her chin trembling, and gives me a single nod.

"Such a good girl for me," I murmur, wanting nothing more than to devour her lips, but I do not have time, nor do I have the control to keep it at just that. Instead, I say, "I want us to talk tonight," her scent mixed with my wash products driving me just a little bit insane, I feel a little high off of it. "Wait up for me?" her eyes light up like fucking Christmas trees with that, this time yesterday I was telling her she had better be in bed by the time I got back, and I spent the entire conversation trying hard not to stare at her pout. "Can you do that for me?"

She nods then, enthralled, focused on my words, my face, lost in me, I hold her every ounce of attention, and it is a heady feeling.

The control a thrill.

"Words, Little Cub," because I love the way she says my name.

"Yes, Thorne," she whispers, making my dick twitch in my pants.

"Good girl."

With the entire Blackwell clan gathered around Heron Mill's kitchen table, it should feel comfortable, safe, my brothers, my stepsister, Dad. This is where we can each be our true selves, where we can indulge in the darkness, not worrying about what anyone on the outside of the family might think.

Tonight, though, I feel edgy.

I have Ivy St. Clair, one of the most discrete chop shop mechanics around, collecting and crushing Shane's car. His body is in the boot of my own, and I cannot stop thinking about it rotting too much before I am finished with it. It is going to stink the whole car out.

I can feel my brother Wolf's eyes on me, singeing my skin with his wonder. I want to escape, the uncomfortable feeling prickling the back of my neck, but I stay planted in my seat, avoid any unnecessary questions, looks, glares. So I avoid Wolf's stare altogether, focus my gaze on my father, listen to the discussion at the table happening around me. When the conversation is over, the decision on my stepsister Grace meeting her supposed biological father, *after* a DNA test, settled, everyone clears out of the room.

"Brother," I say as coolly as I can, a little hint at the ever-growing tension inside me slipping through.

Wolf tenses as I speak, his warm amber eyes locked on my own, I see my mother every time I look at him and it makes my skin itch. Everything else about him is thankfully different though. He has got a good few inches on me, six-six, broad and muscular, skin tight over bulging muscle, hours' worth of intense workouts earning them. His chin-length black hair is pulled up on top of his head, a looped bun sitting on his crown, some strands in the front tucked behind his pierced ears.

The table stands between us, hands tucked inside my slack pockets, he eyed them at the table, they are not too red or swollen today thanks to the icing I gave them. Nothing obvious about what I did, just last night, showing over the white crisscross of scars already present. What it is I *have* done, though, is still a blurred war inside my head.

"What's going on, Thorne?" Wolf asks, voice rumbling like a cave echo straight into my ears, making my nose twitch just barely, but I know he catches it.

He leans back against the copper sink, stares at me across the space, and lifts a hand towards his face, traces a line down the side of his neck with his finger. The same spot on my own neck burns, the reminder of Haisley's clawing as I thrust my tongue inside her mouth.

Stupid.

My injured shoulder jumps, pain rattling down the bone, I did not make a big deal out of the injury, but it aches like a motherfucker today. The skin tight with glue, too much, but *she* did it for me, and I find myself not minding so much.

I step further into the room, removing myself from my static place in the arched entrance to the kitchen. My shoes tapping lightly over the old, worn stone floor. I sweep a hand down the front of my black shirt, buttons bumping over my palm, hands free of my pockets. I step up beside my brother, less than a year separating us, we have always been very close, the two of us the oldest. He has always been patient with me, even as my younger brother. And after Mum decided my *compulsions* were all a bit too much for her to handle, he supported me, made me feel less *strange*. He is the only one I do not completely hide myself from, he never treats me like I am different.

I lay my hands flat down on the counter, eye the slivers of cuts across my knuckles I had not analysed well earlier. My head drops forward of my shoulders, and I inhale a short, deep breath.

"Thorne?"

"I need your help with something. No one else can know," I peer at him from the corner of my eye, waiting for his reaction.

"Okay…" he says slowly, carrying the word out.

"I need you to come with me somewhere and help me with a body," I state quietly, as calmly as I can, despite feeling a little unbalanced.

"Why is this a secret, Thorne?" he questions quietly, frowning, we do not tell lies in this family.

"Because of *who* it is," I state, my words hard, my jaw ticks, thinking of Shane, of his filthy fucking hands on what is *mine*.

His mouth parts, then closes, a silent question on his lips, one he is building the courage to voice, a crease of tension knitting his brows.

"Who is it, Thorne?"

I watch him, expressionless, before I confess, "Shane O'Sullivan."

His lips pop open then, mouth too wide to be anything but shock, and I know what he is thinking, the panic, but he has not heard the half of it yet. My brother is going to be so mad. I see the moment he is going to speak, so I cut in before he has the chance.

"You can't ask any questions."

"The *fuck?* Thorne, I-"

"Really, Wolf, you need to trust me on this one, no one will find out it was me, no one will ever know," of this, I am sure.

He sighs hard, but I am not finished.

"This isn't a disposal," I inform him, the idea forming suddenly crystal clear inside my head.

"I'm sorry, what other help is needed with a *body*, that *isn't a disposal*. What in the fuck does that even mean?"

"It means we're going to collect the body and we're going to make a statement with it."

"Why do you have that?" Wolf asks me warily, running a hand over his tied hair.

He was not happy about collecting Shane's body from the boot of my car and transferring it into another of the family's vehicles, just so I could drive straight back to Rook Point after we are done here.

Silence on the reasoning *why* did not go down all that well either.

I eye the bone saw in my leather gloved hand, the silver metal glinting in the occasional flash of the full moon, more heavy rain clouds passing over it. As I bring the blade up, I lick my lips, think of the bone deep ache in my shoulder and internally wince, this is going to hurt me more than Shane fucking O'Sullivan.

Without another word, I lean forward, wrench the body in the trunk of the old car forward, thick plastic sheeting beneath it. I yank his head back with my hand in his hair, his face almost unrecognisable, skull concave, my fists having successfully pummelled his bone structure into dust. I flex my knuckles, tight, sore skin stretching over them, the smallest splits in the already scarred flesh.

When his head is hanging over the back bumper, neck stretched out, tarpaulin sheeting beneath him, covering the paintwork, I line up my saw with his Adam's apple and start carving my way through.

"Jesus Christ, Thorne!" Wolf hisses, his voice in my ear, where we both huddle close over the car.

Force is the only way to drive the saw through, my muscles burning after the activities of last night. I hear Wolf at my side, but I cannot make out his words, focusing my thoughts instead, on the girl this man laid his hands on. Something I will not, *cannot* forgive. Corpse or no corpse, this is a message, to the entirety of the Irish mafia, the five leading families, The Kellys, Doyles, Murphys, Byrnes, O'Neills, and anyone else who needs to witness it.

None of them are untouchable.

"Get the cleaner, Wolf," I mutter absentmindedly, feeling blood slipping off of the plastic sheeting, splatting on the tarmac at my feet, the icy temperature assaults me in a gust of wind as he moves away.

Spreading my feet further apart, fleshy pieces flicking up as I carve my way through his neck. Tendon and bone and flesh making wet snicking sounds, the teeth of the blade snagging bone as I force my way through his vertebrae.

Wolf returns just as I curl my fingers through Shane's short hair, his lifeless eyes yellowing in their sockets. I tilt my head, a slick smugness flushing through my veins, revealing itself in a sick smirk, I could not hide if I tried, curling my lips.

"Now what?" he grunts lowly, eyes flicking over our surroundings as I flick my own up onto his.

He looks down at me, the blackness of the night discolouring his amber eyes, reminding me more of our father than our mother and I find it easier to push thoughts of her away.

"There is a metal pike on the back seat."

"Of fucking course there is," he exhales, not waiting for directive to retrieve it, he stalks around the side of the car, pulling open the door and bringing it out. "There's cameras," he mutters quietly.

We are deep in Irish territory here, there are likely ears everywhere, despite where we are. One of The Kelly's safe houses, usually filled with drugs and cash, sometimes other items of interest. It is not armed like some of their other, higher priced locations, but it is their largest in size, I want them to know I am not afraid.

"Now," I say, straightening up, wiping my leather gloved hands on a dark coloured towel, before throwing it back inside the trunk. "I am going to place this head, on that pike," gesturing at the long metal pole in my brother's hand with my own. "And plant it in the centre of their perfectly manicured lawn."

"Thorne," Wolf says anxiously, a thread of worry revealing itself in the soft squint of his eyes. "What's this about?" it looks like he wants to reach out, touch me, knowing he cannot, *will not.*

I think about her enthralling jade eyes, wide and watery and wet, the bruising on her perfect skin, those fawn coloured freckles obscured from my view with purple plumes of blood gathering beneath the surface of her skin.

"Do not worry about the cameras," I say instead, avoiding the truth, by offering up this one instead. "They are already looping."

"Thorn-"

"When I walk away from here, you clean the tarmac, get in the car and go straight back to Cardinal House," I lick my lips, taste iron and salt and grit my teeth at the taste of this piece of shit. "Get rid of everything, tonight."

"This isn't my first fucking job, Thorne," he growls lowly, a thrumming vibration of threat in his wide chest.

"It is better you do not know everything, brother," I glance at him, side eyeing him as he swallows down his rebuttal, offering me a nod of understanding instead.

"Keys," he mutters, pulling my car key from his pocket, slipping into mine, the ones for this vehicle still in the ignition. "I don't care what you say," he says then, watching as I heave Shane's decapitated head up into my arms. "I'm waiting until I see you get away. We're Blackwells and we don't leave each other behind."

It is a programming. That phrase, the thought, provocation behind it, it has been tangled up in our DNA since the very first generation of Blackwells were born hundreds of years ago. It is just this generation, though, that I think, truly feels it.

Our uncle, our cousins, more Blackwells, Dad's brother and his four boys, they do not share the same beliefs, feelings, about the family business, as we do. It is why Dad introduced the one thing we all live and swear by, *Blackwells do not tell lies.* His brother would scoff at that. It is why I worry about Raine visiting their establishments, The Crypt being one of many.

I swallow, heart swelling, the love I have for my brothers steeling my spine. I look into his eyes, face hard, and nod.

It only takes a moment to find the perfect spot on the front lawn, creeping from the shadows. Large red brick house looming, all of the front windows in darkness, I am bold, stepping straight out onto the grass.

Head clutched beneath one arm, pike in the other hand. I slam it into the earth, soft from all the rain, close my fingers around the pike and push it in deep, checking its stability by shaking the top of it. Sure that it is not going to topple to the ground with added weight, I grip Shane's head between my hands. Glance up at the darkened house, think of the hell he put *my* fucking girl through last night and slam his skull down onto the spiked end of the pike.

Without wasting another second, I walk around the head, keep my pace strong and even, and make my way back to the car that Wolf is waiting in. Sliding into the passenger seat, he starts pulling away as soon as my door is closing, he drives us back to my car in silence. I can feel the questions, the confusion, I am not sure I have ever not told him something before, and I do not know how he feels about that, but my mind is loud, and I need for it to be quiet. That, too, is something he knows.

When we make it back to my car, I unclip my seatbelt, but I do not move, taking a few breaths, sensory overload crippling. Wolf waits patiently, his big hands loose on the wheel, gaze peering out into the dark, a light drizzle now dusting the windscreen.

"Thank you," I say quietly, my eyes, too, locked on the view through the front window.

"I wanna help," he says next, rough voice low, "If you'll let me." He sniffs hard, turns his gaze onto me, "If you need me, Thorne…"

It is an open-ended offer, one I would offer him, we have and will always have, each other's backs.

"I will tell you if I need you."

He nods, turning back to face out of the front window. I get out of the car, walk around the back bumper of it, disappearing into the hollow of trees to get into my own. I watch Wolf's taillights disappear before starting my engine and then I veer off in the opposite direction to get back home.

CHAPTER 23
HAISLEY

Gravel crunches beneath car tyres, my nerves have been like a frazzled electrical cable the entire time Thorne's been gone. And just because this vehicle has pulled up outside at a slow speed, seemingly unurgent, does not mean it is Thorne.

I place Clover down in his box, the name I decided on because he's lucky. His little whiskers painted white with a dribble of milk, he yawns, stretching his front feet out of his cocoon of white towel, he wriggles around until nothing but his snout is poking out. Pushing to my feet, I place the little milk syringe down on the couch cushion, sweep my hands down my thighs, thick black tracksuit swamping me, but it smells like Thorne, and I wonder why, because I have never, and probably will never, see Thorne in a tracksuit.

I step up beside the front door, my back pressing to the wall, hiding me from view when it opens. I stare at the orange glow cast from the fire, spearing out over the dark wood flooring, watching for his shadow to take form. When it does, my breath leaving me heavily, I sag forward a little, step out from my hiding place as he closes the door at his back.

He doesn't turn to look at me right away, but he knows I'm here, he always knows, always feels me there, in the same way I always feel him. His shoulders are high, spine stiff and his breath is hardly noticeable. I find I hate it, in the moment, the tenseness of him, the strain of the day. I know he took Shane's body away when he went to see his family, I watched from the open door as he threw the corpse into his boot. He turned, his dark eyes on me, and then he rounded the car, drove away.

We didn't speak about it, about last night, what happened, what he said, the pretty words he blurted out in the heat of the moment. Ones I wish he hadn't given life to, hope an unfurling thorned thing inside my chest cavity, pricking and bruising and bleeding the sensitive organ caged there. I want it to be true, the things he said, the way they made me feel.

My face is buried in his back, torn lip smushed against his spine, before I even have time to really think anything through. My arms come up between us, fingers curling into fists in the back of his shirt, the soft black fabric bunching between my knuckles. I breathe him in, the scent of chemicals threading through his own, metal, leather, salt. Danger, storms and sea. All of it easing my taut muscles, the stress in my head quieting.

"I was worried about you," I murmur, my lips brushing his shirt.

"I told you I would be fine."

A statement, factual, clearly, because he looks perfectly fine.

"I was still worried," I swallow down the whisper, far too much vulnerability in my words.

His body only stiffens more, the longer I cling onto him, and I feel like a piece of shit when I let go, release his now crinkled shirt.

"I'm sorry." Heat flares bright in my cheeks, staring guiltily at the creased fabric.

"I think we need to talk," Thorne says, his words cold, something I thought we were moving past.

His gaze on the room, mine on his back. He steps away from me, and I take a further step back, swallowing hard, worry flooding my insides. I was looking forward to him coming back, I feel *safe* when he's here and he takes care of me and I realise, I think I've forgotten what it is that I am doing here. I feel stupid, realising it, this weird false sense of security I seem to keep coiling around myself. I am just a death in waiting. Thorne is just the killer taking his time to strike. That is all we ever should have been to one another, and it feels unfair, like much of my life, that a man like this has been given to me, only to be taken away. To imagine what it could have been like, had this man, maybe wanted me, is the worst torture of them all.

"I am conflicted," he says to the room, drawing me back in with the smooth intensity of his voice.

I am flush with the wall now, back arched away, hands flat against the icy stone, so cold it feels damp beneath my clammy palms. He turns, so slightly, to peer at me over his shoulder, those dark eyes pinning me in place.

"I have never not followed an order before," he says lowly, his mouth hidden behind his shoulder, the one I glued together just this morning.

I made a mess, and I think I used too much adhesive, but he didn't say anything about it as my cold hands pinched together his warm skin. He just watched me, his gaze intent on my face, it made me flush hot all over, but I never once glanced up at him.

"Rebellion does not come simply to me, Haisley, you understand?" he queries quietly.

Trapping us in that fragile bubble of gloom again, instantly making me feel safer, despite not knowing where this will lead. It's in his most dangerous moments that I find myself feeling the safest, even when that danger is directed at me.

"Yes," I answer, my voice, too, quiet. "I understand, Thorne."

"My brain does not work in the same way as everyone else's; it needs to count, to know everything is clean, to have-"

"Control," I whisper, finishing his sentence for him, fingertips clawing into the rough, painted surface of the wall, its chill creeping its way down my spine.

"Yes," he whispers in agreement, and it's as though his voice claws its way inside of me with desperate relief, coiling through the vertebrae of my spine like thick, coarse rope, binding. "Come here," he breathes.

The fire crackles and spits beside us, its flames dancing across his shadowed features. My feet take me to him before I give myself even a moment to decide. He turns to face me as I step up to him, nerves alight with unease. His hands not touching, they glide over the outline of my body, as if he's feeling out my shape, my presence. His chest is heaving where my gaze is focused, unable to bring myself to look into his eyes, sometimes they make me feel like I'm drowning in them when I stare for too long.

"I do not know how to navigate this," his chest inflates slowly, deflating even slower, "What has been happening here... Last night," he pauses, "Last night should never have happened," he says, just like that, and another little piece of me fractures.

I knew this was coming, and yet, I think, perhaps, I still hoped...

"He never should have been able to follow me. I should have been safer, more observant, cautious. I was sloppy," he sighs guiltily, my eyes filling with tears, "I hate that you got hurt."

I glance up then, resigned to my fate, the reason I was placed in this beautiful man's hands finally becoming real, more than an idea, a job, something dark and scary, but also much like relief. This is the cresting moment.

"But what I regret most of all, Little Cub," he says

in a rasp, my eyes closing at the use of his endearment for me.

I think of our kiss, the tender touches, our silence in the gloom. The way he obliterated me with his mouth, tore me open, squeezed my heart, made me really *feel*.

"Is that I waited so long to admit to myself that I am in love with you, Haisley Kelly, and I will raze the world for you, if you so wish it."

Heart thrashing in my chest, I blink, glance up, his hand moves between us, knuckle hooking beneath my chin, he steps in closer, body almost flush with mine, but not quite, his breath a warm tickle on my skin.

"You are someone finally seeing me and not rejecting it." I bite back my sob, tears splashing down my cheeks. "I am going to ruin you. And I am not sorry."

There is silence between us, it feels cold and thick and heavy, but light and warm at the same time. There is always tension here, between us, an unspoken, looming thing, something that has been ready to snap for what feels like an eternity.

How far do I push, push back, submit?

How far will he go, push, push back, dominate?

Thorne needs carefully crafted control, I can offer him that. I am naturally more docile, and The Kelly men have been carefully crafting a submissive mafia princess out of me since the day I left the womb. I rebelled against it my entire life, but with Thorne, I want to give it, my submission.

It is reckless, the moment his teeth clash into mine,

fury and power and pain. His body slams into me like a battering ram, his arms banding around my waist, keeping me on my feet, crushing my softness to him. His lips are soft, movements firm on mine, his tongue persistent in seeking entrance, he spears it between my parted lips, licking over the sharp points of my teeth to tangle with my own.

I fall into him then, this wild, feral monster feasting on my soul through my lips, my hands work their way up between us, fingers curling into the open collar of his black shirt, fingertips on the tail end of ink. The fabric is wet in places, clinging to his skin beneath, making me pull back, forcefully breaking our kiss with a frown. He dips back in, attempting to reclaim my mouth, but I crane back further, looking down between us.

"What is this?" I murmur, lips swollen, I swallow, pulling the shirt fabric taut, trying to see it in the dark.

I flick my gaze up, glance between his dark eyes, he stares back, devouring every little piece of me. He licks his lips, tongue rolling over his bottom lip, eyes flicking down to my swollen lips, the top one split open by his teeth, before glancing back up.

"Blood."

Lowering my gaze, I swipe my fingertip through the wetness, twisting it away from his shirt to see. Red stains my pale skin, sticky and thick, and his eyes flash with want when I lock my gaze with his.

"How much blood will you spill for me, Thorne?" I breathe the question over his mouth as I raise my chin.

Body bowing towards him, folding into his chest,

letting him take my weight in his arms. I blink up at him, his hollow cheeks sharp in the gloom.

"All of it," he whispers back, lips ghosting over mine. "Every last drop," he hushes, pecking a kiss to my mouth. "From every person that has ever hurt you," he breathes long and slow, "And anyone that has ever thought about it." His dark eyes flick between my own, "But not yours. Never yours, baby girl. I am going to keep you."

I gasp, inhaling his scent, his tongue sliding over my lips, slipping inside. His big hands cradle me to him, fingertips driving into my spine like barbed hooks. I claw at his wet shirt, pulling at the buttons that hold it closed, tearing it open to push it off of his shoulders.

"I want to get it off of you," I breathe between kisses, thinking of his desperate words to me just last night, *"Him."*

Thorne's hands sweep down my back, fingers gripping the flesh of my thighs as my hands tug to unthread his belt. He lifts me up, my core grinding down his exposed abs, my hands curling over his shoulders, patterns and swirls of black ink revealing themselves under the lambent light of the fire as he moves us away from it.

From the hollow of his throat to the tip of his chin, I lick up his neck, sucking on the underside of his jaw. A low, feral sound rips from his throat, sending a vibration rolling through me, straight to the fiery heat unfurling in my core.

The bedroom door bangs open at my back, ricocheting off the wall. Thorne's hurried but controlled footsteps take us quickly down the two steps into the room. He slides me down his body, teeth grazing my throat, my hands going back to his waistband, he pauses, breath sliding down the side of my neck, caressing my shoulder with warmth as it slips beneath the thick fabric of my sweatshirt. I feel the sudden change in him, his careful control locking back into place. He lost it for a moment there, the noises he made, frantic hands with desperate touches, but that's gone now.

I understand it, but I... I swallow, throat tightening, my eyes boring holes into the wall at his back.

"Haisley," he murmurs into my skin, teeth still nipping in little teasing pinches, "I am going to shower." His hands smooth up my back, one coming to the underside of my hair, "Alone," his forearm resting along the length of my shoulder, he tangles his fingers into the curls at my nape, dragging me closer. "Get into bed," he says gently, forcing my eyes unto his.

He draws back, grip on the back of my skull, manipulating my attention onto him. He licks his lips, gaze momentarily dropping to my mouth as a bubble of blood from the wound, caught on his teeth during our kiss, dribbles over my lips. He dips his head, tongue rolling over the trail of red, sweeping over my flushed skin.

"Wait up for me," he whispers, his lips caressing mine with every formally pronounced word.

I nod, nerves taking flight in my belly, anticipation of the unknown drilling deep into my core, because this is *more*. The gloom, the small, confined space, the absence of light, our skin exposed, flesh and blood and bone. It's more intimate, private, personal. I both hate and love it. The insanity of it all setting my soul on fire. It doesn't feel like rejection, it feels like acceptance.

He undresses me, his sculpted, bruised body something crafted from the darkest sins. Defined lines of his Adonis belt peeking out from his low riding slacks, belt loose, shirt unbuttoned and skewed where it was tucked into his trousers. His warm hands slide beneath my hoodie and t-shirt, fingers crawling their way up my back as he gathers the thick layers of material in his hands, looping them up and over my head, hair whipping down my bare back. He tosses the clothes into the wooden chair in the corner, eyes burning into me, he hooks his thumbs into the rolled over, elastic waistband of my bottoms and pushes them down. Dropping to one knee, he lifts each foot, the heat from his fingers gentle and soothing over my painful muscles, bruises and injuries he already checked out last night, as he works the material free of my ankles.

He looks up then, my chin flush with my chest where I peer down at him, his black eyes firmly on mine. It's like being captured, shackled, my bones like welded iron, and until he breaks eye contact, his eyes dropping to the floor where his fist aids in pushing him to stand, I can't look away.

"Pyjamas," he instructs, and I feel the smirk that doesn't appear on his face.

My cheeks heat, but I do as he says, seeing him fully

remove his shirt from the corner of my eye, folding it neatly and placing it in the chair. Once I'm dressed, I turn to watch him peel back the bed covers, stepping back just enough for me to slide inside the sheets. He pulls them over me, covering my cold skin with the even colder sheets, and then he walks away. My eyes track him through the gloom, the bedroom door wide open, I listen as he closes the bathroom door, the room beside mine, the walls too thick to hear the rush of water start in the shower but I imagine him in there.

Pulling the curtain closed once he starts the spray, steam collecting behind the thin white plastic, billowing out over the top in dense white clouds. Thorne peeling his slacks and boxers down his legs, muscular thighs, toned calves. I think of his tattoos, how I still haven't seen them properly and I want to inspect them, dot by dot, line by line. Trace them with my fingers, *tongue.*

Legs restless and squirmy, I flip onto my back, squeeze my thighs together, black cotton pyjama pants soft on my skin. I feel warm, there's heat in my cheeks, a flush on my chest, that feels like fingers crawling down my breasts. Breathing fast, I glance at the open door, darkness beyond, fingers slipping beneath my bottoms as I eye the doorway. I glide my hand over my hip, across my pubic bone, think of Thorne in the room next door, his naked, wet body tightening as he strokes his fist along his hard shaft. *To thoughts of me.*

The thought is like a lightning bolt to my core, my finger runs down to my slit, pressing straight onto my clit. I bite back my moan, teeth clamping down on my bottom lip. Back arching, the crown of my head driving into the pillow, I trail my finger down lower between my lips, collecting the evidence of my arousal, dragging it back up to my swollen clit. Eyes wide, I stare at the door, fingertip swirling and circling, watching the darkness. My ears strain, listening for the bathroom door, and it becomes a race to finish. My mind on Thorne's dark brown eyes, framed by thick fans of lashes, big black circles that see too much. Fingers firm in their pressure, slippery and wet, I circle my clit, the heat in my pussy spreading through me.

I arch back, my eyes slipping closed, my breaths quick, sucked in through my teeth, sharp exhales through my nose. I am so close, my knees drawing up, feet flat to the mattress, my ears start to buzz and then a chill sweeps over me, like a shadow across the sun, my eyes snap open, my hand freezing.

Thorne stands in the doorway, hands tucked in his pockets, pockets of what look like black jogging bottoms. His chest bare, ridged muscles shadowed, I can see the darker patch of skin across the front of his shoulder, that I know is the purple bruising from the stab wounds, curling over his arm. His posture is as statuesque as it usually is, his dark eyes on my face, my legs start to lower, my fingers sliding up, just far enough away from where I really want them to be.

"No," he says quietly, my breath held, chest still. He cants his head in that curious, dangerous way I like so much, and then he says, gravelled voice smooth and seductive, "Keep going."

My breath rushes out of me, bent legs splaying open, knees flat to the mattress, thighs wide. Embarrassment heats me further, my cheeks must be turning crimson. But he doesn't move, he does not laugh, and I watch him, my hand paused, relaxed over my pussy. He licks his lips, teeth tucking his bottom lip between his teeth. He can't see anything, the layers of thick bed covers still smothering me, but he knows what I was doing, and my legs close, my hand sliding up the curve of my belly.

"No," he whispers then, but there's no mistaking the order, my throat working hard to swallow. "Please," he says gently, always so polite, but still not moving closer, and I'm unsure if I want him to or not. "Keep going."

My stomach clenches, core muscles curling tight, my belly jumps, and with my eyes locked on his, my mind thinking of nothing but him, I trail my hand back down, the soft sound of the shifting fabric loud in my ears.

"Such a good girl for me," he praises, it makes me jolt, his words, as my cool fingers return to the slick heat between my thighs.

I rub small circles over my swollen clit, cautiously, shyly, my heartbeat pounding in my ears. Thorne watches me without expression, his head cocked, eyes solely focused on mine. A whimper catches in my throat, my middle finger sliding between my pussy lips, slippery and wet as it comes back up to my clit.

"Show me," he breaths next, my fingers pausing again, "Push the covers back for me, Haisley."

My teeth sink into my bottom lip, the way he says

my name, gravelly and rough and desperate. It's strange, because I always think of his voice as this smooth unbreakable thing, but in reality, it's always a little gravelled, but it is so distinctive to him, that it sounds smooth all the same.

I think of the way he kissed me, ragged and filthy, his breath on my face, my neck. And I let fingers continue, my clit pulsing like it has its own heartbeat.

Breathing hard, chest swelling, I put the flat of my free hand against the weight of the blankets and fold them back before I have time to think about it too hard. Icy air chills me instantly, Thorne's eyes slide down my body, my nipples puckering beneath my loose t-shirt, the band of exposed skin between my top and bottoms, hand slipped beneath them.

I watch him watching me, my eyes heavy, adjusted to the dark, so I can see him through the gloom. He licks his lips, his hands retreating from his pockets, to hang loose by his sides, he takes a single step down, further into the room but still too far away. I want his hands on my flesh, he is always so warm, his skin both soft and rough, a conflicting touch, but he is always firm with it, too harsh, the pinch on my skin something I find myself craving more and more. My back arches then, and my neck cranes back, the crown of my head driving hard into the pillow, and I feel it crest, that sudden rush of heat-

"Stop."

It's a crack through the air, my chest stilling, breath held, I slump down to the mattress, my fingers obeying his barked order before my brain even has time to register.

He takes another step down, one more and his bare feet would finally touch down on the wooden flooring, but he doesn't take that step. He glances down my body, hidden beneath my dark coloured clothing, the darkness of the room shielding me too. It's too much, to be in this position, my fingers flexing with the need to finish, to come for this dangerous man, share an orgasm with him, without him even touching me, but he is the biggest part of it despite that.

I have never touched myself to thoughts of another man before.

"I want to watch you come," he says quietly, almost innocently, despite his dirty words.

Black eyes like vortexes, fingers loose at his sides, uncurled, seemingly relaxed, but I can see the hardness of his cock bulging in the front of his jogging bottoms.

"Will you let me see?"

His head is still cocked, his chin dipping, eyes flicked up through his lashes, even though he stares down at me, it is dark and intimidating and I want him closer. The heat, the danger, all of it flooding this room in great swirling waves.

I am drowning.

Using both hands, shyness flaming in my cheeks, embarrassment so thick you could choke on it, I push my pyjama pants down, exposing my bare flesh beneath. I look away as I gently kick my legs free, unable to watch him watching me when I'm so exposed, no longer lost in the heat of the moment. I keep my legs tight together, thighs squeezing, my hands down by my sides, fisting the soft sheet beneath. They are different to the ones that were here when we first arrived, not scratchy or rough or worn, fresh and new and soft.

I have a moment of panic, because I feel suspended, in the unknown, that thin veil between life and death feels like it's looming again, and I wonder which side of the knife this is pushing me further toward.

"Were you thinking of me, Little Cub?" he asks quietly, a strain to his tone, but his body is soft and relaxed even in his rigid posture.

I stare at him, too much of me exposed, tongue dry in my mouth, I can't find the words to confess, but the blush of my skin, even in the dark, is enough of an answer.

"I like that you were," he whispers, it sounds cold, but it feels like restraint, and I find myself flushing even hotter. "I think of you," he whispers, and it's like a shock to the heart, something I didn't know I wanted to hear, lighting up my insides. "Just like this."

His head tilts further, so curious, so boyish. He is older than me, that much is obvious. I don't know by how much, but it feels as if this man has lived an entire life before me. The thought makes my blood run cold, something inside of me rejecting the idea that Thorne had a life before me. It feels like jealousy, and I quickly find myself heating up all over again.

"Just like this," he repeats in a breath.

It's like reassurance, as though he read my mind,

knowing my thoughts were drifting away from him, to the women before me. How did he treat them, what did they look like, did they always do as he said just like I do?

"Haisley," he says lowly. "Come back to me," it's a soft command, one I find myself wanting to bow to, but I don't move, watching him instead. "Keep going," he encourages, like it'll be enough, but I can't bring myself to do it.

"Did you do this with anyone else?" I ask the question too loudly, it shatters our bubble of gloom, but he doesn't look put off, if anything, he looks excited.

"Are you jealous?" he whispers, and my cheeks heat with irritation now.

Yes, yes, yes.

"Well? Did you?" I repeat, ignoring his question as anger creeps its way up my throat.

"I am older than you."

That's his answer and I find myself quickly becoming enraged with his casualness. For a man who does not tell lies, he is very good at avoiding the truth.

I am too patient with this man.

Ignoring his enjoyment at my uncomfortableness, his feet firmly planted on the same step. I go to sit up, to pull on my bottoms, cover myself with the blankets, but his words are suddenly snapping through the cold air, hitting me like a whip to my flesh.

"*No,*" he takes the final step down, clinical and practised. "I want to watch you come." He stalks closer to the end of the bed, his shadow looming over me as he stops at my feet. "Keep going, beautiful girl, let me watch you touch yourself." His tongue slides across his front teeth, the tip catching on the sharp point of his canine. "Spread your legs for me, Haisley. Touch your pretty pussy for me."

Everything blurs in my brain, lust and anger, the pulsing between my thighs, his quietly spoken orders, all of it colliding and swirling into a big mess of black. I shake my head, my body trembling, nerves, the cold, anticipation. My want to please him, seemingly over-riding everything else. I know he wants me. Thinks about me. He has just said as much. I think of his kisses. The way his tongue took over my mouth, his lips soft and harsh, his fingers bruising where he held me. And the split in my lip… *fuck*, I am so gone for this man and his unusual ways. I think I maybe love that about him.

"I waited so long to admit to myself that I am in love with you, Haisley Kelly, and I will raze the world for you, if you so wish it."

Those words thud like an audible heartbeat inside my head, heavy and truthful. I did not say it back.

I don't understand it.

I have never seen it before.

I am unsure what love even really is.

Is it supposed to do this?

Have my fingers sliding back down the length of my body, like phantom hands are guiding it. Thighs spreading slowly apart on the soft sheets, his dark, consuming eyes intent on my own as I slide a finger through my wetness, circle my clit and arch my back.

His heated gaze drops down the length of me, rolling from eyes to tits to cunt, and yet, his focus always comes back to my face. The crease in my brow, the purse of my lips, the noises that freefall from my throat as intensely as the watchful gaze burning my cheeks.

"Not yet," he whispers and a whine has my throat aching.

My fingers slow to a stop, my pussy clenching on air, but then the nod of his head, encouraging me to continue, has me viciously circling my throbbing clit again. All of me swollen and wet and desperate. Desperate to come, desperate to please, desperate for his hands to finally fall on me.

"Please," I beg, "Please, Thorne," he shivers.

His bare chest prickling with goosebumps, he is never cold. I know that this is not a reaction to the low temperature inside the small room, but to me, it is a reaction to *me*.

It feels heady, the power, *I suddenly hold,* a smile begins curling my lips at the thought, he spots it instantly, and as my fingers start to ache with quickened, jerky movements, my orgasm like a wave, climbing and climbing and climbing.

"You are only going to come because I allow it," Thorne says, "But be a good girl for me, and hold it off, Haisley, I want you to come when I say so." He swallows, glances down at my exposed pussy. "And I am not ready for this to end just yet," he whispers, and my entire body clenches and trembles, my finger slowing.

I pant, my chest rising and falling quickly, my

breathing erratic. A desperate whine claws its way up my throat and if I wasn't so crazed with lustful need, I would flush crimson with the embarrassment it brings, but as it stands, I'm nothing but a desperate, pleading mess. The muscles in my bruised thighs are burning, my legs squirming and the watchful way Thorne stares at me makes me want to kiss him and punch him all at the same time. He's holding me off, keeping me on the edge.

I think of the white cliffs, just beyond the house, think of the way my body would fly through the air if I were to fling myself off of it, and it makes me groan. The thought of my death.

I wonder if he would fly too.

With me.

"Good girl, keep going," he hushes and it has every nerve ending in my body lighting up like fireworks. "Do not come."

I whimper, but manage to hold it off, think of his belt, secured around my wrists, banded to the metal rungs of the headboard, mere inches, behind my head. His clothed body on top of mine, warm breath on my face.

"*Thorne,*" I breathe, hard and fast, his name falling from my tongue, like it, too, free dived off of the cliff.

"Beg me," he says coldly, but it feels hot, his words, a rush of heat flowing over me, projected and manipulated in a way that is all Thorne.

I don't even have to think about it.

"Please, Thorne, please, *please,* let me come."

He assesses me slowly, too slow, my lungs on fire as I

suck in short, sharp breaths, my hand cramping and aching, but the pain just makes me all the more desperate. His dark eyes are focused on where my fingers meet my clit, violent circles over wet, swollen flesh.

"Thorne," I say, desperate to have his attention, "Please, I need to come." His dark eyes unfocused, I whisper, "I want to come for *you*."

And the taut spring holding him together finally snaps.

"Come for me, Haisley, come now," he barks it like an order, wild and desperate.

My spine clicks straight, legs straining wide, back bowing and curling up from the bed, I come. The orgasm floods through me, heat and pressure, a pain in my head as it's all too much and not enough, and I crave my captor's touch. It never comes, my eyes open, his, focused on my face, jaw tight, body tense, he watches me finish, my body coming down, relaxing, melting into the mattress.

I'm so out of breath, I don't bother moving my hand, don't attempt to cover myself, I feel nothing but exhaustion, thrill still thick in my blood. Sweat on my brow, hair sticky on the back of my neck, I shiver in the cold air of the room. Thorne steps forward, stretching over the bed, across my body, his hands finding my pyjama pants, silently threading them up my legs, bed covers following, he folds them over me, tucking me in.

When he leans down, my eyes heavy and half-lidded, his usually hard gaze, soft, *for me*. He presses his lips to my sweaty temple, his warmth and scent enveloping me in comfort.

"There was never anyone else who meant *anything* to me, Little Cub," he whispers against my cooling, sweat slicked skin.

Limbs heavy, I reach out from beneath the blankets, fumbling wet fingertips against the hard, lower muscles of his abs, grazing his warm skin, my fingers hook just inside his waistband, only to keep my hand up, stop it thunking back down to the bed.

"Stay with me," I whisper it, "Please, stay with me tonight, Thorne."

CHAPTER 24
THORNE

The days all start and end this way now. Haisley and I sharing the same bed, our bodies always too close and untouching. Our combined body heat like an inferno trapped beneath the sheets we share, but we never cross the line, as though an invisible fence is wedged between us, the threat of an imaginary punishment for either one of us crossing it.

As I lie here on my side, watching her sleeping form, the house in silent gloom around us, it is early February now, the mornings brighter, but it is early. I am usually already up by now, a tactic to avoid temptation, but this morning there are too many things rolling around the inside of my skull. I think of breakfast, just last week, at the mill, the announcement my father made, something that had happened much before it reached his ears, but the Irish, much like every other mafia family, kept it to themselves for a while. Most likely scrabbling around trying to work out what had happened. I knew he had not told anyone when nobody came hunting me down with their pitchforks. I smile at the thought.

"Shane O'Sullivan has been found," Dad announces.

I do not look up, instead, pushing my knife and fork together on my now empty plate. Wolf sits opposite me, and as I raise my chin, eyes flicked onto my Dad, I feel his warm eyes on me. Raine sits beside me, Arrow opposite him, beside Wolf, an empty seat on the other side of them. Our stepsister Grace at the very end, babe in arms, toddler in his highchair; River, banging his bowl with a thick plastic spoon.

"Outside of The Kelly's largest safe house," Dad continues, cutlery scraping over his plate.

Arrow starts pouring a glass of dark pink juice, picking it up and placing it in front of Grace. Raine fidgets beside me, leg jiggling beneath the table, coming down from whatever it was he decided to take on the job last night. He had to sleep it off in the car, the four-man job down to three. I wonder if Dad knows what he gets up to and just does not know what to do about it. Perhaps he thinks now we are grown, he should not interfere.

"Decapitated head displayed on a pike."

A tense silence falls, everyone's cutlery stalling, Grace's mismatched eyes wide on Dad. Wolf looks up at the same time I do, diverting my attention from our youngest brother's movements to Dad, Wolf and I glancing at each other as I do. Dad's dark eyes focus on mine, and I wonder if he is trying to work it out.

My guilt.

My sins.

My secrets.

Is he watching me closely to work out if I am the one who disposed of Shane's body, or because he thinks I may have been the one to put it there. Either way, he does not ask, so I do not tell.

Secrets kept silent are not lies.

There is a tension waiting to snap here, instead, it dissolves when I ask, "What do The Kelly's want us to do about it?"

"Nothing," Dad shrugs, his dark eyes seeing too much, but there is no guilt where there is no confession. "Just keeping my boys up to date," he says it with a false casualness, and despite wanting to smirk, I refrain.

This morning, I just watch her like I am so very used to doing.

I feel dishonest, her not knowing how I have done so, watched her, for so long, protected her from the shadows where I was able, trying not to intervene but sometimes unable to stop myself. I wonder what she would think, what she might say. What she *will*… I cannot keep this a secret from her. I will tell her when the time is right. She cannot leave me anyway, so I suppose it does not really matter how she feels about it. What is done cannot be undone.

Her plump lips parted, I listen to her soft puffs of breath, I stare at the glowing pink scar, speared through the top of her delicate cupid's bow, the scar I put there. I should feel bad about it, causing her damage, marking her. But I do not. Plus, it only really scarred the way it has because my girl would not stop picking it open and making it bleed.

I think she likes it.

She lets out a soft sigh, her tiny nose wrinkling on her face, and whilst her eyes are still closed, I allow myself the smile I so desperately want to show her, but cannot. It feels too much like it shall be required of me, once she has seen it, and I am not someone able to provide reactions upon demand. I think of my mother's scoldings, her words like venom infecting my happiness, cancelling it out, even as a small boy.

'Make eye contact, Thorne.'

'Look at me.'

'You are not a sad boy, smile, Thorne.'

'Smile!'

'Smile, smile, smile, smile, smiiiiiile.'

"Thorne?"

The smile is melted from my face, eyes blinking into focus, I flick my stare up, Haisley's warm gaze on mine, a soft curve to her lips, a mismatched crease between her arched brows. I can hear the question in her mind, to check on me, to ask me what is wrong. But it is as though she knows me better than anyone else I have ever encountered when she avoids all of that and instead, she shyly drops her eyes, sucks on her bottom lip, lets it pop free.

"You're still here this morning," she whispers it, as though this were something she longed for, always waking with disappointment at my absence.

It makes my heart swell a little, having pleased her unintentionally.

"I am," I reply, unmoving, even as my cock twitches at her closeness.

She beams at me then, dark pink lips pulled up high, round cheekbones tinted with a soft blush.

"That makes me really happy," is what she replies, dropping those beautiful eyes from me once again.

"I am glad," I reply softly, my insides feeling full of satisfaction, as though I were built to please her, it may be the only thing in life I am proud of, seeing a smile that I put there, it is unfamiliar, but I like it.

She turns fully onto her side, hands pressing like a prayer beneath her cheek on the pillow. She wriggles down, burrowing further beneath the sheets, too warm, soft, slightly humid, but it is her and I together, a warmth *we* created, and I find I do not mind it so much. I have never shared a bed with anyone before. I have never slept in a bed with someone else, fucked in a bed. I have never even lain in a bed with another. I need it to be clean, and I never know where anyone has been. The thought drives me to the brink of insanity, so I avoid the bedroom altogether.

Haisley blinks those long pale lashes, green-blue eyes wide and glittering.

"It's Valentine's Day," she says quietly, shyly, a thread of embarrassment in her features, but she holds my eye, without dropping her gaze.

"It is," I want to smile, it is right there, but the muscles in my face just do not seem to comply.

That is when she drops her gaze, eye contact too much to bear, I know it all too well. I have spent my life working through my aversion to it. It still feels horrendously foreign, but I do it so well now, it is so practised, perfected, it is unnerving to anyone I lock eyes with. Perhaps they realise how unnatural it is for me, and that intimidates them further.

"You're staying home?" she queries tentatively, trying to smother her want for exactly that.

I have been working more than I would like, it is hard, knowing I have her here, hidden away from a world that did not want her. My visits to the mill, multiple clean ups requiring my specific attention, it has all been very full on. Which is why tonight I made plans. For my girl.

"We can have dinner," I offer, her attention slowly gliding back to mine, her knees bending, tucking up to her belly. "I have a place I want to take you," it has been thought out, planned, I am fortunate to have so many trusted contacts.

Blackwells are death.

But with death, apparently, comes loyalty.

"We're going out?" she sits up so abruptly I almost startle.

"Yes, if you would like."

"Like?!" she squeals, pressing up on her knees, the sheets falling free, her hands coming to the side of my upper arm, warm fingertips curling into the muscle. "Of course, I would like!"

"Okay," I chuckle lowly, my skin heating where she touches me, so innocently, naturally, without reservation, it feels good, the comfort level we seem to have found with each other.

She stops jumping on the mattress, her smile wide at my quiet laughter.

"Oh," she says then, quietly, a rush of breath, her cheeks pink.

"Oh?" I echo quietly, something souring her mood, which in turn sours mine.

She fidgets with her hands, having retracted them from my skin, it feels cold, the absence of her. I remain still, lying in the same position, watching her emotion shift, all of her feelings reflecting on her face.

"I don't have anything to wear," she looks up at me through her lashes, chin dipped, almost flush with her chest.

She has been living in tracksuits, baggy jumpers, my shirts, I love it all, but I know she is used to dressing differently. Though she never once complains. About anything. The house, the state it is in, the ugly cardboard box and old towel currently swaddling *Clover,* the little beast she declared is most definitely a *boy.* But mostly, she does not complain about being trapped here, locked up, the small space, the lack of electricity. I think I love that about her. A girl cursed with mob royalty, the obligations it comes with, but also the things, shiny, pretty items she could hoard like a treasure-seeking dragon.

Haisley is so very different.

I told her that I loved her.

A truth so heavy it weighs on my soul. But she did

not shy away from it. She does not shy away from anything I seem to throw her way.

"That will not be an issue," I think of the items in my car, having sat there for the last few days, a solution to her current predicament.

She looks up at me, eyes glowing, cheeks flush.

"Okay," she whispers.

"**S**he's tearing the city apart." Archer pants down the phone, the pounding thud of his bootsteps on slush-covered concrete reverberates through the phone.

The snow has been heavy, but we have not seen much of it here, an hour outside of Heron Mill.

"What is the actual situation, Archer?" I run a hand through my damp hair, drop my gaze to the tops of my bare feet, cooling quickly against the wooden floor.

"Charlie's missing."

"Missing?" I repeat, an eyebrow tracking up my forehead.

"Yeah, dude, missing, like *poof*, he's gone, vanished, disappeared like a fucking mag-"

"A grown man is *missing*," I interrupt with an almost sigh, Charlie Swallow has never gone missing, well, except for that one time, but he disappears regularly, of his own accord, nothing ever needing to involve us.

"Jesus, Thorne," Archer puffs out a breath, and I can hear him slowing his pace. "I wouldn't be calling you if we hadn't been summoned, but Boss Lady is tearing people apart left, right and fucking centre. We're gunna be busy as fuck today."

I lick my lips, take a breath, swipe my hand over my hair, smooth it down.

"I am busy today, I will not be able to come," I tell him, voice unwavering despite the pinch to my brows.

He laughs, a deep, raucous chuckle that has my hackles rising, but I bite the inside of my cheek, keep quiet.

"Yeahhh, that's not gunna fly, bro. She's literally called in the cavalry, even the fucking Albanians are keeping their ear to the ground, and look at that strained relationship. Dude, I think something may actually be wrong this time."

This time. Meaning exactly that, numerous times, false alarms, too much fuss, it is a constant battle, but we do a job and our job is, unfortunately, to obey. I do sigh then, silently, reluctantly, resigning myself to the fact that I am going to fuck up my evening plans now, and disappoint the only person, I not only want to please, but actually want to make *happy*.

"Fine."

"Thorne, can you like, maybe hurry, because I've got our boys, in all corners of fucking Southbrook and we're struggling with body count already. You might need to make a call to that police woman that fancies you."

"You mean the commissioner, and she does not *fancy* me."

He chuckles again, carefree and boyish, "Sure, bye, bro."

Placing the phone down on the side of the sink, fingers curling over the edges of the condensation coated porcelain, I flex my joints, knuckles popping. A job like this… realistically, I could be gone for days, having no legitimate excuse to leave. I am the leader, eldest boy, heir, it all falls to me. It is all I have ever wanted. To be in control, to work hard, to live up to my name. To make my name the one, the one people are afraid to whisper in the dark, in case it brings forth death, The Blackwells. We are death and disposals. Pitch and harsh and true.

But now, things, Haisley, everything is different and I wonder if it was easier when my objective was to kill her. Because, despite us not yet having that exact conversation, surely she knows, understands, that she still must be *dead*. I am conflicted. And it feels uncomfortable in my chest to be hiding something so big from my family. This feels bigger than the secrets I have about Mum. The guilt feels like a ball of stone I cannot force myself to swallow.

Dressed and put together, I walk up behind her in the kitchen, stopping just far enough away that I would have to reach out to touch her. Her long, red curls hang in wild spirals down her back, flared hips swaying slightly where she washes dishes in the sink. I find it hard to keep my hands away from her, my feet shuffling me back just another inch. I slide my hands into my pockets, avoid the temptation to wrap my fist in her hair, snap her neck back, feel the click of her spine vibrate down the corded muscle of my forearm.

"Hello, Thorne," she says quietly, her arms still moving, hands submerged in the bubbly water.

My lips curve, eyes dropping, her feeling my presence in the same way I feel hers. So in tune with one another, neither one of us need breathe to alert the other of our arrival.

"Little Cub," I respond, fingernails pinching my palms as I flex my fingers.

She sighs, and I feel the disappointment wafting off of her in waves of cold, it makes me feel bad, my insides all churning, it is unpleasant, and yet, there is nothing I can do to change what is.

"You're leaving," a knowing statement, unfeeling, so very cold, my chest rises sharply, breath stilling in my lungs.

"I am sorry," and I am, but I cannot undo what is done.

"It's fine."

My eyes tighten, squinting at the back of her head, anger filling me, not at her, just… at everything.

Our lives are all wrong. Fucked.

"I will get back to you as quickly as I can," it is a promise, it is a shitty one, but it is all I can offer.

"Okay," she says it, but does not mean it, but she does not argue and I do not know if I really like that or not.

I step into her, hands sliding free of my pockets, I think about snapping her fucking neck, how she would probably like it and I shove my body against hers. And the thought is not about hurting her, it is about this tentative thing we have here. We both want to hurt.

Palms flattening on either side of the sink, my hips forcing hers into the counter, I press my nose to the crown of her head, inhale her deeply, plum, pepper, *my* fucking shampoo. That settles me, the rage, the feral fucking need. All of it too much and not enough. To own. To love. It is all the same.

Her hips are crushed into the counter, pelvic bone flattened to the cabinet, my cock hardening so rapidly it makes my head spin, to be so close to her, too many clothes between us. There is always too fucking much between us, too much *skin*, I want to peel it all off, bury her inside my chest, trap her beneath my bones, keep her there forever.

I feel her sharp inhale through the heave of her back, my chest flush with it as I bow forward, my chin dropping to her shoulder, nose trailing the sensitive skin behind her ear, through her thick red strands. She is so perfect it sometimes hurts to look at her.

I am not deserving, but I shall keep her all the same.

"I will make it up to you," I whisper, teeth grazing her earlobe, speaking the words directly into her ear. "When I get back, no matter the time, I shall make it up to you."

She attempts to spin in my hold, her neck arching and twisting to look back at me when that fails, nose brushing mine as she looks up at me. I could move, but I do not, liking her trapped in my arms.

"How?" she blinks, big jade-green eyes on me.

"How?" I cock my head, chin still resting on her delicate shoulder, the bone in my face pressing into her joint, lips slanting over hers.

Her breath hitches, my lip tucking between my teeth, canine snagging the skin, I glance at her lips, the top one torn, scarred by me.

God, I want to fuck you.

"How will you make it up to me?" she breathes the question into my lips, her mouth brushing mine, I think of all the things I want to do with it, *her*.

"Any way you want," I let my tongue flick out quickly, over that delicately curved top lip, immediately bite my own, to avoid devouring hers.

Her body is so tight to mine where I crush her into the kitchen side, I can feel her every breath, every rise and fall of her chest, my chest to her back. My heart thuds against hers, and I feel when hers picks up, thudding hard and fast, mine feeling it, begins to mimic, our bodies instinctively synchronising. It is hypnotising, the way in which she responds to me, and now, I to her.

And yet, I am almost loath to touch her properly, despite desperately wanting to.

I will ruin her, brutal hands and violent nature. It is inevitable, but I do not want it to happen so soon.

I want to retain my control, but I am unsure, once I give in, if I will be able to.

I stare at her face, the pale skin between her light

freckles darkening, that pink flush rippling its way across her flesh. The corner of my lip curls, hands still pressed flat to the kitchen counter, her eyes glance down, to her own hands submerged in bubbly water.

"You already know what it is that you want, Little Cub?" I breathe down her neck, my words licking her skin.

Her skin darkens, eyes flicking up to mine, dropping again almost instantly, she turns her head away from me, facing forward once more. The thin column of her throat works as she swallows, dry and nervous, my cock slotting nicely between her cheeks as she shifts on her feet. She gasps softly, sleet tinkling as it starts up again, hitting the thin windowpane set high in the wall before us.

"Hm?" I hum against her skin, the sound echoing in her own vocal cords as I press my mouth to the underside of her jaw. "Tell me."

"You," she sighs, licking her lips, her eyes rolling up slowly to meet mine, they flicker between my own, nervous excitement, something that looks like hope. "Just… I want *you.*"

I breathe in deep, nose pressing so firmly against her skin that I cut off my own air, let my lips sloppily graze down the side of her neck, chin angled so I am buried in her neck.

"You already have me, Little Cub," I whisper against her goosebump covered flesh. "I am at your disposal," she trembles in my hold, my hands still not touching, my hips grinding, just once, into the small of her back.

She bends at the waist, pushing back against me, trying to force me to give her space. I lift off of her a little, let her turn around in my hold to face me, her wet hands curl over my shoulders, dragging me back in. It would bother me greatly, had it been anyone else, the soap and warm water soaking into my fresh shirt, wetting my skin beneath, but as it stands, Haisley could do whatever the fuck she wanted to me and I would like it.

Her fingertips dig into my shoulders, thumbs pressing in the hollows of my collarbones, her eyes on my shirt covered chest. She licks her lips again, my head cocked, chin dipped.

"You would do anything?" she questions then, wide eyes flicking onto mine, hard, unblinking. "Anything?" she repeats, her voice so quiet, so soft, it soothes me, the constant storm raging inside of me calming.

"Anything," I whisper, breathy and a little desperate, even to my own ears.

My fingertips drive into the cracked worktop behind her, her curvy body wedged between my locked arms, it would be too easy to draw my elbows inwards, squeeze her until her rib bones crack.

"I want you," she whispers again, her perfect skin pink, warmth settling high in her cheekbones. "Tonight, Thorne."

Stupidly, that is when it finally dawns on me, after making my promise of anything, which absolutely, cannot involve sex.

I have wondered since I got her here, what I would

do if she needed something I could not provide, something she wanted but was too afraid to ask for. I was looking at a much smaller picture then. She was to die. And now, that is, well, it is not happening. But there is likely only so long we can live in this fictitious bubble of deluded safety. Never once has it occurred to me that she might one day ask for this, I thought it would be I, that would decide, initiate, it is all a little much to think about. This is not a straightforward process. I cannot fuck with only my dick, it goes far beyond that unless I am full of liquor, those women, I was not kind to them.

I blink, swallow, Adam's apple bobbing hard in my dry throat, I hold her gaze, having spent the entirety of my life practising to do just that. Hold someone's eye, even though it feels unnatural and intrusive. But it is easier with her. She has me in a chokehold.

"Haisley," I say softly, and that is precisely when the shutters drop down, gaze guarded, hardening for rejection.

She turns in my hold, hands dropping from my shoulders to my left forearm, nails biting into my skin even through my long sleeves as she tries to break free of my hold.

"Let me go," she hisses, and it is venomous, it pumps blood straight into my already pulsating cock and she notices. Immediately. "Oh?" she smirks, releasing my arm, she leans back against the kitchen counter, my arms still barring her in. "So, you don't want to fuck me," she inhales deeply, short and sharp with anger. "But you're still getting fucking har-"

"Do not speak to me that way," I say quietly.

Her temper drawing a new redness to her cheeks, a glistening to her eyes.

It is magnificent.

The way she comes apart so easily with rage.

She laughs, it is raucous and fake and much too loud, her head thrown back, arms bending, hands running up and over her face, through her hair. She drops her hands, her gaze, her eyes alight with blue blistering fire.

It just gets me all the harder.

Which in turn, gets *her* all the angrier.

Hunter always said I liked the angry ones.

Guess he was right.

"You are unbelievable," she jabs her pointer finger at my chest, digging it in, my chin still dipped, head canted to one side. "You make me so fucking agg-"

"Haisley," I say lowly, interrupting her once again, "Please, do not speak to me that way."

She stops, body stiffening, eyes wide, nostrils flaring, and I swear to Lucifer himself, I see the devil in her. Suddenly, she slams her balled fist down onto my forearm, almost severing my grip on the counter at her back, but it doesn't and the noise that is expelled out of her is something otherworldly. She grits her teeth, hands balled into fists at her sides, her chest heaving, she tilts her face up towards the ceiling, flares her nostrils and shuts her eyes.

I cannot help myself, watching her lose control, trying desperately to claw it back, I lean further into her.

Smaller frame trembling in her rage, it is beautiful, and it is so familiar to me that an unusual smile flits across my face, not a smirk, a real smile, fleeting, but it is there, and she misses it.

I think of how it will be. When I fuck her. How I know it will not be like anything I could dream. I am violent, and I lose time. I will not be able to be soft for her and I worry that is what she needs. She tells me she wants to hurt. But she does not know what that means, with someone like me. Control issues, black outs, rough hands and a sinister nature. I am death. It is how I live, breathe, and fuck.

"Haisley," I speak quietly, trying to keep my voice controlled, low, deep, I am naturally a loud, gravelly toned speaker, where she is all softness and quiet, so to see her like this, well…

Her eyes snap open, pupils blown, she stares up at me, but I am most definitely the one theoretically on his knees here.

"*What?*" she spits, spewing poison, in my head she is frothing at the mouth.

I lick my lips, bury my hips into her lower belly, bow over her, dominate my position. She does not back down, her finger and thumb coming up to my face, pinching my chin, *hard,* and I swear to Christ, I almost come in my fucking pants. But she does not give me even a single second to answer her, instead, she tightens her pinch, mashing my lip into my bottom teeth with the pad of her thumb, snaps my face down with a violent tug, her lips curling as she slants them over mine.

"I never ask you for anything. All I want is you, and I thought I understood, but I don't. I don't understand. I sit here all day and all night," she breathes between us, her voice trembling with simmering disdain. "*Waiting.* Always. *Fucking.* Waiting. For you. And you *promised* I could have *anything.*" Her narrowed eyes flicker between my own, my vision of her blurry where she holds me so close. "And then you took it *back.*"

She releases my chin, shoves at my chest, and I step back, letting her pass, and she stomps past me, up the steps and out of the kitchen. I listen to the heavy forced thud of her footsteps, her socked feet echoing up the bowing wooden floor of the hall. Then the bedroom door slams closed, and I take, what feels like, my first breath since I entered the room.

CHAPTER 26

THORNE

Bad to worse.

That is how my day is going.

My brothers and I spend the entirety of the day creeping our way through the city. Every alleyway, underground business, bar, club, speakeasy, and mob frequented location is scoured. The Swallow's soldiers are crawling across the city, venturing into its outer rings, all in search of Charlie Swallow. I do not think there is anything nefarious here, nothing that makes it appear to me he has been taken. I am not sure either of the infamous Chaos Twins could be abducted so easily, not without an obvious struggle left in their wake. I am ninety-nine percent positive the man has disappeared of his own accord. And if that is the case, then we are not going to find someone that can so easily blend in with the shadows.

Two men sit before us, just two of many we have played with today, both looking a little worse for wear.

I glance at Arrow, standing along the opposite wall, blood on his hands, his neck, and I know how much he hates it. His dark eyes on our brother Hunter, mine following his gaze to do the same. Hunter's back towards me, he hunches over one of the men tied to a chair in the centre of the room.

"So sorry, I didn't hear you," Hunter chuckles, "Could you speak up?" hand cupped over his ear, he leans further into the man, wide feral grin plastered on his face.

Archer whistles lowly, black hair flopping forward into his eyes, back pressed against the wall, one foot kicked up, leg bent at the knee.

"What's the matter, big boy? Cat got your tongue?" he smirks.

Hunter straightens, muscles flexing in his back, he turns, so he's side facing our guests, he cocks his head at our youngest brother Raine, who immediately mimics the gesture.

He steps forward, circles the chair, stopping beside Hunter, he bends his knees, dropping into a crouch and holds up a hand to the beaten man number one's face.

"Not a cat," he laughs tauntingly, dangling the severed tongue in front of the face from which it came.

The man groans, long and low. Blood and saliva trailing thickly from his lips, dangling and dripping off the point of his chin. The smell of burnt flesh sits heavily in my nose. It is unpleasant, the stench in the air, almost as unpleasant as watching Archer cauterise the wound when Raine cut out the appendage in the first place.

The other guy, beaten man number two, babbles incoherently, shaking his head to himself, cheekbone split open, blood trickling down his cheek.

Hunter flexes his fingers, curling and uncurling his fists as Raine steps back, discarding the tongue to the far corner of the room. It splats down at Wolf's feet, a curling snarl to his lips in distaste. He too, like the rest of us, is dressed in black, painted and slashed with red, his hair pulled back in a looped bun, he shifts his stance, arms crossed over his chest.

He, like the rest of us, wants to wrap this up and get the fuck out of here as quickly as possible. We all have shit we would rather be doing, places we would rather be, *people* we'd rather be with.

Slowly, unbuttoning my cuffs, I fold and roll up my sleeves, smoothing the folds as they reach my elbows, exposing black lines of ink curling and trailing along my arms. Muscle flexing as I stretch my hands, I step up beside Hunter, eyes narrowing in, on what I hope will be our final victims of the night. I sniff, wrinkling my nose in distaste at the smell and sight of them bound and bloodied. Standing before beaten man number two, I eye him, canting my head, running my predatory gaze from broken toes to weepy eyes.

"Anything?" I ask lowly, my deep voice a rumble in the wide expanse of the empty warehouse.

He looks up, head wobbly on his neck, *"Fuck. You,"* he sneers, spitting at my feet.

I flick my gaze onto Hunter, his dark eyes speared with gold, already focused on me. We nod in unison, unspoken agreement to end this shit. Curling my fist, I draw back my arm, slam my knuckles into the guy's cheek, I draw back, hit him again. Think of Haisley punching my forearm, the flickering flames of rage in her eyes. Me, letting her down. All because I cannot control myself.

I have been so distracted by her, *by me*, my thoughts of her, my eyes on her, my entire focus. All because I do not know how to handle this thing I have always wanted and inevitably been gravely gifted. Something that puts my entire family at risk. And they do not even know it. They do not know there is a proverbial guillotine hanging above our heads. And I hate that, perhaps, self-ishly, for the first time in my life, I am going to keep something that endangers them, to myself.

"Thorne."

I drop my arm, take a step back, blink to clear the blood beading in my lashes. The man slumped in the chair before me, now nothing but a bloody, mangled corpse. I lick my lips, iron and salt, draw in a breath, flex my knuckles.

"Let's clean this up and go home," I say to the room, all five pairs of my brothers' eyes on me, watching me closely for just a second too long, and then everyone is shifting gears, and doing as they are told.

I let Hunter and Arrow leave. Hunter for his boys, for Grace, and Arrow because his face turned the sickliest shade of green when he picked up Hunter's victim's spinal column.

"This shit sucks," Archer murmurs, kicking at the black wrapped tarp beside his feet, as he and Wolf finally load the first one into the van, Raine still inside the warehouse cleaning the concrete. "I should be getting fucking laid, dude, it's Valentine's Day. All those single lonely women drowning their sorrows in bars. That's where I should be. Not chasing the ghost that is Charlie fucking Swallow, I mean, dude, the man's a machine, he's probably taken himself off somewhere to carve someone up for a few days. I don't get the fucking urgency of torturing and terrorising the entire fucking city over it," he mumbles around a spliff.

I arch a brow, folding my suit jacket over my arm.

"It is not our job to question, only to do," I tell him, opening my passenger side door and placing my jacket down on the leather.

"Yeah, well, our boss's pregnancy hormones are driving me insane and I'm not even fucking living with her," Archer scoffs and even though my back is turned, I hear fist meet flesh when Wolf undoubtedly jabs Archer in the arm.

"That's basically treason, you fuck'ead, keep your fucking opinion to yourself," Wolf growls, as if someone might overhear us in the abandoned gravel lot we're parked in.

"Whatever," Archer mumbles, plume of dense smoke clouding above his head, sleet and rain falling at the same time, cold and wet, soaking into our blood drenched clothes. "I'm out-"

Wolf's phone ringing cuts him off, the second body now inside the van, Wolf slams the back doors closed and pulls it from his back pocket.

"Yeah? Arro- oh… What?" Wolf blinks hard, brows dipping into a low frown, lips turning down in unison. "Yeah," he flicks his gaze up, caramel-yellow eyes finding mine and holding. "We're all still together, is she…? Fuck, okay, and the boys?" I straighten at that, thinking of our three young nephews, my heart hammering wildly in my chest.

Is this because of me?

"The boys are safe. Someone has taken Grace," Wolf announces, pushing his phone back into his pocket.

"From the mill?" Archer asks with disbelief, stepping in closer, the three of us in a tight circle now, Wolf nods, pushing a hand over his hair.

"We need to check cameras," I say, thinking of the things that need to be done in order to find our sister. "Get Raine," I nod at Archer, who immediately starts to jog back towards the warehouse doors. "We will go to the high-rise office in Bethnal Green," I say then, eyes on the slushy gravel beneath my feet, focusing on what needs to be done, shoving all of my thoughts and emotions down into a concrete box, needing to be the one in control here, strong.

"Thorne," Wolf murmurs, my gaze sliding to his, his

eyes full of worry, the rushed bootsteps of my brothers approaching at my back.

"It will be fine," I say confidently. "It is going to be fine."

CHAPTER 27

THORNE

Raine sits in a cracked, faux-leather desk chair. It squeaks every time he inhales, exhales, fidgets, which he does a *lot* of, and it makes me grind my teeth until they, too, squeak, but he is doing a job the rest of us cannot do nearly half as well, so I do not say anything to interrupt him. He flicks his head to one side, attempting to get his wavy black hair off of his face, out of his eyes, the curling ends of it covering the burn scars down the side of his throat.

Archer swings his legs, perched on the desk adjacent, usual cocky smirk absent, a frown in its place, he watches Raine. Twelve screens of security cam footage pulled up and displayed across each, traffic cams, hacked doorbell cameras, one screen showing fifteen tiles of Heron Mill feeds.

Dad got a ransom call from our stepsister Grace's biological father Michael, making me breathe easier. This was not my doing, not something *I* did that put my family in danger. It has nothing to do with the Irish. Which means I am in the clear. For now.

Phone pressed to my ear, Arrow on the other end, in the passenger seat of the car that Hunter is driving too fast. I know that because I have the information displayed on the tablet in my other hand, speed, fuel level, tyre pressure, map tracking, everything that connects me to them without me being directly in the car alongside them.

Raine taps his finger to an address displayed on one of his screens, an aerial view of a large building. I bend forward, over his shoulder. Wolf stepping in closer to Raine's back, whose fingers are flying over the two keyboards connected in front of him.

"It's a gallery, Fernsby Hall. That's where Raine's traced the call back to," I tell him, words a little rushed.

There is a pause. My eyes fixating on the map following the boys' journey. I input the address to the gallery, syncing it to their dashboard navigation screen, before Hunter's voice comes through again.

"I'm going to fucking kill him," is what he says, his speed increasing as he no doubt forces his foot down harder on the accelerator, now that he has an exact location.

Thinking of anything happening to that girl makes me want to tear apart the world. She is my sister, not by blood, but that means very little. If anything were to happen to her, well, it would be the end of Hunter, and it would simultaneously destroy us all.

"Not if you kill yourselves first," I say sternly,

breathing evenly, I straighten my spine, roll back my shoulders, keep calm for my brother.

It is what I do.

Hunter laughs, the sound a little tinny, echoing through the car speakers.

"We're good," Arrow tells me, a thread of anxiety in his tone, but he holds most of it back, focuses on our brother, knows he needs to be the calm one in that vehicle, even if it is not real.

The car tyres screech, my eyes dropping to the tablet in my hand to monitor their speed.

"You're pushing one-ten," I say indifferently, but I am not happy about it.

Reckless.

Silence follows, our call staying connected.

My eyes flick between the screen in my hand, the monitors on the desk. Raine slouches low in his seat, fingers working hard, he cracks his neck from side to side. Drags the mouse across the desk, switching it out between both hands, tapping keys with whichever one is not on the mouse. Looking for anything. Any clue. Any hint. We do not know what we want exactly, but we will note anything and everything.

"She'll be okay," I hear Arrow almost whisper.

Hunter snapping back with '*shut up*'.

Wolf watches over the top of Raine's head, eyes scanning everything he can, Archer doing the same from the other side of our youngest brother as he works.

I hear Hunter and Arrow murmur apologies to each other, Arrow's quiet questions about how Michael,

Grace's biological father, would know we were not at the mill today. He must have known. There is no way he got that lucky. Grace and Rosie, Heron Mill's housekeeper, home alone with the three boys, Rachel's, their nanny's, day off.

I am unsure how Michael even found Heron Mill. It has been years since we had anyone visit, apart from The Swallows. They are no threat and we trust them inexplicitly. No one has been to the property since Atlas, Hunter and Grace's eldest son, was born, but before then it was only ever close alliances. That is what Raine is looking at now, searching for anything that might indicate who the fuck Michael is working with. That is the only way he could have found the property.

I tell them what we are doing, why, looking for a vehicle to track, and then, "You're fifteen minutes out."

Raine taps on a feed, dragging up still shots, zooming in on the number plate. I call it as I see it, the image of a black van, rattling off the make and model, the number plate. Arrow confirms he is listening with the occasional *okay*.

My mind sort of fractures then, trying to understand what it is that I am seeing as Raine tracks any and all camera footage of the van. Some still shots from a road traffic cam start to ping up, compiling on the screen, sort of stacking on top of one another as he searches the source photograph and lets his system hunt for more.

My head spins, the call to my brothers still connected, Wolf takes the phone from my ear, puts it on loudspeaker, holds it in the open expanse of his large palm. I clear my throat, shift my weight from one foot to the other.

I hear Archer's low whistle, but it sort of hums through the buzzing in my ears.

"Who ran checks on the nanny?" Raine's very quietly spoken question, that comes through the static, the shock.

Me.

That is what happens, the shock floods through my system like an ice-cold tsunami, my chest stills, heart cracking, sweat beading like thick gel on the nape of my neck. I stare at the photographs of two people holding onto each other intimately, lips locked, standing beside the black Mercedes van.

Michael, the man who has taken my stepsister, with the nanny, Rachel, someone that knows exactly where Heron Mill is because she has been *living* there with my family. The nanny is the proverbial *bad guy* in this situation, the nanny that *I* hired. Which in turn, makes this-

"THORNE!" Hunter barks and it physically rattles me, I jolt, almost as though my soul was drifting free of my body and my brother's bellow snapped it back into place.

Wolf presses in closer to my side, to comfort, but I could not think of anything worse in a situation like this. I need space. I feel sweat trickle down my temple, the urge to pat it dry, smooth my hair, slide my hands into my pockets, all of the needs overwhelming, but I do not do any of that. Slowly, I place the tablet in my trembling hand down onto the surface of the desk. All three brothers in the room with me have their eyes on me, but I cannot bear to look at any of them. To see their reaction to my mistake.

This is a colossal fuck up.

And it is mine.

"How have you fucking missed this shit?!" Hunter bellows through the phone, and if he were standing in front of me right now, he'd have his fist colliding with my cheek.

"I…" I furrow my brow, glance down at my feet, feel so. Fucking. Hot. That I feel like I might collapse, my knees like jelly.

"THEY'RE MY FUCKING KIDS!" he screams then, so loudly his rage crackles through the phone speaker, momentarily blocking him out.

"I've fucked up," I lick my lips, swallow the dryness in my mouth, "I don't-" I stutter, having to place my palm out onto the wall at my side. "I'm sorry."

I hear Wolf say something, likely sticking up for me, though I do not deserve it. Archer telling us he will call Dad, find the nanny, hold her until Hunter decides what he wants to do with her.

"Two minutes," Arrow announces, and I swallow, straighten, take in a breath.

This is not the time to fall apart.

My mother's voice in my ear, *everyone makes mistakes, Thorne.* The way she was pleading, placating, I did not care.

"Keep me on the call," I tell Arrow and silence is all I get back, but I am kept connected.

I need to keep Hunter calm enough to wield his rage, keep Arrow calm enough to not make a mistake, slip up and get hurt. This is what I do. I *can* do it.

I pick up the tablet I had placed down on the table, Archer closing the door at his back as he speaks to Dad on the phone, leaving to find Rachel. He and her have been fucking, much to Hunter's disapproval, and I know Grace did not like her, said there was something wrong with her. Grace was right, I fucked up.

I hear the wind howling through the phone, imagine the large snowflakes falling and whipping their faces in the gusts. It is the coldest February we have had in as long as I can remember. And we never get snow down South, not like what we have had the last few weeks, thick flurries and storms, lightning cracking through dense snow clouds, none of the real stuff making its way to Rook Point. I am enough storm for that place, Haisley even told me so.

I think of her anger at me, disappointment, and it feels like a knife to the gut. The way we left things, she thought I was mocking her with my smirking, my smile, even though she did not see it. It is not that at all. I am just not that good with expressing, with words, how I feel about something.

But I want to get back to her.

Bury myself in her, let her take care of me.

Maybe tonight I will finally break, perhaps that is not good for me, for her, but I need her so desperately, I do not know how I will be able to hold myself back. I feel as though, perhaps, tonight, we could talk, whisper secrets, I could wrap her up in me, spill all of my sins, confess them. Infect her with my darkness, ensure she could never leave, because a piece of me is stitched into her soul. Make it so she *wants* to stay. Not just to be kept safe, but because she *wants me.* Because although I desperately want to hurt her, I want to keep her just as badly.

Mum always said I enjoyed breaking pretty things.

I got that from her.

"You 'ear me?" Arrow's voice comes through then, breaking the spell, cutting through the sour fog of memories.

I switch from loudspeaker, clear my throat, place the mobile back to my ear.

"Yes."

"Sweet."

I know, even though Hunter is pissed at me, and he should be, he still needs me to be here right now. And if my brother needs me, whilst he sees this through, gets back the other half of his soul by whatever means necessary, then here is where I shall be. I can deal with my own issues later. Hopefully with the other half of *my* soul.

It is on the car ride home, that I let it all hit me.

Hunter and Arrow having successfully rescued our sister, although, from the sounds of it, rescued is a loose term for what was required of them. Other than unlocking a door, she seemed to have it all handled, relatively unharmed and perfectly happy. I felt relief. For a moment. Knowing, that despite fucking up the background check on the nanny, everyone was safe.

Grace dealt with her abductors, her biological father Michael, no one will be hearing from any of them again. Archer has Rachel locked away for now, until, between him and Hunter, they decide what they want to do with her. We have numerous untraceable jailing facilities at our disposal, so there was zero issue in locking her up somewhere until they decide. I hope they take their time. There was a lot more to that story and all of its delicate little details, but I do not have the brain capacity to think about any of that right now.

Raine's parting words to me, as we left the office, lingering, echoing around inside of my skull, *'Not so perfect after all, huh, bro?'* Shoulder checking me as he went to the passenger side of Wolf's van, not looking back at me as Wolf gave me that *look*. Pity. I hate it.

It makes me feel dirty.

My skin itches and I want to claw it off as much as I want to take a knife and skin the flesh from my fucking bones. Instead, I just grip the wheel tighter, hear the leather squeak beneath my hands. Clammy. Because I have dealt with more than I had expected to today. Or rather, yesterday now.

Valentine's Day officially ended two hours and eleven minutes ago and I feel even worse.

That impenetrable weight on my shoulders finally

drops then, hitting me like a ten-tonne of lead, it is crushing. To be this way. To always be perfect. Presentable. Un*ruffled*. It is fucking exhausting the way my brain works.

She can soothe me though.

The flame-haired girl in my tower.

I know she was upset with me this morning. *Disappointed*. And I fear she will forever be that way. I cannot change my life, or the tasks I am set, not whilst she is a secret. Something that also makes my skin crawl. To keep her hidden, to myself, is my idea of true perfection. But she cannot live that way, and I cannot live that way. I need my family's support with her, to protect her, they would keep her safe if I told them. They would go to war to do so. And if anything happened to me, before they knew, and I could not get back here, *for her*. She would be alone in a world that does not understand. Just as I was before I got her.

I breathe hard through my nose. Trying to clear the dark clouds inside my head. I am going to apologise to her. And despite what was said this morning, I will make it up to her. She got upset at, what she thought was, my rejection. If only she knew the brutal way in which I need to fuck. She would see then, how it was not rejection but protection. I am unsure how to really put it into words.

I do not want to torment her, I just want to love her, but my love is destruction and I am not sure how to navigate it.

The warm orange glow of the fire flickers in the

ceiling high window beside the alcoved front door, vines with flowers will start growing there soon, a curved trellis over the arched wall. I watch the dim flames dance as sleet hits my windscreen. The car parked, engine off, me, still sitting in the driver's seat. I am not sure how long I sit for, my thoughts as wild and erratic as my heartbeat.

I think of her inside the house. Alone. All fucking day. And now, all night. And I feel like a piece of shit. Her temper this morning, something beautiful, that rage in her eyes, venom in her words. It hurt me. I deserve it. And it makes pride swell in my chest, knowing she will call me out on my shit.

I do not know how to tell her all the things I think inside my head.

How fucked up I am.

But I think she sees me.

I think of her pinching my chin this morning, jabbing a finger into my chest, punching my arm, it makes my cock swell in my blood soaked slacks.

And I feel dirty all over again.

I have *hope*. Something I have not had for years. Something I thought I would never have again.

It is a pressure she does not deserve.

CHAPTER 28

HAISLEY

T error.

That's what hits me first.

Hearing vehicle tyres on the slushy gravel out front. I don't know if I'll ever get used to it. But I know it's Thorne. The way he sits in the car and doesn't get out. I wonder if he's thinking about me being asleep in bed, him sneaking in, hoping my unconsciousness would be enough to avoid this whole conversation.

The longer he sits out there. The angrier I get.

He bought me so many clothes, unloaded them all this morning before he got the call to leave. Well, that was yesterday morning now, seeing as it's just turned three-am, officially making it February fifteenth. Which is absolutely *not* Valentine's Day. I went through all of the bags after he left, angry that everything was my size, the colours I like, dark greens, reds, lots of black.

I like that about him, too. How he just *knows* stuff

about me. Some might find that creepy, I probably should, but I don't.

I like how he, too, always dresses in black, albeit the items a lot fancier than I usually would wear. I like dark jeans and black boots, metal band t-shirts with their names scrawled across the front in unreadable fonts. Oversized cardigans and t-shirt dresses, thigh high socks, black ones with the single white stripe circling the top. All things he got, and more, it's not a coincidence, he just knows, and I hated it as much as I loved it. Especially when I unzipped the garment bag with, what should have been, my Valentine's attire. A spaghetti strap dress, a low-cut cowl neck in a deep, dark red silk. Gold hooped earrings, strappy gold heels to match. It is stunning.

In fact, it's what I'm wearing now.

As I sit here, red dress, heeled shoes, gold jewellery and tasselled black shawl, I tap my foot on the warping wood floor. Clover wrapped up inside his box, placed in the bedroom, he's getting so strong now, bigger, I will be sad to release him when he's grown enough.

The fire roars, spitting and cracking, the air still enough of a chill to prick goosebumps along my flesh. Awareness does that, too, when Thorne finally, over twenty minutes later, pushes his way through the front door.

His eyes are on his feet; instinctively that's where my eyes drop too. Scuffed, marked, smears of something, splatter marks blurring the mess, likely from the still falling sleet outside. I wonder if further from the coast they have real snow, not this wet slushy shit. I'm kinda jealous, but I like it here. At the lighthouse. With Thorne.

He doesn't look up, palm of one hand moving behind him, fingers splaying flat against the door, he pushes it closed at his back. Eyes still downcast, chin still dipped, he twists the lock, slides the bolts. It makes me want to squirm in my seat, his lack of attention. That's what I always have of his, if nothing else, his unwavering attention. It is wrong of me to crave it so much. But I do. And I don't care.

I have so many things I want to say, anger running like lava through me, I have spent all day winding myself up more, overthinking it all. I know he has a job to do, I know I am the only one he has ever had that he has not followed through with. It makes me feel strange, like the odd one out, the anomaly, but I am alive, and if he had done his job properly, I would not be.

I suddenly feel embarrassed, sitting here, in this dress, make-up on my face, hair in smoothed spirals, they're still wild, I like them that way, just with less frizz. I had a plan, for when he got back, I was going to tell him exactly what I thought about him letting me down. But now I just… the wind has left my sails and I'm sitting stuck in stagnant water.

My eyes bore into the top of his head, his usually slicked back black hair, wavy and soft, is flopping forward over his forehead. The remnants of the wax he uses in it to keep it back, still a little shiny in some parts, droplets of water too, hanging in the strands, melted sleet. He doesn't lift his chin, he doesn't face me. I tremble with the urge to speak, but I feel as though he should speak first. *Say sorry.*

"Go to bed, Haisley."

My mouth pops open, jaw slack, the fucking cheek of that, no eye contact, no apology, no fucking *sorry.* An order, one that cracks down my spine like a whip, it compels the muscles in my legs to flinch into action, but I suppress it. Curl my fingers into the edge of the couch cushion, rough and scratchy beneath my sweaty palms. I squeeze the fabric, grit my teeth, feel my temples pound.

I realise I don't want him to *say* sorry.

I want him to *be* sorry.

I don't really think he knows how.

Not really.

"No."

The word comes out surprisingly strong, my legs uncrossing, I straighten my spine, curl my shoulders forward, dip my chin, eyes flicking up, I lick my lips.

"No."

I repeat my answer, louder, crueller, because maybe I want him to be disappointed in me, the same way I am him, maybe it will hurt less. Maybe *I* will hurt less. If we are on even ground.

My chest heaves with the words tumbling around inside my skull, all of the things my dry mouth refuses to let escape. I heave a breath, irritation spiking because he still won't fucking look at me. And I *need* his fucking eyes on me. I fucking crave them. And I fucking hate it. I hate myself, I think, maybe, just a little bit more because of it.

He doesn't look up, I hear him exhale deeply, his chest rising and falling with it. Retracting his hand from the door at his back, he stretches out his fingers, arms loose at his sides. His clothes are dishevelled, as much as Thorne would ever allow, and I see the slightest shake of his head. Then he pushes a hand through the wavy blackness, pushes it off of his face, straightens his posture out, squares his shoulders with a roll of the joints.

"Bed."

I scoff loudly, dramatically, shrug off my shawl, push up to my feet, the heels unstable on the warped flooring but I take a couple strong steps forward despite that.

"I am not your *pet*," I spit at him, "Do not treat me like one."

That's when his eyes, having still been averted, leisurely roll up, onto mine, locking me in place. They drop almost immediately, something akin to shock, perhaps surprise, as he roves his gaze up my body, taking in every inch of me. In the outfit, he chose, because he wanted to see me in it. The heat that licks my flesh as he takes his time surveying me makes me want to shrivel, but I don't, I hold my ground, make sure he takes his fill.

His dark eyes settle on mine, and in the light of the fire, it is hard to see any white in his eyes, their darkness blown, shadowed by heavy lashes, the flicker of flames from the fire at our side. The fire *I* kept going all day because it is fucking cold, sleet and snow and rain, howling wind, and Thorne wasn't here to insist on doing it himself. He holds my gaze unwavering, but then his head cocks, slow in its angling, but it makes me wonder what he sees when he looks into my eyes.

Can you feel what you do to me, dangerous boy?

I take a further step forward, closer, closing the too great distance between us. I know what it feels like to have his hands on my body now, and I want it again. I want him to lose that carefully curated control. *With me.* I want to be his undoing. As he is mine.

Play with me.

Love me.

Fuck me.

Hurt me.

Kill me.

"Haisley, I really th-"

"I don't really care what you have to say unless the words about to drop out of your fucking mouth are an apology."

I know what I'm doing, it's the tightening of his eyes as he stares at me, darkness swirling in the gloom between us, I'm getting a reaction. His tongue rolls out, over his bottom lip, saliva glistening on the dark flesh, his top teeth pulling it into his mouth. He looks like he's about to speak, to say something, I know he hates when I speak to him that way. It's exactly why I did it.

He takes a step closer, mere inches between us. His head still cocked, hard eyes on mine, gaze of black fury. I step in. Eradicating the distance between us. Angle my head so his lips are slanted over my own, my neck arched, head tilted back, eyes flickering between his. He smells like iron, it is overwhelming, the scent of blood, but I still get him through it, cutting through with his leather and salt. I breathe him in, intoxicating, over-whelming, suffocating. I want it all and more.

"You think you can cancel on me, leave me here, *again,* and then order me, like that," I lick my lips, the tip of my tongue catching his mouth. *"To bed?"*

His nostrils flare, but he doesn't speak, he doesn't even breathe as I move my head, straighten it, my neck curved back, to keep my eyes on his. I don't know where I'm getting my bravado from, other than anger fuelling me, but I think it feels good, to be like this.

"I don't think so," I whisper the words into his mouth, my lips brushing his. "I don't *fucking* think so."

I have no time to react as his hand flies up between us, clamps down around my throat. Crushing my wind-pipe, he lifts my feet from the floor, slams me back into the wall beside the door, ceiling high window above my head. My hands come up automatically, curling over his wrist, forearm, nails curled in towards his skin, but I don't gouge at him.

He presses his body into me, crushing me against the cold stone, his clothes wet, sticky against my skin. His nose drops to the curve of my neck, inhaling deeply as he runs it up the side of my throat, passing over the bumps of his squeezing fingers. My heels scrape the floor, the tips of my shoes barely grazing the wood, his forefinger and thumb grinding along the length of my jawbone. It makes my ears buzz, my molars ache, then he tightens his grip further, and a strained whimper gets lodged in my throat, his palm and fingers too tight for me to breathe.

"When I tell you to do things," he whispers against the skin beneath my ear, his nose in my hair, "It is to keep you *safe*." His teeth graze my earlobe, nipping at it overly hard. "So that is what I need you to do right now," he says with a hissing snarl.

His lips mouthing against my cheek now, mashing hard against my cheekbone, I can feel his teeth through his lip. My eyes close tight, because the oxygen caught in my chest is burning, my lungs on fire and I want to look at him, but I am suffocating, and I hate that I don't hate it.

I want you to hurt me.

Devour me.

Ruin me.

Kill me. Kill me. Kill me.

"You look beautiful in this," he whispers, and my eyes flutter open, but he's not looking at me.

His hand loosens on my neck, caressing down my throat to my chest as he releases me. And my body sucks in breath, my nervous system instructing it to, survival. When will it realise, I don't give a fuck about that?

"Go to bed, baby girl."

My feet touch down, hands falling from his wrist, he steps back, turns away without looking at me, and heads towards the kitchen. He expects me to do as I'm told.

Why would he not? I always do as he says, like a little doll, his puppet on a string.

I think of Shane, the way Thorne cracked through his skull with nothing but rage and fists and it heats my blood. Thorne killed for me. He told me he's in love with me. Told me I could have anything I wanted, but I don't know if that's really true. I don't really know if anything he's ever told me is true. Maybe I'm just a silly little girl playing house with the older, dangerous man, who wants nothing more than something to control. A possession. That's kind of what I am, *all* I am, I have nothing to prove any differently. It bubbles something up inside me, hot and heavy and my chest swells with my temper. I can't recall ever having such a confusing mess of emotions in my life.

I stare at his back as he takes the two steps down, turns right, disappearing into the dark kitchen. And for a second, I think I might want to kill him. I think I would go with him if I did. My heart hurts. And I feel sad, something heavy and oppressive suddenly infecting me, and I hate it. I swat a rogue tear from my cheek, sniffing overly hard. I turn towards the dark hall, our bedroom on the right hand side, the hexagonal dead end at the bottom of it. The candlelit sconce is, in fact, not lit, so it's like a black abyss at the end of the hallway.

I think of the mirror there, picture the reflection of Shane appearing in one of the darkened alcoves. I haven't been back down there since, tried to open any of the other doors, see where they go. Fear closes my throat, my breaths a little too sharp, the anger I had for Thorne mere moments ago, melting away. I blink hard, my lashes a little heavy with dark mascara, painting the usual pink-white hairs that surround my eyes black.

No one has ever fought for me before.

I've never fought for me before.

But Thorne has.

I drag my hands over my head, through my hair, bite into my lip hard, think of the scar there, the one I picked and gouged at to ensure the wound left a scar behind. Something of Thorne, permanently etched into my skin, forever.

Forever is a long time.

But it's not, not really, not for me.

Thorne might say he loves me, wants to keep me safe, but he has a family, priorities that are far above me. Something like guilt threatens to choke me, even though this isn't my fault. What Cian did to me is not my fault.

I killed him.

I'm a fucking mess. I don't know who I am. But I think I know what, *who*, I want. I need to be less combative, it is kind of exhausting, being angry. I worked hard at it all day, holding onto the rage, but now it's as though I shouldn't have bothered as it slips through my fingers like dry sand.

I turn in the hall, shoes clicking over the wood, I trail back through the living room, past the fire, down the two steps into the kitchen. Shadows and gloom and the dangerous man, I think maybe, could in fact, really love me.

"I told you to go to bed," he says lowly, in a tone I have never heard from him before.

His back to me, shirt and jacket stripped off now, shoulders hunched, head hanging forward, he has one hand flat on the farthest kitchen counter, the darkest corner in the room, beside a locked door that I've never been through. I see the glint of glass as he lifts it to his mouth. I hear him swallow, the slosh of liquid as he places it back down.

"I don't want to go to bed," I whisper it, but there's anger laced there, an impatience I didn't realise I still had. "Alone."

Thorne sighs, and it doesn't even sound like exasperation, it sounds like he's seething.

"I am not going to bed yet," he finally says, not much louder than a whisper.

I swallow, shift my weight from one foot to the other.

"Then I want to wait up with you," that, I do whisper, because I feel fucking stupid, and embarrassed, at my neediness.

I hate girls like that, always feeling like they need a man's validation after spending my entire life telling myself I do not. I breathe hard, eyes hot, my molars grind and pinch the inside of my cheek and the tears gathered in my lash line threaten to fall. Which is ridiculous. I have nothing to fucking cry about. The longer he's silent, the more I'm resigning myself to the fact that I should just go to bed, leave him to do whatever it is he's doing in here. Without me.

"Well, I do not," he says curtly, as though it has

taken all of his energy just to make his words sound that nice, and they don't, they're not.

"Fuck you," I spit the words at him, my entire body trembling again and I wish I hadn't come back here now. "Just, fuck you, Thorne."

He laughs, low and cruel and it is demonic, a chill tearing up my spine, the little hairs on my arms, the back of my neck, all standing up on end. I watch the muscles in his back shift beneath bare skin, tattoos in lines and swirls of black that are too hard to make out in the blackness of the room, rippling. I watch as he pushes off of the counter, slow to turn towards me, his eyes instantly locking on mine. There must be fifteen feet of space between us in this galley shaped kitchen, but I feel him as though he were pressing his body into mine, a heated wave of danger emitting from him.

"That is what you want, no? That *is* all you wanted from me this morning, is it not, Haisley? For me to come home tonight," he curls his top lip, his words spiteful, "To *fuck you*." He huffs a laugh through his nose, shaking his head, spiking something painful in my chest. "You are that desperate for attention that you really want your *captor* to fuck you?" the snarled words almost silent, I flinch, it feels like he just backhanded me across the face.

I feel pathetic, hurt, confused. My face scrunches, brow puckering. He prowls towards me like a predator, my body trembling, feet frozen to the floor, even though I know I should turn and run. This is the type of man I had expected when I was bound and gagged and given away by the Doyle brothers.

God, I fucking hated them, but I suddenly wonder if it might have been better if they had sold me, my death would have been quicker. I never would have seen a Valentine's Day to be upset about. No more than two weeks into a sale is when most girls end up dead, either by some violent sex act gone too far, or by their own hand in desperation. I've heard it all, seen some more, and it's something the women in my family have been worried about since we were the tiny age of ten years old.

Always do as Father says and you won't end up at auction.

I don't know how many times I have heard that disgusting phrase in my twenty-three short years. Something to instil fear into us. Keep us in line. Not that it worked for me. Clearly.

I'm not sure I've ever been more afraid of a simple sentence, not until Thorne speaks again. Suddenly right before me, those black eyes unblinking, staring through me, like he's checked out, leaving nothing but a monster behind.

"Let's give it a go then," he whispers, words not much more than a muttering beneath his breath. "See how well you take it," he speaks robotically, like a tape player is just rolling through, he reaches out, licking his lips, tucking a lock of red hair behind my ear, so gently it brings tears to my eyes. "See if you *survive* me."

I jolt back, his hand striking out like a viper to grab my throat, but I'm just out of reach, lunging back. Wobbling on my pin heels, I shake my head, his arm dropping back to his side.

"Thorne," I whisper, choking on the name that usually makes my insides churn with something like *love*. I shake my head, swallow down the lump in my throat, "You don't mean that," it's pleading, I want him to take it back so desperately, I disgust myself, pathetic shame flares hot in my cheeks.

My stupidity. Jesus Christ. I wobble back another step, tears threatening to spill. I look up at him, his head cocked in the way I like, but it's different, he's not...

"You're not yourself," I whisper, lick my lips, straighten my spine. "Let's just go to bed, okay?" I draw in a shaky breath, roll my shoulders.

"You frightened, *Princess*?" he mockingly rasps.

Because I've never been a princess, not like I should have been, had I been born to a different family, daughter of a mob boss, maybe it would have been better. Maybe it would have been worse.

My entire body trembling now, that fucking nickname reminding me of what I did. I squeeze my eyes closed, swallow back the bile clawing up the back of my throat, set fire to the images of Cian flitting through my skull. His grabby hands, the way he always called me *Princess*, some sick, twisted endearment only meant to mock, to threaten. I breathe hard through my nose, roll my shoulders, my bottom lip curling back between my teeth. I'm always cowing to a man, bowing and obeying, *yes, master*.

"I don't need this," I say then, louder now, breaking the silence.

Heat lashes my skin like a cane, anger simmering, bubbling, boiling.

"I DON'T FUCKING NEED THIS!" the words tear out of me like an exorcism. "I don't need *you*, your fucking games. I don't need to stand here and have you intimidate me, try to frighten me. I didn't fucking do anything to you!" I pant for breath, my outburst tearing through me. "Why are you being like this?" I'm almost whining now, confused, Thorne has never hurt me, not in a way I didn't like. "I don't understand. I thought…" I shake my head again, my eyes on his, he doesn't give me a reaction, silence, his head cocked, dark eyes on mine, but not really seeing.

"You thought what?" he breathes the words, his warmth sliding across my skin as he moves in even closer, twists his neck so his face is level with mine in the cant of his head. "You thought you understood me?" he pouts his bottom lip, mocking and teasing, nasty.

It is the most foreign thing I have ever seen cross Thorne's face. I drop my gaze briefly to his shoulder, dark and shadowed, healing from stab wounds, wounds he took for me, to save me. I cling onto the memory, look back at his face.

"You think you have some sort of control over me? Some sort of say in what happens here, *with me?* Hm?" he hums, cold, cruel. "You thought you meant something?"

Something?

I never meant anything to anyone before I met you.

I thought I meant everything… to you.

Fucking stupid.

I shake my head, look into Thorne's black eyes, the pretty ribbons of gold swallowed by his darkness. I stare into his dark orbs, trying to find him, get him to really see me, claw him back to me, because this isn't Thorne. But it's like he's gone, overtaken, swallowed whole by The Devil possessing his body. My lip trembles and he grabs my chin, sharp pain bolting along my jaw as he squeezes my face.

"Let me show you how *much* you really mean to a man like me, princess."

"Fuck you," I breathe, licking my lips, burying the pain, the hurt, calling forth a shield of fury. "Fuck *you.*"

I yank my head to the side, cracking my neck as I tear out of his grip, I shove at his chest, hands slamming into hot, firm muscle, but he's too fast. Grabbing my wrists, passing them both into one of his big hands, yanking me forward, wrist bones burning as he twists and grinds the skin. He gets in my face, nose nudging mine harshly, forcing me backwards, his teeth bared. He looks like a fucking animal. Savage and out of control. And real fear, fear I felt whenever I was around Cian, fear I felt when Shane was approaching, fear at another beating ordered by my father, fear that was like razor wire wrapping around my organs as I swallowed it down by the mile.

"You push me, and push me and push me," Thorne growls, squeezing my hands, his other hand fisting in the back of my hair. "You waited up for me," he whispers the words over my mouth, my lips parted on a panicked exhale, "Just to fight."

I try to shake my head, the accusation all too true, but I wanted this to go differently. I just wanted to sit with him. Sometimes, in the evenings, we sit together, and he strokes my hair, and I feel love. For the first time in my life I felt it, and it was because of him.

Eyes watering at the pull of his fingers in my hair, my scalp burning, I try to catch my breath.

"I didn't," I swallow, with difficulty, the angle of my head, the curving arch to my throat, it makes my breath shallow. "I didn't, Thorne. I just…" I glance down, a tear slipping over my bottom lid, *don't say missed you.*

I'm always alone.

I've spent my entire life alone in a house full of people and no one ever saw me, until you.

"You forget, I am the one in control here," he says quietly, pressing his forehead to my own, rubbing our heads together, his grip tightens, my breath catching. "I own you," he whispers, nipping my ear, his teeth too hard and biting to be anything but rage, and I hate that I love it.

Even this.

All of this negative attention, all of his anger, his rage, the turmoil, all aimed at me, it's still attention and I hate that I want it.

Crave it from him.

I fucking hate myself.

"You still like me, don't you, even when I am like this," he chuckles darkly. "You are *sick*," he laughs, huffing breath against my cheek, it half sounds appreciative, as if he'd actually quite like that to be true.

My body heats all over, a roaring blush in my cheeks, I feel extending its way down my throat, my chest, my nipples harden, and I want to hide myself. Even in this dark room, I want to bury my head in the curve of his shoulder, let the gloom we exist in, swallow me up. Both of us, we're always happy in the gloom.

Kill me.

It occurs to me then, that I am. Sick. In so many twisted ways, I don't even exist for me anymore, just for him, his attention, his eyes on mine, his heat, his hate, his love. It is insanity. But I can't deny it's true.

"You have ruined me," he breathes then, shuddery, full of disgust and I tense all over again as his fingers twist aggressively in the roots of my hair. "Everything is fucked up," he blows out a breath. "You drive me insane," he snarls, his teeth savage as they bite into the skin beneath my ear, fingers tightening around my slight wrists. "You have infected me like poison," he hisses, biting me again, this time I whimper at the pain. "You have made me fuck up," his mouth sucks and pulls at the curve of my shoulder, "Distracted me," teeth too sharp, they sink into me, and it feels like a punishment.

"Thorne, *stop*," I beg, my chest heaving, breathing short and sharp with panic.

The air changes like the flip of a coin, charging with his storm, lightning zapping and thunder booming, but it's all inside this kitchen, all inside of this dangerous man. All I can hear is Thorne's sanity dissolving as though it were dunked in a vat of acid. Sleet pelting the little window above the sink, the thin pane of glass thrashing in the wind, rattling in its frame, none of it penetrates, just him. I squirm in Thorne's hold, strands of hair snapping free from my scalp, I pull on my arms, the joints jarring as he holds firm.

"All of it," Thorne hisses, stilling me with his tone, "All of this is your fucking fault. I cannot fucking *breathe* without thinking of you!" he roars in my face, making me shrink back even in his hold, trying to free myself of his iron grip. "I put my family at risk, because of you, and your needy fucking attention seeking. If anything had happened to them, I swear to God…" he trails off, his chest heaving, eyes fierce on mine.

"Thorne, I'm so-"

"SHUT UP! SHUT THE FUCK UP!"

He rears back, releasing me, I crash backwards into the dining table, the back of a chair cutting into my spine. Thorne grips his hair in his hands. Yanking and twisting at the strands so hard, some of them tear free, loose in his fists, I see my own, long red curly strands caught around his fingers. His entire body heaves, his breathing heavy and fast. His head dipped, eyes flicking up, he stares at me, and it feels all wrong.

I step back, around the table, the sink on my left, the door a few paces back on my right. I shift further, my heel catching on the uneven wood, the air in the room sending a chill down my spine.

"You think you are going somewhere?" his death glare sticks me to the spot, freezing me in my escape. His dark eyes flick up from beneath his lashes, "You think you can just leave me here now, now that you have done this to me?" his curled fist pounds on his chest, the echo of the thud resounding in the kitchen.

Tears prick my eyes, "I don't-"

"RUINED ME!" he bellows, spittle flying from his mouth, my feet take me back another step.

He takes a step forward, shaking his head, bowing his body forward, mumbling beneath his breath, head in his hands.

"I just need to get her out of my system," he says under his breath, but I hear him, even over the erratic pounding of my heart, mumbling as he jerks his head side to side with his hands fisting in his hair once more.

It forces me back another step, my shoes too loud in the silence, the gentle click of my heel has his head snapping up like a bloodhound on the hunt. We eye each other for a weary moment and then I turn to flee at the same time he advances.

His long arms cinch around my waist, effortlessly tearing me back into his hard body with an oomph. Air flies out of my lungs as his arms constrict around me, my feet lifting from the floor. I thrash in his hold, drive my fingernails into his forearms, throw my head backwards, desperate to connect with some part of him, any part of him.

"Thorne!" I scream through my teeth, "Thorne, stop it!"

"You are all I have up inside my head," he snarls, slamming me down over the table.

One of his hands cuffing my wrists, his other smacking down hard against my spine, he folds me in half over the table. His fingers splayed, each tip like a hot poker burning through the silky, thin fabric of my dress, searing heat down my spine. I tremble, desperately trying to shove myself up, legs kicking uselessly, but Thorne's hips become flush with mine, the thick hardness of his cock pressing against me like a threat. I still, breathing ragged, I twist my head to the side, cheek flush with the splintered wood of what was once the garden table, glancing over my shoulder, my eyes searching for his.

But Thorne isn't looking at my face. His eyes are laser focused on the splay of my hips, the curve of my arse, the red satin dress pulled taut across my flesh, displaying all of my dips and curves.

I swallow hard, my breath stuttering, *"Please."*

His eyes roll upwards towards my face, but he's not here, his body might be, but Thorne's not. I am all alone in this room with a monster in my captor's place, a captor who feels more like my protector. A man who confessed his love for me.

Thorne takes care of me.

"Thorne," I lick my lips, his name a whisper, he shifts his hold on my hands, moving them so my own knuckles are digging into my back, replacing the one on my spine. *"Please."* I swallow, the scrape of razorblades in the back of my throat.

"Once this is done, I will be able to think clearly again," he says the words mechanically, like this is so easy for him because it's all a process, part of his process, to regain control.

"Thorne, *no*," tears fall then, the clink of his buckle, as he threads the tongue of his belt free, is deafening.

My body trembles, eyes squeezing shut, all of this is too familiar.

"Thorne, please, I'm sorry, please, stop. Let's just go to bed, okay? Just you and me, and you'll feel better in the morning," my voice cracks, he presses closer, and the rushing of blood in my ears is almost a comfort.

He's almost too gentle, the way he pushes my dress up and over my thighs, the curve of my arse, his hand gliding reverently over my skin. Pinning the fabric beneath our conjoined hands, exposing me to him. The back of his hand grazes across my flesh, rough, scarred knuckles that I love, because there are scars on his hands for me now. I don't struggle anymore, letting myself melt into the table, the wood tearing at my cheek, because it's old as fuck and is only really good enough for firewood. But Thorne brought it in out of the rain and it felt like it was for me, because I like to eat all of my meals at a table so I can use cutlery because I don't really like getting my hands messy, and he doesn't either. We laughed about it, right here, in this kitchen, at this very table. Like he *knew*.

A sob tears out of me then, the feel of his hand shoving down his trousers and boxers, I feel his heat on the back of my thighs as he presses against me. And none of this is being done in a flurry of violence, there's no fight in him or in me. And I wonder how I'll feel tomorrow, after what's about to happen here, because it'll be my first time.

And I know I'm twenty-three, and I didn't disagree when my father called me a whore for seducing my cousin, I let them all believe, before I killed that mother-fucker, that he had raped me. I had all the evidence, the torn clothes, the knifed bedding, the broken lock on my bedroom door. All I had to do was smear the bloody back of my hand between my thighs and let them come to their own conclusion. I don't care about virginity, it has been nothing to me but a death sentence my entire life.

I've been desperate to get rid of it for my entire life.

But I thought it would go differently.

Thorne doesn't know. But it shouldn't make a difference. Rape is still rape whether you're a virgin or a hooker, it doesn't matter if you've willingly had sex one time, no times or a thousand. Consent means everything.

And I think this might actually kill Thorne. When he realises. Thorne might be a dangerous man, but he is a good man too. And whether he will ever believe it or not, I do, I believe it, I know it to be true. I will believe it enough for the both of us.

And I love him.

I love him even as I feel the head of his cock pressing at my entrance, dry and tight and so not ready for what's about to happen. Tears track silently down my face, my cheek burning where it presses into the rough wood and I swallow down my sob. Chest heaving, mashed into the table with the weight of his fist on my back, containing my wrists. My shoulders ache and my arms burn, but I stop pulling now, go lax.

I want to save this broken boy, but I think, after this, he won't believe he can be saved.

But he saved me.

He saved me, even if he's going to kill me. Something we have not properly discussed, but I don't care about that anymore. Even if I have to die, he doesn't.

"Thorne?" I whisper his name.

He stills, but his breathing is even now, calm, he has me under control, himself, and he feels better. His body instinctively knowing it has the upper hand, he might be checked out mentally, but his body still knows, relaxing.

"It's okay," I say, my lips trembling, eyes streaming. "It's okay."

I let my body fully relax, muscles loosening, I let the table hold my weight, I just feel numb, to all of this. The anger I felt minutes ago dead in the water. I listen to the sleet now, I can hear the waves, violently crashing into the base of the cliff, all of it suddenly soothing. Even his breathing, his warmth, all of it helping me fall into the numbness.

"It's okay, Thorne," I say then, licking salty tears from my lips. "I love you," I whisper it, my words almost silent, for myself, to hold onto the feeling of loving Thorne.

The real Thorne, who I want to hurt me, I do, but not in this way. Not like this. He would never.

"I'll still love you," I promise with my whole soul. "I will still love you."

And then my hands are released, a deafening roar sounds at my back, my arms free, fizzing with pins and needles. I spin around so fast as I stand that I almost trip over my own feet. Thorne throws his half full glass against the wall, the shattered pieces falling like raindrops as he crashes down to the floor. His knees hitting it hard, his hands fisting in his hair, and the howl of pain that tears from his chest threatens to shatter me. I'm shaking, quivering really, all of me is crashing, adrenaline dying in my veins as quickly as my body created it, but I make my way over to him on trembling legs, regardless.

His entire body heaves, his trousers still open, thighs spread where he's collapsed onto his knees, he sobs, the most heart-breaking sounds I have ever heard anyone make, tear out of him. Tears spill down my cheeks, the broken man before me making my heart wrench in my chest.

I step closer, his body heaving with sobs, his hands splayed out before him, shoulders hunched, head bowed. He looks up when my feet come into view, his big brown eyes wide and wet, and it's Thorne in there now, I can see him, *feel him.*

My beautiful broken boy.

"I am so sorry," he splutters, "So sorry, Haisley," he chokes out, tears and saliva, all of it mixing on his face.

He looks like an angel banished from heaven, his

olive skin, dark features, black hair, swirling ink, all he needs now are obsidian feathered wings.

"It's okay," I whisper, even though it isn't, even though nothing about this day has been okay, and I don't know if we can come back from this.

If *he* can come back from this.

"I think…" I swallow, lick tears from my lips, his wide, watery eyes blinking up to mine, looking at me like I hold all of the answers.

I stare down at him, stroke the back of my curled finger across his cheekbone, salty wetness against my skin.

"I think you need to get some help, Thorne," I whisper as more tears fall.

"I will," he says, swallowing the broken sound of his words. "I will get help," he sobs again, catching it in his throat. "I am so sorry," and it's those words that break the dam.

He bows forward, pawing at me, fingers curling around my legs, tracking up the backs of my thighs, digging into my flesh, wrapping himself into me. I take in a shaky breath, his hands gripping the backs of my thighs, lightly press my fingertips of one hand to the top of his head, sweat and leftover hair grease mixing in his wavy black strands. I run my fingers over his hair, gently place my palm on the crown of his head, cupping him to me as he presses his forehead into my lower belly, I curl my fingertips to press gently into his skull. I hold him tight to me as he sobs, tears and saliva soaking into the silky fabric of my dress. My own tears tracking down my jaw, sluicing down my neck.

I try to control the tremble of my chest, the shaking of my body. My free hand hangs down by my side, limp, my legs feeling like jelly as Thorne's weight is leant against me. He holds me to him so tight I can hardly feel it. I'm not sure what I can feel besides his grip on my legs, his head pressing into my belly.

"Let's go to bed, Thorne," I say quietly, listening to the waves outside, his cracked sobs, the mumbling apologies I don't even really register anymore.

I get him to his feet, drape his arm over my shoulders, his heavy weight slumping entirely onto me as I teeter in skinny heels. We make our way to the bedroom, my free hand slapping against the walls as we go, helping to propel me forward.

I turn, drop Thorne to the bed, his head and shoulders slumping, he's still apologising, like a broken record stuck on repeat. I lift his legs into the bed, the covers already pushed back, his left leg first, then his right. I untie his shoes, placing them beneath the chair in the corner of the room.

Coming back to his side, I stare at his trousers, already unbuttoned, I swallow, and draw the covers over him, unable to bring myself to remove them. His eyes are already closed, and even in the dark, I see the glistening wetness on his hollow cheeks. I step back towards the chair, slumping down into it, when my legs hit the wood, and watch him, even in sleep, his brow puckers.

Nothing is the way it was when we woke up

yesterday morning, the last time we were together in this room. Both of us waking up together in bed, smiling, even Thorne, that delectable curl to his lips that is so often absent on his mouth.

We were happy.

And we weren't whole then, but we weren't completely broken either. But now, now I'm not sure there are enough splintered pieces of us left to really make us into anything at all.

P ain pounds through my skull, the echo of
Haisley telling me she will still love me, ringing
in my ears.

Even if I had defiled her.

Ruined her.

The same thing I told her she had done to me.

I remember parts, mostly my begging, when I came
back to myself, saw how I had broken her. And she still
comforted me, even after what I almost did, that much I
am sure of. She comforted me, telling me that it was
okay.

Fucking *okay.*

None of this is okay.

Nothing about this is ever going to be okay again.

My fingers tighten around the leather strap, creaking
as I heft the duffel bag up, passing it into my other hand.
I carry it through the almost empty rooms, the old,

decrepit stone building, one that has started to feel like home, just feels cold this morning.

We exist in the gloom, this dense, tense bubble of shadows, something heavy and light, just for the two of us.

It is all gone now.

I drop the bag lightly to the floor beside the front door, light filtering in through the ceiling high window. It is cold, clouds heavy and white with snow and sleet readying to fall, brightening the sky before the sun has even fully risen. I add wood to the fire, stack fresh candles upon the mantle, stand them on top of wax already dried, long trailing drips of it hanging down, towards the fire, more of it splattered on the hearth beneath.

I inhale deeply, memorising it all, the smell of the wood, wax, fire, *her*, pepper and plum. She is embedded in everything here now; a permanent mark on what has quickly become my favourite place. She is safe here, *was*, will be again. I push a hand through my hair, stare into the lick of orange flames, stare into its core, violent blue. I think of her eyes, jade blue-green, wide and wet. Because of me.

I do not think I can ever make this right.

Hand resting on the wooden mantle, wax silky beneath my fingers, I hear her at my back, her soft padding footsteps. Those thick thermal socks muffling the sound, ones she says are ugly but wears every day because she is always cold. She stops so far away and I am glad, as much as I hate it, she is frightened and I do not blame her. It is probably for the best.

"Thorne?" she whispers, the sound choked.

She swallows loudly, and I hear her wringing her hands together, her skin dry, chapped, because she spent too long outside in the wet and cold, without wearing the gloves I instructed her to. She had beamed at me all the same, that bright white smile, dark pink lips pulled up into a high curve, round cheekbones and tip of her tiny nose, stained with a blush pink.

I cannot bring myself to say anything, everything about this is wrong to me, but good for her, and I am trying to do the right thing here to protect her. She is not safe whilst I am under the same roof as her. She needs someone who will take care of her. Someone who could love her better than I.

I have ruined her life.

"Are you going to work?" she asks quietly, my eyes squeezing closed at the tremor in her voice.

"My brother is coming," I say quietly.

Thinking of Wolf, our telephone conversation, just a few hours ago, when I woke in the bed, saw her asleep in the chair, exhausted, drained.

Because of me.

"Okay," she says quietly, still unsure, but there is less panic. "Is he… are you… you don't need him for the job?"

I shake my head, unable to trust my words enough not to tremble on their way out. I keep my back to her, unable to look at the pain in her eyes. Something I put there. Fear.

God.

"You're coming back," she swallows again. I imagine her licking her lips, glancing around the room, her gaze falling to the bag beside the door. "Right?"

"Wolf will keep you safe," I say first, it is a truth and I am so very good at being honest, I cannot tell lies, but I can mould and manipulate truths in avoidance.

I hear her then, a step closer, still unsure, but she is so much stronger than I am.

"Thorne," she breathes, the space between us too great a distance, but I am glad she does not approach further. "Tell me you're coming back."

A tear slides down my cheek, but I manage to keep my breaths even.

Blackwells do not tell lies.

"Thorne," she says desperately, her voice cracking in the same tempo as my heart. "Thorne, it's okay," she promises urgently, but I hear that fearful tremor in her tone.

I shake my head, letting my eyes slide shut.

"None of this is okay, Haisley. We both know that."

"But I... we can be better," she moves closer, I feel her like she is an extension of myself, but where I am darkness, she is light, and we are becoming too much of a muddled grey the longer I stay. "I can be better," she stutters.

"You are already so perfect," I breathe the words,

raspy and thick, my throat tight as though a hand is constricting around my neck.

"For *you!*" Haisley's hands fist in the back of my shirt, her face burying between my shoulder blades, pressing all of her softness, all of herself, into me. "Only for you, Thorne, I don't want to be here without you, please, *please.*"

Her sobs muffle in the fabric of my shirt, I do not dare turn around, take her in my arms the way I want. I stand stock still, muscles taut, I do not give her what I so desperately want to.

My brother is coming.

Her tears soak into my shirt, wetting my skin, and I drive my teeth into my bottom lip so hard, I split the skin.

Tyres crunch over gravel, puddles and slush sploshing and splattering up the sides of the vehicle as Wolf pulls in.

"Are you…" Haisley sniffs, "Are you at least going to get-" she hiccups then, cutting herself off, a tiny, distressed sound before she recovers. "Are you going to get some help and come back to me, Thorne?"

I glance at the door as footsteps stop on the other side of it, unlocked already. I focus on the depressing of the brass handle, the wood opening inwards, my brother Wolf appearing in the doorway.

"Yes, I am going to get help," I whisper, telling my first ever lie.

CHAPTER 30

HAISLEY

H ollowed.

That's how it feels new.

The empty cavern that is my chest.

It's late March, the beginning of spring. There are lilacs and lavender, honeysuckle knotting with wisteria, all of it starting to bud where it grows over the front of the old house. It will bloom soon, so many shades of purple, the honeysuckle looks to be white as far as I can tell from the small oval buds, but I think it'll look beautiful whatever colour comes in.

The air is still cold, whipping through my long, red curls, where I stand a few feet from the edge of the cliff. White, sandy pebbles and stones beneath my feet. I scuff the toe of my grey boot into the dust, watch it swirl in the breeze, land on the soft suede of my shoe like powder.

I glance over my shoulder, Wolf, Thorne's brother, younger than him by less than a year, there are four more, six of them all together. A lot less siblings than I have, but when he speaks of them, you can see how much he loves them. Very different to my experience with my own siblings, but it's nice to imagine what it's like.

Wolf is quiet, which was unexpected, I thought, because of his large size and stern face that he would be loud, brash, something completely opposite to Thorne, but he's not. He takes up a lot of space, he is so tall and broad, the house we occupy is so small, narrow halls, short door frames, low ceilings, it's almost comical how big he really looks in the space. But he is softly spoken, and kind, he smiles with warmth and is insightful, clever, he fixes things, and takes care of things. *Mainly me.* And I enjoy him, having him here, his presence is nice, calm, protective. He is the type of man I always dreamt of one day having, belonging to, a partner, someone who would love me in all the gentle ways I never saw my own mother treated as a child.

But he doesn't set me alight inside, exist with me in the gloom, he is not serious or silent, he doesn't speak his words as though he were a poet. He is not Thorne. As much as they look alike, they are worlds apart in the other ways, the ones that matter, *to me*.

I miss the low simmering violence, the tension that clouded my head like smog, the feeling inside of my chest that demanded I give in, submit, be consumed.

Wolf's strange eyes, a little like an actual wolf's in their yellow, honey-brown colouring, flick up to mine. Bare chest, broad shoulders, thick muscles bunching beneath his naturally olive skin, tanned much darker from the sun, all exposed, covered in a glistening sheen of sweat despite the icy wind as he works. He drops my gaze, lifts the axe, brings it back down on the next log with a sharp thunk, the wood splintering in two. And then he looks up at me again. Checking on me.

I sweep a lock of hair behind my ear, try to offer him some semblance of a smile of reassurance I don't feel, but I can't find the will. Everything is an effort now. I don't really have much energy for pleasantries.

Looking back out over the cliff, the sea a violent navy-grey, swirling crashes of foamy white. I breathe in the sea air, let the salt fill my lungs, think of *him* and imagine the scent of leather, metal, ozone, and, more often than not, blood. I let it fill me up for one torturous moment and then I breathe it all out and let it go, even as it chokes me.

Clover paws at my calf, his sharp little teeth tugging on my shoelace, a grunting growl as he attacks it, yanking on it like a tug-o-war. I scoop low, replace my laces in his mouth with a finger and lift him up into my arms. He has gotten so big, his dark brown baby fur quickly being replaced with a beautiful fluffy ginger, his nose elongated, short ears pointed, he looks like a real fox now. He chews on my finger, pawing at the ends of my hair, and I glance a few feet away, following the trail of small chunks of yellow to where he has 'killed' the bad kitchen sponge. The third one this week.

Wolf hacks up another piece of wood at my back, the thunking and thudding sound loud over the crashing waves below. I stare out to where the sea meets the sky, wonder what's beyond it. If I were to meet that curved crease of the earth, where would I end up? Lost in a wave of oblivion, I wonder if I would like it, better than being here.

Clover bites into my finger hard, my surprised yelp making both of us jump, he looks up at me with a whimper, blood beading on my freckled skin. I stroke over his head, smooth down his ears, and then my hand is being snatched up by a much, much larger one and for a split second the entire world stops moving. But then I feel him, Wolf, he is always warm too, like his brother, but his presence is something gruff and large and nothing as eloquent as his older sibling.

"You'll get fucking tetanus," he grumbles, drawing my hand up to his face, his warm eyes squinting down at the pin prick wound before sucking my finger into his mouth.

"Wolf!" I yell, tearing my hand free, his saliva shining all over my finger, "*Eww,*" I complain, wiping my hand down my black t-shirt dress, thick forest green cardigan thrown over the top. "And I won't get tetanus," I mumble, screwing my nose up.

"That thing's a wild animal," he tells me for the thousandth time, eyes narrowed on Clover. "My brother must really love you to allow that thing inside," his eyes instantly snap to mine. "Haisley..."

"It's okay," I say quietly, swallowing around the searing iron bar lodged in my throat.

"It's not, I didn't think," he sighs then, stopping

himself, one of his large, calloused hands gripping the back of his neck. He dips his chin, flicks his eyes onto mine, "Wanna make lunch, kid?"

I roll my eyes, punch him on the shoulder, turn away, back towards the house, and then call over my shoulder.

"I'm not a kid!"

"I'll have ham and cheese, please, *kid*," he yells back.

"You'll have what I make you and I'm spitting in it!"

"*Mmm*, my favourite!"

I get that warmth in my chest, a light feeling lifting in my belly, something urging me to laugh, crack a smile, let myself be happy, if only for one single moment.

But nothing comes of it.

Night falls, the lightbulbs work now, a new lamp in each of the two corners of the living room, my candles on the mantle fresh and clean and new, unused atop the scraped away, melted drips of their ancestors. I miss their glow, flickering in the gloom.

I stare at Thorne's black leather journal in my hand. Closed with a binding leather string, gold pen pushed beneath it. My fingers itch to claw it open, seek out his words, his secrets, slither inside his mind like a parasite. But it feels like a betrayal. And I would never betray him. Even though he isn't here. With me. And maybe I would feel closer to him if I read his words. Crawl my way inside his head. Like I attempted to do with his heart.

Instead, I grip it tighter, shove it back down the side of *his* chair, and fold my hands in my lap.

Clover, having finally worn himself out, lays on his back before the fire, having learnt in his very early days that fire is hot, he keeps a good distance when warming his belly. I sit in the armchair, stare at the two-seater sofa that once was *my* place to sit. I would prefer it, I think, not to be enveloped by a piece of leather furniture that, for much too long, smelled like my captor. It just smells like me now, my blanket, currently pulled over my legs, usually thrown over the back of the chair. I think I miss my couch, but I, too, think, that it may be more painful to stare at this chair with someone else sitting in it.

As it is, Wolf takes up both seat cushions on the couch, his knees spread wide, thick thighs covered with baggy silver basketball shorts, his chest bare, as is normal for him, he is never cold. But a shiver still works its way up my spine as I sit here, a book I have read too many times open in my lap, not being read. The pain in my heart hurts more today, each day the longing gets worse. I was sent here to die, and it is the most torturous thing, to still be breathing.

It was my destiny to die.

Yet, here I am.

Forever, it seems, newly destined to live in limbo.

I think of telling Wolf to do it. How he must want to go home, not be stuck here babysitting me, and it is, babysitting, the way in which he watches me. I know I can't be here alone, I'm a threat to their family, a risk if anyone discovers me, perhaps they think I may run away, if given half a chance. I wouldn't. I have nowhere to go. No one to run to. And even if I did, I would not. I do not care enough about myself to bother. I never meant anything until I meant something to Thorne.

I know you shouldn't put your worth on someone else, you should have enough respect for yourself to mean something regardless of any other factors. But I don't care about societal norms, what they mean, what they say I *should* think, feel, do. I don't really give a fuck about anything except for Thorne fucking Blackwell. The man who does not tell lies. *But did.* I knew when he left, without so much as glancing at me, that he was not coming back.

It has destroyed me.

And just as he told me I was to him.

His ruin.

He is my destruction, and my heart is cracked and bleeding and dying.

I am hollowed out, decaying, rotting, and he is not here to put me back together.

Kill me.

Kill me. Kill me. Kill me.

My fingers tighten over the corner of my book, the old paper crinkling beneath my hold. Gaze locked on the flames of the fire, my body trembling softly like a hummingbird at the very end of its life. So much pain and torment. I just want it all to end. I think of that leather belt cuffed around my wrists, the want of having it close around my neck, pulled tight, cutting into my skin as it cuts off my breath. I feel the haunting pounding in my temples, the slowing of my heart rate, the darkness closing in on me instead of the comforting gloom.

A tear rolls down my cheek, one I could not have stopped if I had tried and I hate it. My weakness, something physical to show the world the aching in my chest. I am not much more than a breathing corpse and it is all just too much for my mind to handle. A runaway train that still has one track in mind.

Death.

That is all I long for now.

But I want it to be *him.*

I don't think that I can leave this world if not by his hand.

And I hate myself.

For all of it.

For loving a monster who does not know how to let himself be loved.

And for being a strange girl that craves the kind of love only a monster can give.

"Haisley," I blink hard at my name.

Wolf's voice so similar to the one I long to hear, I let my eyes close, just for a moment, imagine it were *him* and then I look up and let it all dissolve into reality.

"Mm?" I hum in answer, words all feel like too much tonight, and when I give my attention to Wolf, the way he is sitting forward now, elbows on his knees, gaze intent on mine, I clear my throat. "I'm going to bed."

I shift my legs, close my book, place it on the wide arm of the old chair, curl my fingers over the hem of the blanket and-

"No, you aren't," Wolf says gruffly, not smooth at all, and I feel my lungs seize, trying to suck in a breath rather than choke on one.

"I don't want to sit here any longer," I say then, pushing the throw off of my legs, balling it up instead of folding it.

"Sit still," Wolf sighs, dropping his head so he can run a hand down his face without having to lift an arm.

It is a compulsion of fatigue, rather than one of commandment, that I sit still, my socked feet, still cold, pressing to the wooden floor.

"I want you to talk to me," he says lowly, my eyes on the floor space between us. I can see his feet, grey ankle socks, in the top of my vision, but I don't lift my eyes to his. "I didn't want to pry," he says quietly, and my eyes bulge with my lack of blinking. "But I need to know what happened here, Haisley. If I'm going to try and help you, I need to know."

I swallow hard. This is the first time he has ever asked me about the events that transpired here. I'm not sure I can cough up enough words to tell him how his brother broke my heart, and not even because of what happened less than forty feet away from where we sit now. It was his lie that gutted me, finished me off, left me like this.

So instead of saying any of that, the information he thinks he seeks, I say, "No one can help me, Wolf." I swallow, lift my watery gaze unto his, like sparkling gold in the too bright light of the room that was once nothing more than flickering fire and gloom. "I don't want help."

I don't even want Thorne to get help.

Make him come back to me. I don't want to fix him, I just want him to be happy. With me. *Tell him to love me. Tell him to save me. Tell him he is my everything. Tell him I will die without him. My heart is broken, Wolf, tell me how you will fix me.*

Instead of saying anything, he nods, solemnly, but he does nod, as though he could ever understand what is happening inside of my head right now. My hands shake and I clamp them down onto my thighs, curl my fingers savagely into my flesh, nails carving through my cotton pyjama pants.

"I'm here," Wolf tells me with a bit of a swallow, my eyes lifting to his. "If you want to talk to me," he shifts, like this is an offer he wouldn't usually make. "I'm a good listener."

I nod, drop my gaze, see the smallest hint of red bloom through the pale grey cotton on my thighs, my nails biting into my flesh, and I forcibly relax my hands, watching it form.

There is a silence between us, but it is not uncomfortable, so I don't move from my chair, resettling back into it.

"He killed someone," Wolf says cautiously, "Close to us," he almost whispers, breaking the slow lapping comfort.

He says it like it hurts him to, but not because of

what that means, but because he is spilling a sacred secret of his brotherhood, something, I think, hurts him to do so.

Slowly, I lift my eyes again, gaze flickering over his face, dropped head, hunched shoulders, eyes on the floor space between his feet. It looks like it pains him just to utter the words, a betrayal to his very private brother. But he does not take them back, shake his head, bite down on his lips to seal his tongue inside his mouth. Instead, he glances to his hands, hanging between his parted thighs, curls his fingers together, lacing them in an unusual way, the back of one hand sliding inside the palm of his other, fingers crossing over the top of each other. It flexes his elbows outwards like the head of an arrow, and I wonder for a second how it can feel comfortable.

"Thorne doesn't remember what he did, only that he *did*." Wolf's eyes are on mine, the air dense between us and I daren't move as he clenches his jaw. "I loved her," he swallows, as though he is betraying someone with those words, perhaps himself. "But I think I was the only one."

I can't help staring. This large man with an even larger heart, I have seen it for myself already, since he arrived here, the kind way he treats me, even when he holds pity in his gaze. He is almost soft, such a sharp contrast to Thorne and I like it as much as I hate it. Just because he's not the man I want to be here with.

"He thinks we don't know. What he did to protect us," he swallows, I'm not sure he really sees it that way, but Thorne does, so he doesn't disagree with it, their loyalty and love is thicker than the blood they share. "Thorne is a protector, he just doesn't realise that sometimes there are people who can protect him too, *want* to. He doesn't know how to let go, he needs to ha-"

"Control," I finish for him.

Wolf nods, "I know something happened here, Haisley," he speaks softly. "I know it wasn't just something to do with the body."

Shane.

He looks right at me, and I cannot look away, my skin prickles with a chill, and I think of Thorne's warm hands caressing down my spine.

"My brother hurt you," a statement of knowing. "He would never leave you unless he thought *he* was the danger."

The sob that lodges in my throat threatens to choke me, and as much as I hold it back, tears streak down my flushed cheeks anyway. Unbidden in the rivulets they fall in, I don't wipe them away, I don't try to hide. I'm just... *tired.*

"Thorne holds onto guilt because he's a protector. He doesn't know how to break down barriers and forgive himself. I'm not sure he can, Haisley," it is so resigned, factual, a sigh of something like devastation leaving him.

I just nod my head, swallow thickly, use the heels of my thumbs to wipe my cheeks.

"What happens to me now?" I whisper in the

echoing silence, Wolf's sad eyes lifting back to mine. "We can't stay like this forever."

"I'm not going to let anything happen to you," Wolf states matter-of-factly.

"For how long?" I almost laugh, "You can't stay here with me forever, Wolf."

He shakes his head, drops his gaze back to the floor.

"I'm too tired," I whisper instead, a confession, "I'm too tired for this, I'm not even supposed to be here."

"Where are you supposed to be?" he questions, genuinely curious.

Dead, dead, dead.

"Not here," I swipe a hand over my head, down the back of my hair.

Not anywhere.

CHAPTER 31

THORNE

Bass pounds through the speakers, my ears buzz, thumping of my own heartbeat burning inside of them too. Lazily, I circle my fingertip around the rim of my glass, elbow and opposite forearm resting on the polished wood of the bar. I slip my fingers around the crystal cut tumbler, bring it to my lips and knock the watery dregs back.

Over the last seven weeks, I have been here most nights, a place I used to frequent when I wanted to drown out the world, thoughts of the girl, much too young for me, with haunting jade eyes. She is all I think about, even now, our history twisted, because we have forever been connected and she does not even know it.

But that has ruptured now.

Fragments of the picture in my head, something I imagined, longed for with her, a delusion, really, because there was never any way this would end well for either of us, especially not together.

People like me *work* for people like her, we do not have the luxury of marrying them. Something Dad has reminded me of always, harsh but true.

But despite this. I am in love with her.

Forbidden and wrong and frowned upon.

And I did not care, until I hurt her.

We are not supposed to hurt the people that we love.

I suddenly wonder if that is why my father always swore me off, made sure I kept a distance, made sure to keep me away.

Because he knew I would ruin her if I ever managed to lure her in.

And he knew that I would try, if given half the chance.

After all, I inherited my sickness from him. Obsession is in our DNA.

Siren's gleams in bright neon blue letters behind the bar. Mirrors running the length of it, liquor shelved along them. The bartender glances at me as I let my head drop onto my open hand, fingers gripping my cheek. I raise a finger in signal, and she purses her plum-coloured lips, but grabs the bourbon regardless. Stopping before me, she places down a folded royal blue napkin, just another thing that matches the blue and chrome décor. A modern industrial feel to the place, high end, exclusive, not somewhere the average guy would stumble upon. Not unless you know someone. The *right* someone. MCs are not usually keen on hosting too many outsiders, but they do still need somewhere to rinse their money.

One of her hands tight on the bottle, warm dark skin, pale pink painted nails, the other, stacked with gold rings, dips beneath the bar top, bringing out a fresh glass, placing it down on the napkin, unscrewing the bottle, she starts to pour. No ice this time, because it is after one and this has become some sort of self-pitying routine. She flicks her ebony eyes up onto mine. A heavy crown of dark brown braids piled high on top of her head. She re-screws the bottle cap.

"You were here yesterday?" she asks, an arch to her brow, disapproving.

I could lie.

Because *she* was not here yesterday, Melanie was instead, and she never pours my drink right, too busy adjusting her perky breasts inside, or rather, *outside*, of her low-cut black work shirt. But I do not look, I do not care for them, or for her, I only come here to drink.

Alone.

To drown the ache in my core.

I raise a brow at the same time I lift my glass, knock the warm contents back in one, let the burn heating my oesophagus consume me.

"Maybe I was, *Gabrielle*."

She scoffs at my answer, uncaps the bottle once again with a heavy roll of her eyes, refills my drink, but she does not correct my use of her full name. *Yet.*

"You're just as irritating as your brother," she says then, sighing.

Placing the bottle back down, her long fingers

remain curled around the glass housing honey liquid, spinning the cap in her other hand.

"He tips less," I shrug, not needing confirmation of that, I used to drink here a lot and Archer only comes for the women, not that I've seen much of him lately.

Or any of them.

Especially not here.

"He also never calls me anything but *Gabby,*" *there it is.* "Don't you got somewhere you're sposed to be?" she raises both sculpted brows, lips pursing.

"Nope," I pop the P, slide my glass closer to her, rucking the neat napkin up beneath it.

She cocks her head and I know she is trying to get me to leave, before any of *them* get here, but I am not so sure I care. It is possible I *need* the shit kicked out of me just to make it through another day. Even if it is by a fucking motorcycle club. Perhaps, that is exactly what I came here for.

"It's like you come here to get smacked about," Gabby says, echoing my thoughts and I smile then. "Jesus," she mutters, shaking her head, "Just..." she blows out a breath, "Don't get blood on my bar or you'll be the one cleaning it up."

"There won't be any fucking blood," a dark rumble half-barks at my back, the body it belongs to approaching the seat beside mine, right on time to monitor the place for closedown.

My head slips in my hand as I cock it to take in the new arrival, readjusting my fist, I slump my chin onto it.

"Thorne," Slade sighs.

His six-foot-eight frame folds itself effortlessly onto the royal blue velvet barstool, thick shoulder brushing the top of my arm. I think of the mess there, red raised scars and the occasional pinch of pain. I do not mind seeing them, knowing who I took them for. Slade's grey eyes find mine, pale concrete grey reminding me of gravestones, a cold contrast to his warm brown skin. He lifts a brow, top lip pulling back slightly in a half-snarl as the vice president of The Reapers flicks his assessing gaze over me.

"Scourge," I greet using his road name, one of his tattooed hands scrubbing over his short beard, dense black afro curls cut close to the skin.

"We're not doing this tonight," he growls lowly, his deep voice thick and loud even over the drowning bass. "You wanna get fucked up and beaten to a bloody pulp because you think you deserve it, or some fancy people shit, that I'll never even *pretend* to understand, then get the fuck out of my bar and do it elsewhere. I got a lot going on right now, and you, *Mr Blackwell,* are not gunna be adding to it, capiche?"

His eyes roll onto mine, both brows lifted, just daring my half-drunk arse to argue.

I nod and he blows out a breath, shoulders deflating.

"Gabs," he grumbles, gaining her immediate attention where she hovers a little closer than before, she grabs a bottle of beer, plants it down in front of him. "I don't appreciate you coming in here to do anything but drink, Thorne," he swigs from his bottle, swallowing down half of its contents before he looks at me again. "I don't have to let you in here at fucking all. So, remember *that* next time you come in here looking for trouble." He finishes the bottle, looks to me with exhaustion, "Go home."

It hurts more than it should, those words. I want to tell him I don't have a home, not anymore, but that I almost did. I carved it into pieces and set it on fire. There is no going back for me. You cannot build a foundation out of ash. And that is all that is left for us there.

Because of me.

So, without argument, I take his advice. Slumping off of my barstool, I drag my arse to the mill.

CHAPTER 32

THORNE

April thirteenth, it is late, the eve of Hunter and Grace's wedding.

This is one of only three singular visits to Heron Mill I have made over the last eight weeks, choosing instead to stay in my penthouse in the city. I sit in my usual place at the kitchen table, always to the left of Dad, the rest of the seats empty, a plate of untouched food before me. It churns my stomach, the thought of forcing food down my neck when it is already so constricted with self-loathing, makes me want to vomit. I push it away with the barest of touches, my fingertips moving it back.

I am tired.

Fed up of moping about something that is a fault all of my own. I am not good, and I never wanted to be. Not even for her, but she is so different to everyone I have ever met before. I think she loved me despite it all. Then I ruined her anyway.

My heart clenches in my chest, a harsh grip of barbed wire coiling and tightening around it like a boa constrictor. Pain so sharp, it rips my breath away, and for one panicked moment, I cannot fucking breathe. I picture Haisley bent over that rickety old table in the kitchen, wind howling outside, sleet slashing the windows. Me, my *cock*, pressing against her.

I squeeze my eyes closed, drop my head, press my curled fists to the inside of my thighs, drive my knuckles into the flesh, push harder and harder until I cannot feel any of it at all. And I wish for a drink. Something to take the edge off. It makes me think of Raine, his struggles with addiction, and I wipe all thoughts of liquid numbing from my brain.

"Thorne?" it is the lilt to her voice, something so soft, fragile, an appropriate angelic shield for a demon of darkness, she captures my attention all the same.

Like for like.

That is what we are.

I open my eyes, draw in a soothing breath, glance to where my stepsister, soon-to-be sister, stands in the doorway.

"Grace," I greet her.

Tiny body dressed in white, long silk pyjama pants, a thin strap vest, white knitted cardigan over top of it all. Blonde hair surrounds her entire frame like a golden cloak, wavy tresses hanging all the way down to the middle of her thighs. She tilts her head, mismatched eyes, one a warm hazel, the other, icy blue, drag slowly down the parts of me she can see, exposed above the table. She blinks, lashes fluttering and stares straight at me.

"There is a moth," she tells me quietly, blinking again like it is something practised rather than natural, as though she has to remember to do it, *act normal.*

I know how painful that can be for people like us.

We are all strange here.

It is after two, but she looks just as wide awake as I, except she looks fresh, and I am sure that I do not. I do not usually sleep well, but since I left Rook Point, it has been barely manageable. The nightmares shred the inside of my skull like hooked talons, then the memories of the things I have done twist and warp into the fiction, leaving me a panting, sweaty mess when I wake with a start. I can count the hours of sleep I have gotten this week on one hand alone.

I glance up, realising I was lost for a moment, Grace still waiting patiently in the archway. Without further information, because this is how she works, it is how *we* work, there does not really need to be many words spoken between us. Something natural we have built over the last five and a half years. I nod, push my wooden chair back over the stone floor, untucking myself from my place at the table. I stand, and she turns, and I follow her silent steps as she glides down the sconce-lit hall.

When she takes me into one of the many living rooms, a singular light on in the far corner, the ceiling high, I see it then, a large brown moth fluttering around the bulb. It makes my skin crawl, insects, wings, especially inside the house, but Grace turns to look at me. Her big mismatched eyes wide, expectant. Approaching her, I take her hand, cold and bony, in mine, she steps up onto the couch, using me for balance, bare feet on the cushion. Releasing her fingers, I hunch forward, bending my knees, then help her swing herself up onto my shoulders.

Her small hands grip the top of my head lightly for balance, my hands going to her silk covered knees. I hold on tight, her back straight, I take her over to the dancing moth shadows in the corner. I hold still, gold floor lamp before me, I let her take her time, her insignificant amount of weight strangely comforting where she straddles my shoulders. She does not panic, or rush, she just breathes, the soft movements of her working through my spine, and I find my own lungs synchronising with hers. She leans forward then, and I glance up, her arms stretching forward, cupped hands closing gently around the large moth.

"I have it," she says gently, low and slow.

Reaching up, I twist her around so she straddles one shoulder. A leg dangling either side of me, one down my chest, the other my back, and then I grip her waist, curl of my fingers sliding her down and off my body. She stands before me, staring at her closed hands, an almost smile on her face.

"Thank you," her eyes find mine, the darkness and shadows surrounding us.

It is hard, in this moment, picturing the things I know she does so well down in the basement. There is death and rot and decay in the underbelly of this home and she thrives inside of it all.

A flower blossoming from a corpse.

I lead her through the halls, back into the kitchen, moonlight flooding in through the large window above the copper sink. It is a clear night. An almost full moon, and I watch as the gentle, bloodthirsty girl with the unusual eyes, pads barefoot down the three stone steps. Wandering out into the grass, she releases the captured moth with nothing more than a lift of her arms. She tilts her head back, watching it go, fluttering up high and disappearing off into the dark.

She turns back to me when she loses sight of it, trailing closer with a small curve to her pink lips, curious tilt to her head. The distance closing between us as she makes her way up the steps, back into the house, through the doorway I step aside for her to enter through. And then her arms wrap around me from behind as I bolt and lock the door, she presses the side of her face into the centre of my spine, whispering as I breathe deep.

"Tell me about them, Thorne."

I put distance between it all, brain from heart, razor sharp and cutting when they are too near, but I look down to the floor, my shined shoes glittering against the dark stone and I think of the last time I saw *her*. Her eyes much the same. Glittering, wet, sad, so fucking sad, my heart bleeds a little more, decay seeping into my bloodstream.

I look down my body, Grace's icy white hands

knotted tightly across my sternum, knuckles prominent like hidden claws beneath her pale skin. I lift my own, place them atop hers and then I let my head bow. Her warmth against my spine, the tightness of her hold around the cinch of my waist. My sister, probably the only sibling I have that perhaps could understand, because we think differently to the other dark creatures inside of this house. And even if she does not, she will pretend to, *for me.*

I blink, sniffing hard, pry her hands loose and turn, keeping her fingers in my own.

"Is it a girl?" she asks inquisitively, "Or a boy?"

I smile down at her, her chin tilted up, "You mean a woman or a man."

She bites the corner of her mouth, eyes tightening with a suppressed smile.

"Yes," she nods, dropping her gaze. Eye contact is still a little much for her, after the trauma of her past, but I do not mind, eye contact is hard for me too. "Did they hurt your heart?" she whispers, glancing back up, her fingers still locked within mine.

I stare at them, long and thin, bony and pale, they are almost ghostlike, a ghoul, something frightening and unusual. I like that a lot about her.

Holding both of her hands in one of mine, I lift my other, sweep it over her head, cup the crown of her skull, cradle it in my palm. She tilts her chin, further capturing my gaze and blinks hard, just the once.

I shake my head, "I hurt hers," I confess, smoothing

my thumb over her silky hair, feeling the curve of bone as I apply a light pressure.

So many people have hurt this girl, including my brother, albeit for a short time, one I do not think he will ever forgive himself for. Clearly, we are not cautious men when faced with our obsession. I think of when she was locked in St. Michaels, her mother hiding her away from us, the way Hunter tore out an orderly's fingernails, shoved them so far down her throat she vomited in her own mouth, and he made her choke on them, and it, for ripping out his Gracie's. She is so very perfect for our family. For Hunter. I cannot picture our lives without her.

"And now you are sad," her light brows pinch, a crease forming between them, one I reflect in my own.

"I am," I swallow, keeping focus on her knuckles, free of scars, unlike my own.

"You love her?" she probes, her head tilting inside of my palm.

"Very much," I confess, emotion raw in my chest.

"Then you must fix it," she breathes simply. "Hunter did," she smiles softly as I glance up, voice like a haunting, "Don't give up, big brother." Her mismatched eyes fly between mine, "If she is meant to dance in the shadows, too, you will fix it. Show her you're sorry. Show her you love her. If she is right for you, she won't mind the hurt. *From you.*"

CHAPTER 33

THORNE

The pergola glitters in the darkness, solar charged fairy lights strung across the wooden slats, stars blanketing the sky above, the moon, round and full, beaming down. I stare at Wolf across the outdoor table, baby Roscoe snoozing on his chest, his thick arms cradling him there, one big hand smothering our nephew's head of black hair. Wolf glances up, his own black hair pulled up into a topknot, his light eyes bright beneath the moon's rays.

Archer and Arrow took the older two boys to bed, Atlas and River, whilst Raine has disappeared off somewhere else for the night. Our youngest brother will never conquer his demons the longer he feeds them.

I have had too much to drink, it is the only thing I can do to numb my mind, the pain in my chest, other than the distraction of taking on another job. Corpses' decaying organs are much easier to deal with than my own, the blackened one oozing inside my chest holds far too much of my attention.

My eyes are glazed, burning in their sockets, yet I lift my glass all the same, bring it back to my lips, swallow its contents. Fire lights its way down my throat, pooling and heating in my chest, the warmth of it expanding, spearing out like splaying fingers with toxic talons driving into my flesh.

Hunter and Grace, the newlyweds, are off running in the forest, although they are most likely fucking by now. Their wedding was beautiful, no one but our family here, it was perfect. I think of marriage, something that should be my duty as the eldest Blackwell son, but I am unsure if that could ever be on the cards for me. Marrying the other half of my soul one day, what it would feel like if that were a possibility. I am not sure that it is, so I push the thought aside.

I suddenly remember the nanny I have locked up in one of my many underground safe places. An acting prison for Rachel, rotting away down there in the darkness, where she will stay until my brother decides on what he would like to do with her for endangering his family. The longer she survives only extends my sentence of suffering. A fuck up I cannot escape whilst she still breathes. But it is not for me to decide her end because of my guilt. So I pour myself another drink.

Tugging on the collar of my shirt, I free another button at my chest, everything feels suffocating. After my conversation with Grace last night, my thoughts drifting back to Slade and his triggering word. *Home.* I feel a bit all over the place today. Because I know what I have to do now.

"Thorne," Wolf says lowly, dragging me out of my own thoughts, my heart thumps a little out of rhythm and then I knock back my fresh drink, placing the glass down, too hard, on the wooden table. "The fox finally went."

It is as though a blade slides into my heart like a knife through hot butter, we knew this day would come, had to. Clover is a wild animal, he needs to be free, but I picture my girl's face and I feel my own crumple.

"She, uh, it didn't go well," Wolf shrugs loosely, but his shoulders are tense. "She wasn't great when I left," he says almost to himself, a pinch to his brows, he twitches his nose and I feel my heart quicken.

"You care for her?" I breathe out, the question too fast, almost silent as my breath rushes from my chest.

His eyes snap onto mine, a muscle thrumming in the back of his jaw.

"Of course, I fucking do," he snarls as though he is insulted, and another blade suctions its way through my chest.

I do not know why I am so surprised.

It was a half hope. That she would fall for my brother, he for her. Wolf is much better than I am, at, well, all areas of human contact, really. It is only natural that the young woman who needs, *craves*, affection would fall for a man, only too willing, to give it.

He stares across the table at me, face blank, and I see too much of my mother in his features. I wish he looked more like me, like Dad, our brothers. It almost hurts worse. Thinking of her, *Matilda Blackwell*, her warm eyes and soft smile. The noises she made beneath the water. Bubbles and splashing and then silence.

"Did you treat her well?" I whisper, the words slipping free, and I desperately want to claw them back.

Turn back time to before I was sitting here at this table tonight. To before I ever laid eyes on Haisley Kelly. But they are out there now, unable to be unheard, unspoken, and as sick as it is, I need to know how he was with her. He would have treated her better than me. It is why I never really touched her.

"What?" Wolf whisper-barks, my eyes slowly rolling up in their sockets to look at him once more, his own flicking to the sleeping babe in his arms, before rising and resettling on mine. "What the fuck are you talking about?"

I swallow, can hardly bring myself to ask it but then I get this roll of nausea flipping inside my stomach and I bite out the vicious words before I really have time to think about them.

"When you *fucked* her? Were you good to her?" Wolf stares at me across the dark space, the night air crisp, and then his eyes narrow.

"Fuck you, Thorne," it is savage, the way he hurls the words at me, low and deep, simmering violence flaring in his eyes.

I raise a brow, straightening my spine in the wooden slatted garden chair, lean forward.

"So you were a beast then?"

He laughs instantly, a sharp short bark, the slumbering tot stirs in his arms but he does not wake, Wolf's eyes sticking to mine.

Shaking his head, he scoffs, "Listen here, *brother,*" he spits the last word like he despises it. "I shouldn't have to sit here, defending myself to you, for comforting a lonely, scared woman that *you* abandoned, *and* left *me* in charge of protecting. So don't get on your fucking high horse, you piece of shit, *especially* when it comes to this. I don't fuck what doesn't belong to me, and I don't fuck women who are insanely in love with another man. *Especially* when it's with my own fucking brother. So take your goddamn head outta your arse and get back to that fucking lighthouse, Thorne, because if you don't, it is going to kill you both."

I stare at him, and something like grief ripples through my veins, a shuddering down my spine.

"Grace gave me similar advice," I admit, slouching back in my seat, allowing my body to slump.

"I'm sorry," Wolf says after a long moment, shaking his head as though to clear his thoughts. "Did you say *Grace* gave you advice?"

"Yes," I answer, a little disbelief in my own words.

"Christ," he mutters, lifting his own glass to his mouth and swigging it down. "Well, don't leave me hanging, what did she say?"

"Something about, if the girl is right for me then she will not mind the hurt," I glance up, his eyes focused on mine, "From me."

"Jesus," he huffs a laugh, looking down at our

nephew in his arms, then, "I'm not going back to the point."

"I know."

"You are."

"I know that, too."

"Tomorrow, brother, not tonight."

"First thing."

"Don't say you're sorry," he flicks his gaze back up to mine, his hand cradling Roscoe's head. "Just prove it, Thorne. No more holding back."

No more holding back.

Nerves race through me, heart pounding, palms of my hands getting slick.

I think of all the ways I hurt her, most without actually doing anything to her at all. The lack of affection I showed, attention, the craving to love and destroy her, so consuming, that I chose to keep a distance, to keep her safe.

I thought I was keeping her safe.

Until I hurt her worse.

"What if she cannot look at me the same?" *Because I cannot look at myself the same.* "What if I have already ruined everything so badly that she does not want me anymore?" *Because she shouldn't.*

I look into his eyes, my brother expressionless as he takes me in, eyes roving over my face, analysing the flaws I vulnerably allow him to see.

"She can," he says gruffly, "And she does."

CHAPTER 34

HAISLEY

Sleep feels foreign to me lately; it's something I used to love doing, naps in the sun, naps when it rained, on the bed, sofa, chair. Really, I could fall asleep just about anywhere and be happy while I dozed. Now it evades me like smoke drifting through tightly curled fingers. It's unobtainable. Much like getting a grip on any singular emotion.

My chest feels like fire. Agony, searing hot, carving through my breastbone. It feels like my rib bones are contorting, curling into my decaying organs like razor sharp constrictions. Everything inside hurts like physical pain. I have felt somewhat lonely my entire life, even though I grew up in a house packed full of people, but nothing has ever felt like this.

The sun is just starting to rise, the sky clear, a dull blue. My eyes focus on the curve of the earth in the distance, where sky meets water, and there's that slip in between. That's where I want to go. To see what is there, to *be* what is there. To sit in the view, see it from the inside. Anywhere has got to be better than here.

Wolf has been gone a day and a night, I am sure he will be back later today, because he told me so. Wolf is a Blackwell, and as such, does not tell lies. I want to laugh, because my experience with that says different, but my eyes burn with tears instead and I have to hold my breath to choke down my sob. And I don't really want Wolf to come back, to have to see his face anymore. Not only the way he has so many similarities to his brother, but I can't take the saddened expression on his down-turned features.

Watching me cry the day that Clover finally didn't come back in at night. I waited on the front doorsteps, in the half-hidden alcove until daybreak, just waiting, half hoping, half praying, but he didn't return to me. I know it's because I did my job right, caring for him, giving him strength to survive without me. And I'd been leaving him to roam freely without me the last couple of weeks, hoping he would be able to recognise where he should be and just disappear into nature. And then he finally did, and it hurt.

It still hurts.

I am by myself again and Wolf is my babysitter. He is not a captor, but he would not have let me go, had I asked, which I didn't. It would endanger his family, which I would never want to happen. Besides, I don't have anywhere to go to. No one else to keep me. No person that is out there somewhere missing me, waiting for me.

Because he was *here*.

The person I thought was for me.

Thorne.

Breathing life into my corpse, as we existed together in the gloom.

But Thorne is not coming back for me.

I know that now.

And to go on, barely existing without him, is not how I want to survive. Life is for the living and I am not that. I am supposed to be dead. Officially, I am already dead to my family. The world. I was dead the moment I severed that blade through my cousin Cian's neck. My old life is nothing but ash. I am lost. Floating. Caught somewhere between worlds, the veil of our gloom was always so temptingly seductive when we were in it together, now it is just cold. And I desperately seek out the darkness instead. Bleak and solid and permanent.

The morning air is cold, but I hardly feel it whipping at my wet cheeks, my hair assaulting me as it flies about me in the wind. Stones and gravel press into my bare soles, prickling my feet, gouging at my skin. White dust clouds around my ankles, tips of my toes hanging over the crumbling edge, I look out at the view. I am so high up here, the water below so violent, but far beyond, out at the earth's curve, the sky and the sea, all of it meeting, breaking now with a haze of deep orange as the sun starts to climb.

I think of how cold the water below will be, how I think I will catch my breath when I finally hit it. How it will probably feel like knives puncturing deep into my flesh on impact, peel away my skin with the pressure. I wonder how quickly it will fill my lungs. If I will struggle. If I will try to surface. If I will just sink. Then days later I'll bloat, perhaps I'll float then, perhaps when all is said and done, I will be one with the sea, food for the fishes and crustaceans that creep along the sand on the bottom. But it will be dark. Wherever I end up, it will be dark, and I will be free.

I shudder with cold, pulling in a breath, watching as it exhales in a cloud of white. It is April, but it is cold, especially up here.

I think of the first time I got to see inside the lighthouse, the rusted door protecting the rooks nesting high above. I can feel that tower looming behind me now, like it's a living, breathing thing. I think of Shane's ghost haunting those collapsing stairs for all eternity. I wonder if when I fall, I will be stuck here too. It's almost enough to put me off. This plan to just end it now.

But then I think of Thorne, and I feel colder, but warm.

The way he brought me out here, how I got to see the sea. For the first ever time, *with him.* How he watched me closely but let me wander, warning me away from the edge when he feared I got too close. I wonder what he would think of me now, swaying over the edge like this.

I wonder if he would care.

I wonder if he would smile.

I wonder if he would shove me right off.

A shudder ripples up my back, through my spine, rattling in my teeth. I squeeze my eyes closed tight, clench my jaw, bite down on my tongue, wish that things were different.

We were fractured and bleeding and sick. We are a sickness, and it is wrong, and yet, I wanted it all the same.

I loved him all the same.

My captor, my monster, my love.

I want him to find happiness. I want him to find love. I want him to find peace. I want him to find someone that will accept him for him and love him the way I never could.

I want him to find life.

But above it all, I want him to find home.

Something that I don't think we ever found together, but I think, perhaps, we were starting to. Maybe we were always doomed. Perhaps that's why we couldn't exist outside of the gloom.

A pitter-patter of raindrops hit my skin, mixing with my tears, ice and salt. I lick my lips, shuffle a little further to the edge and finally look down. The sun is warm, even as the clouds close in, the orange rays spearing through the grey. Light icy raindrops plop down onto the dusty ground around me, the white cliff I am stood on, eroding beneath my bare feet, pebbles and rocks crumbling beneath my wriggling toes, crashing into the swirling white waves below.

Navy-grey swirls and foams below, I take a deep breath in, staring at the waves and then I look up, watch the sun clawing through the clouds. Arms extending out by my sides, I let myself relax, my breaths even, and even though uncontrolled tears rush down my cheeks, I feel myself smile, finally, something, just for me.

"Little Cub, please, come away from the ledge."

A tearful laugh bursts out of me, because of course he would be here.

Even in death.

"You are even more beautiful when you cry, baby girl," his gravelly, smooth words feel like silk caressing my ear.

I can feel his warmth, his breath on the side of my neck, his large body looming behind me, but he does not touch me, and I fear this is some sort of sick joke.

"Did I jump?" I whisper into the wind, my words drowned out by the buzzing inside my head, flies readying to feast on my corpse.

There is a long silence, my arms dropping slowly down by my sides, and I blink the burning in my eyes away.

"If you jump, Little Cub," he speaks lowly, "Then I am going to jump with you."

A sob tears its way up my throat, my teeth clamping shut to keep it down. I shake my head, squeeze my eyes closed, flex my toes where they hang over the edge, press them hard against the crumbling rock.

"No," I shake my head, drop my gaze, stare at the dark ocean down below. "You're not supposed to be here, you're not coming back."

"I am already here, Haisley."

My breath stutters, rain falling steadier now, droplets of water coiling their way through my curls, soaking into the fabric of my black cotton dress, heavy knitted cardigan.

"But you're not. You're not supposed to be here, this isn't how it's supposed to go. You left me," I cry, tears slipping down my cheeks.

He moves nearer and he is so close I can smell him. His scent cuts above everything else, despite him, too, also smelling like the sea, I can still smell his salt above the roaring ocean below. Leather, metal, ozone and salt, he is harsh and brutal and overwhelming. I crave it like nothing else. It is instinctual, this incessant need to breathe him in like he is the only air I need. It is a curse.

"I did leave you," he agrees, but there's still no emotion in his voice, until there suddenly is. "But I am a selfish man, Little Cub," his voice cracks and it is the first time I have ever heard it do so. "And I cannot, *will not*, get you out of my head, my heart, my soul. I was wrong to let you go. It was never my intention to hurt you in that way and if you throw yourself over this cliff edge, I do not blame you, I understand what I have put you through and it kills me to know I have hurt you this much." I feel it, in every word, the tremble of his body, the bleeding of his heart, his pain and his passion.

His love.

"But, Little Cub, you are not going to get a chance to do that," he snarls, his teeth grazing viciously over the shell of my ear, still not touching me with his hands. "You do not get to leave this world without my say so. I am your captor, and your life belongs to *me*," he hisses, and I think about flinging myself off of this fucking cliff just to spite him.

His feet appear in my vision. Shiny, laced dress shoes on either side of my own, bare and pale, smothered in tawny freckles, toenails painted in a deep plum. He boxes me in, the toes of his shoes overhanging the edge too and I hold my breath as he closes in on my back. His chest almost brushing my spine, I try not to touch him, arch my body forward, hold the air in my lungs.

"I will not hurt you," he breathes against the side of my neck, "Never again," it's a promise that has a tremor ripping down my spine, my next words slipping free unbidden.

A confession.

A declaration.

Something that should remain unspoken.

Like, I'm sure, so should most of the other things brewing inside of my head.

But I'm tired of being silent.

Tired of only being seen as this fragile, delicate thing.

"I want you to, Thorne."

He stills at my back, breath held, and we are still teetering on this crumbling edge, and I wonder for a moment if we should just throw ourselves over anyway. If it would be better for the world.

Two depraved souls, a forbidden love, I thought of, once upon a time, as unrequited. It is a sickness, a disease, a blackened, decaying plague, the love I have in my soul for him, something similar echoing in his own, *for me*, and I do not want us to be cured.

"I want it, Thorne," I breathe out, a pressured weight lifting from my chest. "I want the hurt. I *need* it. *From you.*"

There is a moment, in the immediate quiet that follows, the crashing waves, splattering rain, thrashing wind, that I wonder if I am wrong.

And then his arm clamps around my middle so suddenly that I choke on air as it *oomphs* free of my lungs, his other hand securing itself around my neck, collaring me into submission. I'm breathing hard, panting sharply, my breath sailing thinly in and out of my lungs, my back brushing his chest with every inhale-exhale.

"I don't want you to treat me like I am broken, like I am precious. I want you to hold me too tight, I want you to hurt me and love me and fuck me. *Use* me."

I almost scream it into the wind, the sea, the rising sun, the rain clouds as they lower, the rumble of thunder and then I groan as his fingers tighten around my throat, cutting me off from saying anything further. His breath harsh and ragged in my ear, hot on my jaw, my neck.

"Are you sure you want to know what you really do

to me? How you really make me *feel?"* he says with something like self-disgust.

And it only makes me hotter for him.

Needier.

Desperate.

Luckily, with his hand around my throat, my answer needs no words, I push myself back into him, his arm around my waist constricting once more. And I can feel him. All of him. His firm warmth pressing into all of my soft, cool flesh, the thick, pulsing hardness between his carved hips digging into my lower spine. I suck in a sharp breath as he pulls me into him harder, my head knocking back against his chest, fingers flexing looser on my throat. And there is no space between us, no air, and that familiar dense bubble of gloom starts to descend around us once more.

"I love you, Thorne Blackwell. And I am not deserving. But I want you and your sick, deviant, black heart anyway."

Thorne groans in my ear, it is primal and wanting, something thick in his throat, and he holds me so tight, I swear I hear my bowing ribs crack under the pressure. Abruptly, he releases me, and I tip forward, unbalanced, my arms swirling and flapping in the space before me, my feet slipping off the cliff edge and my heart constricts like it's preparing to shatter. But then, in a flurry of movement, he's there, his big hand fisting in my shirt, one in my hair, he wrenches me back from the dissolving ledge, my feet barely grazing the floor.

Thorne slams me down into the dusty earth, his

towering body crashing down on top of me, his weight on my back. I gasp for breath, side of my face pressed into the gravelly dirt.

"You want me like this, Little Cub?" it is a sinister whisper. "This uncontrollable monster? You think you can handle me? *Tame* me?" his mouth is to my ear, his scent in my nose and I want more.

"Smother me," I choke out, "I don't want to tame you. I want you out of control, Thorne," I pant the words free, his body crushing me into the ground, I whisper, "Let that monster free, Thorne, come play with me in the gloom."

Thorne rears up, knees bracketing my hips, one hand savage on the side of my head, mashing my face into the ground. I watch him from the corner of my eye, staring up at him. Rain splattering down around us, I don't feel it anymore, his big body looming over mine. Concentration on his face, his free hand rucks my dress upwards, bunching it around my shoulder blades, tangled in my cardigan. His dark eyes swirl with madness as he watches himself free his belt, he works meticulously, unthreading the leather through the buckle. When his slacks gape open, his gaze flashes onto mine, a needy whimper working its way up my throat.

He leans forward, intense pressure pounding through my skull. He dips his face low, his breath on my cheek, a tear leaks from the corner of my eye, and I watch as he tracks it with his eyes, following it down my skin. Then his tongue is there, lapping it up, his fingers digging into my face, the side of my head, his thumb carving an imprint of itself into the apple of my cheekbone.

"So beautiful when you cry," he whispers against my slick cheek, his saliva feeling like a gift, "*For me.*" I suck in a sharp breath, his cock thick and heavy against the middle of my spine, his thighs spread wide, knees digging into the earth on either side of my hips. "You want this?" he whispers, and it almost sounds like a real question, as though he would allow me to change my mind, let me say *no*, but we both know that's not true, it's all part of our game.

Slowly, his weight lifts off of my head, his hand gently smoothing down the side of my face, over my hair, brushing the wild curls back from my face. Almost like he's trying to be gentle, but I know him now, I know he cannot touch me with anything but brutal hands. And that is what I crave. All of his dark, deviant parts, I want them to be entirely focused on me.

"*Thorne,*" I breathe, his name a curse, a prayer, a wish, a hope, a sin, "Thorne."

He hums, something dark, a deep rumbling in his chest, his eyes flick over my head for a split second, onto the view, immediately darting back to mine. They're blown black, a cruel smirk lifting one corner of his lips, he tilts his head to one side, that curious, predatory stare. Time slows down, and then speeds up at double pace, his hands close around my upper arms, lifting my chest from the floor, he shoves me forward, my head hanging over the edge of the cliff.

"Thorne!" I yelp in shock, staring down at the foamy

rapids below, my chest barely touching earth. "Thorne," I breathe, his hands planting on the middle of my back, fingers splaying over my exposed skin.

"Mm," he half hums, half chuckles, his lips brushing the centre of my spine.

He breathes hard, his hot breath puffing against my skin, almost like a warning, before his teeth are driving into my flesh, sinking in and around the bone discs in my spine. My breaths are too sharp, too quick, my heart erratic as it pounds too fast in my chest.

"Thorne," I groan as he finally releases my flesh, excruciating pain radiates down my spine, and I am sure he must have broken skin. "Thorne," I pant, and I wonder if he can hear me above the crashing waves, the heavy pound of rain. "Thorne, *more.*"

It's like my plea breaks the dam. His fingers hook into the low waistband of my underwear, tearing them halfway down my thighs, my legs squeezing together where he still straddles me. His big hands grab hold of my arse, gripping a cheek in each hand, hard enough to bruise. Then I feel the burning hot flesh of his steel cock flop heavily against the back of my thigh and I stiffen. My fingers curling over the edge of the white cliff, gripping as hard as I can, gravel and wet dirt sinking beneath my nails.

He arches over me, one hand still gripping a cheek, the other sliding beneath my hips, pressing into the centre of my pelvic bone, he hefts me up, my breasts grinding into the harsh edge. Face hanging precariously over the cliff, all I can see is my death in the waves below. Heat unfurls in my lower belly, thighs tremoring, wetness seeps slickly between my thighs. And I realise how much I love this. Life and death. Give and take. The fear.

I get hotter as Thorne lines the head of his cock up with my pussy. Not checking to see if I'm ready first, because he doesn't care, and then, thighs tight together, he works his way between my restricted flesh and thrusts inside me. He drives his cock deep, brutally, in one dangerously punishing thrust.

I cry out, eyes squeezing shut as he shunts me forward with the jolt of his hips, a strangled roar bellowing out of him. Everything burns, tingles tear down my spine, goosebumps erupting all over my flesh. I crane my head back, neck arching, and the earth beneath my squeezing fingers gives way, arms slipping over the edge, but Thorne's weight keeps me steady.

"Fuck," he hisses, bowing over me once more, his upper body, too, leaning over the edge. "You are so tight, Little Cub, you feel so good, strangling my dick, *fuck*."

I've never heard Thorne sound like this, strangled. Caught between pleasure and pain. His cock burns between my thighs, breath harsh and hot on the back of my neck, my hair trapped over one shoulder, strangled beneath my heaving chest. Tears squeeze out of my eyes, burning as they track down my cheeks. And a warmth expands its way through my chest, spearing outwards like a fast-acting poison. He drops his forehead to the back of my neck, his lips nipping and sucking harshly between my shoulder blades.

"You're the first," I breathe out, the words sounding foreign to my own ears.

He goes still, his teeth still sunken in my skin, pinched between his teeth, his tongue rolls over the flesh in his mouth, before letting me free. He rests further forward, rocking us dangerously over the edge, there is nothing supporting my body from my navel up. His cock still not having moved inside of me, mouth pressing to my ear.

"*What?*"

Chills race through me, the wind whipping around us, the sky is dark, rain heavy and I blink down into the swirling depths below.

"You're the first, Thorne," I breathe, raspy and thick, quiet, "You're my first, my only."

"Jesus fucking Christ," he murmurs into my ear, sagging against me more before he rears up, hand splaying over my spine.

He pulls out, only his tip nestled just inside, my inner walls clamp down, trying to keep him in, I twist my head, try to peer at him over my shoulder. His eyes downcast between us, his free hand reaches down, his scarred knuckles brushing against my skin, and then he lifts his fingers into the air. Head canting, he rubs his forefingers and thumb together, sticky and red on the tips. He stares at it in a trance, and my entire body trembles with the ache in my muscles, the pull at my core, trying to keep myself up on this disintegrating ledge.

"Thorne," I whisper, my voice carrying on the wind, rain splattering down over my back. "*Thorne*, come back to me."

His dark eyes snap up, both hands curling around my hips, and it's like he suddenly slams back into his body. The first real thrust of his hips has me shunting forward once more. Again and again, merciless, harsh thrusts, driving his cock deep into my cunt, until only my hip bones, his long fingers grinding the bones in his grip, are resting precariously over the edge. My hands grapple down the side of the cliff, my upper body hanging completely over the edge, when one of his hands releases my hip, fingers knotting into the back of my hair, he wrenches me backwards with a sharp crack to my neck.

I groan, tingles racing up my spine, the angle of his thrusts hitting deliciously inside of me, and I feel it low in my belly, a rush of warmth, my pussy so wet, I can hear it.

Bowing over me, my back plastered to his front, his cock plunging in and out of me, both of us soaked from the rain, he snarls into my ear, groaning, his grip punishing and painful.

"If you come before I tell you to, we are going over this edge, Little Cub."

I pant for breath, body burning, muscles screaming, teeth biting down on my tongue enough to make me taste iron. Thorne's hand slips from my hair to the base of my throat, strong fingers gripping my neck. My entire skeleton locks up tight, desperately trying to hold off on my impending orgasm, a sob tearing its way up my throat. Thorne snaps his hips into me one last time, groaning between his clamped teeth as he drives them into my throat. A rush of heat fills my insides, his hot, hard body smothering my back, only his weight angled backwards keeping us up on this cliff.

I feel like I've won, his teeth biting into me so hard my eyes spark with white orbs, his tongue lapping at the wound as he draws his teeth away. I relax forward, body aching and jelly-like, I feel content to just go over the edge now. Now that I have finally had all of this dark and dangerous man.

He bows further forward, and I feel the top layer of earth giving way beneath my pelvis, his cock still buried so deep inside me I can feel him everywhere.

"Your turn," he whispers, and like a flash of lightning, he pulls out of me.

Cum rushing down my thighs, he flips me onto my back, spine slamming into the wet ground, only my head now hanging over the edge. He rips my underwear the rest of the way down my legs, flinging them over my head, I watch them drift down towards the sea.

"Thorne!" I gasp as his hands tear my legs apart, his head disappearing between my spread thighs.

The flat of his tongue swipes up my centre in one long, languorous lick, nose brushing over my clit, before he drives his tongue inside of me, licking as deep as he can. He lashes my clit with his tongue, licking and nibbling, sucking himself out of me. It's sloppy and messy and wet, mouth open wide, suctioning over all of me. He sucks so hard it hurts and it's the bite of pain that has my orgasm tearing through me like a jagged blade ripping through my insides. He keeps sucking, swirling his tongue over me until my muscles go lax, my body lies limp, and the sensation is too, too much. But I like the feeling of his attention too much to stop him, even as I start to numb from being overstimulated.

Kissing my pussy, he rears up, our joint mess smeared all over his perfect face, hollowed cheeks, dark eyes, sharp jaw. My lips part as I stare at him, a complete uncontrolled savage and a thrill rips through my soul to see him this way. *For me.*

"Thorne," I say with awe, his face shining, patchy pink slick smeared over his chin, cheeks and jaw, evidence of what I gave to him.

He looms over me, gripping my waist in his big hands, he drags me down sharply, bringing me fully back onto solid ground, strong thighs still straddling me. He reaches up, fingers clamping and squeezing my lower jaw, forcing my mouth open. Leaning down, those deadly dark eyes on mine, pupils blown, wet hair plastered to his forehead, the rain continuing to beat down. He drives his tongue between my parted lips and opens his mouth, filling my own with a mixture of him and me, my blood, his cum, *us.*

He kisses me, and it is a resurrection, *of us.*

Our tongues tangled, the mess of us both seeping out from between our fused lips, dripping down my chin, running down the side of my cheek. Thorne draws back, his lower face smeared, mine probably much the same, he laps at me, cleaning up my face. Holding my jaw with one hand like I'm something to be cherished, the other stroking down my temple, his fingers light. He dips back down to me, my lips automatically parting once more, and he pushes the rest of our joint mess into my mouth.

"Swallow us down, Little Cub," he whispers, and I am dying to obey.

Face dipped close, head tilted to one side, long fingers stroking lovingly along the bone of my jaw, his thumb resting over the centre of my throat to feel when I swallow. I stare up at him, and I can feel it thrumming like a living breathing thing inside of me.

My love for him.

It is ripe with poison, layered with something dark, sharp and controlling and deadly. And I do not care. It makes me want him all the more.

Perhaps we are death combined, he, the maker, I, the bringer.

Salt and copper thick in my throat, I swallow, slowly lick my lips. Thorne groans so deeply it sounds like an echo of the grumbling thunder roaring overhead.

"I will love you in life and in death," Thorne whispers, his lips over mine. "I may be your captor, but you, too, are mine. Cage my heart between your dainty fingers, weave my soul through your spine. I am yours, Little Cub, I am yours." His dark eyes flare between my own, my chest heaving between us. "Will you be mine?"

Eyes filling with tears, breath stuttering in my lungs,

I nod slowly, arching my neck to press my forehead against his.

"Hate me and love me and fuck me. Kill me. You own my heart, my bones, my soul. I am already yours, Thorne Blackwell. And I, too, will love you in life and in death. May it come for us together."

Beneath me, the leather squeaks as I try not to shift again, my thighs burn and my pussy's sore, and I'm trying my hardest not to keep looking at Thorne.

It is next to impossible.

He is a God among demons, and I am nothing but a willing sacrifice at his altar.

"Little Cub," Thorne hushes, a tilt to one corner of his mouth, his lips a hot slash of sinister across the lower half of his face.

One hand resting easy on the gear stick, the other loosely gripping the steering wheel, he glances at me, catching me watching him *again*, and heat floods my cheeks, forcing me to drop my gaze to my lap. I'm in a black t-shirt dress that just covers my knees, an oversized black knitted cardigan and dark green Chucks. My hair is wild, although I attempted to tame it, the frizz is a little less, so I guess I don't look completely feral. I gnaw on my bottom lip, dragging it in and out of my nibbling teeth.

"Is this okay?" I ask quietly, smoothing my fingertips over my thumbnails, freshly painted in a deep plum, in my lap.

"Is what okay?"

"What I'm wearing," I flick my gaze up, peer at him from the corner of my eye.

"Yes."

"Are you sure? I'm not sure about my shoes, what I-"

"Haisley," Thorne says, rough and smooth, cutting me off and drawing my full attention to his side profile. "You look beautiful," he says quietly, my thoughts echoing the same thought about him. "You *always* look beautiful, in anything you wear."

Cheeks burning hotter, I suppress a small smile, my eyebrows knitting together.

Huffing a laugh, "That's absurd, you have literally seen me in tracksuits."

I say it lowly, shaking my head, at the same time he mutters.

"You need more purple."

I feel my head tilt, eyes narrow.

"Purple?" I echo, twisting around in my seat to look at him properly, I kick a leg up onto the seat, tuck my foot beneath my opposite thigh, curl my fingers over the seatbelt to tug it off of my throat.

Thorne is silent for a moment, expressionless, but his eyes seem to brighten as he keeps his attention firmly on the road.

"Yes," he finally says, "Purple. Like that dark plum dress you wore on your seventeenth birthday."

I blink, my lips open and close and there's a high-pitched ringing rattling around inside my ears.

"You think, because you did not know me before I brought you to Rook Point, that it automatically meant that *I*, too, did not know *you?*"

I stare at him, his hollowed cheeks, a dark shade of light stubble across his jaw, dark eyes, blank expression, he is so very beautiful. Wrinkling my nose, brow creasing slightly, I glance down at my hands, pale skin, tawny freckles, round nails and slim wrists.

"I do-"

"I first saw you when you were six years old," he whispers and my tummy churns like riptides in white rapids.

It feels like the bottom of my stomach falls out, goosebumps smatter across the surface of my skin, my breath hitches and I feel... *hot*. Too hot. Sweltering. I remain silent, staring at the side of his face, waiting for disgust to roil somewhere in me, but the longer I sit, the further we drive and the less I really feel anything, except...

"How old were you when I was six?"

"Almost seventeen."

"So you'r-"

"Thirty-three."

"You've followed me all this time?" I ask in some-what disbelief, how could I have been so ignorant as to not see, or notice or *feel*...

"No," his eyes still fixed to the road. "I tried to stay away from you," he says almost whimsically. "But I was there, the night of your seventeenth birthday, in the shadows at Bar Castellum, I watched you then," he pauses, finally glancing at me when he says, "All night."

My stomach knots at that, eyes blinking, gaze dropping back to my hands in my lap. I think about that night, my sisters, Shane, *Cian*. How the entire night was ruined before it even really began. My heart clenches in my chest, thinking of Thorne witnessing all that.

"I almost tore him apart then," he whispers sinisterly. "And I did not even hear what he snarled in your ear," making my heart thud hard. I look up, his eyes back on mine, "But I did not want to frighten you." I open my mouth to speak, closing it as his eyes flash back and forth between me and the road. "And I would have," he says lowly, "*Then*. So I followed you all night instead, made sure you were safe under my guard. I was waiting for him to try something, I would have stopped him, Haisley."

There's a lump in my throat, thinking back to that night, Cian's whispered words of insanity, telling me about all of the sick little things he was planning to do to me. Once I was *his*. How I had better *wait* for him or else. How frightened I was of him, when, little did I know, I didn't need to be.

Because of Thorne.

My monster stalking me from the gloom.

"I don't think you would have frightened me," I

whisper, wondering how true that statement would have been back then.

"I watched you up on the balcony," he says instead of disagreeing with me, staring out of the windscreen, nothing along the winding road but thick, green forest. "I wondered what you would look like if you had flung yourself off, your pretty little head splattering all over the pavement at my feet."

I swallow hard, thinking about that night, tears, sickness in my belly, fear blooming lava red in my cheeks. How I really did consider jumping.

"Did you always follow me after that?" my heart thumps hard, the sick want for his answer to be-

"Yes."

I almost breathe a sigh of relief.

"How often?"

He glances over at me, holds my gaze for a long moment, "As often as I could. But always on every birthday after that."

I cannot address that in any way, shape or form, because I feel overwhelmingly happy about it. Having his attention even then, when I did not know, could not see... I am absolutely a fucked-up mess. I cannot find it in myself to care.

"What if they don't like me?" I blurt out loudly, my cheeks really reddening now.

"What?" he asks loudly, as though we both just snapped into consciousness, travelling back from the past.

We're driving to a place called Heron Mill. Thorne's

family home, where all of them wait for us. Thorne called them this morning, too early for normal people to be up, but they were. His brothers, sister, father. I do not know what he told them. Why we are going.

"Your family," I say quieter now, clearing thoughts of Cian Kelly from my brain. "I think I'm dressed wrong," I sigh again, staring at my foot, dark green Chuck, white laces, poking out from beneath my folded thigh.

"You do not have anything more to say about what I have just confessed?" he asks a little slowly, fingers around the gear stick flexing, I keep staring at my lap.

"No."

"You are not upset with me?" he queries, eyes flicking between me and the road ahead once more, I don't know why he bothers, I haven't seen another car in over an hour. "For not telling you sooner?"

"Nu-uh."

"That is it? *Nu-uh?*"

I snort a laugh, "That sounds funny when you say it like that."

"Like *what?*"

"All posh."

"Posh?" he sounds outraged.

"Are you a parrot?"

"What?"

"Why are you repeating everything I say?" I ask with a straight face, and I can see him from beneath my lowered lashes, the confusion on his face, something I *never* see from Thorne. "It's something babies do, ya know, copy words they hear."

"Are you-" he licks his lips, blanks out his expression. "Are you calling me a baby?"

"Mayyybe."

"You are a very strange girl," he says then, and I know he means it in a nice way, the way he glances over at me, a curve to one corner of his mouth.

"Thank you," I say with a suppressed smile, twisting around in my seat, dropping my foot back to the floor.

I smooth out my dress, tug my cardigan back up my shoulder, Thorne's hand shifts from the gear stick to my knee, pushing the thin cotton of my dress up, his warm palm making contact with my cool skin. I watch the trees fly past as Thorne refocuses on the road, my mind wandering, wondering about all the places he watched me when I didn't know he was there.

I'm sure most girls wouldn't ever want to find out they've been stalked. But that's why I didn't want to address it further. I kind of think it's romantic. That he wanted to watch me. Protect me. Maybe sometimes he just wanted to look at me. I wish I knew he was there. Maybe I wouldn't have felt so alone.

"By the way," Thorne says a few quiet minutes later, dragging me back into the car from my mind, I look at him, his hand flexing on the top of my knee. "Wolf already thinks you are wonderful." I snort a laugh, shaking my head. "Why is that so funny?"

"Oh, it's not, it's very sweet. I just can't imagine

Wolf ever using the word *wonderful,*" I chuckle, Thorne's grip tightening on my leg.

"I suppose not," he smiles then too, looking at me as he slows the car, "They will all love you, Little Cub."

"How can you be sure?" I bite my lip, worry it between my teeth.

My own family didn't even like me enough to protect me from the raving lunatic that was my cousin, let alone *love* me.

"Because I do."

eron Mill is spelled out in old gold lettering on a black plaque, hanging on one of the stone pillars at the mouth of a wide cobbled driveway. Hidden from the road by trees and fluffy ferns, Thorne pulls the car up the winding drive, light gravel spits beneath the tyres as he brings us to a stop in front of a towering stone mansion. I peer up at it through the front window, leaning forward in my seat, my breath fogging the window as I practically press the tip of my nose to the cool glass.

Ivy smothers one side of the house, a huge set of stone steps leads up to a double-wide front door. Windows half hidden by the vines growing up the walls, a deep green, fresh and blooming as it snakes up the grey building.

"Is it a working mill?" I ask, my gaze still locked on the large home, it doesn't look like it, but looks can be deceiving.

"You could say that," Thorne says, making me frown.

I open my mouth to ask for specifics, but he's already getting out of the car, rounding the bonnet, pulling open my door.

Still staring up at the house, I twist to get out, one leg dangling over the edge of the open door, my seatbelt yanking me back making me yelp in surprise. Thorne leans across me, forcing me further back into the seat, the leather squeaking once again. His hand slides over the top of my thigh, down the side of the seat, the tip of his nose almost brushing my own. His scent invades me. I had gotten used to it in the confined space of the car, but opening the car door, the quick rush of cool air blowing in, renews it all. Salt, leather, ice and ozone, gunpowder.

I blink, my seatbelt popping free, Thorne's eyes flicking back to my own.

"Do you have a gun on you?"

Thorne blinks at me, my vision of him blurring at his closeness, but I catch his smirk as he cocks his head, lips slanting over mine.

"Why?" he breathes against my lips, "Planning to use it on me when we fuck later?"

I want to laugh, but my cheeks heat instead, and I drop my gaze.

"*Nu-uh,* eyes up," he whispers, warm lips brushing my own, curled finger hooking beneath my chin. "So beautiful when you blush, *for me,* Little Cub."

His words have heat surging through my body, and I

know my cheeks are reddening even more, but it's the rush of heat gathering in my lower belly, further down at the place between my thighs, that has me really wanting to drop my gaze. But I don't, *can't*, Thorne's eyes pinning me in place, swirling black, flecks of gold. I could get lost in them if I stared any longer.

Thorne's hand slides from the side of my seat, over my thigh, his splayed fingers dipping beneath my dress. I tremble as his strong fingers brush the edge of my knickers, the crease of my thigh, his eyes on mine holding me captive like a blade through my heart.

"You wet for me, baby girl?" he hums in a whisper, but it is darkness swirling us into the gloom, the way his words feel like a prayer to The Devil.

His finger brushes over my centre, his lips plucking lightly at mine as he does so, I gasp against his lips as he pushes against the wetness seeping through the fabric, and then he's pulling away. The Devil *in* him now, he straightens up, staring down at me, sinister and breathtaking and unpredictable. He lifts his hand, brings his middle finger to his mouth, he swirls his tongue over the pad of it, and I know that it's *me* he's tasting.

And then like nothing has happened, like he hasn't just worked us both up into the start of a blurred frenzy, he swipes his hands down his thighs, over the soft creases in his trousers from sitting in the car so long. Then offers me his hand like a true gentleman, not the demon that lies in wait beneath the pressed black suit.

"Come, Little Cub," he says quietly, the gloom engulfing us once more, protective and safe.

Thorne closes the door at my back, the sound of it echoing around the damp courtyard. The air is damp, the clouds are low, the breeze is cold making me shiver a little, the looming house feeling like a living breathing organism. It makes me feel welcome, and not, all in the same moment and then Thorne does the strangest thing. He links our hands.

His long fingers sliding between mine, lacing us together, it feels like our skin is being stitched, and I don't want this man to ever separate from me. This just feels like such an un-Thorne thing to do, but he does it so naturally, so easily, walking us up the wide front steps, hand in hand, just a demon and his sacrifice. His warmth, my coolness, my palm growing clammy and cheeks growing red, I let him lead me.

I squeeze his hand tight as we reach the top step, a large knocker on the cherry red wood front door, some sort of gargoyle type creature, dark stone grey, its eyes following whoever stands before it. It unnerves me, making me think of my cherub twins atop our gold mirror back at home, how they, and this, make me want to fidget, but before Thorne has the chance to use the scary knocker, the front door flies open.

A woman stands before us, short, but still a little taller than me, thick greying hair curled into a braided crown on her head, a long navy dress cuts off just below her ankles, revealing the toes of her white lace plimsolls, a white apron tied around her waist. I glance up, her sharp green eyes on me, making me swallow hard.

"Rosie," Thorne says, a little louder than normal.

Attempting to release my hand, he wriggles his fingers, stepping closer to the older woman, but I just squeeze his hand tighter instead of letting him go, planting my feet. The woman stares at me like she's trying to tear her way into my soul, analysing me, taking me in, her eyes flicking up my body, already judging. She stares at our joint hands and it makes my belly flop, my eyes drop, and that embarrassing flush of heat relights in my cheeks. I want to go back to the car, to the lighthouse, Rook Point, *home*.

"This is Haisley," Thorne says next, pulling me in closer to his side, not pushing me towards the woman guarding the door, but I don't look up, I keep my eyes down, stare at my feet, wish I had worn different shoes.

Thorne is so well dressed, so perfect, and I am a wild mess.

"I know it is," the woman says, softly, politely, and somewhat familiar.

Chin dipped, I glance up, gaze at her from beneath my lashes, take in those green eyes, and then I tilt my head. This time it's me analysing her. I wrack my brain for a memory, something, anything, but come up short. I don't know this woman.

"I knew your nanny Fiona," she says, making me blink, *God*, I'd almost forgotten about her, a warm smile, tight hugs, firm hand, she left me long ago.

Then Rosie's pulling me from Thorne, wrapping me up in her arms like she really knows me and she's so warm, smelling of lavender, that I find my arms lifting to encircle her too.

Squeezing me tightly, she draws back, small hands cupping my cheeks, "Such a beautiful young lady. I suppose you don't remember me, child, but that's okay, I remember you, always covered in mud and attacking your unruly brothers," she clucks her tongue. "Such a handful," she chuckles and I find myself laughing too. "I'm very happy to meet you again, dear Haisley, and with my Thorne," she says quietly, happily, glancing up at him with reverence. "Come, come in, out of the wind."

Thorne enters behind me as she pulls me inside by my hand. The foyer is grand, dark polished wood flooring, deep red patterned wallpaper, stone statues and marble busts on pillars. Paintings in ornate gold frames, and a large gold chandelier overhead. I stare up at it as Rosie closes the door, shutting out the wind, but the house is not much warmer, it makes me feel more comfortable, the absence of heat.

Rosie hurries down the hall, calling back over her shoulder, "You know where they are!" before hustling up the corridor and disappearing from view.

I take a deep breath in, feel Thorne's fingers appear on the base of my spine, his body drawing in close to my back, he looms over me as I stare down the seemingly endless hallway.

"You are wanted here, Little Cub," he presses the words to my skin, his kiss to the shell of my ear, he brings a hand around me, resting it over the curve of my belly. "Always welcome, always wanted."

I blink back tears, my breath held, I nod in response,

letting him retake my hand, press a kiss to the top of my head. We start down the hall, and I cannot help but continuously glance at him as we go. Our fingers laced, casual contact, I thought Thorne not capable of, yet he is, because my pale freckled fingers are locked between his and it is not to hurt, his hold. It is to comfort.

Our footsteps echo, Thorne's more than mine, but the sound seems to ricochet up the wooden floors, reverberating in the walls, like this old house is stealing a little piece of our essence as we wander our way through it. We stop in a large round, open archway, a kitchen *full* of people beyond it, and I don't want to enter, stepping over the threshold suddenly seems overwhelmingly daunting.

Ominous.

I squeeze Thorne's fingers so hard between mine it feels crushing, but he does little more than squeeze gently back. Comfort licks up my spine, reassurance forming around us in a bubble similar to our gloom and I exhale, breathe out deeply, my chest trembling with nerves.

There are six men in the room, all dark hair and black eyes. Only one of them familiar. *Wolf.* He offers me a slow smile from his place towards the far end of the kitchen.

It is a large room, stone floors, a copper sink, window above it. A large wooden table in the very centre, where one man faces away from us stood in the entrance, seated at the head of it. My eyes catch on a petite girl with masses of blonde hair, peering around the brother that looks the angriest. All of these people have something in common though, something more than their similar looks. Danger. It wafts off of them all like a visual cloud of colour, and as each of them turn their attention onto me, I feel like a bleeding lamb wandering blindly into a lion's den.

"If you could all sit," Thorne says calmly, all of their eyes flicking to their eldest brother, instantly making me feel cooler.

Everyone shuffles into seats, the blonde girl and the angry man sit at the furthest end, the remaining three I do not know take various seats in the centre on either side of the table. The man already seated, still, does not turn and I think this must be Thorne's father, although he never speaks of him, I wonder about his mother, where she might be.

Wolf approaches, making his way down the table towards us, where we stand sentry. I feel horrendous, nerves rattling through my chest in a violent tremor, but Thorne is at ease, his hand, the one not in mine, rests in his pocket. It makes me think I should be relaxed. Thorne will not let anything happen to me.

"How are you?" Wolf asks me, gruff and a touch loud, but he is happy and smiles down at me when he stops before me.

"I'm okay," I whisper back, trying to keep my voice from cracking with nerves.

He chucks his finger under my chin, smooths his thumb over the point of my chin and then looks to Thorne, giving him a knowing nod, before taking a seat at the table. Thorne steps forward, leading me around the table, two empty seats opposite Wolf, but we don't sit yet.

The man seated at the head of the table peers up at us, placing his phone, screen down, onto the tablecloth, a thick, wipe clean plastic with yellow and white flowers on it.

"Dad," Thorne greets, the man smiling warmly at his son, his dark gaze dropping instantly, *to me.*

His eyes are as dark as Thorne's, without the gold flecks, but he has creases around the outer corners of them, happy lines, from smiling and laughter, I realise, when he does just that to me. His lips pull into a wide smile, shaped, neat stubble peppered along his chin and jaw in perfect lines. His wavy black hair is thick, and considering this man must at least be in his fifties, he has very little silver running through it. His white dress shirt sleeves are rolled up to his elbows, olive skin dark over his forearms and hands, green veins snaking beneath. His sons look just like him.

"Ah," he says then, relaxing back in his seat, the wood creaking slightly as he does. "A Kelly." Factual, not unkind, and then, "I knew we would wind up here eventually, Son," he looks up at Thorne, and there is quiet in the kitchen.

As though everyone is holding their breath, waiting for what comes next.

Thorne gently squeezes my fingers, and my other hand comes up, curling around the inside of his elbow, shirt and jacket between our bare skin, but I curl myself into him all the same. His dad watches the move, and hair prickles on the back of my neck as he nods to himself, then indicates to the empty chairs with a dip of his chin.

"Let's make some introductions," he says cheerily, a smile back on his handsome face. "I'm Stryder," he reaches out, straightening in his seat, to offer me his hand, just before I sit in mine.

I shake his hand, dip my chin, "Haisley."

"Ah, yes! That's it. Beautiful name," turning his attention to the rest of the table.

My bottom finally making contact with the cold wood of a chair, Thorne pushes me in, sitting himself beside his dad.

"Boys, introductions," Stryder orders.

I swallow hard, my eyes finding Wolf's unusual hazel-amber ones first, and he smiles broadly at me, white teeth flashing.

"I'm glad you're finally here," he tells me, making heat flare in my cheeks, because it feels nice, because it feels honest.

The man sitting beside him cocks his head at me, an unsure look on his face, dark brown hair streaked with ebon, coal black eyes on a soft face, he looks young, more innocent, a little nervous.

"Arrow," he reaches up, palms the back of his neck, glances to his father, Thorne, then back to me. "Nice to meet you."

I offer him a smile, turning my head to the next Blackwell brother on his other side.

This man looks the youngest, but still looks older than me, he has black wavy hair, messy and choppy, flopping across his forehead. There are rough white scars down one side of his throat, trailing down into the neck of his holey black t-shirt. Heavy violet circles sit beneath his dark brown eyes, narrowed as he stares back at me.

"Raine," he voices roughly, introducing himself, with not much more than a grunt, before turning his eyes onto his father.

At the head of the table the angry brother sits beside the petite blonde girl, she is tucked beneath his thick arm as he lounges back in his chair, his dark gaze narrowed in on me like a predator. Straight black hair covering one brown eye, a scar through his right eyebrow, snarl on his lips.

I blink quickly, looking away, towards the girl instead, safer, I think. Her fingers weave a side braid through her Rapunzel-length hair as she watches me, her mismatched gaze on mine, she tilts her head, blinks hard, unnaturally.

"I'm Grace," she almost whispers, sounding like a ghost, spectre, haunting and light, something innocent to draw you in. "This is Hunter." I glance back to him, his eyebrows raised, I glance back at Grace, offer her a brief smile and then I turn to the guy between us.

"Archer," he grins, black hair, shaved on the sides, long on top, sparse strands flopping over his eyes, brown with bright spots of green and gold. "At your service," he purrs, my eyes widening before I quickly twist away, look up at Thorne, who's glaring over my head at his cocky brother.

"Why don't you tell us what's going on, Thorne," Stryder says cautiously, knowingly, I'm sure, because he looks like the type of man who doesn't let much get past him.

His words echo my own thoughts, because I have absolutely zero idea why it is we're here. And getting Thorne to respond to a question he doesn't want to answer is like trying to get blood out of a stone.

Thorne looks down at me, me, up at him, and his head tilts just a little, blocking out his father from my view. He doesn't ever need to try, he always has my complete focus. His face is blank, but serious, and it makes my belly flutter with moths. Something that exists in the gloom, butterflies are for sunshine, neither Thorne, nor I, are made for the light.

"Do you love me, Little Cub?" he asks me quietly, but it is so very loud in my ears, because everyone in this room just heard his question, his name for me, despite his volume, it was intentional, and it makes my entire being flush with heat.

We do not openly talk about emotions in my family, we do not cite love or feelings, we are empty vessels to be bought and bred, and have pretty, empty, little heads. But I stare up into his eyes, gaze into obscurity, dark and heavy and eternal and I find myself answering far easier than I would have ever imagined with an audience.

"Yes."

It is a finality, the last hammered nail in our coffin,

because I am not letting this man go, not without death, and even then, we will go together. By his hand or by mine. We are bound. Irrevocably. And the way he looks at me now, in this kitchen, the eyes of everyone he holds dear focused in on him, he only has eyes *for me*. And I know, he feels the same.

He turns away, his hand finding my thigh beneath the table, loose and warm and possessive. He looks at his father, who is already shaking his head in a *no* motion, as though, because he knows his son so well, he predicts the words before Thorne has even begun to utter them.

"I need to be publicly exiled," Thorne says casually, slowly, careful but sure. "Gather as many families as you can to make the announcement. Everyone needs to know I am no longer associated with this family."

My head snaps up so fast I give myself whiplash, "*What?* Thorne, *no.*"

The table erupts into loud discussion, protest, and I feel the eyes of everyone on me, poised like tips of daggers directed at my organs, because this is *for me*. It is my fault their beloved brother is doing this.

Choosing me.

Over them.

A public exile gives any and all mobs, gangs, mafias, assassins, anyone with an itch to hurt Thorne, get revenge, free reign, a green light to do whatever they want to him without repercussions. So that any crimes he has committed do not fall on the family. Our bylaws forbidding action or punishment to be exacted upon a family for the crimes of their exiled. To keep his family safe. Remaining untouchable, under the protection they have always had. To try and keep me safe. To keep me breathing.

He is breaking centuries-old contracts, agreements, handshakes and blood oaths made in the darkest of shadows in the Blackwell name, *for me.*

My insides tumble and I tune everyone out, I can't grasp onto anyone's words but there are so many that hurt my heart I can hardly breathe. I don't want this, not because of me. We wouldn't last more than three seconds out there. Blood is always thicker than water when it comes to the mob, family is *everything*, which is why I cannot let this happen.

I'm pushing out of my chair before I can even think not to, the sound of it screeching over the stone floor louder than the multiple conversations.

"No!" I shout then, hands slapping down onto the table, my body trembling, vibrations rushing through my arms, my legs, tingling in my spine. "No. No. *No.*" my hands fly to my hair, clawing into the strands. "Stop!" I order, and I do not even know who it is I am addressing.

I can hardly think, everything is silent now, but the buzzing in my head, coffin flies waiting to feast, is so loud, it is terrifying. And all I can see is Thorne's dead eyes inside his sullen face, staring up at me, unseeing, and it tears a cry from between my clenched teeth, because that is what nightmares are made of. Fear eats through me, something sludging through my veins. I am not okay. None of this is okay. And I cannot believe he would ever think it so.

I need him to embrace me, to take this all away. Thorne and his control, something I think I need, can take selfish comfort in because I do not need to think, make decisions, have to worry about things he can deal with for me. He protects me, keeps me safe, and he has done so even when he was strictly my captor.

The goal has always been my death and now I want to live.

With him.

Only with him.

My heart seems to soar and crash all in the same breath and they are coming so sharp and rapid that I wonder how my lungs are even working. Contracting and expanding. I feel sick and I push back the idea of vomit with a clenching of my throat. I feel his heat come to my spine, his fingers barely grazing me, and I flinch away so hard I knock my hips into the table, water sloshing over the rim of someone's glass.

"No, *no,*" I suck in a sharp breath, my breathing and pounding heart the loudest thing inside this house. "Kill me, *just,* kill me, Thorne. I'm not- we're not doing that, *you're not* doing that. This is insane," I gasp breathlessly.

That's when I finally look up at him, sound in the room like a vibration just humming, everyone still and quiet, but it is not anyone else I look at. Unshed tears are blurring my vision, and I am unsure whether the lump in my throat needs to be coughed up or swallowed down, but I *am* sure of just one thing.

"You are needed here, Thorne, wanted, *loved.* I love you enough to let this go, for *you* to let me go," I say all of these words, and I mean them more than anything I have ever felt, but I wish I did not have to speak them this way.

In this place.

At this time.

"I am just a girl always destined to die. And you are just the man cursed with the task," I whisper it almost silently.

Teeth skewering my lip, tears spilling over my lower lashes, I look up into his handsome face, my fingers just grazing the sharp angle of his jaw.

"I am ready to die for my sins, Thorne," and I am surprised by my words, how honest they feel, how very clearly, I am able to speak them when my heart is tearing apart inside my chest. "And you are forever my greatest one."

Thorne stays silent, his face blank, those dark eyes flickering between my own, and I wonder for a second what he sees. Abruptly, he tears away from me, my arm thudding as it drops back down by my side.

He flips the table.

Glass shattering, china cracking as it hits the old stone floor. Everyone throws themselves up out of their seats, scattering out of the way as chairs clatter to the floor. Stryder stands last, slower than the rest, wary, as everyone remains silent, all eyes on the oldest Blackwell son.

Thorne's back heaves, my own breaths matching his, my chest rising and falling rapidly. I am not scared but I *am* sorry.

"Thorne," I say softly, knowingly, we have been here before. "*Thorne.*"

Like a flash of lightning he spins to face me, his eyes wild, pupils blown, the force of him knocks me a stumbling step back, his hand snaring my throat.

"Do *not*," he snarls, too loud, too close, the tip of his nose touching mine. "Do not *ever* tell me what to do, when it comes to this," he hisses in my face, his head tilting, mouth slanting over my own. "I keep you safe." His eyes flicker between mine, my breath cutting off further as his fingers tighten, pressure pounding in my temples. "I will forever keep you safe, Little Cub, even if that means we are separated from my family for the rest of my life. They understand," he says softer, lips brushing mine with every word, "What it means, to feel *this*."

He is so close, but he does not kiss me, he does not loosen his grip or uncurl his brutal fingers. He stares at me, looking deep within, waiting. Finally, when my eyes start flashing with white and I see someone shift in my peripheral, he sees what he wants in my eyes.

Submission.

Thorne places me down, flat on my feet, his hand caressing the abused skin of my throat as he finally allows me to breathe. Vision spotty as it comes back to me fully, he presses his lips to my forehead, a fierce kiss, consuming, he drops his forehead against my own, closes his eyes, breathing me in. But I keep my eyes open, wide and focused on the blurred sight of him and I think about what it is we do now.

Where we run to.

Where we hide.

Who will hunt us to our deaths.

I wonder how much time we will have together now. Now that we have found each other. Now that we are finally *this*.

"No son of mine is being exiled, not while I'm still fucking breathing," Stryder says sharply, shattering the moment, Thorne's eyes flash open.

He holds my gaze, just for a moment, and then he's pulling away, tucking me into his back with one arm, holding me to him with a splayed palm. Turning back to face his father, the destruction of the kitchen. I drop my gaze, fists curling into the back of his black suit jacket, I press my forehead to his spine, breathe him in, feel him calm, his heart rate slowing, it makes me breathe a little easier. Like we're physically joined, connected, his heart is my heart, his breaths, my breaths, our souls tangled and weaving, stitching together all of our frayed edges.

"She was meant to die, I was supposed to do it, and I cannot, *will not*, she is mine," Thorne says calmly, his words strong, the kitchen in silence.

I squeeze my eyes shut tight, tighten my fists, clenching around expensive fabric, I press my face further into his back.

"Thorne," it's Wolf's voice, deep, melodic, gruff. "I think I speak for everyone in this family when I say this, brother, but we are never going to abandon you. No matter what. *Especially* not over you finding your heart," the last part is spoken softly, as if not to frighten, and I feel Thorne tense briefly before he relaxes.

"It will mean war," Thorne says solemnly, a tremor in his tone that seems foreign for Thorne.

"Not necessarily," Wolf says slowly, analysing his brother.

I feel silly, like a small child hiding behind a parent, as I blink my eyes open, turn my head, loosen my grip. Thorne's hand tightens against my spine, holding me flush to his back, making me squirm to step around him, into his side. I look up at him as his arm curls over my shoulder, sharply drawing me into his side. He looks down at me, a crease between his black brows that I desperately want to smooth out.

"The boys," Thorne says, eyes glancing up and over my head, directed towards the back of the kitchen.

"Will be fine," the low voice replies, the angry brother, *Hunter*.

"We love you, Thorne," *Grace*.

My heart clenches in my chest. The support, even though it could destroy them. Their love for their brother supersedes it all.

The risk.

The threat.

The blood.

The death.

I look around at all of the faces in the room, everyone looking so similar, the expressions on their faces determined and decided. I open my mouth to protest, tears in my eyes that I hold back. Before I can speak, think up words that I could use, to even attempt, to show my gratitude, my confusion, hesitation, Stryder speaks as the patriarch of this family.

"Blackwells do not leave each other behind," he addresses me, the muscles in Thorne's arm tightening over my shoulder. "And if Thorne has chosen you, and you have chosen Thorne, then that makes you a daughter of our family, Haisley. Whether your last name is Kelly or Blackwell, we will embrace you as our own. *Protect you,*" he pronounces clearly, "Just as fiercely as we do each other."

I stare back at him, unblinking, a lump in my throat that feels like concrete.

"You don't care…" I glance around the room, all eyes intently on me as I whisper, "About what I've done?" I finish.

The possibility of having to explain myself, be judged for it, before I've even told Thorne the full story, is extremely daunting, my cheeks blaze at the prospect.

"No," says Arrow, quieter than his brothers, timid almost, and I think I recall him now. Whispering words of comfort in my ear, kindness whilst I was a captive, bound and gagged beneath a hood as I passed between hands. "We all have sins here, ones we wear with pride. There is no room for shame within the Blackwell name."

"Thank you," I shudder out the words, my hand fisting into the back of Thorne's jacket in an attempt to keep my trembling legs from buckling, he dips down, lips pressing a violent kiss to the top of my head.

"War it is then," Archer says, drawing my eyes to his

at his excited tone, a cocky smirk on his face, no worry or concern, but there is a darkness in his gaze, something unspoken.

It doesn't feel good, but it doesn't feel bad either.

It feels like an omen that might not necessarily be in our favour.

CHAPTER 37

THORNE

Brendan's Pool Hall is more than unimpressive. Sticky floors, hazy ceiling full of stagnant cigar smoke and the scent of stale sex, thick in the air. If I was to ever show a look of distaste in public, it would be this place that forced it out of me.

Archer is to my left, Hunter my back, Wolf my right as we gain entrance to the curtained door in the rear. Passing by tables of watchful eyes, an Irish owned establishment, that is, unfortunately, a haunt of Cillian Kelly, supposedly the next in line to serve as the Kelly's King. Once the current leader is... *dethroned*. Something I would like to see happen sooner rather than later.

We pass through the tunnel corridor, yellow strip bulbs buzzing to light the way. Eventually, the confined space opens up, my brothers filing into the larger, emptier room, behind me, retaking their flanking positions.

This room is still full of green felted pool tables, gold lamps hanging over each one, windowless walls painted a murky maroon, but only four men rattle around this space.

A man lines up his cue stick, chest flush with the polished, dark wood of the table's edge. His ginger streaked, strawberry blonde hair looks pink beneath the yellow bulb overhead, curls hanging across his pale green eyes, focusing on the stripes as he draws his elbow back, shoots his cue forward and pockets three balls with a smooth *click, click, click*.

That is when he glances up, body still flush with the table, he eyes each of us clinically, and slowly, he smirks. It rubs me up the wrong fucking way, my hackles rising, knowing what is it at stake, but Archer is laughing. A low, deep chuckle, menacing really, paired with a cocky smirk of his own that I catch from the corner of my eye.

"Still shit at pool, Cillian," he chuckles, it sounds light and carefree, a friendly banter that I know is not forced.

"And still better than you, Arch," he grins, lips pulling into a maniacal smile full of straight white teeth, to anyone else it would be unnerving, but as Blackwells we deal in death, and as such, I am eternally unfazed.

Archer shrugs in that casual way he always does, muscles and joints loose and unwound, lazy smile permanently teasing one corner of his mouth.

Cillian stands then, the two men, with whom he seems to be playing, step away, further into the shadowy back corner of the space where a cluster of beaten leather furniture stands. He rounds the pool table slowly, resting the back of his thighs against this side of the table. He plants the end of the pool cue onto the floor, right fist curled around it as he holds at his side. He flicks the curls lain haphazardly across his forehead back, sliding that same hand casually into the pocket of his black slacks. His white, long sleeve, button up shirt tucked into them, pressed and clean, silver belt buckle and shined shoes cared for, I respect that about him instantly. Appearance can mean nothing or everything, but I believe the latter.

He cocks his head, runs his pale eyes up the length of me, a small tip to his head, as though he is assessing me, the same way I were him. But we are not the same.

"You want something," he says lightly, aloft almost, but he still has wonder.

"I do," I nod, "If you would not mind speaking with me," I raise a respective brow, "I can make it quick."

That grin reappears on his face, thin lips curling high, "Oh, T'orne," he chuckles, "Now I really am intrigued."

"This tub is so much bigger than ours," Haisley says quietly.

Her fingers drift through the hot water, steam

curling up and around her forearm, dusting the light hairs on her skin with fine droplets of water. I watch, transfixed, everything about her is addictive, fuelling my obsession, its poisoned hooks dragging against my heart. The bathroom light switched off, April rain battering against the small window at my back, the darkness of night beyond. Candles flicker on the windowsill in the alcove of the window, offering just enough glow to be able to see further than a hand in front of my face.

We are in the gloom.

And it is the closest thing, I think, that may ever feel like perfection.

"Ours?" I speak against her, smothering the small smile on my lips in her hair.

I huff a light laugh through my nostrils to the crown of her head, her curvy body cradled between my spread thighs, her head beneath my chin, back to my chest, water gently lapping at our naked bodies. We are sharing a tub, at her request, and it made my skin itch, but the compulsion to make her happy, after everything, was far easier to concede to than my uncomfortableness. As it stands, it is not so bad.

I breathe her in, her thick, bright curls tickling my nose with my inhale, smoky plum, sharp black pepper, there is a little salt, too, and it makes me think of home.

Home.

Rook Point.

Somewhere decrepit and abandoned for many years, a place of solace when the world became too big, too loud. A place of punishment. The sound of the waves overwhelming the noises in my head. I think of her then, Mum, how she sounded, gasping and spluttering for breath.

"Thorne?" her voice brings me back, not an angel, something a little darker, less white, gloomier.

Mine.

"Mm?" I dip my chin as she raises her own, her head craning back, face angled up towards me, tendons in her neck straining with the effort to see me.

"What are you thinking about?" her hands are now still in the water, draping over my bent knees, bracketing her in.

It feels nice and I sort of want to hate it, the vulnerability this girl unintentionally draws out of me. I feel like I am constantly bleeding whenever we are near. And I love it. The torment of keeping myself in check. It is a deviant self-inflicted torture, caging a beast. I could so easily tear her pretty little face to shreds, and it scares me. Above all else. Not my ability. Not my hedonistic desires.

Her.

Haisley fucking Kelly.

Because she would let me.

She would fucking *let me*.

Do any and all things to her.

It is why I am unable to stop myself from spewing the truth. Why my mouth seems to move before the words register for either of us. Time is suspended. The way she stares up at me, beautiful, scarred lips parting. We are in an upper floor guest suite inside Heron Mill, the opposite end of the third floor to where my old bedroom is. A room now occupied by the newly wedded couple, their two youngest sons, their eldest in the room next door to them. This floor is mostly silent.

"I was thinking about the day I killed my mother," the words flow without stutter or hesitation, I do not feel sadness or regret, mostly I just feel... relief.

The silence is loud, but she does not react, the steady thudding of her heart can be felt through her back, against my chest. Soothing. Calming. My own heart slowing to match hers. Synchronising. Her freckled skin is soft, a delicate plumpness beneath that I find dizzying, the way her flesh sits on her bones gets my dick fucking hard. Her curves make my mouth water. One of my hands is tucked around her waist, holding her to me, fingers splaying over the gentle curve of her belly. It feels *right*.

Her face makes me want to be tender. The way she stares up at me, breath picking up when she feels my hardening cock against the base of her spine. Twitching with desire, the need to claw my way back inside her, her tight little body such a perfect fit for me. I cannot wait to get back inside.

"Did you want to talk about it?" she asks gently, softly, coaxing and luring, a voice she uses just for me.

I do not have to hear her speak to anyone else to know. This is just her with me. It is a thrill, knowing it is just us. The way in which I can just *be*. It is intoxicating and dangerous, my fingers start to clench over her belly, tightening until my knuckles crack, and she does not even flinch. She holds my gaze, knowing now, that I have killed someone who was supposed to be the closest person to me, my mother. The woman who birthed me but never gave me life.

I wonder about Haisley's mother for a second, wonder how she feels *right now*, thinking her daughter is dead. Does she miss her? Does she care? There was no funeral. No place for a grieving mother. If there is one. I have never heard her speak about her mother before. Haisley Kelly no longer exists. Never did according to public records. But she did. She does. To me, now. She is my everything.

And yet, I still think of coughing and spluttering, water churning, my own ears buzzing. And I think of Haisley's dainty little neck, the fingers currently not trying to claw their way inside her belly, stroke down her throat, stilling at the pronounced hollow at its base. I think of flipping us over in this tub, her spine crushed to the porcelain, beneath the water, my hand on her face, holding her below the water, my cock in her cunt.

"Mors Mea," I murmur, lovingly, I live, breathe, and gift death, it only makes sense that I would have my very own.

"Thorne," she whispers, a nervous tremor in her voice, the monster in me snarls with excitement. "Do you?"

"Do I?" I repeat back to her, even though I know what it is she is referring to.

"You know what," she sasses, but she keeps her voice low, quiet, soothing.

Always soothing me.

"I drowned her," I say almost absently, my fingers drifting up and down her throat gently close around her neck. "In a bathtub not too dissimilar to this."

"Oh," she says softly, swallowing beneath the firm hold of my hand, I feel her throat work against my palm, a dry swallow, nervousness, it sets me alight inside.

"Oh?" I echo, index finger pressing beneath her chin, holding her gaze to me.

Her green eyes flicker between mine, and in the dark, the blue in their jade colouring is striking.

"There is nothing more you would like to know, no questions, background, just *oh?*"

I do not know why I pry, urge her to question me. I do not want to talk about the woman I saved my brothers from, but I am unable to stop myself.

"If you would like to talk about it then we ca-"

She splutters as my hand closes around her neck, cutting off her words as the air in her lungs punches free like I hit her in the gut. She only struggles against me for a single shocked moment, then she is relaxing into my hold, her body slumping back against me. She trusts me and I feel nothing but a wild, uncontrolled, feral need to hurt her. But I *am* controlled.

My lips ghost down her temple, over her fluttering eyelid, lashes blinking against my skin as she closes her eye, gives in to the kiss I place there. I loosen my hold, allow her to catch a breath, cut it back off again. She squirms against me, my teeth nip her skin in violent little pinches at the corner of her jaw, her breaths short and sharp, fingers digging into my knees, the tops of my shins.

"My mother hated me," I say spitefully into her ear. "She loathed me, for not being *normal*, for being *strange.*" My teeth graze across the length of her jaw, sucking at the curve of her chin, "She used to call me her *little weirdo*, like it was some sort of endearment." I think of the way she would say it in front of her friends, laugh it off like it was something cute. "I hated her because I loved her." It is the first time I have ever admitted this, out loud, to anyone, including myself, but it is a truth, I feel down to my very marrow.

Haisley lifts her chin higher, my hand resting loosely over her throat, the other still splayed across her belly. Her head rocks against my chest, neck craning even further back to catch my eye. I stare down at her, big jade-green eyes gleaming in the low light, flickering candle glow illuminating one side of her pretty face.

I draw Haisley's body closer, the warm water sloshing around us, lapping at my chest as her back squeezes the water up between us. My knees tighten around her, as though my memories pushing forward implore me to keep her safe.

"She used to hold cleansings," I whisper, lips pressed to her temple, she flinches beneath me, no doubt wondering what I mean, but knowing it is not something good. "There was a trough, out back, closer to the stables, far enough away from the house that Rosie would not see from any of the windows."

I think of the mill looming in the distance, obscured by trees. Even in the winter, the water was always cold, full of leaves and blossoms, sometimes a frog or a newt would be sitting in the bottom of it. I liked it better when there was, something to direct my attention too.

"She would make us line up, the naughtiest boy last," my breath feels too tight in my lungs, but I push the words out. "The first naughty boy was held under for only a short amount of time, then the next for a little longer, so on and so on. I was always the naughtiest boy, even when I did nothing wrong."

I think of when the six of us would be punished, I was held under for long minutes. I learned to stop struggling when I understood that only made it worse.

"They were always held on a day my dad was away from the house, sometimes we would have one cleansing a week, sometimes every other day. Especially when we were home from school in the summer, those seven weeks stretched out like years. They only stopped when I grew to be bigger than her. Then I could keep my brothers safe. But she found new ways to make us suffer."

Raine being burned.

Arrow being locked in the dark.

Hunter being sent away.

Archer's mouth taped, hands bound.

Wolf's long hair shorn off to the scalp.

My love for water being used to punish me.

"She sent Hunter away," I swallow past the lump in my throat, the fear of not having my brother ever found and returned to me still shoots a shiver up my spine. "When we got him back, Mum was gone the day later. Dad threw her out, sent her away."

I stroke my fingers down Haisley's throat, her hands curling around my calves, skin so soft and warm. I could shift my hand down her belly, find an even warmer heat between her thighs, but she will ask me too many questions if I do not continue.

"I waited until I turned seventeen to find her again."

I think of those yellow curtains in her studio flat, bumble bees on the fabric, the sound of rushing water as I entered the open living space. She was already in the bath, even as it filled, I watched her, waiting, through the crack in the door. She did not even know I had entered her building.

"It seemed like it was meant to be, drowning her, it felt like a sick sort of justice. And then it was done, and it did not really feel like enough."

She sighs softly, her breath against my cheek, my head hanging low, curled into her. We sit a while, the hot water turning warm, steam dwindling down until I can feel the cool air of the room teasing my shoulders instead. Haisley turns her face in towards mine, chin resting on the crook of her neck, eyes blinking open, hers already on me.

"Do you wish you could do it again?" she whispers, staring into my eyes, lips grazing mine with every word.

I feel my head cock, curiosity ticking in my jaw, gaze

dropping to her mouth, thick scar slashed through the slope of her cupid's bow, *my mark*. She shifts against me, my hands, still on her throat and stomach, tighten, tucking her back flush to my chest. I sit up a little straighter, still dipped forward, back and neck curved into her, engulfing her with my shadow in the gloom.

Heart thudding hard, blood pounding like a punishment swarming through my veins. I breathe hard against her mouth, her own breaths quickening, a smirk to my lips as I brush my nose over hers.

"What are you thinking about, Little Cub?" I whisper darkly, playfully, low and teasing, baiting her to bite.

She licks her lips, dragging her teeth over the top one, scar blanching white as she tugs and releases the plumpness. Her fingers glide up from the water between us, little bubbles of it sliding down her slick skin, she plants it against my chest, over my heart.

Thud, thud, thudding.

It sounds like muffled knocking from the inside of a coffin.

That is how I have kept my feelings locked up for so long. The decaying organ inside my chest chained and bound inside a wooden box meant for consecrated ground.

And then I got her.

And now we are here.

She looks up from beneath her pale lashes, water beading on the ends of them from the leftover steam. Glistening jade-green orbs slowly flick between my own, holding my gaze, she cocks her head to match my own, whispering terrifying words that make my brain ache.

"Drown me, Thorne."

I bow over her, my tongue fucking its way between her teeth before she can utter another word. Hands finding the flair of her hips, I lift and twist. Slamming her back into the space I was occupying, she squeals into my mouth as her spine crashes into the porcelain. Water lapping over the edges of the tub, crashing onto the floor in waves.

Spreading her thighs, I crawl between them, my hands sliding down her calves as I bow back over her. I bite her tongue, whilst my fingers curl around her ankles, shoving her legs up, knees bending in towards her chest. I clamp them beneath my arms, planting my hands on the bottom of the bath, I press forward, her legs tucked up between us. Sucking her tongue into my mouth, her hands scrabble up between us, one fisting in my hair, the other clawing at my shoulder.

She yanks my head closer, ripping at my hair, my teeth clamping down on her tongue until I taste blood, her squirming body beneath mine slides around dangerously in the water. I drop my body lower, crushing her, her shins against my chest, tops of her feet pressing against my Adonis's belt. I growl into her mouth, releasing her tongue, only to lick against it with my own, tasting iron. I bite her lips, she bites mine back, squeezing the hand around my throat harder.

I rear back, only her face above the water, her red hair fanning out like spreading wildfire. She pants, eyes on mine, her slippery fingers sliding down to the hollow of my throat.

"You going to go under for me?" I ask her softly, my chest heaving, cock weeping

There is a fire beneath my skin, raging and roaring and sparking when she nods, water droplets on her face, *my mark* on her lip.

"Take a deep breath for me, Little Cub," I say, stroking a finger down her face, taking comfort in the gloominess of the darkened bathroom. "I am not going to let you up until I come," I whisper against her lips.

I thrust my cock into her at the same time she heaves in that final breath, plunging beneath the water, I shove her under, palm to the side of her face, fingers splayed

"Fuck, fuck, *fuuuuck,*" my eyes slam closed, brows crashing together, the feel of her wet, hot cunt clenching around my cock has my head spinning.

I force my eyes open to see her, looking down at her thrashing beneath the water, red hair spiralling out around her. I fuck into her harder and harder, the water slamming between our hips, splashing over the edges. She manoeuvres her feet, kicking them into my chest, spurring me on. The fight, the bubbles exploding from her nose, rising to the violently lapping surface of the water. I fuck into her, cock growing harder, balls tightening, my knees driving into the hard base of the tub.

My fingers tighten on her face, short nails biting into her hairline. I force my way further and further into her tightening pussy, clamping down tight around my thickening cock. Gripping my length, trying to push it out at the same time it wants to keep me. I stare down at her, her eyes opening beneath the choppy surface of the water, locking on me from the corner of her eye. She stills then, relaxing, she stops fighting. The bubbles from her nose slow, her kicking feet drop from my chest to the base of the tub, thighs falling open, knees tight against the sides. Inviting me inside deeper. I thrust, once, twice, three times and I come so hard I swear she will have a piece of me inside of her for the rest of our lives.

I drag her up as I come, cradling her to my chest, teeth sinking into her shoulder, she gasps in my ear, teeth chattering in between hacking splutters. I am still coming, pumping my cock into her in slow, short thrusts, holding her tight to my chest. I drop back to my haunches, keeping her to me, my cock still inside of her. Her hands are hanging by her sides, her body limp and heaving in my arms, legs wide and loose around my hips. I lick over my teeth marks, a darkening bruise in each little indent that I can see blooming even with the gloominess.

Fingers massaging into her wet hair, I pull her head back, palming her crown, so I can see her. Water runs in rivulets down her face, over her cheekbones, dripping from her chin.

"Little Cub," I say quietly, keeping us suspended in our bubble of gloom.

Her eyes are wide, pupils blown, teeth chattering. Shock.

"You are in shock," I tell her calmly, smoothing my

hand up her spine, between her shoulder blades, the other tight around her lower back.

Our wet skin sticks together, my cock twitching inside her, I can feel my cum starting to leak out, dispersing into the water. Pulling her back to my chest, I shift her legs, then my own, until I can push to my feet.

"Curl your legs around my hips, baby girl," feeling relieved when she does, I grip her tighter.

Her teeth chatter in my ear, my fingers of one hand curling over the lip of the bath, using it to push myself to standing, her legs tightening around my waist, I keep her clasped to my chest. I step out of the remaining water, grabbing a huge bath sheet from the rail, I wrap it around her, draping it over my shoulders. Haisley trembles in my arms, goosebumps dotted all across her tawny-freckled skin. I push open the adjoining door to the bedroom suite we are using while we are here.

Tugging the towel around her tighter, I drop my arse to the bed, sheets already turned down, her legs straddling my own, I sit on the edge. Her hands curled up against my chest, ear flush with my heart, her breathing starts to slow.

There is dark green carpet in this room that looks black in the dark, a slate grey damask wallpaper, dark wood furniture and gold light fixtures. It is dark and cool, comforting, like Rook Point. I think of the lighthouse, the sea, the smell of salt, and miss it. Being here.

"Shall we go home tomorrow?" I murmur, pressing my cheek to the top of her head, wet hair beneath my face, because that is what it is, *home*.

I hold her close, let her catch her breath. I feel when her heart starts to slow, beats matching mine, our bodies tangled together. I scoot onto the bed properly, up to the pillows, back to the headboard, dragging the layers of blankets up and over us, Haisley lies over me, but her grip never loosens. Her knees bracketing my hips, hand curled into a fist against my chest, the other curling over my shoulder, nails digging into my flesh.

"Are you okay, Little Cub?" I whisper, her wide eyes blinking.

She turns her head, chin to my sternum, I look down at her as she twists to look up at me.

"Yes," she replies quietly, softly, my body melting with ease into the mattress.

"Did I hurt you?"

"Yes."

My heart thuds hard, banging against my sternum as she licks her lips.

"Did you like it?" I whisper, holding my breath as I wait for her answer, but it is immediate.

"Yes." She swallows, confessing, "I like everything that you do to me." She blushes, dropping her gaze, cheeks flushing, she looks up at me from beneath her lashes. "Home?" she finally whispers, my lips tilting up at one corner.

"Yes, *home.*"

"I miss it."

"Me too."

"I missed you, Thorne."

My insides knot, twisting and churning, heart

slowing and speeding up, having those big eyes on mine, her body crushed to me.

"I missed you, baby girl."

I lie in silence for hours, listening to the rain beat against the roof, the windows, feeling Haisley's chest rise and fall with deep, even breaths as she slumbers. I hold her tight, our hearts aligned, never once loosening my grip, until I, too, find my way to sleep.

CHAPTER 38

HAISLEY

Cillian calls a few days later. Thorne takes it outside, away from me. He has been secretive about his meeting with my older brother. Telling me everything was being handled. But my nerves are fraying the longer I don't know what's happening. I feel pressure to behave, to do as I'm told, cautious and safe.

I feel frazzled, and completely at a loss. I don't have Clover to take care of, there are no weeds left in the abandoned beds outside. Wolf chopped enough firewood to last us all the way through the rest of the year, and the copse of trees just beyond look less and less inviting to wander in as the days wear on. There is nothing to distract me. I am jumpy and on edge, ghosts and ghouls hiding around every corner. I can feel phantom hands tightening like a noose around my neck, and an imaginary hourglass somewhere is on its last grains of sand.

Time feels as though it is almost up and I am drowning.

Thorne makes phone calls all day, always out of earshot, his eyes watching me like a hawk from wherever I stand and watch him. He does not pace, fidget or look even the slightest bit on edge and it somehow makes me feel worse. Although, each time he hangs up, his shoulders seem to wind tighter and tighter, inching up higher and higher. He is strung up, wound like a tangled string puppet, and it makes me even more nervous. Thorne doesn't get ruffled; he is completely at ease, always.

A week after we return home from Heron Mill, it's almost midnight. I'm curled up in Thorne's lap, a book in my hands, his journal open on his thigh, but I do not look at it. Gold pen wedged between his fingers, taps rhythmically against a page. I peer up at him from where my head rests against his bare chest.

Lifting a hand, I trace a finger across the fine-line tattoos inked into his warm olive skin. Each of them representations of his family, a constellation for each.

Cepheus for Stryder on the front of his right shoulder, leading to Lupus for Wolf at the top of his pec. Then Sagittarius for Archer, Orion for Hunter, Sagitta for Arrow, Pisces for Raine, all of them painted across his chest. The newer ones are a little lower, creased in the ripples of his abs where he sits in the chair. He has Cygnus for his sister Grace, Taurus for Atlas, Eridanus for River and Draco for Roscoe. I asked if some were star signs, he said technically they are but none of them correlate with their actual star signs which made me laugh. He wanted them to keep close to his heart without anyone else knowing what they meant.

Just for him.

But he told *me*.

I stroke the fresh scars in his left shoulder, think about what he might place there, if he'll want to cover them. Feel fear roll through me again, it comes in waves, too many things tumbling around inside my messy brain. Trembling, I tug myself closer, into Thorne, my touch cool to his warm. His arm around my back tautens instinctively, like he senses my distress, but he doesn't say anything. I can't shed the feeling of being watched, hunted. Danger looms like a dagger, inching closer and closer, threatening to destroy the tentative safety of our veil of gloom.

Glancing up, I can't help but admire the straight line of Thorne's jaw, sharp angle of his cheekbones, the hollows of his cheeks. I glide the tip of my finger up the side of his throat, hover over the hammering of his pulse. I watch it beat, feeling it thrum against the light touch of my finger.

"Vulpecula," Thorne says quietly, his eyes already on mine as I look up at him.

The lights are off, the fire is burning, pyre of candles over the mantle casting a flickering orange glow across the shadows, and we are once again descendants of the gloom.

"Vul- what?" I laugh, shaking my head.

"That is what I am putting there, the constellation, Vulpecula."

"What does it mean?"

He dips down, brushing his lips to mine, I crane my neck, arching back, trying to get closer as he draws back.

"Little fox," he whispers, nose grazing mine.

Eyelids hot, throat tight, I blink, just catching his smirk before he buries his face in my neck, teeth nipping and grazing the length from neck to shoulder. His hand cinches tighter around my waist, dragging me into the bowing shape of him, his other hand gliding into my hair, dragging my legs over his lap, knees sliding down to either side of his thighs to straddle him.

Thorne's lips find mine, his tongue licking into my mouth in long, slow gives, I try to kiss him back, to submit, let him devour me, but I suddenly feel too hot, too closed in, everything just too intense. How can he not be worried about his safety? Whatever it is that's happening outside of this house, someone's going to come for us and take him from me. *Because of me.*

Cian clouds my thoughts, menacing eyes and sinister smirk, and it is nothing like Thorne's, but I can't stop comparing the two, letting their faces morph together, and sickness churns in my gut.

I throw my hands against his chest, push back, him chasing me as I tear our lips apart, turning my head towards the fire, I swallow hard, breathless and shaky.

"Haisley?"

"I have to pee," I kick my legs down, forcing him back in the chair, using the arms of the chair to shove myself away.

Without looking back, I hurry down the hallway, the

darkness cooling me further, I can hear the house groaning and creaking softly, wind whistling. The wooden flooring still feels like ice beneath my bare feet, despite the warmer days, the nights are always cold. The end of the hallway is lit, the single sconce glowing with soft candlelight. I pass the bathroom on tentative footsteps, my exposed skin peppering with goosebumps, covered only by knickers and an oversized green crop top hanging off of one shoulder, I feel the temperature drop the further I venture into this end of the house.

Stopping at the invisible threshold, one step further would take me into the hexagonal shape room of doors, some that I still have not attempted to enter. I glance left, the huge gold mirror, haunted by the pair of innocent-looking cherubs on the top of its frame, heavy red velvet curtains parted, tied back to reveal it there.

My heart thunders in my chest, blood rushing in my ears, I feel hot and cold, nerves firing through me like zaps of electricity. I find myself moving closer, eyes locked on the golden winged children, watching my approach, staring down at me when I step up to the glass. Little spots of rust at the edges, the reflective surface greying in the upper right corner. I keep watching the eyes above, ignoring my own reflection, it's like a dare to take my eyes from them, glance at myself.

I feel frozen in place, held captive by my own fear. I think of who was lurking in the shadows at my back. A shudder runs up my spine, my scalp tingling, the hair along the nape of my neck standing on end. I hold my breath, wide eyes watering from not blinking in so long and then I feel him step into me, finally letting them close.

"What has you so frightened, Little Cub?" Thorne breathes down the back of my neck, warmth rushing beneath the loose open neck of my shirt, skittering across my skin like the goosebumps springing up in its wake.

I shake my head, squeeze my eyes tighter, trembling in place. Thorne closes the distance between us, the feel of a shirt between our skin now.

"Tell me," he demands, his voice low and gruff. "Open your eyes and look at me, baby girl."

And just like that, I do. My eyes pop open, flashing straight onto his. I bite my lip to hold back the tears, his brows slowly pulling together. He steps into me, both of us staring at our reflection, his arm lifts, a hand sweeping hair back from my face, he coils a piece around his finger, his knuckles grazing my shoulder blade as he twists it down my back.

"Tell me your fears," he whispers, head dipping, eyes flicked up, he holds my gaze, easing a hand around my bare middle, splaying his fingers over the curve of my belly. "Let me feast on your fear, Little Cub," he whispers, telling me exactly what he told me once before. "Let me take it from you," he breathes, hot breath ghosting down the side of my throat. "I will devour everything that has ever hurt you," he promises me again. "Remember what I told you?" he pauses, waiting for me to nod before continuing. "I will be the only thing left for you to fear. But I will never hurt you."

Thorne kisses up the side of my throat, nipping at the back of my jaw, his dark eyes still on mine, he never looks away, bowing over me, shadowing me in him.

"Tell me you understand," he breathes against my skin, the soft cotton of his shirt sliding against my bare skin, his free hand cups my chin, finger and thumb pinching the bone.

I nod slowly, his dark eyes flashing, whispering silently they say, *come play with me in the gloom, Little Cub.* And my insides knot for an entirely different reason.

"I understand."

"Good girl," he praises, flashing a devious smile that disappears almost as quickly as it appeared, he sinks his teeth into the crook of my neck.

His hand slides down my belly, fingertips teasing the frilled waistband of my pale pink knickers. I think of Shane, his ghost appearing in the reflection behind us, Cian manifesting on the other side. My eyes grow wide as I watch them form, flinching as Thorne's fingers glide beneath my underwear. He stills, my breaths panting, chest heaving, he rests his chin on my shoulder, holding me tight, eyes still on mine, but mine are on who's standing behind us.

"Baby girl," Thorne says darkly, loudly, bursting our safety, making me whimper.

I press back into him. Stare at the reflection over our shoulders.

"What is wrong? Tell me," he forces the growling words directly into my ear.

"I killed him because he kept coming for me," I

whisper. "His hands were too big, too strong, and I- he wouldn't stop coming," I choke out the words around a sob. "I didn't mean to. I didn't want to do it. I just wanted him to stop hurting me." My words bubble out of me, unable to stop them from flowing, Thorne's hold grounding me. "Shane waited outside the door, whilst he-" I choke down a sob, tears dripping from my wide eyes. "Whilst Cian tried to rape me. He stood guard," I splutter. "To protect *him*, to protect him while he raped me."

"What did you do, baby girl?" he whispers calmly, soothing me.

"He ha-had me pinned down on my bed," his knees digging into my thighs as he lurched over me, hands clasped tight over my head. "He bit me," I say coldly, disconnected from the phantom teeth in the side of my breast as I screamed. "He clawed at me, hit me, trying to keep me down. He pulled out his knife, and I ju- just froze, and he was flicking the blade free, and I didn't fight him. He cut through my knickers and shoved them in my mouth."

"What happened next, Little Cub?" Thorne coaxes, his voice smooth and quiet, his hands on me soothing.

"He told me he would kill me if I didn't just let him *have at me*, that I belonged to him and he didn't want to wait any longer. That he wanted t-to pu-put a baby in me."

Thorne shushes me, his fingers rubbing calming circles over my skin, his hand on my face cradling my cheek, lips to my temple, but he keeps his eyes on us in the mirror.

"Keep going, beautiful, tell me it all," he encourages, I take a deep breath, swallow down the hiccup in my chest.

"He put the knife down, beside my head, looking down at his jeans, he was trying to get the button open, but he was pinning me down at the wrong angle, and he hurt me more because he was getting frustrated."

I think of him swearing under his breath, muttering to himself, his weight bruising my thighs where he wriggled his knees over me. Trying to move, to free himself from his trousers.

"I- I offered to help him, but he wasn't falling for it, he laughed in my face, so I went lax," letting him think he'd won. "That made him relax too, and his grip on my wrists loosened as he pushed his pants down. I tore my arm out of his hold, fumbled with the knife and plunged it into his neck. I ripped it out and blood spurted in my face, it went everywhere and he fell on me, but I rolled him off, onto the floor. He was cho- choking on it, the blood, and I heard the lock rattling. I knew that Shane was going to get in. So I dropped the knife and I swiped my fingers through the blood, I ran it between my thighs and then spat into my hand." I shudder, drawing in a deep breath.

"Go on," Thorne whispers.

"I grabbed hold of him, of his... and I swiped my hand up it, because it was already out of his pants, and the blood and the wet, I made sure it was on him, to make them think-"

"That he had raped you."

"So that I would hold no value," I whisper back, exhaling deeply.

He nods slowly as Shane and Cian disappear from the mirror.

"I don't want anyone to take you from me," I confess quietly, just as his gaze drops from mine, his eyes snapping back up immediately with my words. "I know you don't want to tell me what's going on, Thorne, but I don't want... I won't let anything happen to you. I would kill again. *For you.*"

We are suspended in silence. Darkness. Gloom. A tenseness settling turbulently like an electrical storm swirling around the room. Thorne is practically bent in half where he holds me close, bowing over my shoulder, his dark brown eyes blown wide. Endless obsidian holds my gaze in the mirror, my breath stilling. And then he's thrusting me forwards, my hands fly up between us, cold, clammy palms colliding with the cool glass of the mirror.

He smashes me up against it, his firm body moulding to my back, one of his hands slaps down onto the mirror above my head, his other hand casually sliding into his pocket as he peels his body from mine. Caging me in, all it takes is one hand to do so, and it's not even touching me. It makes me think about how he told me he doesn't like touch, and now all we do is just that. I feel a tremor of something hot rush through me, my eyes glued to his.

"Nothing," he states lowly, "And no one, is going to take me from you, Little Cub." A sinister sort of violence threads through his smooth tone, his eyes drifting their way down my body with predatory gleam. "But I think, perhaps," pausing to lick his lower lip, he glances back up at me, my fingertips mashing into the glass. "You need rewarding for your devotion to me," his voice drops an octave, my breath hitching at the same time he drops to his knees behind me.

Hands on the flair of my hips, pulling me towards him, my lower spine arching, he nuzzles his face between my cheeks, teeth biting into the exposed lower half of my arse, the crease of my thigh. He laps at my fabric covered pussy, nose nudging against my entrance as he sucks me from behind. I quiver, arms trembling where they balance me.

"Look at me, Little Cub," he demands, my eyes locked on him between my spread thighs in the reflection.

His face dips, neck arching and angled so he can access as much of me as possible. Heat flushes in my cheeks, running tremors through my body, sparking like lightning in my core. Hooking a finger beneath the dampened fabric covering my slit, he thrusts it aside and plunges his tongue into me. I buck forward, hands squeaking as they stutter down the glass, Thorne spears me on his tongue, hands gripping the outside of my thighs, pulling me onto him.

Suddenly, he releases me, spinning himself around, he slides between my legs, still on his knees, looking up at me, his back to the mirror, head cocked to one side. Eyes flickering with mischief, he gives me that half-smirk, lips wet, curling up at one corner, I heave in a breath, hands still slapped to the mirror as he buries his face in my cunt.

I throw my head back, spine arching and curling, I cry out, throat aching with the feral sound that tears its way up from my chest. Thorne's fingers tear my underwear down my thighs, fingers curling into the backs of my knees, he feasts on me. Teeth teasing and plucking my clit, one hand coming up to spread me open, allowing him to push his tongue deeper. Long, luscious licks up my slit, his nose firm on my clit, he thrusts his tongue inside of me, my hands coming to the top of his head, I bow forward, the top of my head against the glass of the mirror, I curl over him.

He teases me, and teases me, getting me right to the precipice before pulling away with a huff of laughter. Torturously, over and over. Sob catching in my throat, I groan hard, panting.

"Thorne," I whine, body trembling with desperation, "*Please*," I cry, breathing hard.

"Please *what*, Little Cub?" he whispers, promptly blowing over my swollen, wet flesh.

I jolt in surprise, my entire being thrumming with the intense need to come.

"*Please*," I sob, "Stop teasing me, I need to come."

"That what you need, baby girl? You think you need to come?" he whispers, lips brushing my sex.

"Yes!" I yelp as the flat of his hand comes down hard over my cunt.

"You think you get to tell me how I reward you?" he hushes, his tongue swiping out, the flat of it lapping me from arse to clit.

"No," I sob.

My sternum pressing against the top of his head, one of my hands clamped in his hair. Reaching up blindly with the other, I slap it down on the mirror, the sound echoing around the closed space.

"No," he hums, "That is what I thought. Are you going to be good?" he rasps, my lungs seizing.

"Yes, *yes,* I am, I will, I am," I expel the words, spitting them out frantically between gasps of breath.

"Good. *Now,* be my good girl and let me feast."

His hands brutally grab at the backs of my thighs, fingers spreading my cheeks where he grips my flesh. He dives back in, sucking my clit, biting savagely along my lips, his tongue fucking into my entrance before he finds my back hole. I tense up. A huff of laughter hot against my core has me falling into him further, my forearms clamping around the sides of his head. Fingers fisting in his hair, I groan, loudly, his face buried in me, then his tongue is dipping out of me before thrusting hard and driving through the tight ring of muscle in my back entrance.

Every nerve ending in my body freezes and pulses,

fluttering and seizing, scorching me all the way through to my toes. My spine tingles as he works his tongue in and out of me, groaning and sucking and licking every single inch of me. His mouth suctions over the entire length of me, teeth grazing my clit and then he bites, *hard.* Tears rush down my cheeks as I come. Knees buckling, core bursting with my release. Thorne keeps biting and sucking, pain thrums through me, his thumb slotting into my dripping entrance, my walls fluttering and grabbing around him at the same time his index finger pushes into my arse, the digits fucking me through my release as his teeth stay sunken in the bundle of nerves at my apex.

Nostrils flaring, I heave for breath, Thorne's big hands holding me up, mouth detaching from me, he laps over me, sucking at the wetness along my inner thighs. Then he drags me down into his lap, burying his face, wet with me, into the crook of my neck, biting and sucking along my collarbone.

"I love you, Thorne," I whisper into his ear, feeling unafraid of the words for the first real time in my life.

Drawing back, my hands linked lightly around his neck, he kisses up my inner forearms, tongue swirling through my elbow ditch. My breath hitches, his attention solely on me, he watches me as he sucks his way back down my arms, my heart hammering in my chest.

"I love you," I whisper again, feeling better now, *lighter.*

"*Mmm,*" he groans, the sound thick in his throat, dragging his nose along the length of my jaw, ear to chin. "Say it again, Little Cub."

"I love you, Thorne," I promise breathlessly, intoxicated, addicted, *to him*.

Dropping my forehead to his shoulder, turning my face in towards his, he dips down, peppering kisses across the top of my cheekbone. *Sweet*, if it weren't for the savage little grazes of his front teeth. Shiver shooting up my spine, I lick up his throat, sucking his pulse, hard and unforgiving. I think of our night in the kitchen. When he wasn't himself. When he frightened me, and I *comforted* him. Ruining everything.

My breath stills in my chest, my monster's hands curling around my backside, fingertips grabbing and gauging at my flesh, teeth biting harder into my throat. I thread a hand up his back, feel his muscles tighten and flex beneath my palm. Fingers sliding into his hair, I suddenly wrench his head back, baring his throat to me.

Knuckles white, I clench my fist harder, his fingers digging into my hips, cruel and painful. His ebony eyes lock on mine, Adam's apple prominent in the curve of his throat, the arch of his neck obscene. His eyes glisten, but it is not from tears. I look into his eyes and see terror staring me back.

"Tell me," I hiss through my teeth.

The pinching of his hands on my hips borderline agony. I tear his head back harder, hearing something crack in his neck, and I don't care.

I want blood.

Devotion.

"Now," I whisper gently, coaxingly, completely at

odds to the way I snap his neck back, shaking his head in my grip.

I feel hairs snap in the webbing of my fingers, the wave of black strands mussed and sticking up. His teeth snag his bottom lip, the hollows of his cheekbones shadowing further as he chews on the inside of his cheeks. Lip popping free, he flicks his tongue out, rolling it across his bottom lip. We are so close, my face hovering just above his, we share breath, we could kiss if I leant in just a little, allowed him some reprieve from the punishing grip I keep on his hair.

Neither of us concedes.

Until we both do.

Darting towards each other, our teeth clash in a flurry of heated violence, Thorne releasing one hand to free himself from his slacks, hand still tight in his hair, I use the other to help push down his trousers. In seconds, I'm impaled on his cock, thick and hard and throbbing. I cry out in his mouth, his tongue licking over my teeth, massaging my own, he fucks me with his tongue like he fucks me with his dick.

Hard.

Brutal.

Punishing.

"Tell me," I pant against his lips, demanding.

As I feel the first hot spurt of his release coat my inner walls, I tear at his hair, wrenching it at the root. His hips bucking wildly up into me, the acoustics of our fucking sharp in the hexagonal space. He comes with a roar, groaning as he sinks his teeth into my top lip. And as the tang of iron fills my mouth, my cunt tightening and milking his cock, I come too. Muffled cry drowned out by the sob wrenching up through my chest, his thumb and forefinger pinching my aching clit.

We're breathing hard, lips touching, eyes open wide on each other, I still fist his hair, his fingers still biting into my thigh, he looks at me, *really* looks at me. Gloom cloaking us, he licks his lips, catching my own with his blood-stained mouth.

"I love you, Little Cub."

CHAPTER 39

HAISLEY

City lights glitter brightly in the dark, the skyline bright in the absence of sun. Darkness having fallen, the early hour of almost one-am. I want to laugh a little, because I find it funny that a one-am meeting time was when everyone was the most 'free' on a Friday night. Little sad, actually, if you really think about it. Then I think about what I would be doing. Sitting in an armchair in front of a fire, the gloom we exist in, lit with nothing but candles... To each their own I suppose.

I have seen many a business meeting, they would take place in the grand dining room of our house. The five families of the Irish mob meeting every Thursday night of every week. Women were never to be present, I would often spy from the upstairs open landing, hands curling around the bannister railings as I tried to listen in. See who was coming and going.

That, apparently, is not how the leader of The

Firm likes to play things, she is, after all, a woman herself. She wanted me present, something that has irritated Thorne to no end. He did not want me to come. It makes me nervous that my life is to be decided in this early hour. By a mostly male-led firing squad. One way or the other, I will be leaving The Tower tonight, be it in this rear passenger seat of Archer's car, or in a body bag in the back of Wolf's funeral home van.

Slow and melodic, a shudder rolls through me, cold chill creeping its way along my shoulder blades. Thorne's hand on my thigh grips harder, but I don't squirm even though it hurts. I know he is anxious, not that he will admit it, the five guns hidden beneath his black suit can attest to that.

I stood in the middle of one of the many armoury type rooms inside Heron Mill, walls stacked floor to ceiling with military type weaponry, as each of the Blackwell men chose their pieces. Thorne's sister passed me a small blade whilst no one was looking, told me to hide it somewhere it was easily reachable. I can feel the warmed metal pressing into the inside of my bicep. She did it all with an innocent smile on her pretty face, a smile that only demons masquerading as angels would wear.

The car ride is silent, Archer driving, Arrow in the front passenger seat, Hunter, Wolf and Raine in the blacked-out Lamborghini Urus at our back. Stryder was already in the city, so he'll be there when we arrive. That makes me feel a little better, like maybe he'll get a read on things before we arrive. Perhaps he won't. One can hope.

"What am I supposed to do?" I ask quietly, staring out of the misted window as high-rise buildings fly by.

Condensation runs down the glass pane, air conditioning set to high, all of the Blackwell men seem to run hot, as it stands, I'm freezing my arse off. But I don't complain. Goosebumps pepper my skin, beneath my high waisted jeans, off the shoulder crop top, oversized knitted cardigan, everything in black, like the rest of the family. It feels like some sort of unspoken uniform.

"Nothing," Thorne says coldly, "You do nothing. You stay close to me, or the boys, that is it, and you listen to me and do as you are told."

Frowning, I turn in my seat, his fingers really biting into my flesh now, but I grit my teeth, refuse to tell him so. He is staring out of his own window, the sharp line of his cheekbone prominent, shadowing his hollow cheek, his nose is straight, not too big, it's fairly narrow, it's almost pretty.

Thorne is beautiful, so much so that it sometimes hurts to look at him, the way his skin is so warm, in colour and touch, his dark eyes expressive even when he thinks they aren't. I have seen this man cry and all I can think about is crying for him.

I know he likes it.

My tears.

For him.

My gaze drops down his body, catching on the buckle of his belt, gliding down his forearm, to his hand on my thigh. Ridged with green veins, tendons, scarred knuckles shining white, even in the absence of light. So *pretty.* I reach over, pinching my forefinger and thumb together, the nails biting into the back of his hand. He growls at me, head snapping in my direction as I twist his skin. I cock my head, lift my brows, his expression blank but I know he is irritated.

"Haisley," he warns, low and thunderous and it shoots desire straight through my body.

"Thorne," I fling back, licking over my bottom lip.

"You are a brat," he spits almost silently, but his brothers, too, are silent and I know they hear.

The way Archer's shoulders jump with noiseless laughter, Arrow's tightening through discomfort.

"You do not have to be so rude to me. I'm not stupid, of course, I will listen to you, you only have to say it somewhat nicely," I half-whisper, but it's pointless.

"Yeah, Thorne, just say it a little nicer, dude. Seriously, what crawled up your arse and died?" Archer laughs, slapping a hand down on the steering wheel.

"It's not funny," Arrow scolds quietly, and my cheeks heat with my own uncomfortableness.

"It's a little funny," Archer responds, but there's a lack of laughter this time.

I drop my gaze, curl my hand over Thorne's, thread my fingers through his as I loosen them, squeezing lightly.

"I'm scared," I push the words out in a slow breath, feel the tension in the car jump, it churns my stomach, glancing up, catching Thorne's eye.

"I will keep you safe, Little Cub." His finger grazes the apple of my cheek, tender and soft, sharp in contrast to only a moment ago. "I will always keep you safe."

"What about everyone else?" I shift in my seat, the cold leather creaking and swooshing beneath my jeans.

"They are here to keep us both safe," he answers casually, matter-of-factly. "It is what we do for each other."

I stare down at our joint hands, feel his gaze like laser beams. The car comes to a stop, my lips parting and closing before I can speak. Looking up through my lashes, Thorne stares at me, and there are no words spoken, but I feel him. In my soul. A gloomy tether of love.

I want to keep you safe.

I want to keep you.

I think it over and over, wanting him to know. Wanting him to understand.

I will die for you, beautiful boy.

The door opens beside me, warmer air rushing in, chilling me and heating me at the same time.

"M'lady," Archer grins, my eyes blinking up at him, the roof light in the front of the car illuminating half of his face.

Hand outstretched, I slip my own into his open palm, his long fingers curling over the back of my hand, I release my seatbelt, twist my legs out of the car and Archer pulls me gently to standing. I swallow hard, looking up at the towering building before me, only the very top floors flooded with light. Thorne steps into my side, Archer shutting the car door at my back as I shuffle a few steps forward. The pavement is smooth, the slabs clean of gum and discarded rubbish. I feel out of place already and I'm not even inside the building's lobby yet.

Arrow hovers at my back, Archer traipsing toward the glass front, pushing open the double doors as if he owns the place. Wolf, Hunter and Raine step up into us. And then there is silence. Thorne does not even breathe as Archer steps inside the dimly lit lobby, speaking to two men that are manning the front desk, and then he spins to face me, his brothers leaving us outside as they enter behind Archer.

Hands closing around my biceps, his chin dipping, my own raising, his rush of breath hits my chin, his forehead dropping to touch my own. His eyes flicker across mine, dark and consuming, certain. His fingers loosen, smoothing up my arms, over my shoulders. Palming the centre of my spine, he pulls me closer, my back arching, chest to chest, we breathe each other's air.

Silence heavy, tears prick my eyes and I let them fall closed, keep my words inside. Things I have said, things I haven't had a chance to yet. All of it seems irrelevant, my tongue twisting into a stubborn knot. I exhale hard through my nose, flutter my lashes open, lock my gaze onto Thorne's. He nods against me, exhaling hard too, the rub of his head against mine like a burning declaration.

This could mean war.

With someone.

With everyone.

Because of me.

It feels impossibly heavy.

The weight of The Blackwell family, not only, resting on my shoulders, but the hands of each family member trying to lift me up. Unease is a swirling, heated, coiling viper and I am either going to be its victim or its master.

Protect Thorne.

Protect his family.

That is my job.

"I'm ready," I whisper, even though I'm not.

Not ready to lose Thorne. Not ready to die. Not ready to leave behind a man I am irrevocably in love with.

My soul is painted black, and it is stitched inside of his.

I love you.

It is eternal.

Forever, you and I, in the gloom.

Neither one of us says it.

It feels too final. Too heavy. Too goodbye.

Instead, my lips brush the corner of his mouth, his scent invading my nostrils, dizzy and warm and strong, and a smile curls the corner of my pout. Thorne releases me, drawing back, straightening out his black shirt, smoothing his flattened palms down the small creases in his trousers along the top of his thighs. He stares down at me with those dark eyes, slices of gold breaking free of the obsidian. His head cants, lips tugging into that half-smirk thing I like, making my cheeks heat.

"Come, Little Cub, let us get on with this so we can go home."

Home.

My chest flutters, tummy tightening with warmth, because he thinks of Rook Point as home, *too.*

With me.

Who am I?

I do not know why the thought suddenly infects my mind, scraping like a beetle scratching its way inside my head through the thin skin of my eardrum. Scratching and scratching and scratching. It's what the nail of my index finger is currently doing. *Clawing.* Deep now, into the fragile skin of my inner wrist. I glance down at it, in my lap, beneath the table. Red and purple, bleeding beneath the weepy skin. It feels like the inside of my skull. Vulnerable, cold, depleting. Perhaps when the tension inside of this icy room dissipates, so too, will the pressure inside my brain.

"You are a contracted disposal man," my father scoffs loudly, Irish accent thick and raspy in the back of his throat, speaking to Thorne, but not looking at him.

Eoin Kelly, Mob leader, husband to seven wives,

seventy-something years old, puffs away on a fat cigar. He is still in shape, broad shoulders, toned arms, flat belly. But his age is starting to show in his face, wrinkles around his eyes, mouth, cheeks, the skin of his neck starting to sag a little. His eyes are a dull green, and his freckled skin is so over tanned it has the textured look of vintage leather that hasn't ever been cared for. Cracked, dry, dark with an orangey undertone. His silver hair is almost white, thick curls cut short on his head.

"You failed at ya job, the evidence is sitting at this fuckin' table," he hisses, chalky smoke slithering out with his toxic words.

It is the look on his face, when he releases the cigar from between his lips, the turned down corners of his mouth as smoke billows out between them, pursed and wrinkled, that really makes me anxious.

"Do not smoke in here when there is a pregnancy among us, have some respect," the dark haired Italian Don, Vittorio Gambino, spits darkly, bright blue eyes flashing as he stares down the table at my father. White shirt pulling tight across his chest, he leans forward, into the edge of the long glass surface, "Get. Rid. Of. *It*."

Nobody speaks as I look up from beneath my lashes, head still hung low, watch my father's jaw grind. He leans forward too, dramatic flair to his movements as he stubs out the cigar, right onto the glass tabletop, making his point. My brother stands at his back, Cillian, pale green eyes on me, I glance back down at my lap, fingernail still clawing at my wrist. Hot, raised skin, blooming wider, the purple and red, ugly and splotchy spreading beneath my small freckles.

"Thank you," the boss of The Firm says, husky, deep, sexy.

Kyla-Rose Swallow. She is severely intimidating, with pale grey eyes a little too big for her face, curved scar along her temple disappearing in her long white hair, pulled back into a high, sleek ponytail. She leans back in her chair at the head of the table, just one seat down from me, Stryder Blackwell between us. Her big, round baby bump pokes just above the table, she rests a hand on it, cocking her head to one side, crimson lips pulling into a broad grin, flashing white teeth. Her tattooed chest heaves a little beneath her black V-neck t-shirt, as she wrinkles her nose, drops an elbow to the table, curling her fingers in a dismissive *get on with it* gesture.

"I think you will agree, *Eoin*, that The Blackwell men are invaluable to us all," she starts, the tone in which she says my father's name nothing more than disdain, but she remains respectful. "I do not think we let this one little... *indiscretion*, speak for the rest of the hard work they have done and will continue to do. Each faction of this," she circles her hand again, loosely in the air, "*Peaceful* arrangement between us all has run extra smoothly more recently with the easy disposal services they provide, *to us all*, no?" A light eyebrow tracks up her forehead, the implication of this wasting her time, clear.

"It is not *your* disobedient spawn that has us all meeting here at an ungodly hour, like she is something *special,* though, is it *Ms Swallow?*" he spits violently. "It is not *your* goddamn fuckin' spawn that has *risen* from the dead, *is it, Ms Swallow?*" Father bangs his fist down onto the table, glasses filled with various colours of liquor clinking with the force. "And it is not *your* deceitful, little whore that has murdered one of ya own fuckin' kin!" I jump in my chair as he once again brings his fist down onto the glass, clamping my mouth shut, tightening my jaw, I hold in my whimper.

"I think everyone seated at this table, *Mr Kelly,* will firstly agree that there is no *God* here. Every hour on this shit-heap of a planet is *ungodly.* So, please, do not insult us with your whining. We are here for a vote, at *your* request, not your childish temper tantrum." She purses her lips, glancing at me briefly, before immediately refocusing her attention on The Kelly family's leader.

Kazimir Ivanov scoffs loudly, rolling his blue eyes up towards the ceiling with a shake of his head, a strand of chestnut brown hair flopping onto his forehead. He crosses his arms over his chest, glancing out at the city of Southbrook, lit up in the dark, through the floor to ceiling windows, ignoring the rest of the room.

"It is a family affair," Liridon Murati smirks, straight white teeth capped in gold like a gleaming crown peeking between his pale pink lips. "But, we do not want to lose services with The Blackwells over this little hiccup." He rocks back on his chair, staring straight at me from beneath his dropped brow. "We should just referee the fight," he shrugs, still staring at me, my skin on fire with his attention. His muscles bunch and flex beneath the long sleeves of his white t-shirt, "What do you suggest, *little one*, how do you wish to fight for your life?"

Thorne turns his head in the Albanian mafia boss's direction, so very slowly it has me holding my breath. It is the first time he has moved, even a fraction, since we were ushered into this room and sat at the table. I don't speak, even as I am addressed, and Liridon does not look away from me. Thorne doesn't utter a word, and when finally, my cheeks on fire, lungs screaming with lack of oxygen. Liridon diverts his attention onto him, the huge guy throws his hands up in surrender at whatever he sees on Thorne's face, a booming chuckle leaving his lips.

"Look," the man sitting opposite Stryder starts, a gleaming scar in the side of his neck, brown afro curls long on his head, he reaches up, tucking one side behind his ear. "How about we let the two families directly involved settle this? We can agree, at this table, that it is a family affair, but one which requires a little intervention... Mediation." He says lightly, I know he's a member of The Firm, a *Swallow*, but I do not know his name, he raises a dark brow, silver piercing glinting under the bright overhead light. "How about you agree on a way to settle this now. We will all wait here for the outcome, see to it that whatever is agreed between you goes smoothly, and then we will part ways, fresh start, clean slate. Business as usual, whatever the result." His dark eyes move to the woman at the head of the table, a warmth in his gaze as he glances briefly to her swollen belly.

"Anyone not in agreement?" she asks the room, my father's head practically ballooning with his temper.

The Mexican cartel's leader, Alejandro, stays silent, completely disinterested in the whole affair as he gazes up at the ceiling, baring his brown, tattooed throat to the room.

Even the head of the other Irish families stay silent, Murphys, Byrnes, O'Neills. But Brádach Doyle looks like he wants to tear me limb from limb and hang my intestines from the ceiling like Christmas tinsel, but, despite that, he, too, stays quiet.

"Eoin, what is it you propose to settle this?" Kyla-Rose asks him, eyes pinched at the corners with irritation.

"Is it not obvious?!" Father booms, jumping to his feet, palms, once again, slamming down onto the table-top. He lurches forward, pointing a finger at me, without looking my way, arm trembling with rage. "She needs ta die for her sins! She is a disgrace ta the Kelly name, I will *not* 'ave her associated with us, anymore!"

"Sit down, Eoin," Kazimir sighs heavily, head lolling to the side to peer down the length of the long table at him. "I did not come for your dramatics. If you wanted the girl dead, you should have done your own dirty work and carried the deed out yourself. Instead, I hear she was paraded around you Irish like cheap chattel. You should have taken three minutes out of your *extraordinarily* busy schedule to see to her end yourself if it was so important to you. No one else here is to blame, so stop shouting, it is boring and unnecessary." He mutters something in Russian beneath his breath, letting his head loll to the other side, fingers drumming slowly on the table. "Anything else to add, *Lala?*" he asks Kyla-Rose flirtatiously, a wicked curl to the corner of his lips as he licks them that makes him look downright feral.

She runs her tongue over her front teeth, sucking on them as she pops a pout with her red lips, ignoring him.

"If the girl is to…" Vittorio flings a hand into the air, interrupting the strange standoff, "*Disappear,* there is no more problem?"

My chest tightens with his words, *disappear*, Thorne's hand not moving to comfort me, he stays perfectly still, a marble statue to my left. Stryder, on the other hand, takes my hand beneath the table, his warm palm halting my incessant scratching. I bite the inside of my cheek, glance at him from beneath my curtain of curls, he offers me a soft nod, a gentle smile, and then turns back to face the table.

"We can make Haisley disappear," he says solidly, a sturdy foundation that cannot be cracked.

I don't understand quite what he means, but I see Thorne's jaw tense, a knot forming just below his ear. I think of his brothers outside, each of them waiting to throw themselves inside at the first sign of trouble. I peek then, to the very end of the table, look at my own brother, nothing but coldness in his features, he stares back at me, pale green eyes slightly narrowed. I am not close with my siblings, but I was never uncomfortable in

Cillian's presence. I always thought of him as *good*. I look away before he does, pulling in a slow, shaky breath.

Fingers flexing around Stryder's, I try to calm my racing heart, the heavy, fast beating, hammering against my sternum. Sweat builds at the base of my nape, trickling down my spine, despite the icy cold temperature inside the room. I lick my dry lips, waiting silently to hear my fate.

"Okay, look," Kyla-Rose leans forward, chair scooting backwards, she places her forearms on the glass tabletop, eyes everyone sat at the table, including me. "If the Blackwells swear to *dispose* of Haisley *Kelly*, keep her *dead…*" she looks up, eyeing my father, "Then will you agree to let sleeping dogs lie?"

"No, I will not," his voice booms, the rest of the room in silence.

Kyla-Rose twists her lips from one side of her face to the other in thought, her wide eyes eerily flicking over every face in the room. Liam Doyle stands at his father's back, gaze locked firmly on the floor, most of his face is a swollen, bruised mess. A lump along one side of his jaw, eyes not much more than slits, purples and blues blotch his skin, yellowing down one side of his neck, his temple, lip split. I can guess it was Brádach who dealt with him. Likely, also, my fault for being alive.

"Then make a suggestion, Kelly, and make it a *reasonable* one, I'm getting *twitchy*," The Firm's leader spits venomously, resting her chin on her curled knuckles.

Father scoffs loudly, rolling his eyes, slumping back into his seat.

"I 'ave a suggestion," my brother's voice slices through the room, sending a chill down my spine like a slithering serpent. He cocks his head, flicks his eyes onto Thorne, "'ow 'bouts a game a cards?"

Green eyes stare up at me, this darkened office two floors down from the main meeting room is cast in gloom, glow from the city beyond the tinted glass the only thing offering a small amount of light. We are to wait until we are summoned. A room being prepared for our game of life and death.

Haisley sits on a cleared desk, nothing but a computer monitor and corded telephone atop it. She removed her cardigan, the black knit tossed over the back of the office chair that I rolled out of the way for her. Exposed, freckled skin pebbled with goosebumps, my hands stay firmly in my pockets, fingertips pressing painfully hard into the tops of my thighs, desperate to claw into her flesh. The obsession in my chest is seeping into my bones, heart pumping it around my body with possessive intent. My nostrils flare, eyes on her, she glances out of the window, lips parted, shoulders slumped. She is fucking beautiful.

"Thorne," she whispers, eyes still scanning the skyline. She licks her lips, cocks her head, turns her attention onto me, "I want you to fuck me."

I blink at her, fingers driving into muscle, short nails pinching the skin through the pockets of my trousers. Turning my attention fully onto her, my head canting to match hers, I stare at her, her small hands knotting in her lap.

"And I want you to be the one to do it, Thorne," she breathes, the quiet, the gloom, the cold feeling seeping beneath my clothes, bathing my warm skin in frost. "Please, don't let them do it."

Her cheeks redden, blooming with a blush that is all too familiar to me, I know it is hot to the touch. My fingers itch to press against her face, the backs of them to her heated flesh. I lick my lips, drop my chin, look up at her from beneath my lashes, curiosity licks up my spine, need burning through me like wildfire.

"It is supposed to be you." She swallows, hands shaking now, the longer I am silent.

My head rolls on my neck, tilting back at a cocked angle so I can look down at her. Her head is tilting back, staring up at me, her pulse fluttering in the side of her throat. My knuckles crack as I flex my fingers, eyes locking in on her dainty little neck. I think about what it is she is saying to me, her death, my hands.

My heart.

"Tell me what you want, Little Cub," I exhale, the words feeling sticky as they leave my mouth. "I shall give you what you need. Just... tell me."

Haisley blinks those big green eyes, thick, pale lashes fluttering over the mix of blues and greens, her hands go to the desk's edge, fingers curling over the lip of it, nails tapping the mahogany.

"I want you to fuck me," she whispers sinfully, heavy and thick and hot, Devil's breath licking down the side of my throat.

"What else, baby girl?" my lungs squeeze, breaths coming quicker.

She holds my gaze, but I know she is struggling to, in the same way I do, but not with her, never with her. I hold her captive, tethered to me, even as it makes my skin itch, an uncomfortable feeling crawling like spiders beneath my skin. The strings of silk holding us tight, wrapping and cocooning, suffocating.

Let us drown, Little Cub.

"Your belt," she breathes, her eyes finally shuttering and my heart stops in my chest, lungs freezing, even as a bead of sweat rolls down my spine. Her eyes fly open, pupils blown, "Put it around my neck, Thorne."

Her cheeks flush redder, a dark stain in her pale skin, bright, even in the shadows. Air suddenly conquers me, my body sucking it in automatically, it whistles out between my teeth as I swallow. This girl, so perfect for me. The way she can soothe me and wind me up tight, knotting my insides. I stare at her, feel the weight of my belt buckle like the weight of a wrecking ball hanging on my hips. Confliction wars in me, whether I can stop myself, from going too far, from giving her the other thing she is asking of me.

"No one is taking you from me, Little Cub," the promise spills out like a slit to my jugular, thick flowing crimson bleeding and gushing out between us. "Ever. Not tonight, not ten years from now. *You* are not taking you from me. You are mine. My hands will be the only thing that take your life, and that will not be for a long, *long* time. Your soul is tethered to mine in sinister ways I do not understand. But this is how it will be. You. And I."

"Thorne," my name falls from her lips like a blessing and a curse, maddening me.

"Take off your clothes."

Without hesitation, Haisley pushes off of the desk, never breaking our gaze, she stares up at me as she dips forward, pushing down her jeans and underwear, kicking off her shoes. Elbows bending as she stands, lifting her loose t-shirt over her head. Thick red curls slap down against her shoulders as she drops her shirt to the floor, one hand disappearing behind her back. Coming away with her bra threading down her arms. I lick my lips, watch every subtle shift, breath, movement, she makes.

Something glints on the inside of her arm, and my head tilts as I assess it. She watches me watching her, blushing furiously as she slaps a hand over the small blade sheathed there.

"Get rid of it," I rasp, and she does so without protest, untying it and dropping it to the floor by her feet with a soft *thunk*.

My jacket slides down my arms, and I throw it to the chair to join her cardigan. Tugging my shirt up and out of my slacks, finger and thumb meticulously working free the small black buttons down the front. I untwist my cufflinks, hear the soft thud of them against the thin carpeted floor as I let them go. My eyes try to trace every freckle, every dimple, stretchmark, scar. All of her curves making my mouth water, and my head spin. My eyes flick to her mouth, the minacious thread of white through the slope of her cupid's bow.

A mark I gave her.

In toxic desperation to own her.

Soft cotton falls down my arms, the cool air pricking my skin, I drop the shirt, nipples hardening, skin sprouting goosebumps. My chest heaves, hers the same, anticipation is thick between us, the comforting gloom heavy, a suffocating need between us.

I step into her, her naked body cool, my chest and stomach pressing against her, her chin tilted high, eyes on mine. I unthread my belt between us, her lower back grinding into the edge of the desk, her hands loose at her sides. The back of my hand grazes her skin as I work my belt free. Deliberate little touches making sure she feels what I am doing. Her breath hitches as I force my thumb between her lips, top and bottom teeth grating over the joint.

I catch her nipple between my other thumb and forefinger, pinching it between my nails, she keens lowly, the sound a husk in the back of her throat. She arches into me, back bowing, every inch of her skin plastering against me. Releasing the belt from my other hand, popping open the button on my slacks.

I run my palm over the cap of her shoulder, beneath her hair, down her back, digging my thumb into the bone of her shoulder blade as I dip my chin, bending forward, I glide the flat of my tongue over her hardened nipple. Sucking it into my mouth, my teeth closing around it, biting into the soft flesh. I flick my eyes up, onto hers, pull as much of her breast into my mouth as I can, and suck, hard. She whimpers, breathlessly, her hands flying up, fingers squeezing around my arms, nails biting into my exposed biceps.

I bite into her harder, my eyes on hers, she pants through her mouth. The harder I bite, the faster she breathes, but I do not want to let go, I want to puncture her soft flesh, sink my teeth in deeper than I should. Cheeks hollowing, I suck harder, she holds my gaze, squeezing my arms tighter, as though she is in pain, but she does not tell me to stop. I do not think I could if she did. I hold her gaze, making myself uncomfortable, but I want to see how far this will go.

My jaw locks, teeth violent, I breathe hard through my nose, both of my hands now tight on her waist. Fingers curling so hard into her plump flesh, tips pinching into the hollows between her rib bones, my thumbs caress her front, my teeth driving in harder. I feel it like a soft pop, when I puncture her skin, canines finally breaking through.

Haisley presses herself into me harder, curling into

my chest, her blood thick on my tongue, I lash it over her tight peak, suck hard and pull back. Lips instantly finding hers, teeth crashing together, pain pulses in my temple, my hand latching onto her breast, I massage the wet flesh, the weight of it like a gift in the palm of my hand.

I think of all the times I watched her, from the shadows, imagining my hand slapping over her mouth, arm around her waist as I tore her out of the light and into the gloom with me.

"*Thorne,*" she whispers, between savage, biting kisses, she squirms in my hold, her tongue licking against mine in her mouth. "Please," her teeth tug on my bottom lip, mine go to her top, pulling on the scar I put there. And then her hand is in my hair, wrenching my head back, "*Thorne.*"

I smooth a hand over the crown of her head, work my fingers beneath the thick spiral curls, clamp down onto the nape of her neck. Thumb on the back of her jaw, I apply pressure, angle her face up, step into her, her lower spine colliding with the wood of the desk. Thumbing her lips open, I lick into her mouth, groaning when she shivers beneath me. Holding her tight, angled just right, my thigh tight between hers, she squeezes them around me, trying to grind her bare core into me. I bite her lip, my free hand running up and down her side, goosebumps smattered along her skin.

I palm her throat, using the hand on her nape to arch her neck back further. Her breathing raspy, my own quickened, I step back, spin her around and slam her forwards onto the desk.

She squeals in surprise as her bare body makes contact with the cold wood. Round arse up, I palm her cheeks, squeezing the flesh, one at a time, my other hand still clamped down over the back of her neck. Bowing over her, my chest to her back, open belt buckle tapping against the back of her thigh as I fold myself completely over her. Teeth finding her ear, the tang of her blood still on my tongue, I lick over her lobe, down the side of her throat, swirling the tip over her hammering pulse.

Teeth nipping at her neck, feeling her heart pounding through her back, punching desperately against my own, our organs thumping to break free of their bone prisons to reach each other. I listen to her breaths, soft and laboured, turn my face into hers, our noses touching, her eyes still wide and on mine.

Holding onto her neck, our breaths shared between parted lips, I am intoxicated. Pepper and plum, smoky with a tart sweetness. Lifting up slightly, I slip my free hand between us, latch onto my belt buckle, start to thread the leather free. I make sure the length of it whips gently against her body as I get it free of my slacks, hanging loose with the button and zipper open.

Using my teeth, I thread the belt through the simple rectangular steel buckle, take a deep breath and stand straight. Cold air oozes between our separated bodies, hers trembling with the cold. I release her neck, and loop my belt around her throat. I hear her sharp intake of breath as the warmed leather makes contact with her trachea. And then I am yanking on the end of it, ripping her up to standing, at the same time I free my cock and slam it inside of her.

She screams, her teeth clenched, expelling the air she had left in her lungs. I tear harder on the belt, coiling it around my fist, drawing her into me. Her back flush with my chest, I drop my chin to her right shoulder, her cunt pulsing and quivering around me as I lazily fuck into her tight, wet heat. She is so fucking hot around my cock that I have to bite my lip to keep my groan at bay. Instead, breathing sharply into her ear. She is silent, eyes wide, body still except for the small tremble when my cock pushes deeper inside of her.

Smirk pressing against the side of her throat, I nuzzle her neck, breathe in deep, let her scent fill my lungs. The length of my forearm rests against her spine between us, hips flexing slow and hard, her body jolting every time I fuck into her. Keeping my gaze on her, chin pressed to her collarbone where I curl over her shoulder, I palm her belly in my free hand, fingertips digging in. Possessive. I am greedy. Wanting to use her like this, but she *likes it.* I can hear the chant rattling around inside of her skull as clearly as if it were inside of my own.

Kill me. Kill me. Kill me.

"Next time, Little Cub," I whisper against her wet cheek, salt bright on my tongue as I lick up her face, swallowing down her tears. "I am not letting you breathe until I come," I whisper sinisterly against her face, my nose pressing to her cheekbone, remembering doing just that, I picture her pretty face held beneath water.

Drawing back, I stare at her, cheeks puffy, tip of her little nose red, eyes bulging, lashes clumped as fresh tears spill down her face.

Fuck, she has never looked more beautiful.

And I am gone.

This is all for me.

For us.

And as her hands finally, *finally*, come up from the desk, curling tightly over my hand and forearm tight to her belly, nails biting into me, where mine bite into her, I move faster.

My cock already pulsing and twitching, I drill it into her tight heat. Bite her cheek. Breathe against her face. Hard and humid, I pant, open mouthed, against her hot skin, passing my hand over the curve of her round belly, my middle finger slides between her slippery folds, finding her clit, I rub punishing circles over it. Her pussy pulses, quivering walls tightening more and more as she tries to push me out with her impending orgasm.

I chuckle against her cheek, biting at the curved bone in her face, "You are fucking devastating, baby girl."

And then I rip back savagely on the looped belt, her mouth popping open as the back of her head slams against my shoulder and we come together. I slam my hips into her, my cum painting the inside of her cunt as her body bows forward as much as it can while I have her head held back to my chest.

The rough pad of my finger is lazy on her swollen clit as we both finish. Her knees shaking, skin glistening with sweat, hers and mine, I let go of the belt, and she flops forward, hanging over my arm banded around her middle. She gasps desperately for air, the noise rough and choking as she heaves in breath, the invasion of cool air burning her lungs, making her cough and splutter. I keep hold of her, my cock twitching as it already begins thickening again, still pushed snugly inside of her.

My fingers glide under her chin, pushing into the loosened leather to make the gap between her throat and the belt larger. She heaves in my arms, her entire body trembling. I peer down at her, my much taller body curled over her. Wet cheeks, dribble of blood running down the valley of her breasts, saliva dripping from her chin, she is beautiful. Perfect. And she is all for me.

I step backwards, cock already hard again, keeping it sheathed inside of her, I lift her feet from the floor, drop onto the leather couch seated in front of the window, and peer out of the glass at the nighttime lights of Southbrook. Haisley lies back against my chest, her own still heaving, legs spread, hanging limply over my thighs. I keep a splayed hand over her belly, my thumb tracing up and down her sternum as I watch the world beyond. Not caring about ever seeing it again after tonight. Because of the girl in my arms.

My girl.

The heavy weight in my heart, an ache, *for her*.

She settles against me, breathing regulating, heartbeat slowing, matching my own. Our synchronicity, something I find myself liking more and more. Appreciating.

It means what I feel is not one sided.

That she feels it too.

The madness creeping through my veins.

It is an infection. A poison. One that, if given the choice, I would never cure.

"If things do not go well tonight, Little Cub," I swallow, glance down at her, big watery eyes already on mine, head tilted back against me. "It will be me, I will make sure of it. Only I will ever end you."

She nods breathlessly, eyes slipping closed, and it feels final. The pain in my heart, in my head, the ache in my gut. All of it for what is about to happen here before the sun rises.

However, this is a finality. Something we have both strung out for too long.

I want to tell her that I love her. That I will never let anything happen to her. That my promises, of such, are truths.

But I cannot guarantee it.

The things I have planned.

The people I have trusted.

All I have left now is hope.

And a macabre declaration of love feels too much like a goodbye.

So we stay in silence, the gloom our protection, naked bodies pressed to one another, her lips moving against mine as I slowly fuck her. Arm banded around her waist to hold her close, other hand on her jaw, our mouths moving together.

Synchronicity.

Her death will be mine.

As mine will be hers.

CHAPTER 42

HAISLEY

Voice hoarse, throat sore, the bruising everyone eyed as we entered this room, stark and bright in blossoming blues and purples, I swallow past the pain and focus on my father.

Eoin Kelly is seated directly across the table from Thorne. Nobody permitted to sit or stand beside or behind either one of them as they play a game for my life. If my father wins, I am to die. Here. Tonight. Something, which, despite some of their reluctances, was eventually agreed on by every important person at the table. I do not blame them. I grew up in this world. I know that this is sometimes how it's done.

It doesn't make it easier to swallow. But I have far surpassed my expiration date. This is all borrowed time.

I was born to die.

My fingers are curled together, pressed up tight beneath my chin, as my heart hammers inside my chest with worry. *For him.* Knowing what he will have to do if he does not win. It kills me, dousing my insides with a shock of acid. I could never picture anyone caring about me enough to suffer from my death. Before Thorne.

I can feel the thrumming pound of my heart against my rigid forearms, pulled tightly into my body, flush with my chest. The bite on my breast grates roughly against the lace of my bra, reminding me of the weeping skin, the pink fluid, I did not wipe away, thickening on Thorne's puncturing teeth marks.

It hurts. And I like it. And I want to keep it there forever.

He is an addiction.

Healthy or otherwise. It doesn't matter. I am consumed by him in every possible way someone can be.

I have never had anyone in my corner before.

And as Wolf presses his front firmly into my back, big hand landing heavily over my shoulder. Stryder prying my hands down, away from my face so he and Arrow can each take one, lace their fingers through my own on either side of me. I feel like I want to cry. Tears fill my eyes, and it is not fear for Thorne as I thought it would be. Instead, it is the love I feel in my heart from all of the Blackwell men.

This is what family is.

Means.

And I desperately want to learn how to reciprocate.

If I get the chance, I will.

The small blade that was attached to my inner arm is gone now. Archer chuckling as Thorne tossed it to him when we emerged from our gloom. He had been outside through it all, our time together, standing guard. But he didn't comment, which I think, from what I know so far about Thorne's younger brother, is a first.

He winks at me now as I glance at him, standing beside my own brother, who is yet to do much more than scowl at me, but Archer looks perfectly comfortable in their close proximity. I look away quickly, not wanting him to see the blush in my cheeks, but from his small laugh, I don't think I succeed.

The two men at the table are playing cards, a game I do not attempt to understand, but Thorne seemed more than familiar with it when Liam Doyle suggested it. His father, Brádach, I am sure, would much rather be using his fists, but he did not argue when my father agreed. Liam doling out the cards and flipping some over in the centre of the table. A different one to what we were all sat around earlier, this one a solid wood, no glass top to enable cheating.

Something the Doyle brothers are known for.

It made me nervous, watching Liam, but there's nothing I could have done to change the process. And as Thorne himself did not protest, so I, too, stayed silent.

Everyone is still here, a cluster of people standing on either end of the table, too many feet separating me from Thorne, but it is the way it is done.

As I scan over the room, ignoring the triumphant grin on my father's face when he seemingly wins the first round of whatever it is they are playing. My vision stops on Kyla-Rose. Standing side by side with Vittorio, their arms brushing in their closeness, something familiar between them. Comfortable. I feel intimidated, by everyone in this room, but especially her, even with her scars, on her face, her chest, snaking up and over one of her hands, she is brutally beautiful. Her height almost rivals the men in this room, she must be at least six-foot and it makes me feel even shorter, rounder, perhaps, subconsciously, a little inferior.

I am short, have always held a little more weight than my sisters, not things I have ever worried about, despite comments constantly made by my mothers. But my freckles, having so many, so close together, I was teased about them at school, bullies always like to find something to pick on someone about, mine just happened to go after my skin. I imagined, more than once, what it would be like to not have them, carve the skin from my bones. Would it grow back without them? Would there be more? But, I realised, as much as other people hated them, that I kinda liked them in the end, because of that. They gave me a power, something repelling to them. It kept me a little safer, being less desirable. It made me like my skin. I do like it. My freck-les. All of me. Even if sometimes I am unsure of who it is I really am, who I want to be. I know that I am *where* I am meant to be.

With him.

Thorne.

He makes me feel seen.

Alive.

Worthy.

I *am* good enough.

For him.

But most importantly, *for me.*

Crashing into me so suddenly, this strange self-acceptance. It makes me want to tell him. That he helped me see. I wonder if I will ever get the chance to.

My cheeks burn brighter, hot, I'm sure, to the touch, but I lift my head all the same, stare at Thorne's side profile, see the small purple bruise darkening just beneath his ear. Pride swirls in my chest, knowing I put it there. My lips, my tongue, my teeth. A marking that *he* wanted. It is possessive, his ownership of me, yet, I find it comforting. A security. But to claim him back, in just a small way, makes me feel like the biggest person in this room.

I feel myself straighten at that. Shoulders pulling back. Steel forming in my spine.

For him.

Arrow and Stryder's hands both squeeze mine at the same time, like they know, can feel it, too. My resolve. I will not break here. Not with them. I am stronger than I think. I've just been suppressed throughout my life, by my family, for so long that I didn't see it. Never being away from it meant I didn't understand. Perhaps, that is why it is done. To silence our strength because the women in my family are likely stronger than every man in this room.

I don't know why this suddenly comes to me. What it is that makes me feel lighter at the realisation. But I turn my head, facing my brother, his face is tilted down, chin almost flush with his chest, but he is looking at me, staring right through me, into my head, and a smirk flits across his face, for no longer than a second, but I see it. It feels like I am a co-conspirator in a secret game I am unaware I am even playing.

Until now.

My father's fist comes down hard on the table, the wood solid, but it groans a little all the same. Forcing my head to snap up at the outburst. Thorne is expressionless as Eoin Kelly throws, yet another, temper tantrum.

"YOU FUCKING CHEAT!" he roars, spittle flying from his lips with his bellow.

He throws himself out of his seat, one hand splayed over the tabletop, the other balled into a fist, index finger out, pointing straight at Thorne.

Thorne, for his part, does not move. His chest rises and falls evenly. His hands are open, their backs resting on the table, fingers curling naturally in towards his palms. His cards face up too, an Ace and a King, but I do not get to see my father's before he dashes them, and the cards in the centre, down the polished wood, scattering them like confetti with his big hands. Some drift to the floor, others just lurch down the table with speed, whipping up like a dust devil.

He leans forward on his fists, chair on its back behind him, he stares at Thorne, his face glowing a vibrant red, he looks like a balloon overfilled with helium. His chest is heaving and I think he is going to say something cutting, to try to hurt feelings, most likely mine. Elicit some sort of violent reaction out of the man I love. But, instead, he lunges across the table, hands going straight for Thorne's throat. His legs are practically kicking in the air as he slides across the table.

There is a flurry of movement, my hands released, strong ones on my shoulders wrenching me backwards, my eyes never stray from Thorne, even as Wolf's scent engulfs me, lilies and teakwood, soft and earthy. I know I am safe. That I should stay where he holds me firm. But watching the scene unfold before me, Bràdach standing back with a snarling grin on his face, arms folded across his huge chest.

Alejandro grapples my father, wrenching him back off of the table by the collar of his shirt. My father heaving like a leashed attack dog, he shrugs out of Alejandro's grip, tossing the man a glare that the Mexican cartel leader does not rise to.

Thorne is standing now, his hands by his sides. There are red marks on his throat. From my father's hands. Something I, too, have had mark me, many times, before. And then Eoin Kelly is whipping a gun out, pointing it in my lover's face. He is shouting, my father, but I am deaf to the words, the noise, a high-pitched keening buzzing in my head. The coffin flies descending again. My body trembles, fixating on the red finger marks on Thorne's smooth skin. Wolf's grip tightens over my shoulders, fingers kneading, to comfort, keep me safe, *keep me back*, but I don't think it's anything but rage inside of me making me shake.

It shocks him as much as it does me. My twisting out of his hold, my feet urging me forward. My hip bone slams into the solid wood of the table as I throw myself in front of Thorne, breathless and gasping as I face down the man who condemned me.

He laughs, an auburn brow lifting on his forehead, wide toothy grin marring his ageing face. Thorne growls lowly at my back, the vibrations of it rolling through me where I am wedged against his chest. He does not reach for me as I place myself between him and the bullet sitting in my father's chamber.

He laughs loudly, his body shaking with mirth, finally deigning to look at me, his green eyes flare as they finally lock on mine. Wild and hostile. Heat flushes through me, uncomfortable and pressured, yet, I hold my ground. Wrap my hands behind me, around Thorne's hips, locking my fingers together at his back.

Nobody speaks and none of them move. No one is intervening now, if I didn't have Thorne's heat at my back, I would think I were totally alone. Standing off against my father.

He keeps his arm extended, finger on the trigger, raised high, at Thorne. Panic flares hot in my chest, belly flip flopping with the stress of it. And I don't know what to do. I am not strong, there is nothing inside of me that fits here. I don't want to, but in this situation, maybe, perhaps, it would help. I swallow hard, straighten my spine, feel my chest puff with a deep inhale.

"Put the gun down," the words come out loudly, surprisingly strong, commanding and I have a moment of pure terror, fear pulsing through my veins like arsenic.

"I will not take orders *from you,*" he spits viciously, sneering at me, he drags his eyes up my body, pausing at my throat with a flick of his brow. "Not some murdering little whore," he scoffs dismissively, shaking his head in disgust.

I flinch at his words, stinging like a slash from his whip. I feel the pain from them, lashing over the bones in my spine, how it would hurt just enough to not break skin. Leave no scars. Mar no flesh. Damage no merchandise.

I think of all the things I could say. All of them statements that would fly over his head. Eoin Kelly does not care about me. Women, his wives, my mothers, sisters, cousins. All we are to him is tradable, sellable objects. Some with a higher value than others. It is why he had so many children, *continues* to have so many children.

We are disposable.

"I no longer belong to you," I say simply, softly, strong.

His arm trembles with his rage, eyes locked on me now, jaw clenching, he huffs breath through his nose.

"Ya are an *embarrassment,*" he spits, "Pathetic. Weak."

I say nothing, even as he goes on, his temper growing hotter, face growing redder, his breaths are raspy and his arm shakes further. My eyes fill with tears, but I don't let them fall. Give him the satisfaction as he tells me exactly what he thinks of me. Thorne shifts closer, his hips against my lower spine.

"And with Thorne *fucking* Blackwell," he tsks, clucking his tongue with a huff of laughter.

That's what has my head snapping back up, my own teeth grinding.

"Thorne *fucking* Blackwell is ten times the man you could *ever* be," I spit back, breath rushing through me, my legs waiver, knees wanting to buckle. I lean forward, fingers splaying over the table, I cock my head, "You lost." It is almost a whisper, my mouth curling up at one corner at the way he stares at me, his mouth popped open, like he cannot believe I dare speak out of turn. "Let it go." I do whisper then and that's when his eyes widen.

Trembling arm going slack, his other going to his chest, splaying over his heart. I glance to my left, see my brother watching, hands in his pockets. He does not move. In fact, nobody but Bràdach moves to check on my father. His gun clattering to the table as he slumps forward over it, a strangled sound falling from his gasping lips. I stare wide eyed, Liam Doyle hovering just behind his own father.

Others do start to move then. The peace-making Swallow member who spoke before, going over, leaning over Eoin Kelly's still form which does not much more than wheeze breath. His dull green eyes bulge, staring up at me as the man's fingers go to his neck, checking for a pulse.

Thorne's arms curl around me, trudging us back a few paces, letting others swarm in. His brothers surround us, moving in on all sides, a protective bubble. Stryder steps forward, not blocking my view, but facing off against the room, his back to us, as the patriarch of The Blackwells.

There are things happening around me, Liridon Murati stopping before us, his huge body blocking my view of everything. I do not look up at him as he speaks to Thorne, my eyes locked on where I know my father lies behind this man's back.

Thorne keeps me held against him, eventually taking us back a little, sitting in a chair that is pulled out for him, away from the table, me in his lap. He caresses my hair back from my face, my heart thudding hard and fast in my chest.

I stare at my father, people no longer fussing with him now, where he is lain over the polished wood table. He looks impossibly human. Nothing of the monster that I am so accustomed. He is small, nothing, meaningless. The fear he inflicted already disintegrating where I store it inside myself.

Breaking my stare, Thorne whispering in my ear, his lips soft against my cheek. I see Stryder speaking with my brother, others speaking, drinks passing hands.

I hear nothing. None of the noise penetrating enough to drown out the buzz of the coffin flies, once again, filling my ears.

But for the first time.

This time.

They are not descending for me.

EPILOGUE

THORNE
JUNE

L ove is not something I ever thought I would have.

Could have.

I thought Haisley was just an obsession. A curse. Something toxic that was born with me, sprouting like a seed of infection, making me sicker and sicker. An urge to have her, to keep. Not to love. To own.

And then we built a home.

She built a home.

She is it.

My everything.

I am consumed by her.

Twilight settling around us. We sit silently. Refractions of light from the sun casting us in an orange glowing gloom. I glance down at her, where she sits beside me on our doorstep. Violet wisteria and white honeysuckle weave together around the curved stone alcove overhead. Haisley flashes those beautiful jade-green eyes up at me, a nervous nibble of teeth on her bottom lip.

"What if he doesn't come tonight?" she whispers, worrying her lip until it blanches white.

Her upper arm pressing into the side of my chest, my own slung over her shoulders, I look down at her, head cocked, lick my lips. I press my mouth to her forehead, not kissing her, just resting my mouth against her as I draw her closer. My other hand takes hers, caressing the bones in her fingers, resting our joined hands on my thigh.

The cliff being beaten by the soft crash of waves at its base, I glance at our lighthouse. Its fresh coats of white paint, new glass, gleaming with the last of the day's sun, fitted in its top. A clean door with new hinges, fresh varnish and a gothic style handle. The structure repaired, spiral staircase inside fixed and coiling its way back to the top.

I flick my gaze over, onto the treeline at the far edge of the white, dusty earth. My hand over her shoulder cradling her crown, lips still pressed to her head, I breathe her in, smoky plum and sharp pepper, let my lips trail into her hairline.

"What if he forgot where we live?" she mumbles vulnerably into my neck, her breath hot, my skin sticky with the humidity of her, our perspiration from the summer day's renovation work still clammy on our skin. "What if he-"

"He did not forget where we live," I promise her, a smile curving my lips as I watch him come forth. "He did not forget you, baby girl,"

"How do you know?" she asks me, drawing away, she looks up at me, eyes wide, watery, she frowns at my half smile, pouting her bottom lip.

Turning her head toward the trees, her free hand fisting into my shirt, sleeves folded up to my elbows, the top few buttons open, the backs of her fingers grazing the exposed skin of my chest, she gasps. I place my lips to the crown of her head, smiling, holding her to me as we wait patiently for him to approach. I turn then, too. Rest my cheek atop her head as she leans into me, watch him sniff the ground, hesitantly step closer, his head down, eyes up, ears flicking.

I can hear her whispering under her breath. Desperate for him to come closer, and I want him to, *for her.* Anything to make her happy.

It is what I live for now.

Her happiness.

Haisley Blackwell.

I huff a soft laugh into her red curls, keep palming the back of her head, holding her close. Never going to let her go.

"Clover," she breathes almost silently as the red fox she rescued stops just a few feet away, ears pricking, he watches us closely, neither one of us moving, Haisley holding her breath.

He dips down, sniffing the dry earth, keeping his eyes on us, *her.* And then suddenly his ears flick, twisting as he hears something else. His gaze going over his shoulder, towards the treeline, where another fox, just like him, waits. He looks back at us, and it feels like he holds Haisley's gaze, just for a second, and then it is over, and he is trotting back in the direction from whence he came, disappearing back into the cover of trees.

Haisley pushes against my chest, knuckles digging into my sternum, she pushes up to sitting, and reluctantly, I let her pull away from me. Her big eyes wet, she stares up at me, sniffling to hold back her tears.

"Oh, Little Cub," I chuckle lightly, pulling her back into me.

"He's okay, Thorne," she murmurs, relief in her tone and it settles something inside my chest, the racing of my heart slowing.

"He is."

"We're okay," she whispers even quieter.

"We are," I echo, squeezing her just a little bit tighter.

We settle in the gloom.

Just a monster and his salvation.

THE END

AFTERWORD

Hello you…

Well, here we are again.

I hope you loved this story, I don't think I will ever get bored of writing unusual people in strange places, or strange people in unusual places.

Thorne was super interesting for me to write. He is so layered, but his delicate violence is what really snagged me. I was surprised actually, the way he evolved on the pages. And I think Haisley was right for him. Haisley was lost, and I think back to when I was 23 and I was lost back then, too. I didn't know where I wanted to be, let alone who.

I think Thorne was lost. For a long time. And now they can start to navigate their lives. Together. This is the end of their story, but it is not the end of their journey. We will see them in the next books of the series. Let's be honest, if you've made it this far, you know by now how much I love a crossover… chapter 40 anyone?

Make sure you let me know all your theories about all of those interesting people! We'll be seeing allllll of them again soon.

Anyway! Thank you so much for being here, I appreciate each and every one of you for reading. I was hoping to have a blurb ready for this part, for Wolf and Cardinal House, but there's so much drama surrounding that man's story that I haven't yet been able to put it into a few short sentences. But I will. And I hope to see you again then too.

ACKNOWLEDGMENTS

Mark. I absolutely fucking love you. Thank you for your unwavering support, for taking TikTok guru lessons and recording filthy lines from my books in that sexy deep voice of yours. All the girls in my office love it! For your encouragement, for wiping my tears and holding me tight. Here's to eleven years, beautiful boy.

Addie. I love you. You are my best friend, my rock, my heart. I love you endlessly. I think you are an incredible and strong woman and I am so blessed to have you. Thank you for everything.

Kendal. You are my favourite person even when you are not! I would be lost without you as my sister. I love you to the stars.

Leah. This one was for you. You give me drive, passion, you push me to push boundaries and be a violent poet. Thank you for your friendship. I love you. Also, I am obsessed with you, in case that wasn't already obvious!

Inga. You are incredible. I look up to you in so many ways, you are so strong and kind and you're just fucking brilliant if i'm totally honest. I don't know where I'd be without you. I love you. (P.S. Thank you for giving Devon a girlfriend called Kristy.)

Raisley. I honestly do not know where the fuck I would be without you. Probably Timbuktu, but honestly, with me, who knows, right? You are a fucking kick-arse, take no shit, give no fucks, boss bitch and I strive to be even half as incredible as you. You are a blessing. There are no other words. But honestly, lettuce pray, *for you*, for having to deal with me for lord knows how much longer. Ramen. I love you.

Kristen. Dude, I don't have mushy words for you because we don't really do all that shit… But, I think you're fucking amazing, as a mom, as a wife, as a friend, anyone would be lucky to have you in their corner. I love you a ridiculous amount.

Gayle. Because I would not be Oprah without you. I am insanely in love with you, I hope you know you'll never escape my web now…

My Street Team. You are an awesome little cult. Where would I be without all of your hard work, encouragement and love. Not here, that's for sure. Thank you for everything you do for me. I hope you know how much I appreciate all of you.

ARC Team, you're all fabulous, thank you for being so passionate. It makes me endlessly happy to know you are continuously excited for my work.

And to you, the reader. Thank you. I could not do this without your support. I hope to see you here again soon.

ALSO BY K.L. TAYLOR-LANE

.

SWALLOWS AND PSYCHOS

KYLA-ROSE SWALLOW

A Dark Mafia Why Choose Romance

PURGATORY

PENANCE

PERSECUTION

CHARLIE SWALLOW

A Dark Mafia MMF Romance

RUIN

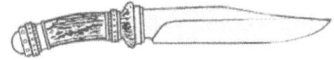

.

THE BLACKWELL BROTHERS

HUNTER BLACKWELL

A Dark Gothic Horror Stepsibling MF Romance

HERON MILL

HERON MILL TENEBRIS

THORNE BLACKWELL

A Dark Gothic Mafia MF Romance

ROOK POINT

WOLF BLACKWELL

A Dark Gothic MF Romance

CARDINAL HOUSE

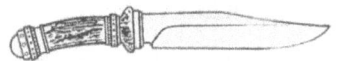

THE ASHES BOYS

A Dark Bully Gang Why Choose Romance

TORMENT ME

BURY ME

(COMING 2023)

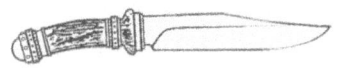

STANDALONES

A Dark College Bully Why Choose Romance

NOXIOUS BOYS

Coming March 4th 2024

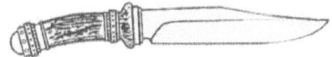

FIND K.L. TAYLOR-LANE

BOOKBUB

AMAZON

INSTAGRAM

TIKTOK

PINTEREST

FACEBOOK

GOODREADS

FACEBOOK READER GROUP